# Praise for Robert Fleming's erotica collection *After Hours*

Named Best Erotic Collection of

One of the Best Recommende
*Black Issues*

Nominated for Best Erotic Anthology of 2002
by the Erotic Authors Association

"An eclectic collection of erotica from Black male writers."
—*Essence*

"You will find yourself immersed in wonderful stories that
will tickle your mind and your sensual bone."
—*Nubian Chronicles*

"Readers and critics discouraged by so much recent mainstream African
American fiction and romances will find plenty to enjoy in this collection,
which aspires to be more literary than smutty and succeeds in exploding a
few stereotypes in the process."
—*Publishers Weekly*

"Robert Fleming's unique collection of erotic short stories
reveals black sensuality that's imaginative and touching as
well as breathtaking and sweat-breaking."
—*Africana.com*

"This is not blaxploitation lit. This is the real thing—
true, sexy, and all of it smart. It's fabulous."
—Erotica Readers and Writers Association

"An impeccable collection of well-crafted stories by some of today's top
male authors. The writing is exquisite, all across the board."
—Erotica Writers Association

**Robert Fleming** has written for *Essence, Black Enterprise, The Source,* and
*The New York Times,* among others. A former award-winning reporter for
the *New York Daily News,* he is the author of *The African American Writer's
Handbook* and *The Wisdom of the Elders.* His work was featured in *Brown
Sugar,* and he was the editor of *After Hours* (both available from Plume). He
lives in New York City.

ALSO BY ROBERT FLEMING

*After Hours*
*The African American Writer's Handbook*
*The Wisdom of the Elders*

EROTIC STORIES
of
LOVE, LUST,
and
MARRIAGE

intimacy

by
BLACK MEN

EDITED BY
ROBERT FLEMING

A PLUME BOOK

PLUME
Published by the Penguin Group
Penguin Group (USA) Inc., 375 Hudson Street, New York, New York 10014, U.S.A.
Penguin Books Ltd, 80 Strand, London WC2R 0RL, England
Penguin Books Australia Ltd, 250 Camberwell Road,
Camberwell, Victoria 3124, Australia
Penguin Books Canada Ltd, 10 Alcorn Avenue, Toronto, Ontario, Canada M4V 3B2
Penguin Books India (P) Ltd, 11 Community Centre,
Panchsheel Park, New Delhi – 110 017, India
Penguin Books (N.Z.) Ltd, Cnr Rosedale and Airborne Roads,
Albany, Auckland, 1310, New Zealand
Penguin Books (South Africa) (Pty) Ltd, 24 Sturdee Avenue,
Rosebank, Johannesburg 2196, South Africa

Penguin Books Ltd, Registered Offices: 80 Strand, London WC2R 0RL, England

First published by Plume, a member of Penguin Group (USA) Inc.

First Printing, January 2004
10  9  8  7  6  5  4  3  2  1

*Page 267 constitutes an extension of this copyright page.*

 REGISTERED TRADEMARK—MARCA REGISTRADA

LIBRARY OF CONGRESS CATALOGING-IN-PUBLICATION DATA
Intimacy : erotic stories of love, lust, and marriage by Black men / edited by Robert
Fleming.
    p. cm.
  ISBN 0-452-28474-0
  1. Erotic stories, American. 2. American fiction—African American authors.
3. American fiction—Male authors. 4. African American men—Fiction.   I. Fleming,
Robert, 1950–

PS648.E7I58 2004
813'.01083538'08996073—dc22                                    2003058011

Printed in the United States of America
Set in New Caledonia

PUBLISHER'S NOTE
This is a work of fiction. Names, characters, places, and incidents either are the product
of the author's imagination or are used fictitiously, and any resemblance to actual persons,
living or dead, business establishments, events, or locales is entirely coincidental.

The scanning, uploading, and distribution of this book via the Internet or via any other
means without the permission of the publisher is illegal and punishable by law. Please purchase only authorized electronic editions, and do not participate in or encourage electronic piracy of copyrighted materials. Your support of the author's rights is appreciated.

*This book is dedicated to Calvin Hernton,*
*a true cultural revolutionary, a master of nonfiction,*
*fiction, and a poet. And a generous spirit.*

*Love does not begin or end the way we seem to think it does. Love is a battle, love is a war; love is growing up.*

—James Baldwin, 1961

*No love is innocent. There does not exist a relationship between a man and a woman that does not have its deep hidden, graying ember of carnality, stubbornly aglow.*

—Frank Yerby
from his novel *Judas, My Brother* (1967)

# CONTENTS

x    Contents

# ACKNOWLEDGMENTS

A book, like a writing career, is a collaborative affair, for no writer could succeed without the cooperation and support of others. First, I must thank Gary Brozek, my editor at Penguin Group, for his patience, assistance, and masterful guidance. As any writer will tell you, agents can make or break a writer's career, so it's with much gratitude that I thank Marie Brown, my agent, my friend, and my co-conspirator for her savvy opinions.

To Donna, my beloved, whose advice and love are peerless. You challenge me to press the limits of my imagination and skill, both with your example and words.

To Ashandra, my daughter, budding actress, writer, and playwright, you have made me very proud of you with your various achievements. Nothing you could do, errors of judgment or any other misstep, could lessen what I feel for you. Love you, sweetheart.

Furthermore, no writer can operate at optimum ability without proper backup from a loving, supportive community of peers and friends, so I send a heartfelt thanks out to them: Angela Harvey, Judy Simmons, Charles Seaton, Michael Harris, Rae Harris, Tonya Bolden, Michelle Paynter, Emma Wisdom, Debbie Uffer, Mondella and Tracy, and Willard Jenkins. A special thanks goes to my creative mentor and friend, John A. Williams, a master writer and one of the strongest black men I know. And I still remember David Jackson, who challenged me so many years ago to come to the Big City and kick butt. You made your transition much too soon and your wit, friendship, and curiosity are deeply missed.

Thanks also to all the bookstores and distributors who backed my books, most notably A&B and Culture Plus. I must not forget the crew over at the Erotic Readers and Writers Association, who opened their hearts to my work and supported *After Hours* unconditionally. Special mention must go out to Helena, M. Christian, Bill Dean, Marilyn Jaye Lewis, the Venus Book Club, and the following websites: Clean Sheets, Venus or Vixen, and Suspect Thoughts.

And lastly, there are a number of people, magazines, and websites that gave my first collection worthwhile play: Carol Mackey of Black Expressions Book Club, Africana.com, *Essence, Black Issues Book Review, Dialogue, Publishers Weekly,* AALBC.com, Mosaicbooks. com, NetNoir, R.A.W. SISTAZ, The Nubian Chronicles, Margie Walker, Rosemarie Robotham, Leslie Esdaile, Shonell Bacon, Dominique and John of Prolific Writers, and Shaunda Blocker of Booking Matters. And a special thanks to Monica Jackson for maintaining my website.

# INTRODUCTION

The purpose of this book is quite simple: to present a collection of superb writing by Black male writers on a range of subjects dealing with love, lust, and marriage. True, much has been written about these subjects, most of it clinical or pop psychology or overly romanticized, but I felt readers would welcome a book of some of the most honest, provocative, sensual stories written about three of the essential ingredients in our daily lives. Bigger, better, and bolder than the first, *After Hours*, this new collection is designed to make you think and make your sexual temperature rise.

In *Intimacy: Erotic Stories of Love, Lust, and Marriage by Black Men,* the writers don't dodge the complex issues of those essential life ingredients; instead they explore them in a way that intrigues and informs while also providing something for almost every erotic taste and fantasy.

What has always intrigued me about editing collections is how they evolve from original concept to final product. What I'd originally conceived was a smart, brassy fictional look by Black men at the natural progression from lust to love to marriage, with all of the stops in between, from the single existence to coupledom. After the project was green-lighted and the call went out for submissions, the stories came in a torrent, many from established, respected writers and others from young unknowns. The best of the stories were startling in their ability to make me rethink all of my ideas of what Black men felt about love, desire, and commitment. As a result, I redrew the boundaries of the book. In the end, the writers dramatically recast the collection into the book you now hold in your hands. Just as no two people's experiences of intimacy are the same, no two stories are alike.

Fortunately, none of the writers hold back in their tales about the loneliness, lust, and dating miscues that go on in the single life. Being alone is not fun. Lovers here love, nurture, cheat, lie, and sometimes abandon the very promises that brought them together. As it is sometimes with men, sex can also be just about getting off, that fleeting thrill after climax when the mind and body seem to go their separate ways.

When the writers speak of matters of the heart involving love and marriage, they do not whitewash the challenges and demands of remaining steadfast in the roles of husband and wife: bills, children, careers, sacrifices, illness, infidelity, boredom, and sex. What we realize upon reading these stories is that there is no manual to guide one through the intricacies of love or marriage; nor is there one path to achieving a good relationship or marriage. The bottom line is these stories are not just about love and sex; they are about life and living.

All of the writers start with a handful of the basic questions: What is love? Why do you love one person and not another? Why does it end? Should it hurt or cause you to doubt? Why should you continue to trust or believe in a relationship or a marriage when the other partner has lost the commitment to the union? What happens when the other person changes during the marriage, either through circumstances, illness, or aging? What keeps the love present when all else is gone? What are the benefits of a good love relationship or marriage? When is anger and jealousy healthy? What do you do when all communication collapses? What makes fidelity so important? Should there be double standards for the man in a relationship or marriage? If a man continually compromises in the relationship, does that make him a punk or a wimp? How many chances do you get in life to find love and happiness?

How does sex play into all of this? Where is the importance of the erotic element in this mix? Although some say sex is not the most important ingredient in a solid, stable relationship or marriage, no one will deny that a union of any kind can't survive without it. In each of these stories, the writers, despite the differences in their ages and backgrounds, underscore the fact that so many secrets, so much mystery still surrounds the most intimate moment a man and woman can share. They celebrate this with a determination to not repeat old plots or scenarios. They seek to cover new ground as they search out many of the hidden truths about love, lust, and marriage in our society today, crafting stories full of discoveries and revelations that go beyond race, gender, and class.

These celebrated and respected writers refuse to believe that writing about the erotic should get in the way of fashioning stories that would deepen an understanding of ourselves. They know that erotic literature can be avant-garde, bold, and even dangerous. Once it is shed of the cheap pornographic element that disconnects it from real life, erotica can even be subversive, revolutionary as well as inquisitive and enlightening. They attack much of the Old School thought about what a man should be, what he should feel, what he should revere, and how he should love.

Stephen Barnes, one of this country's premier sci-fi writers, looks, sometimes comically, at the obstacles of getting it on with a high-profile writer wife, whose busy schedule and intrusive mother-in-law keep the couple out of the bedroom and away from each other's arms in "Jet Lag." "Be Careful What You Wish For" could be the title of Reginald Harris's "Almond Eyes," a wild erotic cautionary tale of a man who covets, pursues, and wins the love of an insatiable woman who pushes him further and further into the outer realms of forbidden sex. In Gary Earl Ross's "Lucky She's Mine," a man takes a chance on love and marriage with an abused, neglected woman from a foreign land, without fully considering the consequences of his actions.

E. Ethelbert Miller, one of our finest poets, details the highs and lows of love found and lost in a lyrical meditation that both tugs at the heart and stirs the passions, with "Giovanni." Everyone seems horny, crazed, and slightly odd in Brian Egeston's sexy screwball comedic work, "The Post-Cock Box," proving once and for all that a mix of delicious food, outlandish deeds, and unbridled lust can be as soulful as an afternoon at a sanctified church. Novelist and screenwriter Trey Ellis gives forth an almost autobiographical turn in his sizzling entry, "After and Before," the story of a worldly writer on the make during his travels while recovering from a shattered love. A Hispanic woman, on the eve of her wedding anniversary to her eager Black hip-hop fiancé, is haunted by the tragic loss of her first love and nagging doubts in Phill Duck's engaging "Cotton Comes to Nina." SekouWrite's "Laser Tag Love" enters the realm of video games and arcades when a young woman's plan of revenge for a perceived betrayal leads her to take a romantic risk and find a torrid sexual adventure away from her lover.

When Edwardo Jackson creates the topsy-turvy world of the first Black female Hollywood studio head in "Broken Rules," he goes deep inside her life of glitz and glamour, brilliantly uncovering not only the racism and sexism she encounters but her refusal to submit to temptation and decadence. Mismatched lovers—a man from an upscale family and a saucy stripper—try to overcome their class differences when passion compels him to take her home to meet his parents after she weaves an enticing sexual spell on him in Jemal K. Yarbrough's "The Drive." Michael T. Owens's "More Than Meets the Eyes" is a sexual romp that uses an updated revision of the age-old Medea myth to offer a few dramatic surprises and lusty coupling, along with a heap of sardonic laughs. Female empowerment is the core theme in Mitchell Jackson's wise "Postscript," which follows a submissive, adoring wife's final break with matrimony after bowing to her husband's permissive sexual whims one last time before discovering her self-worth. David Anthony Durham's sensual prose fuels an intricate yarn of young love blooming in the late 1960s when a transplanted country guy falls for a savvy city gal in a relationship of restrained emotion and Old School romance in "An Act of Faith." In Robert Scott Adams's memorable "Lust Enraptured," the writer delves into the numerous dilemmas posed by infidelity in a long-term marriage when an ongoing affair between long-distance lovers continues their good ole hard loving, spine-snapping ways. Noir veteran Cole Riley returns with a story of a groom, a man enamored with the curvy female body, replaying memories of past failed marriages and dashed hopes, on the eve of his wedding to his fourth wife, in the unforgettable "Male and Females."

In one of the collection's highlights, C. Kelly Robinson draws a stunning parallel between the lives of a father and son, as the older man learns his son has sired a child out of wedlock, much as he had done years before. Now he is forced to confront the mother of his son's girl, the woman who introduced him to the pleasures of sex as a teenager, in "Coming of Age." Satire and sexuality reign supreme in "A Fan's Love," an excerpt from former Richard Pryor screenwriter Cecil Brown's acclaimed novel *Days Without Weather*, where a

Black comic encounters a dogged fan intent on bedding him in a most unusual manner. Kenji Jasper's "In the Wee Hours of the Morning" vividly depicts "the average guy's wet dream" of fame, sexual hijinks, and the high life, with a bit of added social commentary.

Pulitzer Prize author James Alan McPherson's supreme talents as a storyteller comes to the fore in his probing "Private Domain." In it, McPherson evokes the jockeying for power in a relationship between a man and his flirty lover, who seeks the attention of his male friends with her scandalous actions. Age is only a number in Kalamu ya Salaam's "Forty-five Is Not So Old," as an older woman shows that age and experience trumps youth and bravado every time in life and love in this story of lust and conquest. A man is given a second chance for affection and sexual intimacy in his golden years, with his love life getting a boost from a younger woman, in Al Young's perceptive "Vodka and Viagara."

Award-winning writer John Edgar Wideman tackles sexual and racial taboos when he exposes the forbidden fantasies of two joggers, one a Black man and the other a white woman, in the controversial "The Statue of Liberty." Closing out the book with "The Boxer and the Lotus," noted mystery writer Christopher Chambers offers a biting glimpse of a big-time novelist's life and the current publishing scene, using some crackling prose and witty dialogue to describe all of the backbiting, ego-fueled pitfalls, and sexual perks in an ever-changing industry.

And that's it. If you want stories full of red hot sex, keen insights into the sexual mind of the African-American male, and stories that both stimulate and shock, look no farther than *Intimacy*. As a first-rate collection of erotica, it is very hard to put down. Each story strives to outdo the one before it, going into a new territory of emotion and sensuality, providing readers with a very agreeable companion on a long, lonely night.

Enjoy the collection!

Robert Fleming

# Jet Lag

**Stephen Barnes**

My plane arrived at PDX at ten P.M. Monday night, after about twelve hours in the air. I'd been away from home for ten days, working on a television show in Munich, Germany. Ten days, just long enough for my body to totally adjust to a foreign time zone. Then, as it always seems to happen, it was time to come home again.

My wife, Zora, had been holding down the fort at home, which was only right, because I'd done it for her the previous two weeks, when she'd been on tour for her book that she'd written with her mom on the civil rights movement in Texas.

The bad part of all this was that we hadn't seen each other in three weeks. I walked through the door, knowing she was going to take off again in a day and a half. Arrgh.

The flight had been long, bumpy enough to keep me from sleeping but still boring as hell. One of the few things that made it worthwhile was knowing that I would see my baby when I deplaned. Zora is about five-four, with dark chocolate skin and a body shaped by excellent genetics and endless, endless hours in our home gym. She is the sexiest and most beautiful woman I have ever been blessed to bed, and anytime I look at her, the depth of my luck just about slaps me upside the head. She gave me a kiss that helped me to forget just how bad the flight had been.

"Sweetie!" she squealed. She pressed her body against me for a glorious instant, and then peeled away again. Zora can be quite reserved . . . in public. That makes the private Z all the more fun.

"God," I said, less an exclamation than a grateful prayer. "It's good to see you."

As always, her smile dazzled. "How was your flight?"

"Great," I lied. "How's your mom?" Mom lives in Dallas, but had flown out for a few days preparatory to the promotional tour. I looked around the reception area, wondering if the matriarch was back toward the shops, perhaps searching for bargains. No sign of her.

"Fine," Z said. "Looking forward to seeing you."

That was great. I love her mom, an extraordinarily strong and centered woman, unflappable in the extreme. Ordinarily, I'd be eager to see her, but right now I had other, baser thoughts in mind.

We joined the crowd heading down the escalator to luggage carousel seven. "I cannot wait to get you home," I said, putting every bit of sensuous insinuation I could muster into those eight syllables.

"Uh . . . sweetie." Her lovely face suddenly lost a bit of its animation. "I'm sorry to say this, but I've got a shitload of work tonight. We've got to get the notes for the Q and A together."

Arrgh. Publicity tours meant writing essays and articles by the dozen. "When are we going to get some time together?"

"We'll manage it, baby," she promised.

Uh huh.

We walked out of PDX, down to the parking garage, past rows of cars, until we reached our 2001 silver Toyota RAV-4. Sitting in the backseat, reading a manuscript, was her mom.

In every sense of the word, Z's mom is a substantial woman. Heart, intellect, generosity, and physical form are all congruent. Back in the day, she had faced down teargas-armed police with the same aplomb with which she had once, on the occasion of our first meeting, informed me in no uncertain terms that she doubted that I was good enough for her eldest daughter. "I'm not impressed by you *at all*," she had said in her mildest voice.

Without missing a beat, I replied, "It's not your job to be impressed by me. It's your job to protect your daughter." My tone was calm, but I shivered to think how I might have dealt with her sober gaze if I had meant her precious child any harm in the slightest. It took time to win her trust, and things hard-won are those we value the most.

She offered a warm hello, asking me how the flight was, and I responded with the kind of bland, vanilla sigh that has been synonymous with communication about air travel since the Wright Brothers became household names.

"S'alright. I hear you guys are burning the midnight oil."

"Oh, you know how it gets. Seems things just never stop."

We pulled out of the garage. Headed to the payment kiosk, and then to the freeway. In the front seat, Zora and I exchanged longing, heated expressions while Mother started to discuss business from the back.

The first thirty days of a book's publication time is of the essence. That's about all the opportunity you have to prove to the book distributors and store managers that your product should be treated with respect. I could understand why Mom needed to engage Z in intense discussions on matters involving transport, hotels, talk shows, newspapers, reading groups, and publicity agents. Nonetheless, my hands tensed and released on the wheel, but there was no sense in being upset. This was the life of a writer, and a lucky writer at that. Most writers would sell their newborns for their publishers to send them on a nationwide tour, so complaining didn't make a lot of sense. Like Superchicken once said to his sidekick Fred, "We knew the job was dangerous when we took it."

It takes an hour to get from Portland to the little logging town where we currently lived while waiting for my daughter to graduate high school. Nice school, tiny town.

We lived in a two-story house on a quiet street walking distance from the town's largest park. In a town this size, writers are local celebrities, but even if we weren't, it's the kind of place where people smile and wave to you as they rake the summer leaves. Nice folks.

Can't wait for cap-and-gown day.

I hauled my luggage into the house, and then tried to think of a stratagem to get some private time with my wife, which, given the tiny window of opportunity, was trickier than it sounds.

In many ways, Zora is extraordinarily strong, but mothers are special territory, especially around the issue of sex. So her mom, who had a huge number of questions regarding the schedule for the next few weeks, was able to monopolize her. After an hour, my adrenaline was starting to burn off, revealing the bone-deep fatigue below. When a lull in the conversation provided an opening, I pounced.

With the aid of some fancy verbal footwork, I was maneuvering Z toward the bedroom when the phone rang: her editor called from the East Coast. As late as it was for me, it was almost as bad for the editor, and it would have been ungentlemanly of me to grumble as they shared a three-way business conversation.

Z found a few seconds to whisper a promise: she'd come to bed as soon as possible. She followed that with a quick, hot, deep stolen kiss that pulled a bit of lead from my bones and deposited it in my pencil, but that faded swiftly, miles and time zones taking their inevitable toll. For a few minutes, I tried to get a little work done: catching up on correspondence, editing some long abandoned short story project, just to keep myself awake.

Our office space is up on the second floor of the house, with Z at one end of the hall, and me at the other. It's a nice work arrangement, and ordinarily I love it. But this time, I found the sound of their chatter and typing profoundly irritating. Every time I pulled my mind away from the e-mail or the work, a vivid image exploded into my mind: Z walking toward me, tantalizingly naked, her hips moving with the metronomic movement women have perfected since the last ice age. The world suddenly felt bright and hot. I was harder than Chinese algebra, but there was not a damned thing I could do about it.

When we first married, the two of us lived in a two-bedroom duplex apartment. We were pretty broke, but we had love, and hope, and a plentiful supply of buck-ass wild sex anytime both of us were in the mood, which was often.

The place was too small, but we could have stayed there awhile longer if her parents hadn't decided to come to visit. I decided I didn't want to have her mom and dad thinking I had moved their precious girl-child into a slum, and with that in mind we rented our four-bedroom house in a much nicer neighborhood. It was an initial stretch of finances, but the money started rolling in, and we never regretted the decision. We christened every room in that house, and the memory of those fevered initiations drifted through my mind like remnants, mocking me with ghosts of humping past.

I rolled into our double bed alone that night, which was no one's fault, but that admission didn't make me feel any better. Fatigue had eroded my energy more deeply than I thought. I didn't fall asleep. I passed out. When I first cycled up toward wakefulness, at about four in the morning, Z lay beside me, but I was too damned tired to do much about it. As if alerted by some ancient mating instinct, she woke up groggily, and spent a few seconds trying to convince herself that she was awake enough to function. She wasn't, and we gave up and settled for spooning. Warm and comforting, but once again the fire and the fuse were frustratingly far apart.

Despite fatigue, I found myself wide awake at eight o'clock. Z was still dead unconscious, and all I could do was let her sleep, hoping that she would be awake by the time I got back from our home gym, a detached room out in the backyard. It's supplied with a treadmill, a total gym, a set of varied weights, and a television set–radio combination.

After a gradual warm-up, the workout turned unexpectedly fierce, evolving into a combination of martial arts, weights, and angry yoga. I worked the kinks out, but by the time I came back in, Mom was already awake and talking to Z. They had arranged their ride to the airport by Wednesday. I couldn't even drive them down, damn it, having a radio interview at the same time. Life just wasn't giving us any kind of break at all.

Then, two more weeks. Arrgh.

While I was gone, Mom had been doing a little bit of sight-seeing in Washington. Z had promised her a look at our local mass murderer, and this was the last day, so we headed off to check out Mt. St. Helens.

We drove north up I-5, then east along a winding road up to the great gray slopes of the lethal cone. There at the visitor's center, we listened to the tour guides tell a crowd of gawking spectators about the mountain that exploded in 1980, wiping out fifty-seven people and flattening millions of trees and thousands of acres. My interest in geology waned quickly. As the rest of them gazed out of the wall-sized window at the shattered hillside, I sidled up to my wife and put my mouth as close to her ear as possible. "Honey, if I don't get naked soon, I'm going to screw the cat."

A little blue-haired lady next to us seemed to have heard that comment, and glanced our way until my waxy bright smile made her retreat. I felt something brush my side, and realized that Zora had snuggled herself close to me, blocking tourist line of sight, position-ing herself so that Mother couldn't see anything, and let her hand drift down to cup my groin. Her fingers stroked gently and then squeezed, and I groaned. If she did that again, St. Helen's wouldn't be the only explosion the tour guides would talk about.

"I think maybe before dinner . . ." she whispered.

On the way home, I smoldered as Zora and her mom talked about volcanoes and hurricanes. Zora's older sister had moved to Miami some years back, and almost been blown into the Atlantic by Hurri-cane Andrew in 1992. Which was more dangerous? Occasional lava, or seasonal typhoons? The conversation would have interested me if not for the fact that every chance she got, Z took my pulse in a man-ner rarely taught in nursing school.

The last couple of miles, Z had mentioned a favorite movie of her mom's that we had recently acquired on DVD, hinting that said film could occupy her mom for an hour or so while the not-so newly-weds . . . *talked*. Yes, I think that's the euphemism she employed. I re-member watching her mom's eyebrows rise in the mirror. A little light went on in her eyes, as if she finally realized that certain subjects had not been directly addressed. The light turned into a twinkle, and my heart raced with hope that we were all finally on the same page.

When we finally rolled into the driveway, I was out of the car al-most before the brakes were set, skipping into the house with a burst of energy I hadn't felt in days. *Damn damn damn, I'm gonna get laid, yes siree.*

As Z and her mother came into the house, I was throwing our cats off the bed and dashing to the bathroom to brush my teeth . . . when the front doorbell rang. Damn. It was Mindy and Richard, neighbors eager to meet Z's mom. They're friends: he's a tall white guy, an award-winning photographer and avid hiker. Mindy's a slender, viva-cious Latina local cop and community activist. Nice folks, but this was some of the worst timing I'd ever seen in my life. I'd known they wanted to come by, and vaguely recalled Z asking me if it would be all right if they came by Tuesday evening. To my frustration, I re-membered being stupid enough to say yes. Politeness had rarely seemed so stupid in retrospect.

It was all right, I said to myself. They'd leave, and then: movie time for Mom and intermission for the horny kids.

Richard and Mindy couldn't have been there for more than a half hour before, to my horror, the fatigue brought on by switching time zones descended on me like an avalanche. Everything they said or did reached me in syrupy slow motion, and I was having difficulty following the conversation at all. Tears of frustration and fatigue mingled beneath my heavy lids, and each breath began to feel labored. This just wasn't fair! My woman was leaving in the morning. We had spent twenty hours around each other, and been unable to arrange the most basic level of nookie. Memories of sex seemed more and more distant, phantasmal, like mirages glimpsed by a man dying of thirst.

Fifteen more minutes passed. I couldn't keep my eyes open any longer. Z looked at me helplessly as the conversation veered into civil rights territory, and the old war stories were dusted off. Fascinating stuff, but I felt my libido melting as fatigue's sticky fingers clutched at me, dragging me down into a swamp. I was almost crying with frustration. In a little over twelve hours, my wife would disappear for fourteen days, and there didn't seem to be much I could do about it.

By the time Richard and Mindy left, our window of opportunity was gone. Vital work remained on their itinerary, so Zora and her mom worked late again that night. I was swearing I was going to be awake and alert when we came to bed. *Just let me close my eyes for a minute and . . .*

*Zzzzzzzz.*

Morning came too early. I levered myself up, feeling like something that had recently crawled creakily out of a crypt. Beside me, Z gently snored. I knew that look on her sleeping face: total exhaustion. My woman works like a field hand on uppers, and there was no way I could be angry, or try to motivate her into feeling sexy when I knew her whole emphasis would be on getting out of the house and to the airport by noon. I had a bad, bad feeling, and didn't want to project my personal bullshit onto her: she hardly needed the grief. I could feel myself shutting down a bit, pulling back emotionally so that I wouldn't be cranky with my sweetie.

I pulled on my sweats, figuring that if I could get another good workout, I could finally feel like I had adjusted to the time difference and have a decent day, if not a really good one.

It was seven A.M. Despite my best intentions, I was angry. Z would be gone in a couple of hours. I felt not just sexually frustrated but childish and selfish to think that the whole world revolved around my prostate.

To my surprise, after I'd been out in our gym for about thirty minutes, Z and her mom joined me. Z was wearing her two-piece workout suit, the one in which she makes Serena Williams look fat and flabby. "Mom said she'd like to watch us work out together. Would that be all right?"

Her mom was smiling at us, her expression slightly echoing the light that had appeared in her eyes the night before. I said: "Sure." And we started a half hour of torture.

When we're serious, Zora and I work out with kettlebells, cannonball-shaped weights equipped with suitcase-style handles. These instruments of destruction can stretch, strengthen, and push heart and lungs all at the same time. We worked out, hard. Sweaty. Intense. Her mom watched, seeming to take genuine pleasure in the way the two of us drove each other on without mercy.

We did stuff that looked like yoga for masochists, calisthenics for those bored by Tae-Bo on fast-forward. As we worked, Z and I melded into a kind of physical synch, a fleshy, wordless understanding. But beneath every drop of sweat and other moisture lurked a different communication altogether. The heat in the room wasn't all about temperature.

At some point, I'm not really certain when, her mom slipped out of the room.

I remember wondering: *gone for water or . . . ?*

Would we dare? No. I can imagine few things more embarrassing than being caught knocking boots in a sweat-soaked exercise room by a mother-in-law bringing a nice glass of Gatorade.

We finally quit, our sweat and moist exhalations fogging the windows. Mom hadn't returned. Our clothes were soaked. I could smell Z's salty, almost metallic scent and knew that she was more than just working hard. We weren't touching, and nothing overtly had been said, but every sideways glance, no matter how brief, seemed swollen with implication.

Moving in concert, we turned the radio and light off, joined hands, and walked back to the house and directly into the bathroom. Her mother was in the guest room, pointedly watching television. I started the shower running, and watched the mirror begin to mist rapidly.

When Z entered, we locked the door, peeled each other's clothes off, and stepped into the shower. Z leaned back against the wall, the burning water beading against her perfect cocoa skin. Her back arched as I knelt against the tile to slide my tongue from her navel to the tangled forest warm inches beneath. Salty soapy water ran into my mouth, and I heard her groan, then my own echoing as my mind was overwhelmed with sensation. Her fingers wound into my hair, drawing my head down and in. With the water thrumming against my skin, I spent what seemed like hours there, reveling in the slippery velvet tastes and smells, feeling her thighs clutch against the side of my head until I had to grip at them to get room to breathe. I pinned Z against the tile wall, felt her fingernails digging into my shoulders as her sounds grew more guttural, less controlled, and she bit into her hand to keep from screaming.

Panting now, her eyes burning bright, she pushed me back and down until I lay against the tile, kneeling in front of her body. Her reaching fingers found my sack, rolled my balls together gently, then tightly enough to start a spark of pain. As I gasped, she dove down and slipped me into her mouth, her tongue rolling along my underside with a kind of feathery fierceness that let me feel every rough crevice, every bump, every curling stroke before she closed her lips around me and created a seal.

I don't know where she learned it, and don't ask. But somehow Z created a little pocket of saliva in the back of her mouth, then with glottal control that would boggle a ventriloquist she began a sucking-and-pumping sensation that was a cross between a washing machine and a vacuum cleaner. At moments like that, if I had to choose between my soul and another five minutes of head, I'm afraid I'd never see heaven.

The explosion should have happened then and there, but with

practiced strokes with the ball of her thumb, she prevented that release of pressure, and we reversed positions again.

I don't remember everything that happened then, only that we eventually ended up on the rug, the pulsing water disguising our animal sounds as we giggled like a couple of kids worried that their parents might catch them at play, clutching at each other's wet, soapy, hot body as if we had never known each other, and might never again.

Damn, it was gloriously, thunderously fine.

The limo came to pick them up at 9:45.

I hugged Mom goodbye and tried not to blush at her secretive smile. All she said when we finally emerged from the bedroom, fully dressed, was: "Good workout?"

You bet.

I kissed Z goodbye, carried her luggage out, and helped the driver put it into the limo. I watched them drive away. I hadn't brushed my teeth since first awakening, and might not for the rest of the day. I could still taste her.

Two whole weeks until she came back.

No problem. It's the job, man.

Besides, some things are worth waiting for.

# Almond Eyes

**Reginald Harris**

N ow look, man, promise me, I mean fucking *promise* me you won't tell anyone about what I'm going to say to you, okay? Especially not to You Know Who. Promise me, okay? I mean, I thought you were pretty cool when we were introduced and you've been down all the other times we've met. Something, I don't know, something makes me think you'd understand a little bit of what's been happening to me. And I have to talk to someone, man, I have to. I have to tell someone about what's been going on.

You've noticed the collar, right? Most people do. Most people, they don't say anything about it, though, you know? I guess they assume it's some kind of fashion statement, or that maybe I'm some kind of black rocker, I'm Lenny Kravitz or some shit, or in a band. I don't wear this one all the time. Sometimes I wear a small chain with a lock on it. People think that's fashion, too, not knowing I'm not the one that has the key. Sometimes women make comments about it, say something about all black men being dogs. A lot of you gay guys seem to recognize what it really means. Why is that? I catch you-all eyeing me. Well, maybe not you, but you know what I mean. It doesn't matter. Whatever . . .

The first thing I noticed about her was her legs. She seduced me with her legs. It's a horrible cliché to say her legs started at her neck, but there you are. It seemed true. But you know that. Long and shapely, peanut brown, with firm calves and breathtaking thighs. Of course, the rest of her is great, too: nimbus of hair, perfect skin, glorious little breasts, piercingly black almond-shaped eyes, and the

kind of face you'd swear you've seen before, in Harlem or Mississippi, Chicago or Oakland, San Juan, Salvador, or in Africa on a
Benin mask. That sexy gap between her two front teeth drove me
crazy whenever I saw her talking or smiling.

But, man, her legs, her legs are like music. She never wore anything inappropriate at work, but all her dresses were right . . .
there . . . right at the line of acceptability. She showed as much leg as
she could get away with, and that shit got my Jimmy moving every
time. Coming down the street, perched on high stilettos, she looked
like a walking skyscraper. The breeze you felt was from every head
turning as he passed. Only she didn't walk, she strode. You know
that, she marches, man. She could've taught all those supermodels a
thing or two about how to represent. Every street and hall was her
private runway. I always hoped it echoed the way her body moved
when she made love.

Working together made things . . . complicated. First off, it made
going out impossible. She had a strict no-dating-coworkers rule,
which she stuck to. It didn't matter that she was up with the execu-
tives and I was junior in accounting, her rule was her rule. I tried
though, Lord knows I tried. The other guys in the office laughed at
me, told me to forget it, thought I was playing way out of my league.
But you know a guy just has to try. Only there's just so much begging
I was used to doing. I got tired of her calling me 'young-un' as if I
was a kid, of her always saying no. Finally, I realized she was right, it
was for the best. The level of jealousy and hatred I could feel from
the other guys in the office who had also tried and failed would have
been too much to take if we had gone out. And it would've looked
like I was trying to suck up to the boss, taking out one of his staff
members. So I chilled.

Not that she didn't have friends at work, both male and female,
no, not at all. I really wasn't paying all that much attention, don't get
me wrong, but she would have lunch or chat at breaks with a range
of different people. I saw you there, too, coming in to take her out,
or meet up with her after work. A lot of her closest friends seemed to
be like you, the gay guys on staff. I can understand that. She wanted
to be with a guy who was not a threat. Someone who she could talk
to about men, who had the same experiences, and could also give her
real insight into them as well. But some of those guys though, some

of them . . . I saw them. I saw them looking. Even a couple of those guys were thinking about turning in their gay cards because of her, I could tell.

Then one day I come in to work, and the whole place is in shock. She's leaving for a new job, some place where she'll be running things. The Director is devastated, and her gay friends are all broken up. Some women are in tears, others can barely hide how glad they are their most serious competition is about to walk out the door. Guys are cursing about how they won't have anything to look forward to five days a week. But me, I'm thinking, "Okay, here's my chance." I'm already making plans for what to say at her farewell party.

The Director, of course, threw her a big bash in one of the downtown hotel ballrooms on her last Friday, with food and an open bar. You remember, that was where we met. She introduced us. You remember how the Director made that speech about how much the company would miss her, how he would miss her, how glad he was for her to move up to an executive position with another firm, but still . . . she smiled and blew him a mock kiss.

I waited until everyone else had spoken to her, hugged and given her gifts and said their good-byes before making my move. As always, she just stared at me.

"Am I right or wrong? We're not going to be coworkers anymore, right? So . . ."

"And exactly how young are you, again?"

"Twenty-six. And please notice how I don't ask you how old you are."

"Very wise decision."

"See, I know a thing or two about women."

"You also remember the first time you talked to me I told you I was in my forties and damned near old enough to be your mother."

I looked her up and down. "Hey, mama. Wha' up?"

She shook her head. "You're also very persistent, aren't you?"

"Yes, I am. Very persistent—determined, tenacious, relentless. 'Long-winded,' even. Especially when I know what I want."

"So you know what you want, do you?"

I nodded.

"Hmm . . . Do you *really*?"

I looked directly into her eyes. "Oh, yes, absolutely."

She smiled the smile of those who know but do not tell. "We'll see," she whispered. "We'll see . . ."

What movie did we go to? Where did we wind up for dinner that first night? I don't remember. I remember sitting in the dark with her, being washed in the light of images reflecting off a large screen. I remember trying desperately to concentrate and not stare at her in the dark. I remember eating after that, a mix of tastes and textures on my tongue, a warm sated feeling in my belly at the end. We talked. Or rather she said something and I made sounds I supposed were some kind of language she could understand to answer her. I don't know. All I remember is her eyes staring at me, smiling at me, pulling me in all night.

I got myself together enough that first night to take her home, walk her to her door, leaving with nothing more than a long friendly hug. I had a plan, realized I could probably get farther longer by pulling back a bit, denying what she obviously knew about how I felt. She wanted an adult, and so I was going to act like one, like an old school gentleman. She just smiled that smile again, and said good night. I drove home and spent the entire sleepless night on edge. Even beating off didn't help. I'd shoot, try to relax, and still find myself wide awake, still thinking about her, and slowly get another erection again. I lay in bed all night, feeling her almond eyes staring at me from the ceiling.

But still I was determined to play our next date exactly like the first. And it was exactly the same: don't ask me who it was we saw in concert, who the opening act was, what they sang. I remember her fingers tapping in time on the armrest of her chair, my forearm, my leg. Dinner was something hot and sweet, followed by some cool, slightly intoxicating liquid. I dropped her off and said good night, and headed back to my car. This time she gave me a small peck on the cheek during our hug, and whispered something I couldn't understand into my ear. And again, the sleepless night. Only this time, her image over me was even more vivid. I almost felt like she was there in my apartment with me as I beat off again and again.

By our third date, I just couldn't take it anymore. That night after dinner, I didn't even ask. I took her back to my place.

"Are you sure you want to invite me in?" she said, standing in the doorway.

"Absolutely," I said, hands slightly shaking, on the edge of a cold sweat. She smiled, closing the door behind her.

I turned on a light, illuminating my small apartment, and hit the "Play" button on the CD player. The CD I'd had an older friend burn for me especially for this occasion, a mix with everything from Brian McKnight to Coltrane ballads to dance music from Cuba and Brazil, draped a warm sheet of sound around us. We flew into each other. Words caught in my throat as we kissed. The feel of her soft lips was all the conversation we needed. Her heels brought her up to my six-foot height, and our bodies fit together as if we'd been molded for each other. As we wrapped our arms and legs around each other, I felt as though I'd leapt off a great height and was falling, falling, falling, and didn't want to land.

Our third orgasm was the first we had actually in my bed. The first time we'd just ripped each other's clothes off and did it right there in the middle of the floor. The second time we managed to make it a few feet to the couch. After the third time, I lay with my arms around her, dozing as she ran her fingers over my body, stopping when she felt me rising again in her hand.

"Would you like to try something?" she whispered.

"Hmmm . . . yes. Yeah, sure."

"Then kiss me." She pushed my face down and down and down, right into her bush. And that's how I wound up on my hands and knees at her feet at dawn, beating off with her toes in my mouth.

Sorry, I didn't mean to upset you. I'm just trying to tell you that I thought I knew something about sex. You couldn't tell me shit, man, I *knew* how to please a woman. Where to touch and when and for how long, what to pinch and prod and where to poke my tongue and for how long. Some women thought I was a freak because I knew more than two positions. Hell, I knew nothing. She taught me how much I didn't know. Turns out I was strictly vanilla. Every inch of the human body is an erogenous zone. Before meeting her, it was only my dick that came. After three nights with her, she had the hair on my fucking head ejaculating. My body had never been so alive.

I don't have a harmful bone in my body, I really don't, yet I discovered I really liked her in uniforms. This scared me. Here I am a brother who believes that the police have oppressed and continue to oppress all people of color, including me. But there I was drooling over her dressed like a cop, security guard, or correctional officer. Begging for her to cuff my wrists and ankles. CO and inmate became my favorite game. Does this mean there's some fascist hiding inside me? Is it harmless pleasure or a result of my rigid upbringing, or being forced to wear uniforms in school? And where did she get all that shit, anyway? Complete uniforms and all the extras, down to the utility belt with mace and nightstick. All this makes me want to laugh—but why? Once she taught me exactly how to do it, wasn't I happy to prostrate myself on the floor before her, gazing up with longing at the crisp whiteness of her uniform shirt, silver badge glinting in the bedroom light? My hands caressed her calves under the deep blue covering of her slacks as I began to lick first right then left black steel-toed work boot, as a sign of devotion and submission to welcome my woman home.

The things we did together started out as a game for me, a kind of mask to put on to make her happy. Beginning with silk ties and tickling me with a feather, we moved with blinding speed to floggers, paddles, whips. A matching pair of his and hers nipple clamps. Being tied down to the bed was fun. She was right, I did look good with the leather and metal "X" of a harness strapped across my chest. The feel of the leather strap slapping my bare ass was hot, startling, sending an electric bolt of pain through me, turning my jock-bound dick to granite for when she released me and we fucked. I lay back in the tub as she stood over me and drenched my open mouth with her juices because . . . well . . . because . . .

Sorry, sorry. So okay, so maybe, like, things were changing between us. Changing in me. The games were turning into something else, the mask turning into a doorway leading to a deeper truth. A new way of life. After three months of play she wrapped my first collar around my neck, closing it with a sharp, clicking snap. She smoothed down my eyebrows and quietly drew an X on my forehead with her long red fingernail, marking the spot of her coming kiss. I looked up, first at Heaven's Gate, where my face, tongue, fingers, fist, dick had been, then beyond to her laughing face and the deep, quiet pools of her almond eyes.

But, see, now here's the kicker, here's the shit I just don't understand. I felt *better* after we started doing all this freaky shit. Man, I mean I'm sharper, more secure. People noticed I was more "on" at work. I spoke up at meetings, became one of those "High Potentials" bosses love so much. True, some folks thought I was just sucking up, others that I had suddenly found the key to "acting white" and was just trying to get ahead. None of that was true. Giving up my ability to say no, at home, I found myself more able to resist bullshit everywhere else. Belonging to someone else, in taking care of her and being taken care of, calmed me down. Wearing a lock and chain under my button-down shirt seemed to liberate me. Knowing I had to get home to draw her evening bath, scent it with flowers and oils so she could uncoil in the tub while I made dinner, made me more than willing to finish all my work before 5 P.M.

"Let's get married," I said to her one night.

She lifted her head up from where she'd been lightly sucking my left nipple and smiled. With one quick jerk she pulled one of my chest hairs out with her teeth and quickly swallowed it, then kissed the tiny pinpoint of blood that formed in its place.

"Why mess up a good thing?" she asked. "I feel like we're already 'married.' I . . . we've found someone willing to carry out our desires. We're already 'connected' in some way. Don't you feel it?" She moved up to kiss me, and began to wrap her legs around mine again, to ride me, connecting us cunt to cock.

Now she's anxious to take me to this party next week given by some friends of hers at this artist's loft downtown. A whole spectrum of people will be there she says: black, Latin, Asian white, male, female, gay, straight, both, neither. I've been helping her with her outfit and she, of course, will look stunning, in full Army fatigues, pants tucked into boots I will have polished so shiny you'll see the full moon reflected in them. As for me, I'll be wearing nothing but the harness, a pair of boots, and these leather shorts so short and tight they barely cover my ass. And the collar of course, with a short leash attached. The place looks like some kind of sexual clubhouse. After strutting around showing me off, she plans on stripping out of her fatigues, down to dog tags and a bikini bottom. Then, she says, we're really going to have some fun.

A lot of shit is going through my mind about this. Am I jealous? Is it that I want her all to myself (well, yes, yes, of course I do)? Am I going to freak when I see her with some other guy, or another woman? And what is she going to have me do? Who is she going to send me off with? Not that I got anything against you guys, but I really don't want to be with a guy, you know? I'm not sure if I even want to see what you-all do together, no offense, man.

"Just relax," she says, staring at me with those eyes again. "You'll have fun. I'll be there to make sure everything's all right. You just have to realize that sometimes we play and sometimes we make love. This will be one of those times when we'll be playing." She smiles and suddenly seems both younger and older than her years.

But see, there's something else too. It's strange, but I'm not sure what's really happening to me. You see me now, right? I could swear that I'm shrinking. I'm positive I used to be taller, remember? My clothes don't seem to fit me anymore. She just says I'm losing a little weight or something, I should cut back on working out, maybe she should change the mix in the protein shake she makes for our breakfast every morning. I don't know . . . once upon a time I used to be taller than she is, she had to have her "fuck me pumps" on to come up even with me. Now I always seem to be looking up at her, even when she's barefooted. And my shoes don't seem to fit right anymore.

Old stories keep running around in the back of my head, never stopping long enough to become clear. I keep thinking about her cutting my hair every two weeks, how I saw her once collecting clippings from the trash can after I'd cut my nails. The collar keeps getting tighter, our sessions get wilder and wilder, but somehow something . . . I don't know, something doesn't seem quite right. Help me out, bro, you have to have some idea what's going on. You've got to help me, tell me something. I'm happy, you know, I mean, shit, we're fucking or doing something almost every night. I should be ecstatic, but instead I'm just feeling more and more tired. Some nights I just want to go to sleep, but there she is, pulling on me, willing me to come one more time. I just don't know . . .

And when I ask her, you know, I don't get an answer. Not a real one anyway. She just looks at me and smiles and smiles. Her almond eyes stare at me and smile.

# Lucky She's Mine

**Gary Earl Ross**

*The way I feel right now, somebody gon' die tonight.*

I met my wife the rainy April night her husband tried to kill her—her first husband, that is. Though I was new to the apartment building, the sad face in the flashing red and blue lights was not new to me. Several weeks earlier, passing the laundry room one evening, I had glimpsed the same woman loading wet clothes into a coin-op dryer. She was tall and ginger-skinned, with thick black hair, broad shoulders, and long thin fingers. For an instant our eyes met. Mine, I imagine, looked as tired as I felt after a day of classes and meetings that ended with my evening graduate seminar. Hers were a sparkling pale brown and seemed full of a wisdom that belied her obvious youth. She was in her mid-twenties, I guessed, about half my age. I slowed long enough to nod a greeting but didn't stop to speak—the ink was still wet on my own divorce decree, and I had not yet begun striking up casual conversations with women. Besides, her wedding rings would have caught the attention of a blind man. I climbed the stairs to my apartment without realizing that she was half of the couple who lived directly above me, who sometimes awakened me in the night with their enviably loud sex or their violent arguments. In fact, I didn't know who she was until the Tuesday night their dispute spilled down the stairs and I found myself trying to disengage her husband's thick fingers from her throat.

Though I am by nature a shy, withdrawn man, I grew up in a neighborhood that demanded an entry-level toughness to survive. I learned early to hold my own in a fight, but my last fight had come when I was fifteen. I was nearly fifty now, in reasonably good shape but softer in the middle than I would have liked. As a professor of criminal justice, I had visited enough penitentiaries to recognize a prison weight room physique from the thickness of a man's forearms and neck. I was clearly outmatched, but giving the woman's towering husband an opportunity to break my nose, split my lip, and snap my glasses while hissing, "Ol' nigga need to min' his own bidness," gave another neighbor the chance to dial 911. Slumped on the red tile floor, I grabbed at his leg to keep him from returning his attention to his wife and caught a steel-toed Timberland in my side. My broken rib permitted his wife to scramble back up the stairs and lock herself in their apartment. Fortunately, he had left his keys inside. He spent several minutes hammering the steel door with his fists, ordering her to let him in. Then he stomped back down to the landing where I lay, to punish me further for my intervention. The cops arrived just as he delivered his fourth kick.

The husband—Darius Bell, I later learned—went to jail. His wife and I went to different hospitals. Assisted as she walked to one ambulance, she stopped to see how I was, just before I was eased into the other. Looking up at her from the stretcher, I could see the tears on her cheeks catching slivers of the pulsing emergency lights, and I swallowed at the sight of the finger bruises on her beautiful throat.

"You save me," she said, with a vaguely African accent I couldn't place precisely. "You not have to do. Thank you."

"Don't mention it," I said thickly. "What's your name?"

"Lakech," she said.

"Lucky?"

She smiled and nodded, as if to say, "Close enough."

> *Man, this ain't had nothin' to do wit' you.*
> *What you gotta get in my shit for?*

I spent the night in the hospital and came home the next day, the bridge of my nose bandaged, my lower lip stitched, and my midsection taped. I had several visitors that afternoon. My department chair passed half an hour pretending he was my best friend. My graduate assistant, an eager suburban kid, assured me she was ready to cover my classes for however long I needed to recuperate. A police investigator stopped in to ask if I wanted to press charges, to which I said, "Hell yes!" Summoned the night before as next of kin because I had not yet changed the insurance card in my wallet, my ex-wife dropped by to put groceries in my refrigerator. Then she came into the bedroom, where I'd retreated after letting her in, and shook her head at the sight of me. When she asked if I needed anything else, I studied her before answering. Never beautiful, and heavier in middle age, Andrea was still a handsome woman, with unblemished dark skin and the best mouth I had ever kissed.

"This wouldn't have happened if I were still married to you," I said.

"No, it wouldn't have," she said simply. "Now, if you're okay for the time being . . . Well, Charles is downstairs with the motor running."

"Sure," I said. "Thanks." And when she was gone, I added, "The least you could do after I made everything so easy for you." Then I swallowed more painkillers and lowered myself into a throbbing sleep.

I was awakened some time later by a faint tapping at my back door. Dragging myself out of bed, I was surprised to find Lakech standing in the hallway. Thick hair in a braid that hung over her shoulder to her right breast, she was clad in a simple denim dress and hid her throat bruises with a filmy gold scarf. Her left hand was in an oven mitt, balancing a steaming bowl with a spoon handle sticking out of it.

"I bring soup," she said. "Make feel better."

"You didn't have to do that," I said.

"I want do," she said, and smiled so wistfully I felt my ribs cinch. It seemed criminal that a woman so striking should be so sad.

I invited her in and gestured toward a chair at the kitchen table. We sat across from each other, and she pushed the soup to me. It was full of vegetables, noodles, and chunks of chicken. She watched me, waiting for me to try her cooking, her high cheekbones even higher because of her expectant smile. I felt a twinge in my lip stitch as I blew cool air on my first spoonful. The soup was good but hot, so I ate slowly, trying to engage her in conversation so the food could cool.

"Where's your husband?" I asked.

"Still jail." Lower lip caught between her teeth, she shook her head. "No bail. No wait for him this time. We all finish. Through." Her eyes moistened and she lowered them, as if ashamed. For the first time I noticed that the oven mitt was off, that her wedding rings were gone.

"He's . . . hurt you before?"

Eyes still lowered, she nodded. "We meet when I high school. I happy to have American man like me. He have good job then, not like now. We marry. I have no brother, no father, so he beat me when he mad, when he high. He go to prison before, beat when he get out." She wiped her eyes with the heel of one hand. "He beat me, all time say he sorry. Still beat me." She sniffed.

I reached out and touched her other hand. "It's not your fault," I said. "You don't have to put up with abuse. Nobody does." Then I changed the subject. "Where are you from?"

She looked up, her face brightening only momentarily. "Ethiopia," she said, the *h* almost silent. "Beautiful country but too much war. I come here teenager, to other city with my mother. Now mother dead. Different city. No friend. Marriage finish. No place to go. I need help."

"What kind of help?"

"They say you law professor." Her face brightened again, this time with hope.

"No, criminal justice," I said. "Law enforcement, the psychology and sociology of crime." The sight of her hope dissipating pushed me to say more. "But I have friends who are lawyers, and law professors. If you need legal advice—immigration, an order of protection, divorce—I can find somebody to help you."

She appeared to think this over, then smiled slowly. "Thank you."

"No, thank *you*," I said, taking another spooonful of soup.

For the next half hour I listened as she told me the story of her life. I listened to the music of her Amharic accent, felt borne along on its rhythms, despite the sorrows she had experienced. At eight, she had seen her father, a professor, shot to death for his opposition to the government. Forced into the streets when their home was burned, Lakech and her mother and brother had resorted to begging to survive. All three had been raped at one point or another—"By soldiers," she said with distaste. Later, her brother was a civilian casualty in a shoot-out between the army and the Eritrean People's Liberation Front. After his funeral, a U.S. relief agency brought Lakech and her mother to Philadelphia. Her mother lived only two years, long enough to see her daughter wed to a man who promised to take care of her and the children she bore them. But damage from multiple rapes had left her barren, and Darius was disappointed. After three years he lost his job. They moved to this city five years ago in search of new opportunity. The beatings had started soon after their arrival, after she had got a job in an African arts store that paid her more than the minimum wage he earned. The only break in the cycle was the several months he spent in prison for drug possession.

"Stay this time," she said. "I not care."

"Lakech, how old are you?" I asked.

"Be twenty-eight next year." She frowned at my smile. "Is the truth."

"You don't look a day over twenty-three," I said, finishing the soup.

She dismissed me with a wave of her hand. "How is food?"

"Very good. Thank you for bringing it."

She shrugged. "Least I do . . . for friend."

*No, right about now, killin' feel easy, real easy.*

As a professor of criminal justice, I am invited frequently to speak at luncheons and civic associations about crime or the history of crime. My most requested topic in such venues is classic murder cases. After an hour or so of listening to the misdeeds of Jack the Ripper, Lizzie Borden, Leopold and Loeb, and Ted Bundy, most audiences are ready for a touch of comic relief. So I invite them to describe the perfect murder—of someone they know and have a motive for killing. A few usually take the challenge. When they finish outlining their scenarios, I explain how they will get caught. Sometimes, after describing the range of forensic testing or the near impossibility of disposing of all physical evidence, let alone the body, I slap a pair of stage handcuffs on one of the volunteers and lead him or her out of the room. Thus, an otherwise gruesome talk ends with laughter and applause.

The week after the assault, I gave my homicide talk to a Thursday evening crowd in the central library auditorium downtown. I explained my nose by saying I'd had a disagreement with the edge of a door, and the door won. Then I began with a recitation of the abuse Charles Manson had suffered throughout his early life. When the lights came up fifty minutes later, I was surprised to see Lakech in an aisle seat about ten rows back. During the Perfect Murder Challenge, she rose to offer a weak scenario for getting away with the murder of a husband. After exposing the flaws in her plan— mainly, that the basement incinerator would leave enough bone for identification—I marched down the steps and put the cuffs on her. I took my bow in the aisle.

Afterward, we went for coffee. Seated across from me for the second time in a week, she smiled and said, "Before, we talk about me. Now your turn. Tell me about you."

So I did.

> *Who said anything 'bout gettin' away wit' it?*
> *We can all die right here.*

While Darius sat in jail for three months, served with divorce papers and awaiting criminal trial, Lakech and I deepened our friendship. We went to museums and concerts, movies and plays, and over dinner discussed what we'd seen or heard. I found her intelligence even more engaging than her beauty. It was as if her mind had been cloistered and waiting for a special dispensation to open itself to the world. Gradually, the weariness of the wisdom in her eyes began to lessen, and her face lit up whenever she opened her door to find me standing there.

I had not thought of our time together as dating until I took her to a cocktail party at the university president's house one Friday evening and a gray-haired woman from the anthropology department asked to meet my date. When I said, "This is my friend Lakech," somehow the word *friend* seemed wrong. I looked at her as she shook the professor's hand and realized that whether she was in an embroidered caftan with a matching headwrap or a sleeveless dress with matching shoes and handbag, Lakech always dressed to be noticed when we went out. Of course, I *had* noticed the roll of her hips beneath flowing mud cloth or damask, the curve of her legs when she wore shorter dresses. I had seen the touches of makeup and breathed in her modest perfume. But I had not thought of us as dating, because I had refused to let myself do so.

Later, when I walked her upstairs to her apartment, she looked straight into my eyes and said, "Why you never try to make love to me?"

There was so much I should have said. Some were things she already knew: that my wife's decision to end our marriage and take up with Charles had devastated me, that I felt awkward around women, that work took up too much of my time. Some she should have known: that it was probably stupid to begin a relationship when we were both set to testify against her husband, that I was old enough to be her father. What she couldn't have known, however, was that I still had vivid memories of her sex with Darius in the weeks before I entered their lives. Lakech had no idea how much I had heard, how I had lain beneath their bedroom floor and listened to the squeak of their springs and the punch of her breathing. Having had no sex for nearly a year, I was jealous of what I heard, ashamed but willing to strain to hear more. Sometimes I even reached for myself, at my age. I should have told her that I was afraid, afraid I couldn't make her cry out in the night, as Darius had done, afraid that if I failed to do so she would pull away from me, as Andrea had pulled away from me, and I would be alone again.

But she never gave me the chance.

Lakech pulled me to her and put her mouth against mine and slipped her tongue inside, and I could taste her after-dinner mint. She pulled me into the warmth of her body and ground herself against me and whimpered in her throat, and I forgot about Andrea's mouth.

Inside, in the same bedroom she had shared with Darius, I trembled with a mixture of fear and anticipation as I watched her undress in the soft green light of a bedside lamp. She undid her headwrap last, green light glinting off the gold threads, and let her thick hair hang loosely as she crossed the room to me. Her body was exquisite—long arms and legs, heavy but firm breasts with large dark nipples, scars that cried of a past life. She kissed me again and undid my tie and shirt and belt. Smiling, she undressed me tenderly, slowly, holding me up as I stepped out of my pants and boxers. She's so strong, I thought, and then she confirmed the impression by cupping me and leading me toward the bed.

"A long time since I've done this," I said.

"Shh," she said, kissing me and pulling me into bed beside her.

Her skin was firm beneath my hands, her nipples thick beneath my tongue. I touched her vagina, her clitoris, and felt emboldened by her gasp. Kissing her deeply, I inserted a finger, which slid into her moist heat with no resistance. I had forgotten how wet a young woman could be. I began a gentle circular stroking. Pulsing, she came quickly, screaming into my throat, tearing her face away from mine to scream again. I brought her to climax again and kissed her throat and inhaled the sweat between her breasts and felt my skin tingling as she thrashed against me. Then she reached out for me, and I was suprised to feel her fingers close around the hardest erection I'd had in years. "Now fuck?" she said. I was afraid again, but only for a moment—and, as it turned out, unnecessarily.

Two weeks later Darius was sentenced to five years for assault and drug possession. Five months after that, when her divorce was finalized, Lakech and I married in a small civil ceremony and moved into a two-bedroom cottage about two miles north of the university. Feeling fortunate that I was getting a second shot at happily ever after, I nicknamed my new wife Lucky.

*Serious as a heart attack, you black bitch. You gon' give it up right here in fronta him or I'ma cut this old motherfuckah's throat. C'mon, Pops, wake your old ass up.*

The voices and the memories that had been crowding my brain began to recede at the feel of leather fingertips smacking my cheek. I blinked and raised my head, but the back of my skull was pounding and I lowered it again, squeezing my eyes shut against the pain. I swallowed, swallowed again, tried to make sense of where I was and what was happening. My eyes opened slowly, letting the light seep in. It startled me to realize my wrists were bound behind me, my ankles duct-taped to a chair. The last thing I recalled was unlocking the front door and stepping into the living room. The remains of a champagne bottle lay in a wet green debris field a foot or so to my right. The stickiness on the back of my neck had to be blood. When I raised my head and looked across my living room, I saw that I was helpless as my wife's ex-husband, out of prison ten months early, prepared to rape her.

Dressed in oversized jeans and a black turtleneck, Darius was bigger than I remembered. One gloved hand was locked around Lakech's wrist, the other around the haft of a boning knife from the cutlery set in the kitchen. He was forcing her to her knees on the carpet, in front of the sofa. Her whimper cut through my haze, and I struggled against the duct tape.

"Lucky!" I screamed. "Leave her alone!"

"You 'wake, Pops? Good." He grinned. "For a minute I was afraid I hit you too hard, like I was christenin' you, y'know." Grin widening to bare large white teeth, he nodded as if pleased with his own ingenuity. "But I'm glad you back. I figure since you wanted my wife bad enough to get me sent up to make it easy for you, least I could do was show you what this bitch really like." He forced Lakech to her back and released her wrist. "See," he said, "she be all sweet 'n' shit wit' you, but you don't know her like I know her. All she really want to do is look out for herself." He stretched to his full height above her and looked down at her. "Bet if I said she could run, all she had to do was give you up, she be gone like that." He snapped his fingers and chuckled. "But she ain't gettin' off that easy. Neither one o' y'all is." He looked from Lakech to me and back. "Y'all got to pay for what you done to me." His glare fixed Lakech where she lay, propped on elbows, chest heaving. "Sent me to the joint so you could be wit' some old broke-down motherfuckah." He shook his head, then, hissing, backhanded her across the face, snapping her head back to the floor. He rolled his head so that his neck cracked. "Well, it's payback up in here tonight, and ain't nobody gon' call the law."

"Leave us alone," I said, my eyes filling from rage and helplessness. "I have money." I swallowed. "About a hundred dollars in the bedroom, top dresser drawer. Take it and go and nobody needs to know about this. Just leave her alone. Nobody needs to know. I'm a man of my word."

"Man of my word," he mocked. "It ain't 'bout the money. Like I said, we can all die right here. This 'bout payback. You want her so bad, you get to watch me fuck her. You get to watch me fuck her the way you can't, you old limp-dick book-buster." I closed my eyes and remembered what I had heard a few years ago. I'd long since forgotten the sounds Lakech made with Darius. It was enough to know they were different from the sounds she made with me. Now, not only was I was going to hear those sounds again, I was also going to see the two of them together. I had never felt more impotent.

"And when I'm done," Darius continued, "yeah, you gon' gimme that money, and your cards, and all your PIN numbers. Maybe we all live, maybe we all die. Maybe just you two die. I ain't decided yet."

"You know you're the first one they'll look at," I said. "Ex-husband, just out. She married a witness in his case—"

He whirled away from her and swung the knife up to my face, steadying the point near my eye. "Maybe I got me a alibi. You ever think 'bout that, pro*fess*or? Maybe I got me one o' them jailhouse letter-writin' bitches do anything I tell her. Or maybe I'll just kill you and take back what was mine to begin wit'."

"Do you know what I teach?" I said, desperate now, trying to hold his face with my eyes. "Criminology. Murder investigation. They look for motives first. You got a motive and a jacket. And you're leaving clues everywhere. Your shoes, your sweater, your hair. Fibers, DNA. You'll never get away with this."

"That's funny," he said, jerking a thumb toward Lakech. "That's what she said, like she been listenin' to your lectures. Know what I tol' her? I said, who said anything 'bout gittin' away wit' it? You gon' watch. If you close your eyes, she die slow. If she fight, I cut leg tendons so she can't walk. Then she watch you die slow before she die. Your call."

Lakech, who had remained silent through all this, sat up and said, "Fuck me, Darius. Fuck me. Then go, leave us alone." She unsnapped her jeans and began to wriggle out of them.

"Lucky, no," I said.

"Only way," she said.

"Oh, we can try a couple different ways," Darius said, free hand undoing his jeans. He pushed them down, and then his boxers, and worked them over his boots.

By this time Lakech had removed her shirt and bra and pushed her clothes toward the couch. She leaned back, propped on her right elbow, right hand tangled with her clothing, left hand gesturing to her ex-husband. "Off with top," she said. "You know I like with no clothes."

Sucking his teeth, he set the knife on the mantel and peeled off his gloves and turtleneck. When he reached for the knife again, she shook her head. "No need. He can't get. I can't get."

He thought it over for a moment, looking at me, then her, and deciding neither of us posed a threat. He left the knife where it lay and knelt before her. He worked his knees between her legs and said, "Baby, I'ma make you forget all 'bout this geezer."

The sight of my wife naked, spreading her legs and reaching for another man's dick, made me gag. As she milked him into an erection, I rocked and grunted, shook and strained against the tape. I knew that if I were free, I would kill him without worrying about the forensics. I would kill him and spit on his corpse, grind my heels into his eyes, and piss down his dead throat. The smile on her face as she pulled his erect manhood toward her convinced me I would kill Lakech too.

Just then Lakech's right hand flashed with something silver and seemed to punch Darius in the stomach, knocking the wind out of him. With a grunt, he doubled and went onto his side, then tried to get to his knees. "Bitch," he muttered. "Fuckin' bitch!" In that instant Lakech was on her feet, springing toward the mantel. Snarling, Darius snatched her ankle and tried to pull her back to him. She spun and kicked him in the face. They both went down, she to her knees and he onto his back. Then I saw the knitting needle she'd lost a few days ago protruding from his navel. Blood bubbled around it, as if it were the shaft of an oil drill that had just hit a deep reserve. Lakech reached for the first thing she could find, a hardcover that lay on the lamp table beside the sofa. She raised the book over her head and brought it down on the knitting needle as if hammering a stake into a vampire's heart.

As he twitched and begged her to help him, please, she went to the mantel, got the knife, and cut me loose. His hands slick with blood, Darius tried to get a grip on the knitting needle to pull it out. He didn't understand, but I did. It almost seemed as if Lakech *had* been listening to my lectures; she had nailed him just right. I bent down and withdrew the needle for him, knowing it would be faster that way. "You saw it under the couch," I said, and Lakech nodded, pressing her face into my chest. We stood holding each other for a long time as he bled out at our feet. When he was still, his ass dead center in a small lake of blood, she began to cry and said, "What we do? What we do?"

I held her and stroked her bare back and whispered, "You saved me, baby. You saved us both." I thought about calling the police. Three quick tones on the telephone keypad and this could all start to go away. But would it? Home invasion, attempted rape, threats of murder. We could certainly make a case for self-defense, and a good criminalist could reconstruct everything that had happened. But would it stick—or would we luck into a DA eager to make his bones with a foreigner? Or somebody who had it in for a liberal university type, especially the "Murder He Wrote" guy whose lectures were covered in the newspapers from time to time? I lifted Lakech's chin and looked into her wet eyes and saw the old heaviness beginning to return. I thought of her father and her brother, of all that she and her mother had endured. Whatever direction a police investigation took, she would face endless questions, possibly cross-examination, more poking and prodding and pounding. She had seen enough, I decided, suffered enough.

"What we do?" she said.

"Did he come in a car?"

"Don't know," she said. "Inside when I come home." She shuddered and said, "What we do?" as I draped my sports jacket over her shoulders.

"What you're going to do is take a bath," I said, "and get that bastard's funk off you. I'll take care of everything else."

Formulating and rejecting one idea after another, my brain refused to acknowledge the irony of my facing the very problem I had posed for so many students and audiences. I won't go into the details of my solution. Let's just say it involved a bit of misdirection with the knife, plastic drop cloths from the paint supplies in the garage, a four-hour drive—rubber gloves, allergy mask, vinyl raincoat, plastic bags over sneakers—halfway through a neighboring state in a Volvo I later learned was stolen, and a 120-week commitment to double plastic bag one square foot of carpet and put it in the middle of a different neighbor's trash barrel.

But I couldn't have managed any of it alone. Lucky for me, I didn't have to. In our SUV, on the return trip from out of state, Lakech was tired after driving behind me for so many hours. She crawled into the back to sleep as I drove home through rural darkness. Listening to her now peaceful breathing, I felt a shameless surge of pride that she would trust me like that with her life.

# Giovanni

**E. Ethelbert Miller**

*A soft wind at dawn*
*Lifts one dry leaf and lays it*
*Upon another*
  —Richard Wright

## I

I climb into bed and wait for Rochelle to move over to the far end. There is something strange about this, like segregating beaches and pools, drawing a line in the water, or in this case a line down the middle of the sheets. I am waiting for the world to end. That's what this is, the end of the world. My wife's back is a stone even Jesus can't move and this is just another sign like everything else. Earthquakes, floods, tornadoes, and kids killing kids in schools. I think all these things are biblical and that's why I want a divorce. I try to sleep on my side of the bed. There must be more space inside a coffin. Tomorrow is the first day of November. Another fall day and leaves falling, turning colors, filling the ground like tears slipping on the earth. Red, orange, brown. The green of my youth gone. What do I have to show for it? Home and work. I am tired of teaching at a small college in a small town. I hate my job and all the raking necessary to turn students into people who want something more than grades. My two children ignore me. They play lottery with my love. On weekends I disguise myself as an insect.

I feel one day someone is going to step on me.

## II

I am holding a copy of *Native Son* in my hands. The classroom is filled with faces that have no interest in what I am saying. We could all be trapped on a roof in Chicago, a snowstorm coming in off the lake. The white, wet, soft stuff covering our blackness. Giovanni sits in the front chair by the door crossing her legs, and the flesh she reveals has a smile for me. I know what she is thinking. Giovanni holds a pen in her hands like a penis, twirling it like a baton, tapping it quietly against her thigh.

The first time we made love it was in a park near the lake, a place in the afternoon when the weather was changing and folks didn't know whether to stay indoors or go outdoors. Giovanni wore a dress with a dozen buttons and she opened it enough for me to count past twelve. I heard the birds flying overhead, and Giovanni's body fluttered as we collapsed to the hard earth and my own hardness fell upon her.

What do you notice first about a woman? Across a room her hand touches her face. Her face a leaf changing colors. Giovanni was the type of woman whose skin had a European and African history. The curves of her breasts and buttocks were the reasons why wars were fought. Men died but first they killed for her. The wind kissed the surface of our clothes and clouds covered the visible parts of our nakedness. Giovanni introduced me to her lips. The same lips that seldom spoke in class. The silent lips belonging to a character in a book. How much of a man's life is fiction? I read Giovanni's lips looking for an answer or maybe a short story from my life. In the park one of Giovanni's unfastened buttons tells me to stop. It becomes a small eye, a witness, and reader. I wanted to turn back but I couldn't turn away. So I fucked Giovanni and prayed that I would die. I prayed for her to resurrect me and I prayed again to forget every word, sentence, and page I had become. I wanted to be reduced to a fuck. After Giovanni I crawled away from her body like a furry animal looking for something else to fuck. It was either fuck or become fiction. A fictional fuck.

## III

Ring! The alarm clock goes off and I feel my wife's body depart from the bed like an early morning train. A slow movement out of the station, the daily crawl, the same destination and checking of tickets. Cold air greets my body where the blanket has been pulled back. I keep my eyes closed as my wife pulls her body into the bathroom. She knows I'm not sleeping but she prefers to take a piss first before speaking. When was the last time we made love? I lie in bed thinking about my morning lecture. It's going to be a long day, with a faculty meeting around three o'clock. I feel myself becoming hard as my thoughts change to embrace Giovanni. I place my hand inside my shorts, protecting my penis from the sound of a pissing Rochelle. It has come to this. Yet for the first time in five years I feel excited about teaching Richard Wright. I am tired of Ralph Ellison. Toni Morrison is like bad seafood for my freshman students who read nothing but black romance books and memoirs by women who always cover their heads as if they were living on a plantation.

My wife and her female book club read these books. Her girl friends are middle-aged black women who have lost the battle with their weight. They resemble aunts who sit in the corners of rooms during weddings and funerals. I sometimes come home from work and find two or three of them in the kitchen. My wife laughing and stopping only for a moment to laugh at me. Someone has been telling one of those black men jokes about how we don't act right and treat them well. Who can blame me for stroking myself every morning and thinking of Giovanni? Or how sometimes my penis becomes a tall tree in search of her forest. My thoughts are interrupted by the flushing sound of the toilet. Rochelle is running water. My own wetness spills threw the gates of my hand. "Giovanni," I whisper, wishing she was real. On the floor by my bed the books I need for class. The alarm clock goes off again. I rise.

## IV

The water in my shower changes temperature. It prevents me from taking a long shower. I like to wash, relax, and think about philosophical questions. Are all stories true? Our lives fictions like Borges believed. I love the tile in the bathroom. Dark and light blue. The color of the sky when you're young and your head is always turning to follow the sun, moon, and stars. A blue color of coolness. Blue notes coming from a horn. A Blue Monday when you can't remember the last good thing you said to your wife. I remember blue tiles like a crime.

I'm standing miles away, perhaps in another city, in a hotel or a woman's bathroom, getting ready to shower. I need to get away from it all because the sex is too filled with guilt and it keeps undressing me and seducing me and I stop only long enough to wash and scratch the dry remains of a woman's pussy from my skin. The flakes also flutter before they fall into the tub. I stand with soap and washcloth, washing myself. I feel the water on my back, and maybe if I were a slave running from the hounds, this water would be the river telling me, "Boy, you still gotta swim, this ain't freedom yet." I reach out and place my hand against the tile to support the weight of my body. The water on my back and shoulders turns cold and I realize this is not home. The woman in the next room is not my wife. I wonder if she's real. I emerge from the bathroom with a towel replacing a shirt and pants. Where is she? I sit in a chair across the room from the bed. I'm naked. I look like a musician who is listening to the music while the other members of the band are playing. I'm waiting to take my solo. I want to release this pain and song that comes from deep within my soul. It's the place where my heart once was. It's the church where I took my wedding vows. It's the corner where the light ends and the street bends and I see Rochelle walking with another man. Nothing will ever make me believe or pray again. I won't ask God for explanations. Let me play devil music. My horn is on fire. My life is hell.

## V

If I were a character in a book I would betray myself. I would be waiting for someone to end my misery. Instead I'm a teacher, a man teaching books to people who can't read in between the lines. I'm living with my wife and dreaming about Giovanni. She might be in my class next year or maybe the following year. I want to walk with her along a beach or maybe make love to her in a park. I want her body to turn and speak to me. Tell me a story and I'll tell you one. My story begins with a man trapped inside his marriage. It begins with leaves falling somewhere.

# The Post-Cock Box

**Brian Egeston**

I won't have sex with my wife. I love her too much. Intercourse, making love, whatever people choose to call it. I've always disagreed with the term *make love*. If people need to make it, does that imply it didn't exist before it was made? And why do those same people who profess their love to each other have to make it over and over again? Does love come in batches with expiration dates? *Best if screwed before August '03*. Love can't be made. It's derived, isn't it? Cultivated and nurtured, I think. Forgive me for saying so, but it's work more than anything else. And I'm good at my job, I don't mind telling you. Excuse me for a moment, will you?

"Yes, dear?"

"It's almost time, darling."

"Thank you, love. I'm just about ready." That was her. Isn't she wonderful? Does things like that every day. Reminds me of this, helps me remember that. I can't count the ways I love her. We're expecting company again. It's the fourth time this month and quite honestly I'm a smidgen tired of entertaining, but for her anything.

I get so much grief from the guys about my adoration of her. But they have plenty of problems in their own marriages and could learn a thing or two from us. They're probably love-makers anyway. With fast expiration dates, I'll bet.

"Dear, is there anything you'd like me to do in the kitchen?"

One second.

"No. I think the chef has it all under control. Won't you check with her? If she's done, send her on. She's got a big evening planned as well. Has the maid left already?"

"Yes. I do believe so."

"That's fine, my darling. I'll be down shortly." Amazing isn't she? Don't know what I'd do without her, or what she'd do without me. We're a hoot, the two of us. I really can't babble on like this all night. Although I could carry on about my wife for days.

We're having French cuisine this time. Our chef is simply the most wonderful cook on the earth, I swear. My wife caught her off guard once and demanded that for dinner we have neckbones, collards, yams, and pig's feet. You should have seen the chef's face glow. I thought she was going to faint. Oh, it was an absolute rage. Truthfully I would have fainted if I'd eaten that garbage. My palate hasn't been tortured in such a manner since I went to the country for the last family gathering I will ever attend. Shameless Negroes, all of them really.

Forgive me, I tend to get a bit flustered when I think of the old world in which I used to live. Oh heavens, I must hurry. It's nearly five of seven and I haven't a stitch of clothing.

This one is her favorite. Black and red unlined mesh bra item number 158–827 with matching garter belt item number 158–828, and the thong is item number 158–824. She likes to see this. I've memorized all of her favorites from the catalog. She absolutely loves to see these. I have a devil of a time getting them on without her knowing. But once she sees them it's like releasing an animal. A wild boar, a mad dog. Oh heavens, not a mad dog. Oh dear, I didn't mean to call my wife a female dog. Good lord. I must get dressed.

She likes this beige suit more than the others. Quite frankly I can't tell the difference between this one and the other five she brought back from Italy. I try so hard to keep them sorted out by closets. Light to medium dark colors are kept in closets 1 through 3 and dark to funeral director black are all kept in closets 4 and 5. It gets so hard to match shoes that way. Having to look at a suit in closet 1 and then having to walk all the way down the hall to shoe carousel number 1B to try and match square toes or wing tips and God help me if I decide to wear suede loafers. I'd have to practically take a train to the basement to get into the climate-controlled closet.

Well, I'll just have to compromise and throw on whatever. If I don't hurry I know she'll discover the bra and panties before it's time and the surprise will be absolutely ruined. I hate it when that happens.

Once we were having company and she walked right in when I was trying to get the underwear on. It was a pink lace demi-bra, item number 159–576, and matching lace tanga, item number 159–579. I'd seen the new catalog before she had and knew the outfit would drive her mad. She walked in just as I was getting the panties on. When she saw, she immediately ripped them off. Of course she loved it, but it's just so sensational when clothes are peeled off when we're into it. That's when she gets so—

"Someone's at the front gate, dear!"

"I'm on my way down. Five minutes. I see them on the monitor up here. By the time they're at the front door, I'll be down."

See what you've made me do. How will I ever get the underwear on now? I really must go.

"Hi, how are you? Great to see you again. Come on in. Dinner's ready. You remember my wife?"

"Of course I do. You're looking wonderful as usual. What a gorgeous strapless dress."

"Oh, thank you. My darling husband picked this up for me while he was in France. And this must be the gentleman you've been raving about."

"It is. He's been waiting all day to meet you two and see this fabulous house."

"Darling, let our guests follow you and your gorgeous dress into the dining room. I'll get drinks for everyone. Scotch for the ladies and cognac for the men?"

"Sounds good. You two follow me and my dress."

She's such a wonderful host. I've done thousands of parties—others, not my own—and you and I have never come across anyone more gracious, pleasant, sexy, funny than she is. Strangers are family around her. Can't you see why I love her so and why I wouldn't dare have sex with her?

I took the drinks into the dining room, where she was already whirling around in that fabulous gown and preparing to serve. Sure we'd have the chef or the help take care of it on any other occasion, but tonight was special. We try to be . . . well, common every now and then. It's hard, but we try.

I swear she must have been some type of manual labor person in another life. The way she carried the soup from the kitchen to the dining room, it was too natural. As if she'd actually served someone before—it was almost frightening. The guests looked at the soup then at each other. Beautiful people, but so sheltered, so unexposed.

"The soup is *Velouté de Potimarron*. My darling wife didn't make it, although I'm sure she could. You'll love it, trust me. It's made from potimarron, a variety of pumpkin with a light chestnut flavor."

I'm sure the sight of soup that looked like nothing more than scrambled egg yolks startled them, but the instant they sipped, we could see the enjoyment. They were aroused. A good sign.

"Dear, would you like me to get the *Salade d'Automne*. Don't I get a chance to serve?" I must have sounded like a complete whine.

"No, lover. You sit and enjoy." Off she whirled behind the swinging door then reappeared with some type of . . . a tray with plates on it. My God she looked like a servant.

Again the two with their puzzled looks.

"Not to worry, it's nothing more than lettuce, tomato, apple, avocado, artichoke heart, radish and finely shredded red and white cabbage. Even better than the soup, I assure you. My wife loves this, don't you, dear?"

"I must admit, it was my favorite last time we were over."

"See? If a woman in a dress such as that adores it, you'll die for it."

They loved it, of course. Each morsel brought them more bliss, more passion. I was hoping they could hold on.

"This is a beautiful home. I'm glad I got a chance to see it. Been thinking about it all day."

"Why, thank you, old chap. My wife picked it out. Saw it from the road one day when we were driving. Told me how much she admired it. I stopped the car, walked up to the front gate and made the previous owner an offer."

"Well, I think you made a good investment."

"Investment? Good man, this was a steal. Turns out the poor sap was a day away from bankruptcy and two days away from suicide."

"My husband has a gift for business deals like that. Uncanny really."

"Oh, thank you, love. You're too kind. Can I help with—"

"Hush, I'll be right back."

"Oh what a life, what a woman. You two should be so lucky as to have the kind of love we've found."

"So what is it that you do?"

"Shhh. Never before dessert, my good man. Never before dessert."

"I need to go and powder my nose. Where's the little girls' room?"

Ah, This was it! Just what I needed.

"Allow me. It's right this way. We'll have to go upstairs; the facilities downstairs are being redone. The gold plating on the faucets is wearing. Follow me."

My wife came through the door as we left the table.

"Where are you two going?"

"Oh. Darling, she needs to use the little girls' room. Won't be a sec."

"Well . . . hurry. I'm serving the entrées."

She's just so perfect. Perfect timing. Perfect host. It's no wonder she was too good for the Baptists. We had a long talk on the way back from Indonesia before we converted to Catholicism. It was the right thing to do. Although lately I've had some concerns with the scandals and what not. Yet I have resigned myself to the fact that no man is perfect and man is the custodian of religion, therefore no religion is perfect. However we've found solace in being Catholics. Sure we got stares and whispers. I assume any dark-skinned person in an all white parish would. The gawking and whispering stopped after we funded the renovation of the priest's home. Then we were invited to all the parties and receptions and christenings and the this and the thats. They love us now.

"Ready?"

"Yes. I feel much better, thank you. We'd better get back downstairs before they start without us."

"They'd never do that. But are you ready? Is everything set?"

"Yes, I got it."

"My wife's going to love the bra and panties I got. Can't wait to show them."

"Sorry we took so long. That elevator is getting slower every month. You didn't start without us, did you?"

"No. Why would I start without my wonderful husband?"

"Thank you, dear. Go ahead, you two. Eat up. My good man, yours is *Daube de Sanglier*. Wild boar's stew, and it will drive you raving mad. And yours, my lady, is *La Millefeuilles de Saumon Fumé Florentine,* smoked-salmon and spinach baked in an enclosing crust of flaky pastry. It will absolutely kill you. Won't it, darling?"

"You'll die as soon as you eat it and be reincarnated as a fork just to poke it again."

"AAAAA HHHHHAAAA HHHAAA AAHHA HAHHHH-HAAA! Oh my! Oh my! Oh my! AAAAHHHAAAAA HAAA HAHHA HAHA. Oh dear! Oh dear! You absolutely slay me! God, I'm crying you've made me laugh so."

"You're such an easy crowd. Our guests didn't have nearly that reaction."

"No, it was funny. It really was. I'm just loving this . . . what is it? Wild Boar . . ."

"Wild boar stew, old boy. And I told you it was tempting."

The entrées always put them over the top. We could stop with the soup and that would surely be good enough, but the entrée makes the work so much easier. We found long ago that dessert prolongs. Therefore, we thought it necessary to serve the cheese and dessert simultaneously.

"I'll be right back, let me get the final dish and we're done."

"You mean there's more?"

"Good man, we feed you until you pop. Never been exposed to the ghastly ways of rural Negro eating, have you? How they bring that deplorable garbage that looks as though it came directly from the pig trough and slap it on your plate? They call it soul food. I call it slopping the Negroes."

"Don't start, honey. They don't want to hear your lecture on *The Color Purple* and its influence on the unlifted veil."

"I'm sorry dear, you're right. Let me help you with that. She always comes to save me. I love you, dear."

"And I you. Now explain the dishes if you will, sir."

"My honor, yes. The cheese dish is *La Faisselle de Pays à la Crème Fraîche*. It's a soft white cheese, or *fromage blanc*, served in a bed of fresh cream. And the dessert is *La Cristalline d'Agrumes au Coulis de Fruits Rouges,* citrus fruit, mandarines and pink grapefruit slices, in a gelatin, lying in a sauce of red berries and fruit. The pale green, star-shaped slices are rocambole, sometimes called Spanish garlic. Don't be shy. Take a bite."

The fair-skinned Adonis spooned a portion of cheese to his mouth and absolutely melted, as I knew he would.

"This is unbelievable! How does everything taste so good?"

"Old chap, didn't I tell you? Venture capitalist, by the way."

"Huh? What does that have to do with how this food tastes?"

"Nothing. You asked what I did. And now dessert is on the table. I make billions by giving people millions to make billions for themselves. I give people what they need to be happy and that makes me happy. Take for instance—"

"Rip your shirt off now!"

"Darling, let the man finish his cheese. For goodness' sake he hasn't even—"

Suddenly my wife grabbed the corners of the tablecloth and gave it a whipping heave. Plates were sliding, glasses were crashing, bowls were turning over, silverware was flying, food was spilling, and clothes were being ripped off.

The long glamorous black dress I'd spent days searching for, spent hundreds of dollars for a translator in search of that designer who didn't advertise but still charged $30,000 per item—was torn to shreds in something like a cat's fury at something that tried to constrain it. I'd known the dress would meet with a fate such as this. They all do.

She jumped on the table, now strewn with remnants of French cuisine and carefully constructed etiquette. A candle was rolling, still holding on to a flickering flame. Burning with the hope that it could live on the wick forever, that its wax could drip and drip until it had lived a full flame's life. I doused it. Just as I had been doused so long ago.

Like the intense blue in the flame, nothing that was pure seemed to go on forever. My flame was pure so long ago, until it was contaminated. Now my flame, my pure blue flame was intensified by poisons. Gasoline, alcohol, and any other mixture that made fires burn out of control. So young, so unaware that my desires would become perversions. I threw a goblet of water upon the candle, protecting it from contaminating flammables. If only it were that easy for me.

"Old boy, I'd do as she says before she—"

"Don't make me ask for anything more than once!" my wife wailed and struck the man across the face with a crushing backhand. My God it was . . . it was . . . it was pimpish, I think. She's unbelievable. A servant, street pimp, an amazing attorney. Oh, how I wish you could have seen her in therapy. Some nights she just took over and ran the group, I swear.

Stunned, I'm sure, the slapped chap just sat there waiting for more. She's not violent, mind you. That's not the way she likes it. Her hand clutched his shirt and ripped it. I could hear the plastic buttons dropping and dancing on the hardwood floor. The maid will no doubt come to me tomorrow asking if she should mend the shirt from which these buttons were lost. Always with a strange look on her face wondering how shirts lost five buttons at once.

Still sitting in his chair, my wife throned his lap and filled the man's face with her breasts. She grabbed a lock of his wooly hair and commanded his mouth over erected nipples. She drove his head while moaning, then looked over at us.

"You two had better get started."

That was our cue. I pulled a chair beside them and sat, pulling the proxy on my lap. My wife tried to keep a careful eye on us while reveling in her own pleasures, her own anticipation of orgasmic symphonies. She was a tenor in the church choir, but a soprano when she came.

I began to peel off the proxy's dress, and I watched carefully for my wife's reaction, hoping it would be the best of all.

"Nuh, huh, huh, darling. Your shirt isn't off. His is, yours isn't. You know I like to see your chest."

"Sorry, darling. Getting ahead of myself."

I ripped my shirt off and more buttons danced. The maid would count all the buttons and wonder what the hell had transpired.

"Your chest is so hairy."

"What did you say?"

"Darling, she was just—"

"Did you hear me say anything about the hair on his chest?"

"No, I just—"

"Unless I say it, you don't say it!"

"Dear, I'm sure she just got caught up. Look. Watch this, love." It was time. I had to show her the bra and panties. The proxy was wearing a blue . . . something. Probably right off the rack in some . . .

godforsaken mall. I forgot about peeling it and tore it off instead. Hoping it would calm my wife and ease the guests. Climaxing was always so difficult with tension.

While still smothering the man's face, she looked over and saw the set. The bra cupped the proxy's breasts perfectly. Her nipples, try as they might, couldn't hide behind the thin sheen of the black mesh. The panties were hugging her waist, disappearing down her crotch, and connecting with the thin line on her backside. The garter belt stretched her stockings and decorated her waistline like the perfect contrast in an abstract. She had slipped them on perfectly while in the little girls' room. Without my help this time.

My wife saw the set and screamed. She looked at the proxy and looked at her Adonis and fed him her warm swirling tongue. The proxy did the same to me and we were all finally synchronized.

Belts were unlooped, pants were sliding off, panties were curled down curves, falling off legs and being flung across the room by feet. My wife moaned and the proxy responded almost with the same pitch. She pulled the Adonis through the window of his boxers. The proxy did the same to me. My wife stood up over his erection and descended on his tip. She rose again to adjust the fit, moaning all the while. Again she rose and descended, just like the elevator in the hall transporting people where they wanted to go. The elevator's was a jerking motion, but just as my wife had managed, it eventually got to a place of comfort. The proxy saddled me quickly and swallowed my warmth with her insides. She duplicated my wife's bouncing and rocking and shaking and grinding and gyrating and screaming and scratching and pulling and pushing and yelling.

The Adonis, somewhere between the lingering taste of cheese and utter bliss, was holding on, fearing the worst if he exploded too soon. I could see him grimacing and releasing and holding and clutching and heaving and blowing and looking and hoping and holding and holding. Finally he looked at me in this man-made mirror next to him. The proxy on me like my wife on him. He looked to me for an answer of when, how long, how many times, why.

I turned away, for I had never been able to answer my own questions. It was pleasurable for him, I'm sure, but riveting pain for me.

Sex is such a dirty, evil, invasive thing. I've heard it's beautiful, but beauty is the life of a child filled with games and good times. Not manipulative molesting. I could never answer the questions in therapy. Never knew why I chose to be the one instead of my sister. Never knew why it didn't matter to him if it were a boy or a girl. It didn't seem right. He was too big for her. I remember thinking that he would crush her, break her in half if he did to her what he did to me. So I took it for her. I was her proxy. The proxy in a life in a family to which I will never return except for these brief moments that give my wife this pleasure. A pleasure corrupted by her father, who could not please his own wife because someone contaminated him.

It was after that session that she took over that we swore our allegiance. She took over the session because it was her turn to confess. To bring out the demon slumbering in her mind. She knew it was her turn so she transformed our session into a courtroom where she filibustered and deliberated and all those things lawyers do to make the truth look like a pure white-dress virgin at the altar.

For the entire night she danced around the confession, never got anywhere near the breakthrough. The session ended and I followed her. Walked several feet behind her and watched as she entered this beautiful building designed in the most amazing Roman architecture.

I sat beside her and said only one thing. I told her that I had the same illness as she. Sick with tainted blood from someone else's tainted blood whose blood had also been tainted. You know that amazing woman said to me, "Fool, are you crazy? I don't have AIDS. Oh Lordy, what a hoot."

I explained to her I'd been violated with a pure blue flame, and I sensed that she had also. She cried and yelled, and confessed. They put us out of the building she was so loud. So we checked into a motel and drowned our sorrows in dirty, nasty sex. Because that's what we do when we're sick, when we're contaminated, when we don't get help. We screwed each other so many times in that hotel on that weekend. But then I fell in love with her and couldn't. It pained her so. And that, my friends, is when we started having dinner guests.

She must have it. Have it hard and have it often, because she never returned to therapy and I don't suspect we ever will. We have our own sessions now, and as you can see, we're perfectly normal. She insists that I have a proxy. Supposedly it's because she loves and wants to make love . . . or have sex with me in some way.

The very same way that she was rocking her Adonis. She was screaming now.

"It's close! It's close! Get ready!"

The Adonis looked over at me with relief. Glad he had lasted. Glad that he could be of service. My wife's breasts were leaping with each thrust. The proxy tried to match her, but my wife's energy was pure. It wasn't paid for, nor could it be contained.

Flesh smacked and collided. Hips danced on pelvises. Hair brushed and danced and merged. Stomachs burned with the heat of friction. Arms wrapped. Hands grabbed. Fingers clinched. Backs arched. Heads snapped. And voices screamed, singing the sweet melodic rhapsody of sexual satisfaction. I longed every time to hear my wife's solo. Her voice was above the others. It held the longest note. It made the sweetest melody.

As we all sat there gasping for breath, instantly hungered, my wife released the Adonis and headed for the elevator. She returned shortly with a change of clothes. It was time to make the session complete. Time for therapy.

"There are towels in your bedrooms if you wish to shower. You're welcome to stay the night if you choose. We won't be but an hour or so. My darling wife makes an amazing omelet."

We drove the Jag to the old building. The Rolls is too much of a target and we just want to get in and out. The building was just the same as we remembered it. Every time we enter, there's the same feeling, the same smell, the same . . . well, commonness if you will. There's hardly anyone here at this hour. We called ahead and had the man ready for us. He's not much of an Adonis, but he suits us just as well.

Our place is in the corner. Off to the side behind a curtain. I sit first and my wife perches on my lap. It makes me want her, makes me want to revert to those sick things, but I always resist. And finally the man comes to join us in the box and we start. Together, holding, touching, we say,

"Bless us, Father, for we have sinned. It's been one week since our last confession."

# After and Before

**Trey Ellis**

After I sat down I saw that there were a few cute girls on the plane, an aging Aero Inca 737, the only jet the Cuban charter outfit could rustle up at LAX. Everyone aboard had some sort of State Department dispensation for visiting Cuba. Most were Cuban émigrés returning home with two or three nylon suitcases, each as large as a loveseat, but several of us were on a cultural or trade mission of some sort. Mayor Willie Brown of San Francisco was up front in one of the two rows of first class. Officially I was permitted entry because I was going to the Havana International Film Festival. However, like most of the other Americans on board, what really propelled me onto the flight was my desire to visit a place that was difficult to arrive at.

*Before landing at Narita Airport outside of Tokyo, it finally struck me, what all my friends had been telling me for months. "What are you, nuts? You just met the girl a few weeks ago and now you're flying all the way to Japan to live with her? I'll give you a week." I had just met Erika, that much was true, but we both soon realized the power of us as a couple so were never more than a few hours apart from each other. At the party where we met she told me that she was moving to Japan to teach English as soon as her visa came through. I think that was what made me pursue her even more than the way her beauty controlled my breathing. Having, stubbornly, not yet fully recovered from my previous heartache, I thought this short-term fling would finally heal me. She would soon be off to Japan and we would never see each other again but she would leave with me the knowledge that my ex-girlfriend was wrong. I could be a person that some-*

*body else could want. Then I kissed Erika, right there in the party;*
*she let me, she did. For a week we made love and ate spaghetti with*
*our fingers. One night, right after she came, she said I love y—but bit*
*her lips together and looked away before she could finish. I told her*
*that I had not been to Japan in years and would love to visit her if*
*she would like that.*

What would Maela be like? She is a friend of a friend, another divorced guy I met in yoga. He said she knew everybody in Havana,
would show me the city behind the *mojitos* and the Buena Vista Social Club. Twice he told me there was nothing romantic between
them so hope lit my belly. After I passed the soldiers in baggage
claim I saw her holding a paper plate with my last name written in
red marker. I knew she would be beautiful because my friend had
prepared me, yet he didn't mention that her skin was as inviting as a
caramel apple.

*I was prepared to leave with Erika but my agent forbid it. I*
*needed six more weeks to finish a draft of a script I was writing and*
*then meet with the director. Almost every day Erika and I would*
*write each other the longest love letters and every week I would fig-*
*ure out the time difference on my fingers and call her at the all-*
*women's hostel she was staying in until it got closer to my arrival.*
*She had told me she had looked everywhere in Fukushima, her little*
*town in the middle-north of Japan, for an apartment for us and fi-*
*nally found one at the edge of town, right where the rice paddies*
*began. She bought a double futon and a used bicycle for me so I*
*wouldn't be too bored during the day while she was teaching at the*
*English Friendly Way School.*

On the way into Havana down a palm-lined road our cab passed
dozens of "Yank Tanks," the vintage Chevys and Fords that I was as
excited to see as naturalists are to see exotic animals. My window
powered down about six inches till it jerked to a lopsided stop but
still that was enough for me to twist my nose outside and smell the
sweetness of the night. Maela told me that with my brown skin I
could pass for Cuban though my Spanish would quickly betray me. I
let my thigh press against her thin skirt. Then she told me that her

Canadian boyfriend also sticks his nose out the window every time he arrives. My thoughts about her had not even had time to grow into full-blown fantasies before wilting and shivering into unrequited, abject defeat. Would I ever again be somebody that somebody else would want? And if they did, how soon would their desire also fade to indifference and, finally, contempt?

*Soon she would be here. I knew it. So I waited at the arrival gate for her to find me. We were to take the next* Shinkansen *bullet train back up to her little town instead of spending the night in Tokyo because she had to be back at school early the next morning. The newness of the adventure, the signs everywhere that I could not read, carried me through the first twenty minutes of her tardiness. Then the voices started. She had changed her mind, found someone here, slipped and fallen on the platform and was killed by the bullet train in her excitement to meet me. I moved to a different chair to wait some more. I had traveled as far around the globe as possible (without it being faster to have gone around the other way) to be with a woman I didn't know yet, not really. What a story I would have to tell my friends when I returned on the next flight back to New York. "What can I tell you? I guess she got cold feet. Yeah, you all told me so but so what? I would do it again in a minute. Really I would. Don't forget that I'm tragically, heroically romantic."*

Maela forgot to ask me if I was tired and now apologized. Her English was beautiful and thick yet I answered her in Spanish that I came here to have fun, not to sleep. She said I had a very Cuban attitude. Then she called a friend on her new and first cell phone and told her to meet us at La Bodeguita del Medio, one of Hemingway's favorite bars and the place where the *mojito* was invented. You will like her, she said. I just met you but I think I already know your type.

*I didn't know who she was when I saw her enter the terminal. What I noticed first was her panic, then the explosion of her hair and the brown of her skin, three things that make a person stick out in Japan. I hurried to her to relieve her pain as soon as I possibly could and we found ourselves holding each other, her heart panicked and fluttering like a chickadee that had suddenly found itself lost inside a*

*very small room. She smelled sour from the sweat of running to meet
me and still her lungs filled and emptied erratically. Between gasps
she tried to explain about the missed trains and the confusing signs.
"Shhhh. It's all right. I'm here now. We're together." She hugged me
so close we walked together to the train in drunken zigzags.*

The cab was rolling so close to the ocean that out my window I saw
only the dark of the water. We were hurrying down the Malecon, the
sea wall, and out the other window we passed mile after mile of crum-
bling cityscape, once ornate palaces now windowless tenements
crammed with squatters and inexorably dissolving in the wind. The
road curved and suddenly fat Atlantic swells rammed the Malecon
and exploded into white spray that splattered against the road, startling drivers and sending nighttime pedestrians running and laughing. I might have enjoyed the view but my thoughts kept running off
to how the rest of the night would develop. G.F.E., "girlfriend experience," is Internet shorthand for the highest rating of an experience
with a prostitute. At first I made fun of the pathos behind the
acronym, as if any sex that you pay for could ever approach the genuine intimacy of consensual intercourse. That was in L.A. and I still
had my pride. Cuba, everyone told me, was a different universe. Like
European women right after the war I had read that you could have a
Cuban girlfriend for the week just by being generous, gentlemanly
and foreign. The friend who knew Maela would not go into details but
his eyes would sparkle and he would just say, "It's fantastic, man. Just
go. You'll see." Back in L.A. I smiled when I thought about taking my
Cubana to the beaches of Playas del Este, feeding each other cheap
lobster on the beach with her giggling at my Spanish and playfully
swatting me when my lotioning hands got too nosy. Then I'd take her
shopping for whatever she wanted at the one sort-of-mall for tourists
and Cubanas with tourist boyfriends. After that I imagined the two of
us dining in a candlelight *paladar,* one of the small, nongovernmental
restaurants run out of private homes. The nice woman running the
joint would tell us that Fidel ate there just the other night and that the
Cubana and I made a very handsome couple.

Cubans are famed for being open to the fleeting joy of unat-
tached, shame-free sex. One of the last times that I had had sex, with
or without shame, was with Erika, eight months before. Our fights

had subsided and I was starting to hope that we had ridden out the worst of our storm. Yet just as suddenly the usual end-of-marriage warning signs would return and dampen my optimism, leaving me in a state of heightened alert. Signs like her insisting on stripping one night at a local gentleman's club's amateur night contest, and her demanding that I take a lover to "give us something to talk about." That last night, however, the free sex between us was so good, meaty and intense, right on the couch, that right after I came I had this thought: "Phew! And for a while there I was starting to think that she was actually going to leave me." Then on the baby monitor I heard the rhythmic thwacking of our son's banging his head into the side of the crib so I pulled out, kissed her and hurried upstairs to drag him to the safety of the middle of the crib. I can't remember if that was actually the last time that we kissed but when I say it it feels right.

*It felt as fast as a bullet, so fast that epileptics are warned against staring out the window because the strobing telephone poles, power lines and rice paddies have been known to trigger an attack. I didn't think to ask but I assumed Erika wasn't prone to seizures, and besides, neither one of us was looking out the window because we were too busy climbing into each other's eyes, first one, then the other, gulping each other like milk straight from a carton. "You look different," she said and I knew exactly what she meant. My imagination had held her in my mind almost as she was but not quite, like an identical twin (because they never are, not really). But we kept kissing, our fingers kept skating each other's hands and arms, her fingernails periodically trying to insert themselves under mine till the irritation made me flinch. Still, her desire to close even this gap between us opened a hatch inside of me to rooms I did not know that I had and I inhaled slow and wide to fill the newfound spaces.*

La Bodeguita del Medio's narrow bar was filled with older Italian men and their young, very beautiful black Cubans laughing at their Spanish in bright, songlike bursts. I'm just forty and the Italians seemed much older, or at least a little older, or at least significantly more round and soft.

I told myself that I was not one of them, an exploitative, predatory sex tourist. I was just a wounded man badly in need of repair.

I'm a nice, sometimes charming guy and a woman stayed with me for twelve years whom I was not paying and she loved me for at least ten of those years so I must have some worth as a romantic partner.

I rolled my carry-on snug between my legs and remembered our honeymoon in Juan-les-pins when a young African had broken into our little rented Renault Kid and stolen all our clothes, our passports, and my laptop with one hundred pages of my latest novel. I was too busy trying to remember the detective who took my statement to notice that Maela had been talking with a very cute young blonde tourist at the bar. The tourist's Spanish was so flawlessly fast and mumbled, Cuban-style, that I was both jealous of her prowess and couldn't understand much of what they were saying. Then they simultaneously slid their eyes at me, which pulled me closer to them. When Maela introduced her friend Yelina I tried to tell her that I had thought that she was a tourist, but I never really learned the subjunctive in Spanish so she just frowned at me until I gave up, told Maela in English and she translated. I had thought that all of the white Cubans had long since fled to Miami but I kept that pluperfect to myself. She seemed naturally blonde, only her eyes weren't blue but light brown and as sparkly as champagne. "I told you she was your type," Maela told me in English so Yelina would not understand. "You're my type," I told her, though I did not tell her that her skin was exactly the same color as Erika's the summer we lived on Santorini. Maela burned her eyes at me then jerked them at Yelina so I would pay more attention to her.

I ordered *mojitos* for the three of us. Touristy, sure, but I had officially arrived at a place that had long lived only in my dreams and here before me was a very beautiful twenty-something-year-old woman who, theoretically, was willing to have sex with me. We talked and talked, she warmed up to my slow Spanish and gradually stopped addressing all her answers to Maela to translate. She said she was a literature student at the university and loved Márquez as much as I did but thought G. Cabrera Infante, my favorite Cuban author, was not serious enough. I could feel my heart gaining weight and as we talked her eyes danced from one of mine to the other. This was a G.F.E. already. Can I extend my trip? She has cousins in Orlando. How difficult would it be for her to come visit me in the States?

*     *     *

*I was in a dreamy state as we stepped off the train. Now it begins officially. Night was just falling as we left the station and headed for the taxi stand. Across the street stood a string of noodle shops, each with a huge ceramic kitten in its doorway raising one paw. Next to them the arches of a McDonald's suddenly turned on and glowed yellow just for us. I tried to open the taxi door but the cabbie yelled something at me quickly, a curse, it sounded like. Erika stroked my arm and said, "They open automatically here." And so it did, as if opened by a ghost. We fell inside and on top of each other and squeezed our hands together until they hurt, giggling and fidgeting at every red light. The ugly white buildings, the signs everywhere, big characters shouting, shouting God knows what. What an adventure, I remember thinking.* I have come halfway across the world chasing a girl. *That was exactly the type of person I had always wanted to be.*

*Erika paid the driver and thanked him. Her Japanese sounded flawless to me. I was so fucking proud. Our white building was at the edge of the rice paddies, just as she had said. She showed me my bike and it seemed right out of an Italian neorealist film, heavy and iron, the kind of bike a child would draw. I loved it and told her so as she was stabbing the keyhole, couldn't make it work, couldn't calm her fingers until I reached around her with both arms and kissed up and down her neck. "It's all right," I said. "We can stay out here and sleep under the stars." But I pulled the doorknob and tried the key again and we entered. As we were taking off our shoes she was already apologizing for everything: the refrigerator not much bigger than a subwoofer, the only hot water a small electrically heated can hanging over the sink. To bathe we had to fill a bucket and dump it into the turquoise soaking tub housed in its own room, dozens and dozens of times.*

*"Where is the bed?"*

*She explained that the saleslady had said that this futon was the softest they had, good for gaijin, Westerners, who aren't used to Japanese custom. I laid down on it and reached up for her to join me and we found ourselves kissing again, too impatiently, as if trying to climb inside each other while at the same time dragging clothes off each other then smearing each other with our skin. She told me she had just bought condoms yesterday and they were by the bed and I slid one on and she held her breath while I entered her but the mo-*

*ment all of me was inside of her she cried and I tasted her tears and
her sobbing was the saddest sound I have ever heard in all my life.
How can one person love another as much as she loves me? How can
I have earned that much luck?*

*When we were finished she laughed at herself and wiped her nose
on the sheets. "I wish you had a shirt with a pocket so I could crawl
in there," she said. "I wish I knew that you were going to love me forever."*

*"I will," I said.*

*"How do you know?"*

*"It's the only thing that I know."*

Maela and Yelina were only wearing thin dresses so when the
wind blew they warmed themselves against my shoulders, hanging
on me so closely that we walked in drunken zigzags across the cobble-
stones of Havana Vieja, the old part of town that looked like Cor-
doba or Sevilla. The girls were both terrified of the police, who
looked more like soldiers, so they explained that their other reason
for clinging to me was so they would not be harassed or even impris-
oned. The eyes of the soldiers we passed never left us yet we three
pretended to be too giddy to care. At the taxi stand I saw a 1955 Be-
lair cab and tried to get us to take it but the girls both grimaced. "Too
slow," they said. Then a Russian Lada as old as I was pulled up and I
was excited to try it but again the girls looked sour. Decay is less
charming when you live it. Finally we found a newish Fiat taxi and
we drove back along the Malecon to the Miramar Playa district
where Maela had found me a *casa particular*. I had wanted to stay in
Havana Vieja but the friend from yoga had convinced me to trust
Maela and allow her to find me a private home outside of town
where you can do what you like and where the police seldom travel.

The mansions along Avenida Quinta could have been mansions in
Palm Beach except that every sixth one had plywood for windows or
was missing a roof. Then we turned down a side street and the
houses suddenly shrank. Mine turned out to be a cement box sur-
rounded by a chain-link fence, more barracks than a home, especially
because there was a guard who let us in and who spent the night on a
cot in the empty garage on the first floor. Upstairs and inside, however, it was clearly a home, done up in early grandma. Everything

was covered with the images of flowers: the walls, the couches, the chairs and the lampshades. Maela turned on the boombox, a brand-new Sony, and played the new Christina Aguilera loud, then she drew a pack of state-owned cigarettes from her knockoff Louis Vuitton purse and pinched out a spindly joint that she had hidden there. Yelina declined but Maela and I passed it back and forth, and I smiled as this thought scrolled across my brain like the news ticker at the bottom of the screen on CNN: *I'm a bachelor and I'm getting high in Havana and I'm about to get laid. I made it through. What do you know, I'm going to survive after all.*

My eyes had closed and the music was dancing my limbs when I realized the girls were whispering. I opened my eyes and saw them standing in the kitchen, talking too fast and low for me to understand. When Maela saw me looking she smiled and they returned and she told me that it was getting late so she was leaving. Maela said she had a key and would let herself out and she kissed me and she winked. I sat next to Yelina on the flowery couch and put my arm around her. Then I nervously counted my breaths until I got the courage to kiss her. And she let me. We both smiled. G.F.E. Both of us pretending well that our courtship was not rigged.

"Where is the bed?" She asked me in Spanish, but it still sounded abrupt. Not so G.F.E. I had imagined us talking more; there were plenty more authors we could discuss. I remembered what Sally had told me, my girlfriend before Erika, near the end of our second date. She was a white model/Ph.D. candidate and Princeton grad, nearly as tall as I was. "Trey, I want to get to know the inside of you before I let you inside of me." Obviously I wasn't the first guy to be delivered that line, but I appreciated the rhetoric. Sally and I talked all night, slept an hour, then made love in the morning. For a month I was drunk with my love of her. I don't know what she was. Then she went back to her second-string defensive lineman and my heart experienced its personal record of pain withstood. A stat unbeaten until the night Erika told me she would be leaving.

I told Yelina that I did not know where the bedroom was so we explored the back of the apartment together. The bedroom was large and an old air-conditioner hung so far into the room that I was surprised it hadn't long ago pried itself out of the windowsill. Yelina took her clothes off and sat on the bed. *Here we go,* I thought. *I won-*

*der if as soon as I come I will burst into tears.* I asked her to leave her heels on, then took my clothes off too and only then did I notice the springy perfection of her body. I forced myself to help remind myself that I was a student of tantra, a very good lover, even Erika said that right up to the end. I kissed Yelina down to the bed and instantly she was pulling and pulling at my prick, sucking my nipples and helping me forget. I reached between her thighs as she reached between mine and she was wet.

"Excuse me." Maela was back, fiddling with the air-conditioner. Yelina and I stopped and watched her. "The knob is tricky. I should have shown you before. There. Good night." And Maela left again. I looked at Yelina and she laughed and me too and my heart breathed and I kissed her more and all over. Finally I pushed off the bed and rifled through my bag for a condom, returned, and she pushed my cock inside of her. *I'm inside her now. She has let me inside of her.* As I started moving I babbled into her ear everything that came to mind, and I don't think it was just the pot talking as I said things like, "Thank you for letting me inside of you. For giving me, a stranger, so much joy. You are so beautiful and this is my first time since my divorce." Actually I told her *despues mi divorcio* which means *after my divorce.* I didn't remember that I should have said *desde mi divorcio* until after she had gone.

I started fucking her well and our bodies fell into a rhythm and I remembered the Taoist tantric ritual of nine short strokes to the G spot followed by one long, then eight short to two long, then seven-three, etc., and judging from her enthusiasm I started thinking that perhaps this night would be as memorable for her as for me; maybe with the next pudgy Italian she fucked she would utilize some of the techniques taught her by me this night. Perhaps she would think of me often, she could get my email address from Maela and I could come back in the spring and she could pick me up at the airport, breathless and vaguely funky from having hurried so she wouldn't be late.

I held her legs out straight like rabbit ears on an old TV set while I kept fucking her, then rolled her over and felt the tightness of her ass on my belly. Tantric seminal retention I've practiced for years, so I can usually fuck indefinitely and told her that we would be gently exploring all night. Yelina then unhitched herself from me, rotated and took me in her mouth while pinching my nipples, her high-heeled mules clacking against the soles of her feet as her toes flexed and pointed. I could almost see the orgasm rising inside of me but I kept breathing, surfing the pleasant electricity of sex. *Maybe next I'll bend her over the balcony or even politely ask her if I could ease myself into her from behind.* (Something my wife had never allowed during the whole of our twelve years.) *Look at me now,* I thought. *I must be over her because look where I am and what I am doing.*

"Please, are you finished yet? I have to go."

My cock collapsed. This was not a girlfriend between my legs. I paid her the $100, what Maela had told me was the going rate. She walked naked to the phone in the kitchen and called herself a cab. We talked a little, about Borges, and Cortazar's amazing book *Hopscotch,* but we both had our ears on alert for the first rumble of the approaching cab. I made myself smile when she hugged me, then locked the door behind her after she left. Thanks to yoga I'm skinnier than I was when I was thirty, so it didn't seem possible that I could house, inside of me, so vast an emptiness. I didn't think that I ever would but sometime much later I slept.

*While Erika slept on the futon, I was too jetlagged and more to join her. Instead I just kept watching the magic of her face, my lungs filling and emptying with a sweetness that tingled.*

# Cotton Comes to Nina

**Phill Duck**

*Three days before the Day*

Warm honey.

I don't exactly smell it, the warm honey, but the aroma of food hits me as I enter the apartment. And knowing my husband as I do I know he's found some use for warm honey in his dinner preparation. He's been on a cooking-with-honey jag ever since the day he came across Nigella Bites during his lunch break. At first I was jealous, but then I put aside the green-eyed beast, realizing Nigella might bite, but I lick, suck, and please this man better than any other woman could ever hope to. Every day except today that is.

I hang my jacket on the coat tree in the foyer. I can hear him humming along to the low-playing radio, a salsa tune he doesn't understand the words to. I attempt to tiptoe my way upstairs to our bedroom without him hearing me.

"Nine," he calls out, "is that you?"

Busted.

I grit my teeth in frustration. I was hoping to avoid a confrontation. I know, just as I do about the warm honey, that he's in there, apron on and nothing else. That's his ritual. Cooking in the nude. I'm not in the mood for this today, three days before our second wedding anniversary. Valentine's Day, the day of romance, the day I took that leap with this man that satisfies my every desire and craving. Satisfies me except on those three days leading up to what I refer to as the Day, and the Day itself.

"Nine?"

Nina, I want to shout out to him, Nina. Call me by my name. He wouldn't understand, though. Wouldn't understand how this precious nickname he's given me can ignite every pleasure point on my body, setting me on fire, every day of the year except the three days leading up to the Day, and the Day itself.

"Yes, Anthony," I answer.

"Come in here," his baritone beckons, "I want you to taste something."

I pat my business skirt and look down at my pumps. My legs look damn good. I can see my nipples pressing through the soft white material of my blouse. I have on my eyeglasses today instead of my contacts. He prefers me in eyeglasses. Loves me dressed in my professional garb. I can imagine the sight of me like this will make him want to prop me up on the countertop, spread my legs, slowly remove my satin panties, and commence to suckling and licking that private space I shaved just for him last week. But that was last week. This is a new week. Our second wedding anniversary is just three days away. The thought of him touching me in that way during this period of the year makes me feel slightly nauseous. Damn, why didn't I make it to those stairs without him hearing me come in?

"Nine, what are you doing out there?" he barks.

"I'll be right in," I say, stalling him. He's extremely forward thinking and ambitious. I can use this to throw him off my scent. "I just need to check my voice mail real quick and see if this couple I showed a duplex to today decided if they want to bid on it."

I can hear a sigh come from his lips. Those lips that I love on my skin every day of the year except the three days leading up to the Day, and the Day itself. "Okay," he says, satisfied by my answer. Unlike many men he isn't put off by a hardworking career woman. He loves it. Loves me. Besides his painting, and maybe the cooking, I'm his only other passion in life.

I go to pick up the phone and dial some fake number, but his voice cuts through my actions. "Make it quick, okay, Nine?"

Nina. Nina Glover. Your lawfully wedded wife. Not Nine, not today, just three days before the Day, three days before I pledged to be yours forever. Nina.

I sigh. He's thrown me off something terrible now. I can't help but think back to the day he started calling me Nine.

I was in front of my makeup mirror, naked, oblivious to his eyes studying me. His voice came from over my shoulder like a summer breeze. "Nina . . . Nine. Real close, huh?"

I turned to him. The passion in his eyes made me want to either rub my hand down between my legs . . . or between his. "What are you talking about, Tony?" He was Tony back then. He didn't become Anthony until after we married. He never explained why, but I think me being one year older than him made him feel self-conscious and he wanted to make sure he measured up to a certain standard he thought I desired. He's always been so attentive like that, attentive to my every need. That's why I love him so. That's why I love the feel of his fingers on my flesh almost every day of the year.

"Nine is only one letter off from Nina," he confided.

I pulled my hair from a bun and let it fall down to my shoulders. "So?"

He took a tentative step toward me. I could feel my pelvic muscles tightening as I looked at this admiring look on his face. "I was just realizing—watching you—that there are exactly nine things about your body that just make me want to spend all day knocking the bottom out of your shit."

My eyes crested. "Are you talking dirty to me?" I asked.

He nodded, took another step forward. I stood from my seated position and pressed my bare ass against the lip of my desk. I was too hot to even be bothered by the coolness of the desktop. I spread my legs, smiling. "What are those nine things?" I asked him, making a play of batting my eyes and flinging my hair as I spoke.

"Your eyes, eyelashes, and eyebrows," he told me. "They're absolutely perfect. Some women have pretty eyes or pretty lashes, pretty brows, not too many have the entire package as you do."

You would have thought he'd told me he'd love me even if I gained a few pounds in a few wrong places. Without being able to help myself I had moved my fingers down to the crease between my legs, cutting myself in half by rubbing two of those fingers through my burgeoning wetness. He looked down at what I was doing, smiled, and inched forward a bit more.

"That's only three things. What else?" I said in wonderment, with the breathy sound of my own voice and the joy my fingers could bring.

"Your lips," he said, "I could suck them shits like they're strawberries or something."

"What else?" I prodded.

"You've got beautiful shoulders. Sometimes when I'm doing you from behind, I catch myself looking at your shoulders more than that plump round ass of yours."

My breathing was ragged by this point. My head fell back and hit the lighted mirror over my desk. It was as if I fell into a fluffy pillow, didn't hurt one bit.

"How many is that?" he asked. "I said there were nine things about you."

I couldn't fault his short attention span; his eyes were trained down between my legs as if nothing else in the world existed, as if there were no moon, stars, flowers, or ocean to gaze at for beauty. He looked at me the same way he did his canvases after he finished a painting. "Five . . . You owe me four more."

He snickered and then took a couple more steps toward me. "Of course your breasts," he went on, "I think your honey complexion and those dark nipples are what set me off. When I lick and suck on them I feel like I'm indulging in some sweet candy."

I'm not ashamed to admit that I stuck a finger deep into the folds of my womanhood at that point and that I then took that finger and did a taste test on myself. I *was* sweet like candy. I just knew that Anthony would enjoy me once he reached me. "Three more," I said, holding up three fingers in case his eyes had taken completely over and his ears no longer heard.

"You know how they say black men have big dicks?"

He shrugged out of his boxers and took another step to me. I looked down at that horse leg dangling between his thighs. In his case the myth was no myth. "Yes . . . and it's true," I acknowledged.

He seemed pleased. "Well, they say Spanish chicks have nice hips. Wide hips."

"And?"

"True in your case," he said.

He was within an arm's reach of me at this point, and I wanted to reach forward and pull him to me, open my legs and just have him push that big black man's dick as far in me as it would go. But I didn't. There would be other times when I wanted this slow foreplay dance before we got into a heated adrenaline-rushed tango. "Two more," I said, keeping score for him.

He stopped. I could feel my heart pounding in my chest. Don't be stopping now, I silently commanded him. I scanned down with my eyes to see what the deal was. He had his thick member in one hand, rubbing the veined shaft, getting it hard for me. My attentive lover man; I appreciated that so much.

"Your legs," he said.

I looked down at them. They weren't as long as the Fifth Avenue models but were just as shapely. "What about them?"

"Don't you wonder why I always put them up over my shoulders right before I nut?"

"I hadn't," I admitted.

"Love them legs" was all he said, shaking his head as if in disbelief.

He reached me and wrapped his arms around my waist. He kissed my chin, my lips, and was about to work on my neck. I stopped him. "One more," I said. He smiled. I swallowed, upset at myself for taking the brush out of his hand right when he was about to paint the Mona Lisa. Still, I wanted to know the ninth factor.

"Maybe I should show you instead of telling you," he teased.

I nodded, bit my lip. Aw sukie sukie now.

He bent to his knees and parted my legs. I was about to tell him to skip this part, go ahead and put that big black man's dick in its proper place, but his tongue silenced mine. The ninth factor pulsed and throbbed and minutes later sent a shock through my system that made my entire body convulse with ecstasy. I hadn't even realized that my eyes were closed and clenched so tightly until after I came and a tear dropped from the corner of each eye. His lips were wet with my juices and for a moment he looked as if he wanted to kiss me. Thankfully, he didn't, though. A quick taste on my finger was one thing, tasting myself on his lips was just icky.

He wasn't finished, yet.

Just as my chest stopped heaving, he took that big black man's dick and plunged into the ninth factor. He grunted with each stroke and I could feel his heavy sack of balls smacking against my ass. As far as I was concerned nine was the magic number.

"Nine, come on baby," he calls from the kitchen now, breaking my thoughts.

I place the phone back on the hook, my pretend call to my voice mail over, and head toward the kitchen with regret.

"Hey," he says as I linger by the doorway. He is smiling, his muscular chocolate build carrying a film of sweat from the heat of the oven, naked except for the apron that only covers his upper torso. If it wasn't three days before the Day I would rush over to him, drop to my knees, and perhaps suck him until that smile on his face turned to a pleasured grimace.

"Something smells good," I say.

He looks at my pumps, my skirt, my blouse, and then my glasses. He licks his lips. I cross my arms over my chest and hug myself as if I were outside in the harshness of a winter day. His eyes on me feel more like a leer today.

"I sliced these cutlets to make chicken fingers," he says. "And I made a honey mustard sauce. You want to taste it?"

"No." I shake my head.

"Come on over here and give me a hug, then, at least."

I hesitate. I know full well what hugs lead to. Him naked like this makes me so uncomfortable, even though I'm used to coming home from a long day of working to find him in the kitchen, cooking, nude. I look toward the refrigerator. The calendar held in place by a magnet on the fridge door. I quietly curse that calendar.

"Come on, Nine," he says.

Nina, I want to shout. Nina.

I walk over toward him and he grabs me in an embrace. "Damn," he says, "you talking about the food smelling good . . ." His voice trails off as his mouth finds my neck.

I work myself from his embrace. He frowns but lets it go.

"I'm going to go take a hot bath and then I'll be back down," I say. I must clarify. "For dinner and then I have to get some sleep."

"Whatever."

I turn to leave the kitchen, thankful to get away so easy.

"Hey, yo, Nine?"

Spoke too soon. I turn back. "Yes?"

"We're going to have a good anniversary this year. Not like last year." He has the look on his face he gets when he's struggling with the paint brush but refuses to let it conquer him.

I smile, even though I know this isn't possible, and turn to leave.

"Nine?"

I wheel back to him. "What!"

He puts his hands up, his eyes widened in surprise at the tone of my voice. I feel bad, but it's three days before the Day. I can't help it. "Just wanted to say that I love you," he says. I nod. "I love you, too, Anthony." And I do. God I do. Where would I be without him? What would I be? My mother always told me the right man will make you be the right woman. There is no doubt Anthony is the right man.

That smirk of his, that I usually love, crosses his face. "You know the second anniversary is the cotton anniversary?"

I look down at my hands, examine my nails, and then raise them so he can see. "Good, you can get me a bag of cotton balls so I can remove this chipped polish and redo my nails."

That smirk reappears. "You want balls, huh?"

I grit my teeth, don't answer. I asked for that one.

He licks his lips and stares at me. "Are we going to fuck tonight? Or make love?"

Now it's my turn to smirk. "*No son nada de esso dos, pero yo te amo,*" I tell him, saying it slow and sensual to throw him off.

He shivers and smiles himself, reveling in what he says is the most beautiful language on earth. Spanish. A language he only knows a few words of which I've taught him. He nods at me, still smiling. "Cool."

I smile back and then leave the kitchen. He has no idea I just told him, "Neither, but I love you," in that beautiful language.

*Two days before the Day*

At work I turn on my computer to check my emails and see what hot real estate listings hit the market today. To my surprise there is an email waiting for me from Anthony's AOL account. Sent this morning after I left the house. I'm surprised that he would bother after the fight from last night that spilled over to the morning. I figured he'd be stabbing at his canvas with a brush instead of emailing me. I open the email and scroll down to read.

Nine,
Sorry I upset you so much last night. I don't know what I did but I don't want us to be on bad terms as we approach our

second wedding anniversary, not to mention Valentine's Day—
the day for lovers.

I smile and scroll further down. I'm so lucky to have Anthony in
my life. If we can just get through these next few days I'll show him
how lucky I feel by donning that pink flowered lingerie set that he
loves me in.

Whatever it is I did to upset you I'll make it up to you. I've attached a picture of something I have for you when you get
home tonight. Remember, this is just for you, you deserve it.
Make sure you're alone when you download the picture. I
don't want your co-workers getting jealous. Especially that
Miah. Love you like no other.

"I love you, too, baby," I say aloud as I hurry to download this
mystery picture. He knows how much I love animals. He knows
Miah's boyfriend just bought her a puppy last week and that I was
beside myself wishing it were mine. I bet he went and picked me up
a cute little shih tzu with eyes like black marbles and a warm little
nose that will sniff at my ankle when I come home at night.

The file is taking forever to download. I tap my fingers against the
top of my desk in frustration.

"Files done," the computerized voice calls out. I click to locate
and open it. My jaw drops. A picture of Anthony's big black man's
dick in all of its firmness is taking up the majority of my monitor. I
delete the file in disappointment and lean back in my chair. Suddenly, I feel a tension headache coming on. The calendar on my desk
is staring at me, seemingly smiling, mocking me. It puts my mind in a
time machine, flowing backward four years.

Donovan Gabriel.

There is something mystical about a man with two first names.
Donovan is my evidence. His skin had a rusty copper tone to it and
he had that chiseled jaw thing going for him that only football players
and bodybuilders seemed to have. He wasn't particularly muscular
anywhere else. In fact, Anthony has a bigger, stockier build. Donovan had the dignified poise you had to have to broker stocks, nothing
like my hip-hop lover Anthony, who'd channeled his graffiti tagging

talents into a legitimate painting passion. Donovan and Anthony were so distinctly different.

Anthony is a grunting, grind-it-out lover. Anthony moves inside me, changing the angle and pressure of his thrusts until I start to moan.

Donovan was more of a measured lover. And Donovan asked where the elusive pleasure spot was, never one to waste his energy on a treasure hunt.

Different types of lovers.

Donovan was my life before I knew Anthony Glover existed. Before I was Nine or Nina Glover. Back then I was Nina Torres, who could eat all the empanadas she wanted without gaining weight. Donovan Gabriel was the most beautiful man I'd ever met up until that time. We had plans to marry.

February 11, four years ago, Donovan came by my place and made love to me with his eyes open and trained on the wall behind me. I didn't question him about it at the time, and that fact hasn't left me since. I wish I'd asked him about it.

February 12 was more of the same. I started to worry but kept quiet.

February 13 is the day that really sticks in my mind.

The vacant look that had held Donovan's eyes for the two previous days was absent. He was smiling again.

That night he made love to me like Anthony does. Grunting, grinding, excavating without the aid of my compass.

"What are the pillows for?" I asked Donovan that night, nodding to the pile of pillows he'd arranged in the corner of my bedroom.

It was as if I hadn't spoken. "Take your clothes off, Nina," Donovan said.

Before I took ownership of Nine and the erotic feelings it brought in me, I thought the greatest satisfaction was Donovan calling me by my birth name. I moved to obey him. I unbuttoned my blouse, slowly, winding my hips for him as I did it. I took off the blouse and flung it to the opposite corner from the piled pillows. I had on the ill-fitting lavender bra I fell in love with at Victoria's Secret. The bra they didn't have in my size but had sold me on anyway because of its beautiful styling. My breasts—that I'd find out in a few short years were one of my nine best features—spilled out of the bra.

"Man," Donovan said.

"You like," I said, cupping them with my hands and pushing them up even farther.

"With a certainty," he said.

I unsnapped the bra from the back and let it fall to the floor. Donovan took a hard step toward me; too eager for my tastes. I put my hand up. "You told me to undress, so wait."

He sucked his teeth like a young boy. That made me so hot I could barely stand it. I loosened the top button of my slacks and worked them down. As the pants crossed my wide Latina hips I purposely pulled my panties off with them, and then covered my mouth in faux shock. "Whoops, I didn't mean to take them off so quickly. I'm taking the tease out of striptease." I made a play of pulling the panties back up, but Donovan froze me with a "Don't you dare" that was so deep and forceful it made the subtle wisps of hair on my arms raise.

I scooted over to the bed with my pants shackling my ankles and plopped down on the soft mattress. Donovan watched me with joy in his eyes. I took my sweet time working the pants off one leg and then the other. Donovan must have shifted weight from one foot to the other about ten times while I tortured him with my bushy pussy. That was the other difference between Donovan and Anthony. Anthony likes me shaved. Donovan liked a thick brush to work his way through.

Donovan sucked his teeth again. I smiled at him and stood, slowly. He rushed me like the football player his chiseled jaw seemed to say he was. I found myself face down on those piled pillows. One of his hands was greedily rubbing over and then through my bush, the other hand cupping my breasts, Donovan worshipping two of what I'd find out a few years later were my nine factors. When I was good and wet, he grabbed my ankles and I was catapulted deeper into the pile of pillows.

"What are you doing?" I screamed, taken aback by the force of his movement.

He pushed his rock hardness into me as an answer and started a hard pound. The smack of flesh and him filling me, leaving me, filling me, leaving me . . . it made me moan louder than I thought I was ever capable of.

He held my left ankle with his left hand and rubbed the small of my back with his right hand. He stood the entire time as he filled me, left me, filled me, left me. I could feel my love box fisting around his hard shaft, my lips down there sucking him like my other lips often did.

I let myself fall into those pillows and turned my head to the side, resting in them. He continued pushing. Filling me, leaving me, filling me, leaving me. A joyous pain took over me. My head felt as if it would explode and my vagina actually did. "Oooooooo," I said. I dragged that one letter out as if I'd recited the entire alphabet from A to Z. A short while later Donovan's hardness grew even harder for a split second and then deflated just as suddenly. He dragged out O as if he'd recited the alphabet forward . . . and then back again.

The next day, Valentine's Day, I got the call that they'd found Donovan's lifeless body in his car, engine running, in his garage. There was a sticky pad note on his steering wheel.

*Love you, Nina.*

*Sorry I couldn't talk to you about this sadness I have.*

Happy Valentine's Day.

The memory still shakes me. Anthony knows about Donovan's suicide, but I didn't tell him all the specifics. Couldn't. Can't. I thought getting married on Valentine's would erase that horrible memory and give me a greater memory to cling to. I was wrong.

*One day before the Day*

I'm in the shower, lathered with my favorite soap, preparing for work. The shower door opens and startles me.

"I can't let you go another day without finding out what's the matter," Anthony says to me.

He's dressed in a white cotton T-shirt and cotton boxers, not wielding that big black man's dick at me as if it's the answer to all life's problems. I'm impressed. "Nothing is the matter," I lie, testing to see if he's going to let it stand at that.

"I love you more than the air I breathe," he says. "I can't take you being like this."

The "air I breathe" thing was kind of corny but he has my attention. I rinse off the lather and step from the shower. He hands me a towel to dry myself and then a robe. He doesn't paw at me once.

"You're going to talk to me," he says.

"Donovan," I tell him. Might as well put it out there.

He furrows his brows, looks shocked and surprised, but his voice doesn't rise and he doesn't storm off. He's as gentle and understanding as he was when I met him in grief counseling. His mother had died of cancer and his father joined her with the swipe of a razor blade. Two parents gone in a finger snap. Anthony and I shared stories of grief and heartbreak. He brought me back from the brink. I did the same for him, but I hadn't told him the full story. And he'd never asked.

"What about Donovan?" he asks.

"He killed himself on Valentine's Day," I say, the words coming out in a rush like the water from the shower head of a few moments before.

Anthony's eyes widen. "Oh . . . I didn't know that. So why—"

"I picked Valentine's for our wedding day because I wanted to forge a happier memory to erase the memory of Donovan's . . ." I leave it at that, unable to finish it.

Anthony's eyes cast down. "But it hasn't worked."

I shake my head. "No."

He thinks for a moment then looks up at me. "Maybe we should renew our vows, pick a different day. We can celebrate our anniversary on the new day and deal with your feelings about Donovan on Valentine's."

I look at him to see if he's serious. He appears to be. Did he say that we would deal with my feelings about Donovan on Valentine's? I'm blown away. This is precisely why I fell in love with Anthony. In my quest to forget Donovan I made the mistake of remembering him and forgetting my Anthony. What a fool I've been.

"What do you think?" Anthony says to me.

What do I think? I think about the wonderful dinner he prepared for us two days ago. I think about the hot bath he had waiting for me yesterday when I came home from work. I think about the beautiful painting that he just completed last week. I know this is the painting that will provide him with his big break, have everyone wanting an Anthony Glover. I think about him now, standing in front of me, fine from head to toe, those boxer shorts unable to hide the bulge that wakes up with him each morning.

"Nine," he says, following my eyes, which are on that bulge, "you heard me?"

"I think cotton is my new favorite fabric," I say.

He's puzzled. "What?"

"Didn't you say the second anniversary is cotton?"

"Yes," he says, remembering.

I move forward to him, reach in through the opening of his boxers and take that big black man's dick in my hand. I drop to my knees and pull it through to the outside, to my waiting lips.

"What are you doing, Nine?" he asks.

"Early anniversary present," I say. "Now shush."

I take it in my mouth as he falls back against the sink. My lips, my touch on this wonderful lover of mine . . . is soft as cotton.

# Laser Tag Love

**SekouWrites**

*M*  *en* never *say no.*
This is the thought that suddenly erupted in the moistened soil of Gail's mind and crotch simultaneously. At the time, she was using the reflection of a video game's large glassy screen to gaze at a man so fine she could feel tremors tickling right at the top of her thighs.

The quote was from Vasken, probably the best male friend she'd ever had, which meant in real-life terms that she was just waiting for him to dump his girlfriend and finally see the light—her light. Not that she would ever push the issue—she did value his friendship—but she knew good and damn well that if it ever came down to a choice between keeping his friendship or finally wrapping that boy up in some satin sheets, she was going with "door number two" every time. But until that magical day came, he was a great friend, and although she'd tried to keep herself distant and standoffish, she'd been dismayed to realize that she liked his girlfriend as well. Not that it mattered right then—right then, she would have gladly humped Vasken's leg till he was horny enough to jump her bones. And she was planning on doing just that—except he didn't answer the phone. Figures. The one time she's ready to go for broke, she can't find him. And, as if things weren't bad enough, she was *here*. The last place on earth she wanted to be.

Gail wasn't fond of arcades, not because she didn't like video games—she was one of the few women around that believed in their stress-relieving properties—but because of Bradley; the X-ed out former boyfriend whose idea of a romantic evening was dragging her to three arcades in a row and insisting on staying hours past her boredom breaking point.

Today she was inside Mega-Machine, a tri-level monster of an arcade located on the fringe of New York's Times Square. She'd dashed in to get out of a torrential rain that had materialized out of nowhere and drenched her to the bone, putting the final cherry on what, at 12:05, was already a bitch of a day. She had a plan, as much as you can call it that. She was going to surf the web, drink some coffee—better make that an Alabama Slammer—and throw sharp objects at anyone that came within twenty yards of her until the rain let up, or at least until she was sufficiently distracted.

This was her plan. But hey, shit happens.

You're sopping wet. You're in your least favorite place. You're desperately trying not to think about the fact that you just tried to surprise your boyfriend for lunch and saw him arm-in-arm with a white woman so pretty her mama must've sold her soul to the devil. You're sitting in front of a computer. Tired, wet, depressed, hungry and trying very hard not to do anything that might land you in the city lockup. So . . . what do you search for? If you're Gail, you search for "sex." Well, actually you search for "guns, FAST, New York," then you scrap that and search for "assassins," then you finally regain some semblance of sense, settle down, and *then* you search for "sex."

It worked for a while, keeping her distracted and all. But then she chanced upon this website filled with testimonials about "my hottest time ever." That's when she got herself into trouble. First she started feeling indignant. She was cute, in her mid-twenties, had a healthy libido, was single (or at least she would be as soon as she confronted Rudy) and she couldn't even come close to the kind of freaky things these middle-aged housewives were managing to wedge between vacuuming and doing the laundry. Then, once her indignation began to wear off, she got horny. The more she read, the more she became convinced that these stories were really told by *real* people, not Rollergirl or *Playboy*'s Ms. February. Most of the letters started with "I've never done anything like this before *but . . .*" and then they went on to tell a tale of some ol' freaky shit. Stuff Larry Flynt couldn't come up with on his best day. It was starting to affect her— the more she read the more heated she got. Then she started feeling like a goddamn nun. Why didn't anything like that happen to her? How come no sexy Italian waiters were inviting her down to the wine cellar when she dined alone? Why weren't there any ruggedly handsome cab drivers offering to show her the sunrise from Jersey?

"Take a risk." As in: "I just decided to . . ." But it was the last three words of that sentence that burned out at her from the computer screen. They were the words of some forty-year-old housewife who had finally succumbed to the urge to answer the door for the Polar Bear Springs delivery guy in her shortest Frederick's of Hollywood robe. It worked too. She'd found herself in her Jacuzzi, getting shagged by the best that Polar Bear Springs had to offer.

Polar Bear Springs. Water. Jacuzzi. Gail. What do these things have in common? Gail mused, as she crossed and uncrossed her legs—occasionally squeezing them together. She was hot now, and the phrase "take a risk" was inking itself all across her brain the same way wetness was inking itself across her crotch. She started playing out a couple of "what-if-I'd-only's," and before she could talk herself out of it, she was calling Vasken, her heart flailing but her mind made up. His voice mail picked up. She hung up, almost embarrassed by what she'd attempted—but really just wishing he'd been there.

Feeling thwarted, she logged off, paid for her time, and headed for the door—she couldn't take any more. Those internet stories were driving her to the brink of suicide by estrogen/oxytocin overdose.

It was on her way out that it happened.

He was standing there playing one of those fighting games. A tall brother with a skin fade and curly hair on top. He was so handsome he looked surreal—like someone had sculpted her perfect man and breathed life into him—and he was dressed to the nines to boot. Black trench, three-button charcoal suit with a silver-gray tie. Brotherman was fine. She slowed her pace a little to get a better look. *Mmph,* she thought then turned toward the door.

*Take a risk.* She stopped.

Every story about regular women and their once-in-a-lifetime experience of extraordinary sex ran collectively through her mind. The picture of her boyfriend strutting through midtown with the blonde goddess on his arm revisited her. And finally Vasken's long-ago quote on the nature of men and sex added its two cents to the pot. "Men *never* say no. Just give them the opportunity and they are all over it."

And here she was, on the brink of . . . something. Just like she'd found herself countless times before. Like the vast majority of people, she usually walked away. That was her poison. She never kept herself near the brink long enough to let something happen. Well, not this time. She would not be outdone by Connie Sweetman of Anytown, USA, dammit. Besides, it was still raining anyway.

She walked back to him while she assessed her appearance. She looked good enough, she thought. She had on her black jeans, chosen because they were too small and therefore grandly accentuated her best ass-et, boots with just a little taste of hooker heel, a plain black baseball cap and a leather three-quarter-length pea coat that ensured she could control exactly who got to see her ass and when. And beneath all that she was wearing . . . nothing. Not a damn stitch. No bra, no panties, no tank top—she was completely freeballing. Her plan had been to try and spice things up with "Romeo Rudy" at lunch by casually fessing up to the fact that just beneath her clingy beige turtleneck and skintight jeans was a completely naked woman. She was hoping that would jump-start things a little bit, maybe even entice him to take the rest of the day off—or at the very least take a *very* long lunch. Instead she found out why things were off-kilter in the first place.

Anyway, the point was she was naked. So despite being a little damp from the rain, she was still feeling kind of . . . sexy. Course, that internet session didn't hurt either—she was still running *très* hot from that. Gail was experiencing what they called in her information technology world a convergence. All these things were impacting her at once and making her react much differently than her usually cautious self. Normally, she would have just stood around hoping he worked up enough nerve to approach her—and that was on a good day—but today she was all the way in the red zone, baby. She gazed at him in the reflection from the video game's screen.

"Nice move," she said, not even really knowing if it was him or the computer that had just dealt out a nasty "KO." He looked over at her and his eyes lingered a little before his attention was drawn back to the game.

"Watch this," he muttered, right before one of the characters flew up in the air and landed on his head. She wasn't really paying attention, but he glanced at her and she took the hint.

"Oh, wow! You're *really* good." Doing the requisite amount of ego stroking required by the male species while secretly wondering if he liked to do it doggy style or missionary.

"So are you."

"What?" She was genuinely surprised. "Good at what?" she asked, wondering if she had the courage to say what she was thinking: *I'm good at a lot of things . . . wanna see?*

"The quickest way to a man's heart is through . . . ," he began as he turned his attention to the next battle.

*His dick?* she thought. "His stomach?" she said.

"Nope. Try again."

Oh, so he'd made up his own phrase. Well, how 'bout, *The quickest man to a man's heart is to tie him down and give him two blowjobs in a row.* She really tried, but in her current horny-as-hell mindset, Gail could not think of one thing that was appropriate to say to a stranger. She demurred.

"I give up."

"The quickest way to a man's heart," he announced dramatically. "Is through . . . Tekken 3."

She laughed, amused by the joke and recognizing its truth all at the same time. Tekken 3 had been high on Bradley's must-play list too.

"Izzat so?" she said when she'd regained herself. This was easier than she'd thought.

"Yep." She liked his easy confidence. He seemed comfortable with himself, if a little cocky. Fully invested in giving this opportunity a chance, she slipped four quarters into the game's money slot.

"Oh! *Major* brownie points." He laughed.

"Yeah? Do I get more if I win?" She delivered her line with a radiant smile and heavy eye contact—getting fully into her role. But he messed it up by laughing a little too loudly before answering, "Yeah, *if* you win."

The diss annoyed her slightly but she was thankful for it. It reminded her that he was just a guy with faults like everyone else, even if he did look like Adonis. Under normal circumstances, that dumb comment would have been just enough to make her lose interest. She had high standards in that regard. But this time she brushed it off. She didn't want a husband here, or even a boyfriend. What she wanted was hot sex on a platter. A story; something to put the ones she'd just read to shame. And she wasn't about to let her usual timidity or high standards nix her out of the race this time. She was out to get *done,* and there was nothing he could do to throw her off.

Gail pressed the "start" button, rather symbolic she noted, and got down to the business of earning some respect. She got him back for the snide comment by whupping his tail with Eddy, a tricky fighter who she knew from her Bradley days was difficult to defend against. After she put him down enough times for him to know it wasn't beginner's luck, she let him beat her silly. Primarily because he was losing his sense of humor about it. The sting of losing to a girl was getting to him and he'd started to get quiet on her. She wasn't having that; she wanted to reel this fish in—all the way in. And by the time he'd trounced her enough to restore his pride and upbeat demeanor, she had an idea.

"Have you ever played laser tag?" She'd played once, and at the time she'd had a fleeting thought that had returned and taken permanent residence in her mind about five minutes ago. He looked at her.

"Why? You wanna play?"

"It could be fun," she said, touching his arm for the forty-fifth time.

"Man, I have just hit paydirt. A woman that likes video games *and* laser tag. Wow. Okay, bet . . . So when you wanna do this?" In his sly smile she saw that he was trying to set her up for the phone number exchange. He was thinking of a laser tag excursion as their first date. Forget that, she might lose her nerve by then.

"How 'bout now?"

"Now?"

"Yeah, now. Unless . . . you have to be somewhere." Immediately, she regretted saying it. It was just like her to give him an out, but it looked like he was hesitating, and if he had somewhere to be, she was gonna let him off the hook.

"Nah," he said after a moment's hesitation. "But I do have a suit on. I don't wanna mess it up."

"Yeah? You scared you gonna get a whupping when you get home?" She was being playful, but she knew her jibe would probably cow him into it. His ego seemed too fragile to be able to walk away from that kind of insult. She was right.

"Ohhhh snap . . . Okay then, let's go! It's on now."

They laughed and joked on each other as they made their way into the basement, where the sprawling laser tag arena was located. Some listless teen in a Mega-Machine T-shirt was chewing gum and generally looking bored out of her mind down there. But soon she had them all suited up in the appropriate gear.

The teenager started her spiel. "This is your vest. This is your gun. These are the target areas. When the laser from your gun connects with one of the target areas on the other's vest, the vest will vibrate, signaling a hit. One round is seven minutes—"

"One round?" Gail made herself sound incredulous, then looked up at her new friend, smoothed her face out and said, "Oh . . . right."

"'Oh, right' what?"

"Nothin'" she said, looking down at her vest and trying to get the timing of her joke right. "It just figures, that's all."

"What figures?"

"Oh, you know . . . that you can only go *one* round." She caught him flat-footed and he laughed loudly.

"Oh see, your mouth done got you in trouble now, girl," he said, handing more money to the teenager. "Make it two rounds . . . Matter of fact, let's go three, unless you can't handle it, Ms. Thang."

"Oh I can handle it. You're the one that's gonna be huffin' and puffin'."

Still laughing, they disappeared into the dark labyrinth of multi-sectioned walls. The moment they stepped inside, she shoved him away and lit off into the maze. They ran around like kids, jumping, shooting, giggling and trying to cheat. Mostly he chased her and she made him work for any shots he got. In the meantime, she figured out the lay of the land and confirmed her hunch that no one else was in the maze that early on a rainy day. Finally satisfied that they were alone, she ran straight to the darkest, most secluded corner in the place and flopped to the floor. By the time he caught up, she'd shed her electronic vest and was sprawled on the floor in what she hoped was a provocative pose. *Take a risk*, she thought. *Here we go*.

"Oh! Look who's tired now!"

Damn. That wasn't quite the response she was looking for.

"I'm *not* tired." She had intended for it to sound sexy, but as it escaped her lips she realized with terror that her voice had gone high and cracked; it sounded like she was pissed and attitudinal. He stood there for a moment, unsure how to read this new sequence of events, and in that instant she got scared. Terrified, she found her mind firing off a fusillade of panicked what-if's. She couldn't go through with it. Quickly, she decided the easiest way to chicken out was to tell him she just wasn't feeling well and was just lying down until she felt better. She opened her mouth . . . but he beat her to the punch.

"So . . . do you surrender?" It wasn't much, but she thought it sounded vaguely suggestive; then she realized that one of her legs was cocked up in the air. She couldn't quite see the direction of his eyes in the darkness, but given her position, it was a pretty safe bet he was *not* making eye contact. Her hopes buoyed. She thought about the housewife and the Polar Bear Springs man. *C'mon, Gail, you can do it.*

"Totally." This time her voice didn't crack and she even managed to sound a bit flirtatious. Slowly she cocked her other leg up as well. He stood still, his glib remarks gone for the moment, and she realized he was hesitating because he still wasn't sure. He was a decent guy and didn't want to make the mistake of reading this wrong. Suddenly, she liked him a bit more for being enough of a gentleman not to pounce on her like a wolf the first chance he got.

*Men* never *say no,* she thought. That was all she needed to push her that final inch. An instant later, she'd whipped her turtleneck over her head, revealing her small but nonetheless naked breasts. There was no misreading the signs now, and he immediately knelt to gently pull one of her nipples into his mouth. The shock was immediate and tremendous.

"Oh, shit," she heard herself say, and even though she was embarrassed, she knew she meant it. It was so hot. So *unbelievably* hot. Later, when she was capable of rational thought, she would try to figure out exactly what created the visceral thrill that had swirled over every inch of her skin the moment his tongue caressed her breast. The risk of being caught in a public place; the raw power of realizing she had created and defined the encounter; the dazzling attractiveness of her newfound friend; the fulfillment of actually getting it on with a sexy stranger—only the number one sex fantasy of women across the world; the daring and heat of being bold enough to leave the house without bra and panties; even the coolness of his plastic laser tag vest against her skin felt colossal. And that was *before* she used her gun to make it vibrate. Lord, she couldn't even think about it without getting tremors and tickles all over again.

It was Gail's show, and she made sure it stayed that way. She assumed there was no condom in the vicinity so she steered them away from actual intercourse. And she also made sure she got hers first. It was so thrilling, being in control—of a stranger—a *gorgeous* stranger, that she found herself exploding powerfully just moments after she'd guided his hand into the bare, copious wetness between her legs. She mounted him after that—pinning his arms beneath her thighs and grasping his tie in her hands like the reins of a spirited horse. She ground her pelvis slowly against the mound in his pants, then faster, then slowly again, until she felt the pulse of his orgasm throbbing in ripples beneath her.

When they finally came out of the maze, they both had just a hint of a smile on their lips and a languid swagger in their gait. If the teenager picked up on anything, Gail couldn't tell and frankly didn't care. They ascended the steps together and stepped out on the street, still not having said a word. It wasn't until they'd been standing on the sidewalk for a moment that she realized she didn't even know his name. The thought gave her a tingle that shot through her thighs, and instantly she decided to keep it that way—an anonymous assignation, how hot is that? Finally, they looked at each other, each trying to decide what came next.

"Well . . . maybe I'll see you in the arcade sometime." Gail felt a little guilty after she said it, but she'd never intended for it to go any further. Her pang of guilt evaporated when a look of relief crept into his face. He knew where he stood now, no guesswork involved. He relaxed.

"Shiiiiiit. I damn sure hope so." She laughed with him, feeling flattered even though it wasn't directly a compliment. "If I do see you," he continued, "maybe we can, uh, play some laser tag."

She laughed again. "Yeah, maybe so."

"So, is this gonna show up in the *Penthouse* letters section?"

She nodded at him, a smile on her face. "Yeah . . . probably."

"Well, just for the record. I've never, uh . . ."

"Yeah, me either."

"That's good to know, lady."

"Likewise."

"'Sides, if you weren't gonna write the letter, I damn sure was."
They laughed together a final time before shaking hands and walking
off in separate directions.

"Hey," she called out, half turning in his direction. He stopped,
doing a half turn as well. "Sorry about messing up your suit."

He laughed loudly. "Are you kidding? Anytime, lady, anytime."
Then they both turned away.

Gail knew she'd forgive Rudy now. She might not even bring up
the white girl at all now, 'cause, no matter what, she knew her lunch
date had been *so* much better than his. Maybe even marriage could
be in the cards. No, that was getting too serious. Marriage wasn't
something you even thought about, especially in your early twenties,
especially when you were having fun. Big fun at that!

Ha! Speaking of big fun, let's see Connie and the Polar Bear
Springs guy top that.

# Broken Rules

**Edwardo Jackson**

## OBSERVATION

That was my job, to notice things. The devil is in the details, they say. If that were so, then I was Queen of the Underworld.

Helen Keller could see how goddamn fine this man was. Details, baby: the curve of his ripe lips as they cupped the edge of his glass; the dimple at the crest of his shoulders as they undulated to the beat; the ripple of his stomach fighting against the black Lycra shirt. Rise, fall, rise, fall, you beautiful black valley of darkness of a chest!

His penis must have been huge.

There is a fine line between observation and obsession, so I diverted my eyes for the first time in almost a minute. Damn if he didn't catch me just as I looked away. No, no, no, no! It had nothing to do with you, baby! Trust me, that was a compliment.

He knew. He must have, because he smiled. Thinly. Well, at least as thinly as those big, pink pussy-eaters could have. Compliment received.

I walked to the other side of the bar, giving myself time to recover. Allowed myself to get lost in the infernal intensity of the techno beat. I couldn't remember the last time I had been so damn moved by a *body*. If you knew me, you would know that's a very big deal.

Call it conceit, but I could feel his dark eyes inside that shaved head follow me around the club. I wouldn't turn around to verify, but I could feel them nonetheless. They disrobed me. If those eyes were hands, I would let them, too.

I toyed with my wedding band as if it meant something. There was one rule I could not break, and it's not the rule you think. There was one rule I could not break and damn me if this black Jehovah didn't make me want to break it. I toyed with my wedding band. As if it meant something.

I joined up with Marcy the second she was out of the bathroom. "Sorry, Reese. Some girl OD'ed and was puking up her guts into the porcelain goddess. I miss anything?"

I had started to say no when I was caught in my own lie. The Brotha from a Planet Like None Otha strode past us, shimmering in the dark, sweaty filth of Sunset Strip nightclub libido like a comet reminder of all that was right with men. Stirred an ember of feeling of what could have been but never will be. Not in my lifetime, at least. His back to me, his aura of sexual supremacy almost past us, he very subtly cut his eyes at me. Leaving me breath*full*—as in so full of breath, my words could drown themselves—he closed his blade, and left the club.

Marcy, in all her blonde glory, couldn't even deny it. "Who was *that*?"

I corralled my smile. Before committing my biggest lie of the year.

"Nobody."

## RECRUITMENT

I'm something of a living legend. Those weren't my words, but the words of some intern quoted in *Variety* a year ago when they did a piece on me. Hollywood's female Jackie Robinson is the one I like best, which is what some CE at Fox had called me in a piece *Newsweek* did four months ago.

I am the first African-American female head of a major studio in Hollywood history.

Believe it or not, that's a big deal. I am in a position to influence American pop culture with the movies that my studio makes. You don't find that in every job description. I would have been the first black studio head period if Perry Ellis hadn't gotten to be the interim head of MGM three months before me. That's right: I was beat out on history by a man named after a *cologne*. Cologne Boy was later replaced by a Long Island Jew two months later (shocking, I know).

Actually, I shouldn't even talk. Hell, *I'm* married to a Long Island Jew. My sister says that we act as a two-way ghetto pass—I vouch for him in black circles while he vouches for me in Hollywood, a notoriously Jewish enclave. Truly, my sister couldn't be further from the truth. I grew up in upper middle class Ladera Heights in LA and went to Harvard B school, while Mike's a Long Island tax attorney. He stays out of the spotlight while I can't escape the profile of this job in its glare.

I'm more than a token hire. Affirmative action never did shit for me. I learned how to swim with sharks while in the damn shark tank. When you've worked your way up from the William Morris mailroom, through the junior agent ranks of both WMA and Endeavor, jumped careers over to the Creative Executive circle at my current home, and then worked your way up all the way to the top *without* fucking, sucking, or ducking from a single executive—male or female—then *that's* an accomplishment in this town. Especially at age forty-one.

But I doubt that's running through the mind of these two pricks in my office right now. If they're respectful, they're maybe thinking, "Damn, that skirt's kinda short, but she sure looks good" and "I hope she greenlights this pitch and makes my career." If they're not, they're probably thinking, "How many cocks" and "Black bitches sure can fuck."

As these two pricks finished up their presentation of the latest bad idea from a midlist screenwriter whose bloated development deal was done way before I took over and desperately needed a hit to validate his ridiculous salary, I nodded and "mmm-hmmed" my way into semiconsciousness. They finished, looking at me with expectant, hopeful eyes, anticipation heavier than the national deficit.

"I hate it."

Not even the dotcom bubble burst faster than their hopes.

"But let's do it."

They were stunned. I had just greenlighted the latest derivative, humorless, pseudo-romantic Hollywood comedy that will eventually require twelve screenwriters, seven producers, fifty-two rewrites, thirty-five million dollars, a bottle of Vicadin, and bad reviews from the *New York Times* to *Vibe,* en route to grossing sixty-two million dollars two years from now but netting the studio five after marketing and back-end deals, yet before DVD sales. Why do it? you may ask. I'm a businesswoman, not a cultural vanguard. No matter what *Essence* may say.

I sent them on their way, happy that they got what they wanted. Now it was time for me to get what I wanted.

Mirrors tell lies. Yes, they reflect, but they also distort. First of all, everything is on the wrong side. Left is right; right is left. They also flatter, sometimes when you don't need flattering. I know I'm beautiful, dammit. I don't need a mirror for validation. Nor do I need it from men; Momma always told me I was, and that's good enough for me. What gets lost in the translation? What gets lost in the space between the reality and the reflection, the flesh and the image in the glass?

"The soul."

I parked my car in our empty driveway. I reeked of sex and couldn't care less. I looked it, too, as I glanced in the mirror, at my whipped hair and melted eyeshadow.

My favorite place in the house was the deck off the master bedroom. Ours was a three-and-a-half-million-dollar home on the cliffs of Pacific Palisades. I could spend hours out here, watching the moon sparkle platinum kisses off the waves of the Pacific. It was lonely and comforting all at the same time, kind of like the touch of a man not my husband.

Mike and I had an arrangement. Somewhat like the military, really. Don't ask, don't tell. And I was cool with that. We spent so much time away from each other, whether it was my incessant flying to put out fires on set, massage some coked out star into doing my picture, or go back to the New York office to step on some necks. He still lived in our Great Neck home, while I had to split time on both coasts, spending most of it on this one. What I did was a necessity, to keep our marriage whole; otherwise I would go crazy from the loneliness, being a woman in a man's job, being on the wrong side of the country from my lover, being the middle of three children and not having a roommate. We never talked about it and he never complained. Being together was as important for my career as it was for his. Appearances. Respect. It just made sense. I never threw it in his face, never brought it to our home, I just did my own thing. Or *things,* really.

Marcy called it a harem. If it weren't me doing it, I'd be inclined to agree. I liked to call them The Collective. If it sounded slightly

Marxist, that's because it was. They were the farmers, and I was Lenin. Lenin with a vagina. They all paid taxes to the state of me and my Conchita. What Conchita wanted, they gave her. And when she wanted them, she got them.

There were rules, of course. Always rules. Compensation, of course. Sex? Most definitely. None of them knew who I was. They were all non-entertainment types but ruggedly handsome nonetheless. Their numbers varied but I currently bankrolled seven men in The Collective; three others had joined voluntarily. I paid rent for the seven and they earned their keep. Whenever, however, wherever I wanted. I would rotate their services as I saw fit. Marcy repeatedly warned of a karmic collapse, but I didn't care. I was having fun with it. It was stringless as a tube top and guilt free as nonfat vanilla ice cream. But at times like this, it was as unfulfilling as bad Chinese food.

I was restless. I was too energetic and craved some excitement. Not someone from my three-year-old payroll. I craved something I had not had before. I needed to get out. I needed . . .

Verve. Hottest club in Hollywood. A starfucker's dream. Music pulsated like an arrhythmic dancer's heartbeat. Cosmos, apple martinis, and Skyy Blue flowed as readily as corny pickup lines. Handsome, built twentysomething playthings grazed about the pasture of taut, sexy fortysomething power brokers like myself. They were fishing for careers, I was scrounging around the tackle box looking for bait. No one was looking for a relationship.

On nights like this, without my blonde bombshell Marcy, the regrettably committed studio accountant, I flew incognito. Dark hat, dark clothes, dark shades—yes, even at night—dark flipped hair pulled back into a simple ponytail, dark attitude. I was on the prowl.

I flirted, I danced, I got sweaty, I got ready. I took a break by the bar to consider my options. One of the three young studs I had danced with—a Tom Cruise look-alike, a white hip-hop guy, and a Eurotrash model—not a single one of them over the age twenty-five, to be sure—was going to get some chocolate cream pie tonight. I sipped on a Blue Motherfucker and played Eenie Penis Miny Moe in my head, ready to add a new Y chromosome to the payroll.

Him again. On the other side of the bar. Tuning out the immature diatribe of some model-cum-actress-cum-waitress. Staring straight ahead at me. Cutting through the space, and the bullshit, like a laser pointer. I put down my drink and came to his aid.

"Who's this?" I demanded.

"Uh, I, uh . . ."

"Adriana," supplied the girl, a little impatiently. "Who the hell is this? Your mother?"

Stringy-haired twat. "What was your name again?"

"Adriana Fox."

Adriana Fox, you will never work in this town again. I smiled through orthodontically perfect teeth. "School's out. Get the fuck away from my man."

I sliced between the two, draping my arm around his neck. Disgusted, Adriana took off. I could've sworn I heard her say, "Tired-ass bitch."

I stroked the tiny black hairs on his large shaved head. He smiled.

"Thanks. What's your name?"

"Sharice." Most people didn't know my full name. I cut it down to "Reese" a long time ago to compete better in my field. Ethnic cleansing.

"Paul."

I caressed the side of his face with the tip of my French manicured fingernail. "I've seen you before, Paul."

He arched an eyebrow at me.

"And I will see you again."

I walked away, positive Paul absorbed every curve. So tempting. I ended up leaving the club with the wrong man—the hip-hop guy. But as I stepped into my car to follow him back to his one-bedroom dump in the shadow of the Hollywood Hills, I swore to myself that if I ever, *ever* saw Paul again . . . I would have to break every rule.

And he would be worth it.

## THE OFFER

The biggest wars you never hear about are fought during preproduction. Many a good film has been scrapped due to arguments over budgets, locations, talent, even catering. I'm not kidding. This shitty rom-com would be no different.

*Love for Free*, as the bad script we had purchased two months ago was called, was hip deep in preproduction. We had producers, a young but expensive director, a hungry line producer ready to atone for his nearly fatal mismanagement of his last film's budget, and a DP whose visuals were like the *National Geographic* of the MTV generation.

But we had no stars.

I can kiss ass with the best of them. It's more than a social skill in Hollywood, it's an essential—food, shelter, kiss ass. So I was more than ready to woo the handsome, impossibly tanned, twenty-eight-year-old flavor of the year, Roman Hoffman.

I sat at Wolfgang Puck's for the better part of an hour, having already known Hoffman would pull some insecure, B-List-trying-to-make-A-List-actor bullshit on me. I had some scripts with me and I made notes, fully anticipating he would try to jerk my chain a little bit, feeling out his power (and newly vetted eight-million-dollars-a-picture asking price) on the heels of his two-hundred-*million*-dollar-worldwide-grossing romantic comedy that had just left theaters last month. Never mind that I was the head of a studio, albeit one in dire need of a major hit next year. Roman wanted to show me how long his dick was and how low I would go to suck it. With just about every major A-List leading man in his age range having quietly passed on the formulaically sappy script, we needed him like Magic needed Bird—contentiously, yet still vitally.

When he did breeze in just behind a scent of beachfront salt air and just ahead of the last five minutes of having any career at my studio, Roman looked every bit the contemporary, cynical, anti-leading-man leading man. Even down to the requisite five o'clock shadow, intensely "artistic" eyes, and shoulders the size of the Great Wall.

I wanted to bite off his head like black widows did their mates, but I was thoroughly professional, even if he wasn't. Like most young actors, he wasn't very smart, although completely self-aware and obsessed with the direction of his career. So let's get down to brass tacks:

"We're prepared to offer you eight million for the role of Porter, Roman."

"I want ten." The little gerbil didn't even hesitate to crawl up my ass and irk the shit out of me. "Plus back end."

I searched the heavens and the restaurant for a shred of self-control. What the—Paul? After two months? Looking hotter than the Mojave on an August afternoon? He tipped his glass at me from the bar. I offered a weak smile in return.

All of a sudden, I wanted this demanding piece of mainstream trash out of my way.

"Eight point five," I countered. "No back end, and you're lucky I don't badmouth you to every studio head in town that wants to hire your overvalued, self-important, indulgent young ass."

I vaguely saw Roman smile. My focus was elsewhere. Paul waved me over without waving me over. Did the man have eyes or what?

"You're begging. Nine mil, against twenty percent of the gross," Roman fired back, unfazed by my very accurate dismantling of his position. "I've got four other dinners with four other studio heads to topline their projects. You need this more than I do."

*Are you going to be late to all of them?* I wanted to scream. Truth be told, he was right. My spies around town confirmed as much. If I wanted this flick to open with a bang that would solidify my sliding ground as studio head after last summer's disastrous box office take, then I did need the sandal-wearing fucker. And with Paul's stare intent on drawing me over to his side like the Sirens did sailors, I had to end this quickly.

"Fine," I snapped, gathering my things. "Contracts will be sent in the morning. If you'll excuse me."

I left behind Roman and his ego-sized sense of self-satisfaction, for the warmer shores of Lake Paul at the bar. I wanted to dive into those eyes and do the backstroke. You know—the back . . . *stroke.* I slid onto the stool next to him.

"Took you long enough," he said, those curved cunnilingus callers wrapping around the rim of his glass.

I ignored him. "Here's the deal. You work with my terms and my terms only, or I file a stalking report."

"Your terms only, huh?" He laughed. "Maybe we have similar tastes."

He ordered me a Jack and Coke to match his. That's a hard drink. Just like I like my men. I cut my eyes at him. "Maybe we do."

"So what are these terms, Miss Sharice?"

He called my name just to show off. It worked. But at this point, he didn't have to work for anything. "I set the times, the places. You just show up and take care of me. Don't call me, I'll call you.

Condoms, always. Compensation, too, if you can keep your mouth shut. Nothing personal, no gossip, no last names, no tongue kissing, no love. And never at my house. Never."

"Do you come with a rule book?" He smiled.

"Just make sure that I come."

"Anything else I should know?"

I paused slightly before telling him this. I'd never wavered on this point before, but I wanted him so badly. I couldn't explain it.

"There's more than one of you, and you can be replaced at any time."

An edgy silence set in. Well, at least it felt edgy to me.

"So that's the offer," I recapped. "Take it or leave it."

Paul looked at me. I looked at him.

## TRAINING

"Jesus, Marcy. I think I almost lost my job today."

I was in bumper-to-bumper traffic on the 405, man's mortal attempt at playing the Devil. My DVD screen was up, playing some Eddie Murphy comedy I tuned out. I spoke into my earbud microphone that dangled near my lips.

"The board meeting?" Marcy buzzed into my ear.

"Yeah. They've given me until the end of next summer."

"What?"

"This summer almost killed us. One of the worst in studio history. Never mind the fact that this summer's slate was ninety percent set up by my predecessor . . . They still thought that my background in marketing would have translated immediately in their performance."

"Both you and I know the dogs that Bill had on the schedule. Dead-in-the-road dogs."

I clucked my teeth, sucking back the real, black truth. "Doesn't matter. Their quarterly reports are off. The rest of their balance sheet couldn't draw flies with shit, and now they're putting the pressure on the media unit to perform. All I was told was that next summer would be my first with my own slate." I didn't have to say it could be my last.

Traffic started to ease up a little north of the 10 interchange. I heard a beep on my phone. "Hold on, Marcy."

I switched over. "Reese."

It was Mike. He told me that he was going to be stuck in Great Neck this weekend, working on a huge project. Mike was supposed to come out to LA this weekend. My disappointment was minimal. I played the concerned wife role enough to ease his mind and switch back over to Marcy.

"Who was that?"

A smile fixed my lips. "Opportunity."

I wanted him so badly. Like how Einstein must have wanted to prove to the world the theory of relativity the second he had cracked it. If I didn't feel as if he was the E to my MC squared, Conchita did. And what Conchita wanted, she got.

But she had to wait. There was a process to these things.

I had called him over an hour ago for an encounter right now. It disturbed my womanhood how much my flesh ached for him. I visualized my arriving at his door, some unexpectedly tony address in beach-warming Playa del Rey for which I would take pleasure paying the rent. Envisioned my demanding, unwavering stare, fully in control of the situation. Foresaw a quick disrobing from both parties. Prophesized a kneeling, tongue-laden tribute to Conchita. Felt the penetration of a future quenched desire.

My sheets were wet from my own making. The ocean breeze snuck inside and stole the light from my candles. A shudder took hold of my body, the result of nature and emotion. I withdrew my fingers and exhaled my longing.

I wanted nothing more than to go over there and fuck the black out of him. He was expecting me to come. I was expecting to come if I came. I just . . . I had already broken a rule with him. I couldn't break any more just to have him because I wanted him.

And I did want him. But I had to make him wait. I needed to follow procedure. Stand him up. Make him mad. Have him try and burn a hole through the bed when he next saw me. Have him so whipped, he would pay me for the pleasure of my dirty bathwater. I didn't get off so much on the physicality of my own desire but on the intensity of theirs. I was every woman. I wanted to be wanted.

I burrowed under the covers and visualized. And shivered. Not from nature this time. From anticipation. From the process.

## DRY RUN

*This better be fucking worth it.*

That thought swirled a million times in my head as I made the trek out to Playa del Rey from our Valencia set. Today had been the first day of filming for *Love* and I was too through.

Disaster would be an understatement's understatement. Roman Hoffman was an hour late back from lunch because he was hiding out in the woods, getting ass from two extras *at the same time*. I quietly paid the whores from my pocket change and dismissed them from the production. Seven grand in union time was completely lost because Roman had a threesome in the sticks. I needed a relaxing diversion like dumb struggling actresses needed a clue.

He hadn't returned my calls in over a month. I hadn't called him in almost two weeks, fed up that the pursued was now doing the pursuing. No man was worth all this trouble. If it weren't for a less than fulfilling weekend of marital sex back in Long Island, I wouldn't have made this call at all tonight.

But I did. And here I was.

He answered the door butt ass naked.

"Jesus," escaped my lips, just under my breath. I didn't know if it was an exclamation or a greeting. I was ready to commit idolatry of the highest order. Conchita began to sweat beyond my control.

I quickly assembled a controlling stare, the controlling stare I had always envisioned would allow me to manage the situation like I managed my job. It would be the last time I would be in control of *anything*.

"May I come in?"

He smiled just enough for a smirk. Pink pussy-eaters parting to project perpetually pleasurable possibilities. He drew me into his house, cupping his hand under my breast.

"Better yet, may I come in you?"

## INTEGRATION

I was late, and didn't even care. I shoved the assortment of roses I found at the front door in the corner of the closet. They were from

Mike. Once upon a time, I would have considered that sweet. We were too far gone in our marriage for sweet.

Ran a shower, stripped naked, let the warm pellets of water rinse the sex off me. As the steam fogged up the glass blocks of my shower, I knew no amount of water could rinse away the feeling. Conchita hurt. Throbbed really. I could never get used to the size of that man. I smiled. Okay, that's a lie.

Over the course of the past three months, Paul had singlehandedly eliminated my harem. Paul *was* The Collective now. I had sex with him at least once a day, twice if I were lucky. I grinned. Today I was lucky.

And late. I dried off and stalked my mirrored closet naked. I saw the bicuspid marks on the underside of my breast. I giggled like an eight-year-old girl. Paul loved nibbling me right there. I'd have to cover that up before my trip back home this weekend. If I made it at all.

This was the first time I let our trysts affect my work. While, yes, I have had him *at* work, this is the first time I let our games get in the way of it. I was late for the wrap party for *Love for Free* because I demanded one more orgasm—and I got it. Number ten. If there were a Hall of Fame for Fucking, his penis would be enshrined.

I slid on a slinky red number. My eyes shimmered with femininity. Who knew one man would make me break almost all my rules? It wasn't love, because I no longer believed in that. I couldn't really talk to him like I used to be able to with Mike, because Mike and I had started off as friends. But it was full-blown lust. If I could combine Mike and Paul into one man, I could be faithful to him forever. Never mind that my dalliance with Paul broke the one rule that Mike and I had established in our don't ask–don't tell policy, the one taboo he was most afraid of, one that I had not indulged in since grad school. And, as it turned out, this would be the one characteristic that would separate, differentiate, and totally eradicate Paul from The Collective, and The Collective from Paul.

He was black.

Albeit late, I stared at my profile in the mirror, a sunny disposition of sexually charged womanhood. If I could always look and feel like this, the cliché was true. And I was never going back.

It never occurred to me that, for the first time in my life, I was truly being monogamous to a man. Just a man not my husband.

## MATURITY

I was addicted to that man. Seven months into seeing Paul, I had to admit I'd had a priority shift. It was now food, shelter, dick.

We had a highly focused test screening for *Love*. Let's just say that it went badly. I didn't notice the popcorn thrown at the screen because I was too busy in the empty upper balcony area, riding Paul like the coin-operated hobby horse outside a grocery store. I had snuck him in once the movie had started, just to scream silent orgasms of my Conchita singing his praises. That was not the first time we had done it while I was on the job, but it would be the first of several times we would do it in public.

Based on the screening cards and my recent glowing, emotional state, I ordered the ending reshot. I did what any mature business like this struggling studio had to do: reduced risk in order to maximize profit. Well-done romantic comedies, outside of maybe non–special effects kiddie flicks, were as safe a bet as you could get in this cyclical industry. So I had ordered the ending reshot to be more romantic. Imagine that.

I had lunch with Marcy at the Standard, recounting the evening over fifteen-dollar hamburgers.

"So is he your boyfriend or what?" Marcy grinned over six-dollar fries. I gave her a look, so she continued. "I mean, you've ended your harem all over one guy. You should marry him or something."

"Not funny." I gazed off while chewing. "I did do something stupid the other night, though."

"I know I'm like a Greek chorus with this, but Mike's a nice guy," piped Marcy conscientiously. "Boring, sure. But that's what you signed up for after hoing around your first year at Harvard."

I ignored her. "I told Paul that I once wanted to be an actress."

Marcy's ice blue eyes bugged out. "You shared personal information?"

I sighed. "Told him I was pretty good, too. Until I stopped, after finding out that the average actor made seventeen grand in LA."

"Why did you share personal information?" Marcy treated this like the watershed moment it truly was.

"Marcy, is it possible to love just one thing about a person? That

that one thing about a person opens you up to exploring every other facet about them?"

She laughed. "Don't tell me Paul's penis is a gateway drug!"

"I think it is. I don't love him. Not in the conventional sense of love anyway, where it's supposed to be totally fulfilling, mutually satisfying, and about mind, body, and soul commitment."

"You mean how you once used to love Mike?"

"Maybe," I allowed. "Mike always had two out of the three. But I always felt something was a little lacking in the 'body' part. Paul . . . he fills that body part. Every damn night. He does it in such a way that makes me wonder if he can somehow get the mind and soul part."

I stopped mid-sip for more pontification. "I know it may not sound very feminist, but at the time I met Mike, he helped save me from myself. Now . . . I believe Paul's here to save me from a life of ennui with Mike."

I never asked why I couldn't do it by myself, or why I needed saving.

Marcy sucked her teeth disapprovingly, much like a sista would. Sipped her Diet Coke and passed judgment all at the same time. "You know what I see? I see a woman who has broken every vow, broken every rule for a taste of the impossible—and to get away with it. But what happens when there are no more rules left to break?"

## DEGRADATION

I was never much for pillow talk, but tonight was a special occasion.

We had just come back from a press junket for *Love for Free* at the picturesque Hotel del Coronado down in San Diego. I wanted to emphasize the upcoming movie's romantic theme to the reporters through the ritzy resort once frequented by old-time LA movie stars. Also it gave me an excuse to enjoy Paul's talents in the studio-tax-deductible four-thousand-dollar-a-night presidential suite. I had introduced him as my personal assistant all weekend, but I wouldn't be surprised if the intrepid reporters had figured out just how personally he assisted me. Their job, and access to my stars, would be enough for them never to dare ask the question or print such salacious speculation. After a weekend of coordinating arrival times, facilitating massive movie star egos, and massaging the press, I was exhausted. Coming home and crashing on the bed, we had enjoyed a quick, relatively quiet lovemaking session before basking in its afterglow.

I felt so vulnerable with him, the way he made me feel. I needed him more than ever now. The typically tepid spring season had been disastrous. Our returns from the first two months of the summer season were negligible. Everything rode on whether *Love for Free* and Roman Hoffman's overpaid, snarkily charismatic ass would be a hit. The editor-in-chief of *Variety* had it in for me, as I could swear he had a spy or something in my studio, feeding him numbers on how our movies were bleeding money. Even Mike was in Europe on a special project for two months. I needed someone in my corner, even if it was just my male concubine. Or was he more?

"Only you can answer that, Reese." He laid his beautiful, walnut brown body next to mine. His sculpted, bare ass looked like South African diamond mines. "It's been a year. I've played by the rules. But now it seems like we're rewriting them."

He was right. He usually was these days. I considered leaving Mike. Seriously. More than ever these days, Paul fulfilled the most important duty of marriage. He was my de facto husband.

"You're the first real man I've met. You make me feel like a real woman."

He laid on top of my back, pushing his love in from behind. My mouth groaned, my mind sighed, my body gave in.

"I only want to be with you," he said.

Rest in peace, Mike. Rest in peace.

"Paul . . . I love you."

As I spoke those unimaginably life changing words, I realized the full weight of my breaking the last rule. I made love to him in my bed.

*Love for Free* opened to horrible reviews. Critics hated the ending. But with the crowd-pleasing trailer and Roman Hoffman's nine-million-dollar looks, it looked to be review-proof. I wanted to go to Century City with Paul and sit in the back row of a packed Friday night theater, making out like teenagers without the braces. I hadn't heard from him since Sunday night, our first night in my bed.

I paged him once again.

## INSTABILITY

"I want a divorce."

"Okay."

At least Mike had the guts to do it in person. I was so toxic these days, I was my own nuclear waste dump. *I* didn't even want to be around me.

Mike tossed a thick manila envelope on the bed. For some reason at moments like these, I always remembered the little things, like the mild humidity in the room or the crease in the top corner of the bed-sheet. When I opened up the envelope, pictures spilled out. All over the bed. Our onetime marriage bed.

I guess now I knew why Mike wanted a divorce.

"You were set up, Reese."

Well, that explained the quality of the photos. I tried not to stare at them. Mike paced the floor slowly, like the litigation attorney he was not. I wasn't sure if he did it to soothe his emotions or to gather up steam for his indictment.

"I put up with your previous indiscretions because I knew you didn't love them. I knew you loved me—well, to the most that I knew you were capable of—but I knew that, with our spoken and unspoken rules in place, it would never get out of hand."

I didn't like being lectured at, but I shut up and took it, evaluating my legal and professional options all the way. With *Love for Free* grossing a paltry seven million dollars in three weeks—a bomb by anyone's standards—this divorce would kill my career. Absolutely kill it.

"But it was brought to my attention some time ago that it *had* gotten out of hand."

The board members were meeting tomorrow. *Variety* ran 40 to 1 odds that I would keep my job. He stalked some more. "Want to know why you haven't heard from 'Paul' in a month? Because I *paid* him."

"What?"

The first pleasure Mike was able to extract from this misery presented itself. "I paid the man you know as 'Paul' to seduce you."

The photo of us making love in this very bed singed my eyeballs in a personal, accusing way. "No way. No possible way."

"He's really good, isn't he? A Broadway actor I hired over a year ago to find you, fuck you, and fool you."

I couldn't push out the word "Why?" so Mike explained it for me. "Paul was a test, a test that you failed. He accomplished his mission: you fell in love with him. You knew when we got married about my insecurities concerning interracial marriage. That, no matter how much of myself I gave you, you may always want something more. Back then, you dismissed it, calling me silly and insecure. Even when you started cheating, you assured me that you would never, ever step out on me with a black man. That was back when your word meant something to me, meant everything to me. So when I heard about your stable of studs, I wanted to see if you still had your word. If that word still carried any weight. If you were still that woman I fell in love with her second year at Harvard . . . or the slut who fucked the basketball team in her first. Now I can draw my own conclusions."

Momma always warned me about marrying a white man. She never disapproved, but she warned me. Said it would be complex emotional and social terrain. For us, it never had been. Until now. I bit my lip. Momma always warned me about marrying a white man.

"You know, in my heart of hearts, I always knew you would cheat on me," Mike calmly accused. "But I never thought you would betray me."

He shook his head softly. "I could have outed you earlier. Should have. But I always thought you'd get tired of him like the others. I always thought he would be replaced. I guess I always thought that if I trusted you enough, you would save yourself and go back to being my wife someday." Snorted. "That's what I get for thinking."

Mike stopped at the door. "Those are the only set. I don't want your money. But I want a divorce. And, for once in your life, some fucking respect."

At that very moment, he had both.

"Goodbye, Reese." And Mike left.

My world felt inside out. So, of course, the phone rang. Marcy called to announce her engagement. I tearfully announced to her my divorce.

## REPLACEMENT

Marcy: "I told him."

It all made sense. The fancy restaurant. Midday. A lot of people around. Marcy's diamond wedding ring reflecting like a shiny promise of a simpler, naive time. She didn't want me to make a scene.

As if I didn't know what she meant already, Marcy elaborated. "I told Mike about your harem. The, uh, Collective."

In the last six months, I had lost my job. Lost my husband. Lost the illusion of the only man I gave a damn about. I had given up the house in Pacific Palisades and now sold real estate in the eastern suburb of Chino, anonymously working under my first and middle given names, Sharice Tyler. I had lost everything. So I'd be damned if I'd lose any more dignity by deigning to ask why.

Marcy knew me so well. "You were out of control, Reese. Mike had been nothing but decent to you, and you perverted the institution of marriage.

"I tried to warn you. I never passed judgment on you, but I tried to warn you that, eventually, it would all catch up to you. I had no idea about Paul, that Mike would go out and hire somebody to expose you. But I always had a feeling your personal life would end up affecting your professional one. And it did."

Marcy, obviously, was referring to *Love for Free,* part of my total undoing at the studio. When I say "part," it's because news of my divorce and the impetus behind it became public knowledge and industry spectacle. The only thing hotter in the trades at the time than my career collapse had been the sudden movie star ascendancy of unknown Adriana Fox. I was no longer the first African-American female to lead a studio; I was now the black bitch who sent the studio down in flames because she was a faithless whore. I would be the first to admit that the truth lay somewhere in between. Despite being aware there were forces at work waiting, itching for a chance to see me fail, I had helped their cause all too much by having been less vigilant. Okay, okay—I had been out-and-out distracted.

"I did what I did because I know you're better than that. Even the wild and crazy Reese I met at Harvard our first year was nothing like the cold, cynical man-eater you evolved into out here. I don't know if it's something about LA, this Industry, or both, but I know that who you were was a product of where you were. What you were doing. What it took for you to do what you did in a man's world. You weren't the same person. Hell, you weren't even a person at times. I did it because, in the long run, this will save you. And maybe, just maybe, I could get my friend back. Someday."

But today wouldn't be that day. I focused on my ice water as if I could melt the glass. I didn't know if I should be mad at her or mad at myself. No one forced me to cheat on my husband. No one made me break the rules that we both had agreed upon. Yet, by that same token, no one forced me to listen to my nature, an invisible force screaming inside me that I was missing something in my life with Mike. Mike was wrong. It wasn't my fault he feared the power of the black man. Shit, I was a black woman! Did he truly believe that I wouldn't experience that power for myself firsthand again someday? In this respect, Mike hadn't divorced me so much as set me free. But free to do what?

Maybe Marcy really did do what she felt was right. I secretly suspected it had been her leaking numbers to *Variety*, discrediting my films' budgets in a covert attempt to extract me from the business. Let's hear it for the blonde bombshell! It worked.

Life, just like business, is cyclical. There is a process. It repeats itself. Mine would, too. I had a boyfriend. It was still kinda new. As far as I could tell, everything was on the up-and-up with him, even though my past was left firmly shrouded in the past. He was no Paul, but then again, not even Paul was Paul. (I think there was something to be said about my only being able to fall in love with someone who wasn't real.) This guy was nice, a gentleman, and black. I didn't dare curse around him. He was super-respectful. Honest to a fault. And he genuinely seemed to care about my well-being. I tried to return the favor. There were no mysteries, no taboos, no rules. I wasn't sure love was in the offing, but this sure beat the hell out of being alone.

"Thank you, Marcy." I was thanking her for her honesty, nothing more. Marcy was a mirror. And, for once, the mirror did not distort.

# The Drive

## Jemal K. Yarbrough

"Relax, baby. Everything will be fine. You'll see," Shelia said, reclining in the tiny bucket seats of my beat-up car and placing her bare feet on the dash. We were halfway to my parents' house in Santa Clarita for Thanksgiving dinner. This would be the first time they met Shelia. From the moment I told them about her, they disliked her. I've always been honest about my girlfriends, and when my mother asked what Shelia did for a living, I told her. She didn't handle Shelia's being an ex–porn star and currently a stripper too well. The fact that she was ten years my senior didn't help any.

"Right. I can just see it now," I said sarcastically.

"Hi, Mom and Dad, this is my fiancée Passion, she's a thirty-four-year-old ex–porn star now on the strip club circuit. Hey, Dad, maybe you seen her in *Passion Unleashed: A Gang Bang!*" I said, chuckling to hide the truth behind my words.

"Naw, they'll be more disturbed by the fact that I don't have any panties on under this dress," she said, smiling and revealing her long taut legs and hairless crotch.

"Tell me you've got a pair in your purse," I said. I wasn't sure if my heart started to race from the fear of my parents actually discovering her surprise or because I was looking at her pouting pussy lips.

"No. You must be preoccupied if you haven't noticed that I am not wearing a bra either," Shelia chuckled.

Exasperated, I replied, "You're just not going to make this any easier for me, are you?"

"No, why should I? I warned you that you were going to fall in love with me," she teased. "Look, you're their son; they have a right to be concerned about you and your future. I understand that. I also understand that my career path isn't exactly normal, but I love you and I'll win them over just for you. I promise."

I glanced over at her exposed pussy and felt less than reassured by her words. She was right though, she had warned me, but I'd ignored her and pursued her anyway. Hell, who wouldn't have?

We met two months ago at a local dive strip club in Gardena. Finals had just finished at USC and I needed to burn off steam. So my best friend Rahiem and I went to the club for a few drinks and whatever else we could get from the girls. We'd been there many times in the past, and each of us had our favorite girls to watch. I usually split my meager $100 between Ebony and Honey. Both of those girls were just my type—young, tight little bodies. Rahiem liked them tall and thick.

But that night was different. She was a porn star and was the featured attraction of the night. I'd never heard of her before, but when I walked into the club and saw her, she took my breath away. Shelia wasn't the prettiest woman in the club. In fact, her looks were just average. She was about five-two, and had a gym club body complete with six-pack. Her breasts weren't overly large, but seemed to fit her tight body just right. To top it all off, she had some of the thickest nipples I had ever seen. I forgot about all of that when she turned toward me and smiled. There was something about her crooked smile. Maybe it was the shape of her lips, but I knew I had to say hello.

Except for her dance rotations, we spent the rest of the evening in a back booth talking. Actually she talked and I listened for the reasons behind the sadness just beneath the surface of her smile. We were both surprised when the announcer made the final call for drinks. Shelia hadn't made any money since I arrived at the club three hours ago. I got up and borrowed $200 from Rahiem to give to her. She refused and instead wrote her real name and telephone number on the back of one of the hundred-dollar bills and told me to call her. Instead, I convinced her to let me take her for coffee after the club closed.

We spent the rest of the night talking about her. She was thirty-four, and her mother was a sad casualty of the drug trade, leaving her to fend for herself and her two younger sisters since the age of sixteen. She did what she had to do to survive and take care of what was left of her family. The more I listened, the more I admired her sacrifice of her life to the sex trade so that her family would stay together and her sisters would have a chance at a regular life. One was now a lawyer, the other in her last year of medical school. Since that night we'd been inseparable.

"What are you doing over there, sleeping?" Shelia asked, nudging my shoulder with a laugh. "Wake up. We can't sit at this stop sign forever you know."

"Oh sorry," I replied weakly. "I was just thinking about something."

"Probably about how much you wish Thanksgiving was next month or that I was not going with you to meet your family for the first time, I bet." She teased. "Well, I've been thinking too," she said slipping a finger into her pussy and retrieving some of her precious nectar. "You should think about how much you like this instead," she said, rubbing her wet finger across my lips.

I sucked her fingers greedily until I couldn't taste her anymore. "I swear you've worked some voodoo on me. I don't know what you did, or how you did it, but I actually crave you," I said, knowing that she was right. As terrified as I was of her meeting my parents, I couldn't live without her.

Playing with her engagement ring, she replied, "Yeah, from the size of this diamond, I see that whatever I did worked. You want to know what it was?" she asked teasingly.

"I bet it was some of that ole freaky stuff you learned doing porn." I jokingly replied.

"Not even close."

"Hmm . . . I know, making me lick your pussy for a whole week. Yeah, that had to be it."

"Shut up," she chuckled. "Besides you volunteered—hell, begged—for that duty. But no, that's not it either. It's because I love you with all my heart, stupid."

Looking at her pussy had made me randy. "Prove it," I said, placing her hand on my stiffening shaft.

Pulling her legs down from the dash, she kneeled in her seat and fumbled with my zipper. "Oh, I'm willing to prove it, but can you handle it?" she asked, mocking me before retrieving my dick from my pants.

"I've been handling it so far, haven't I?" I asked rhetorically.

"You just drive, and remember if we get a ticket, you're going to be the one paying it . . ." She mumbled before running her tongue along the underside of my shaft.

"You know what that does to me . . ." I moaned. The flicking of her tongue on my skin was incredible. My cock throbbed with each lick.

"Yeah, nothing compared to this," she said, sticking the tip of her tongue into the tip of my penis.

My right hand drifted from the steering wheel to the back of Shelia's head just in time to ride the first bob as she pulled my stiff dick into her warm mouth and began to suck.

"Now, if you're a good boy, Mommy will give you some more later on," she said, kissing the head of my cock before settling back into her seat.

"Aren't you going to put him back?" I asked mischievously.

"No. I like him like that; a little soldier standing at attention for me."

In protest, I licked my finger, then slipped it between her legs and ran it up and down her already moist pussy. "Well, I shouldn't be the only one horny, now should I?" I asked as the tip of my finger traced the path toward her clit.

"No," she moaned as my finger finally reached her clit and began stroking it in small circles. Closing her eyes, she lowered her seat back into a reclining position and put her feet back on the dash to give me complete access to her hot pussy.

"Don't tease me" she panted.

In response I slipped my index and middle fingers into her wet body. A low moan escaped her lips as she pushed my fingers further into her. While I was thrusting my fingers into her wet pussy, my thumb stroked away at her clit. Her body shuddered on the verge of an orgasm. Refusing to cum, she pulled my hand away and squeezed her legs together.

"What's wrong?" I asked.

Eyes closed and still holding my hand, she replied in a husky voice, "Nothing, nothing at all." Opening her eyes and looking at me, she continued, "I just want to savor this feeling until I can actually be satisfied by that thick cock of yours." She smiled. It was the same smile that had originally stolen my heart.

"OK, hand me a napkin out of the glove compartment."

"For what?" she asked, starting to lick her juices from my fingers.

"Never mind," I said through a grin. "I forgot you were self-cleaning."

Laughing, she replied, "How could you ever forget that?"

Long after she'd finished licking my hand clean, she continued to hold it near her heart. Finally, she worked up the courage to speak. "I really do love you. I wouldn't be here and wouldn't have agreed to marry you if I didn't. I love you so much it scares me. A part of me still wonders if you will leave me because of my past. That scares me." She turned her head toward the window to hide the single tear that worked its way down her cheek. "I mean, what happens when your friends recognize me from my videos, or your future boss is one of my clients from my stay at that brothel in Las Vegas?" she whispered.

"Or heaven forbid, my parents turn out to be that freaky older couple who would come to you for threesomes," I joked, trying to lighten the mood.

She turned and hit me. "I'm serious," she said dejectedly. "A whore like me isn't worthy of someone like you," she cried between sobs. "You have your whole life ahead of you, and I don't want you to piss it away on me."

I pulled over and looked at her. Taking her face in my hands, I kissed her forehead. "Listen, I know its not going to be easy. Life isn't easy. I understand that. All I know is that when you're not around, my body longs for your touch, your smell. My heart aches for you. And I don't want to lose you, ever."

"Promise?" she asked.

"I already did," I said, raising her hand to my lips and kissing her engagement ring.

Wiping away her tears, she smiled, saying, "I'm being silly."

"Yes, you are."

"OK, OK, is there someplace I can get cleaned up? Maybe a mall near your parents' house so I can buy some underwear and fix my makeup? After all, I have to make a great first impression on my soon-to-be in-laws." It was nice to see her smiling again.

Smelling my hand, I replied sarcastically, "Yeah, I think I need to clean up a little too."

We eventually pulled over at the old strip mall just outside of town. It had a Target, Sears, Wal-Mart and a couple of other little stores. We headed for Target. As soon as we hit the door, I veered toward the electronics area.

Shelia pleaded, "Come on, don't leave me. Help me find something nice."

"If you insist," I said, trying to sound annoyed.

"Don't be such a spoilsport. You always leave me alone in the store and run off. Stay with me, please."

She knew I couldn't resist her pouting and laid it on extra thick. "OK, can we please just make it quick?" Defeated, I trudged along after her to the lingerie department.

Fortunately the store was fairly deserted due to the Thanksgiving holiday and we had free run of the lingerie department. I found a lacy black bra with high cut French panties. "Try these."

"I want to be conservative, not dead, honey. Can you find me a thong instead of that granny underwear?"

"Sure," I replied, thinking about how nice her tight ass looked in a thong, the nice curves of her ass cheeks separated by that little strip of thin black material. Just the thought made my dick stiffen. Self-consciously I pulled my shirt loose to try to hide the lump in my pants. Of course Shelia noticed.

"What's the matter, baby? Is your dick hard again?" she called teasingly from the next aisle.

A gray-haired lady in the next aisle snickered. "You better keep that thing in your pants, young man!" she said, further adding to my humiliation and embarrassment.

"Yes, ma'am," I replied. Pointing at Shelia, I continued, "But that cradle robber over there keeps taking it out and sucking on it."

The lady's face flushed as she spun on her heels and walked away, muttering, "Kids today, no respect."

I turned to try and catch the look on Shelia's face, but was too late. She had already gone into the fitting area. Chuckling, I walked over to the obligatory "husband/boyfriend" seat that all stores seemed to have. It's always placed far enough from the doorway to the dressing area that the ladies don't feel uncomfortable, but close enough for the men to be only a "come here" or "what do you think" away from the lady. True to form, a few minutes later Shelia called my name.

"You look great," I called without getting up from my seat.

"You haven't even seen it, and I wasn't going to ask you that anyway." Shelia retorted. "Will you just come here?"

Sighing, I stood up and moved toward the doorway.

"Come closer," Shelia's disembodied voice called.

Nervously I looked around then stepped into the doorway. "What do you want, Shelia?" I said, peering cautiously around the corner.

Shelia stood in the middle of the fitting room wearing only a sheer black nylon bra which showed every inch of her breasts. The panties were made of the same sheer material and showed Shelia's shaved pussy lips to the world. They looked marvelous. I licked my lips as my hunger for her sweet juices caused my dick to spring back to life.

"You like these?" she asked casually.

"Hell yeah." I heard my words come from some strange voice.

She walked over to me and grabbed my ears. Leaning in close, she whispered, "What I want is that thick cock of yours pounding away inside me." She pulled me toward her dressing booth. I willingly followed her lead, stiff dick and all.

By the time I pulled the door closed, she was reaching for my belt buckle. "Not this time," I said, brushing her hand away. Before she could realize what was happening, I reached behind her and unhooked her bra, releasing her breasts. Grabbing her by her hips, I moved her around to face me as I sat down on the dressing room bench, leaving me at the perfect height for sucking on her breasts. I began softly flicking my tongue across her hardening nipple. Once it was nice and erect, I began gently sucking on it. The quick inhalation of her breath told me she liked what I was doing as I continued to suck while swirling the tip of my tongue softly across the tip of her nipple.

"I've been wet ever since you fingered me in the car," she moaned.

In response, I began to squeeze and rotate her other nipple in my free hand. She moved closer, trying to rub herself against my body for relief. I loved the feel of her hard nipples in my mouth. The taste of her bare skin was intoxicating. I ran my tongue over, under, and across her nipple, making sure no spot was ignored. Then I switched to her right breast. Instead of the soft licking I gave her left nipple, I grasped her right one with my teeth. Not hard enough to hurt, but just hard enough for her to feel it. She grabbed my head and crushed my mouth on her nipple. "Damn, baby, you know I love that."

I bit down a little harder. Her reply was a long low moan of pure pleasure. Keeping her nipple trapped between my teeth, I began flicking away at the top of it with my tongue. Slipping my hands to her crotch, I was amazed at how wet she had become from my licking and biting her nipples. The sheer material of her panties was completely drenched with her juices. I traced my finger along the valley of her pussy lips, gathering her honey before licking my finger.

"I'm fucking addicted to you," I said, removing her panties and dropping them to the floor. Before they hit the ground, I was stroking her clit with my thumb and again sucking on her nipples. Grabbing a hand full of my hair, she pushed my mouth toward her waiting pussy.

"Lick my pussy, baby," she said, somewhere between a whimper and a demand. Instead of replying, I stood up, grabbed her, then turned around and sat her on the bench. Kneeling before her, I spread her thighs with my hands and then placed her legs on top of my shoulders, giving me easy access to her succulent feminity. I took a few seconds to admire the look of her exposed body. It reminded me of a closed flower that held the sweetest of all nectars inside its soft petals.

"Come on, baby, don't tease me," Shelia pleaded.

I smiled, thinking I could spend days worshipping at her fountain. Leaning in, I began to gently lap my tongue across her thick outer petals. I licked and sucked and nibbled at them until they were fully engorged from her passion. As though they had a mind of their own, they separated to reveal the source of her sweet waters.

Hooking her ankles together behind my neck, Shelia pulled herself lower on the seat. At the same time she grabbed the back of my head and forced my lips to the spout of her canal. My tongue darted inside, causing her to shudder. Without removing my tongue, I slid it the length of her petals, up to the bud of her clitoris. Letting my tongue wander, making lazy figure eights over and around her clit, I slipped a finger into her wet pussy.

"Oh, that feels so good," Shelia moaned. "Use two fingers, baby," she demanded in a lusty drawl.

My index finger slid right inside. I continued pumping and rotating my fingers inside her. Shelia started to fuck my fingers and pull my hair. Knowing that she was close to orgasm, I pulled my index finger out of her pussy and pressed it against the tight bud of her asshole. The wetness from her honey allowed it to slip into her ass. Fucking both holes with my fingers, I started sucking on her clit.

"Oh god yes!" she screamed as she came. I could feel the cold fluid of her orgasm on my face and hands. Feeling her response drove me wild. As her orgasm began to fade, I turned her around to face the wall.

"Come on, baby, fuck me from behind. Let me feel that hard cock of yours in my sweet pussy," she said, still horny.

Quickly undoing my pants, I let them drop to the floor with a soft thud. Shelia reached back and groped for my cock that grew even stiffer at her touch.

Lifting her leg to give me easier access to her pussy, she said, "You know this pussy is wet for you," as she placed the head of my cock at the entrance to her flower. I was too excited to respond and instead answered by pushing my cock into her hot pussy. All I wanted was to fuck Shelia, and I did, taking a few long, slow strokes to feel her pussy on the length of my hard shaft.

"Fuck this pussy like you mean it. This is your pussy, baby," she panted. Her talk just served to heighten my arousal, as I began pounding my hard cock into her small, sexy body. Wanting more leverage for my thrusts, I grabbed her waist and began pulling her into the increasingly frantic thrusts of my cock.

"Yeah, just like that," she said, with her voice full of wanton pleasure. Losing myself in my desire to have my cock deeper in her moist pussy, I pulled her head back by her long thick hair. The new arch of her back changed the feel of her pussy around my shaft, driving me to the edge of orgasm. As the need to climax built inside of me, I let go of her hair and grabbed her shoulder to increase the power of my thrusts. My animalistic desire for her spurred me on, until eventually

I exploded, spilling my seed inside her glorious body. Panting from the exertion, I leaned over and kissed her sweat-soaked back. "Thank you, baby. You know I love that pussy of yours."

"Yeah, I can tell," she replied, chuckling. Her laughter caused her vaginal muscles to squeeze out my deflating penis.

Realizing that I was standing ass naked in the ladies' dressing room of the local Target, where my parents shopped, I scurried to put my clothes back on. Shelia was amused by my sudden burst of modesty. "With all that noise grunting and groaning you were making, I'm sure we've been exposed," she teased. I heard footsteps moving away from the front of the dressing area. I blushed at the thought of some little old lady standing there listening to our passionate impromptu lovemaking session. Smirking, I picked up the pussy-soaked panties she planned to purchase and held them out for her. "I can't wait to see you pay for these."

"Just watch me," she replied, smiling, before slipping them on and ripping off the tag. She did the same with the matching bra. As she lowered her dress over her head, I leaned in and kissed her softly on the lips. I wanted to tell her how much I loved her, but the word "love" just seemed inadequate to describe my feelings. Instead, I just looked her in the eyes.

"You're not still concerned about me meeting your parents, are you?"

"Let's see . . . um . . . yeah, considering we both smell like that delicious pussy of yours." I laughed. "They were right, you will corrupt me yet."

"Yeah, but did you tell them that you like my corrupting you?" she replied, patting my crotch. "Come on, it's already three-thirty P.M. We were supposed to be at your parents for dinner an hour ago. I'm sure they will blame me for our being late."

We left the dressing room and walked toward the cashier. She was a thirtyish white female who appeared very conservative, and a little nervous.

"Hi. I'd like to get these," Shelia said handing the price tags to the cashier. "I tried them on, and since my fiancé liked them so much I decided to wear them home. Will that be a problem or do you need actually to see them?" Shelia asked, amusement in her voice as she started to pull up the hem of her dress.

"N-no, I'm sure that will be all right, considering . . ." The cashier stammered as she realized she had just given away the fact that she'd been spying on us in the dressing room. She quickly looked away and fumbled around trying to ring up Shelia's purchase. Knowing she knew about our fuck session caused me to pay her a little more attention. Her name tag read "Francine." She was a cute, if rather plain, redhead, with an average body. She wasn't wearing a bra and her erect nipples were clearly visible. Shelia noticed she was sexually excited too.

After thanking the cashier for her change, Shelia asked where the rest rooms were located. As we turned to leave, Shelia looked over her shoulder said: "I hope you enjoyed the show." I was too embarrassed to turn around to look at the poor woman.

To my surprise, the lady replied under her breath, "Very much."

We both entered the rest rooms and did our best to make ourselves presentable. On the way out, I grabbed a bottle of mouthwash and paid for it at the row of checkout stands near the front of the store. As we neared the exit, two burly men, obviously undercover store security—even though there was nothing undercover about them—came out of a side door. I tensed up thinking they were coming to harass me because I was young and black. Instead, both men smiled and applauded as we walked out the store.

I was aghast. They had seen us. Shelia, however, was unfazed. "That one was a freebie, boys. Just don't let us find that tape on the internet. Remember what happened to those fellows who got the Pam and Tommy Lee tapes," she teased, waving her finger in their direction. I was too embarrassed to say anything.

"Well, honey, it's official, you are now a porn star too!" Shelia teased while rubbing my ass. "I wonder what your parents will think about that."

"Oh god, if my parents ever find out, I'm dead. You too; we'll both be dead," I said, somewhat amused at my new porn star status.

Chuckling as she got into the car, Shelia replied, "Not me. They are already set to kill me today."

We drove the short distance to my parents' house in silence except for an occasional grunt and "um hum" reply. As we pulled up, I noticed a red Mercedes-Benz coupe in the driveway. My heart sank. The car belonged to my high school sweetheart Tamika. My parents had always wanted us to marry. It would be just like my mother to invite her to Thanksgiving dinner. Damn.

Pulling over to the curb, I grabbed Shelia's arm before she could exit the car. "Listen, there's something I have to tell you."

"Are you ashamed of me?" she asked before I could continue.

"*No!*" I shouted. "Sorry. It's not that at all. I love you. I really do. It's just that my parents are the most conservative people I know. Hell, I think they only had sex three times, and that was to have me, my brother, and my sister. When I told them about you—what you do—they hit the roof." I pointed to Tamika's car. "See that car? That car belongs to the girl that my mother has always wanted me to marry. My father and her father play golf together once or twice a month. She's a lawyer now, and I suspect my mother invited her over just to embarrass you."

"Don't worry, I don't embarrass easily. And don't sell me short either. I'm here because I love you. I can handle your parents no matter how conservative they are, and no matter how much they dislike my being ten years older than you or the fact that I'm in the sex trade. That's their problem not ours."

"We can leave if you want to," I said. Deep down inside I wanted her to to say yes so I could escape. She didn't.

"It's Thanksgiving and I've got to meet your parents . . . our parents . . . sometime, don't I? I'm sure that everything will be fine. Just tell me that you aren't ashamed of me."

"I'm not. All that matters to me is that we are together."

"Great. Then let's go meet your folks."

The butterflies were fluttering in my stomach as we headed up the walkway to my parents' house. Shelia rang the bell, then leaned over to me and whispered, "I'll make you proud, you'll see. Don't worry. I love you, baby." Just then my mother opened the door. Screaming, she grabbed me and gave me a big hug. As she let go, I turned and introduced Shelia, while trying not to breathe in my mother's direction.

"Hi, Mom, this is Shelia Watkins."

"Pleased to meet you, Shelia," Mother said coldly but politely. "A good friend of mine was named Thelma Watkins. Poor thing passed away young from cancer. She had three small kids. One of them was named Shelia too, if I remember correctly. I've always wondered whatever happened to them poor kids," my mother said to no one in particular.

Stifling a sob and raising her hand to her mouth in surprise, Shelia replied, "That was my mother!"

"You poor thing!" my mother exclaimed, giving Shelia a hug. Pulling back to look at Shelia, she continued, "Let me look at you." Smiling, she continued, "I can see her in your face, you do favor her so. And your sisters, how are they?"

Smiling like a proud parent, Shelia responded, "I took real good care of them. One is a doctor and the other a lawyer."

My mother looked at me curiously and then stared at Shelia for what seemed like forever. From that look, I knew my mother's assessment of Shelia had changed. My mother finally understood the why of what Shelia did for a living.

"Come let me introduce you to everyone," my mother said, stepping between Shelia and me and taking us by the arms. "You are among family here," she declared. As I thought about the hidden truth in Mother's words, I smiled at the thought of my new family.

# More Than Meets the Eyes

**Michael T. Owens**

The sweltering Atlanta sun shines bright this Thursday morning. Despite the ridiculous heat, twenty-six-year-old George Pratt isn't bothered at all. In fact, he loves the sun because when it shines, lawns grow. When lawns grow, people want them cut, and that's how he makes money. Moving his muscular body with ease, he loads the mower, weed wacker, and the rest of his lawn equipment on to the trailer. He crosses his fingers, hoping his old pickup truck will crank on the first try. He doesn't need anything slowing him down—especially not today. His newest customer, Medea Wentworth, is scheduled for twelve o'clock sharp. To her, that means eleven-fifty-eight. If she weren't his biggest customer, he would've stopped working for her after the first week.

"C'mon now, baby, start for me," he says, placing the key in the ignition. The engine stutters before rattling under the hood. He drives off with a grin on his face.

Thick blades of St. Augustine grass, manicured shrubbery, and an assortment of colorful plants set Medea's enormous yard apart from the rest on the street. After George finishes, he walks up the stone path to the front door of her home and knocks. She answers wearing a blue bathrobe. Her mid-shoulder-length hair and light cocoa skin are still moist from the shower.

"Good afternoon," George says, taking off his Atlanta Braves cap. His low haircut is as fresh as the lawn he just finished cutting. "How you doing today, Media?"

"Will you please learn to pronounce my name correctly? It's not Media—it's *Medea*, as in the Greek play written by Euripides . . ."

Looking Medea up and down, George scratches his chin and says, "Yeah, the Greek play . . . Yeripdees, right . . ."

"Why must you stare at me so?" Medea huffs. "Have you never seen a blind person before?"

George's eyes widen. "I-I wasn't staring . . ."

"Nonsense. Yes, you were. I felt it."

"Okay, I—"

"Here's your money. Good day." Every other week it's the same thing. Medea gets upset at the drop of a dime and usually ends up closing the door in George's face. It's getting old.

"You got some serious attitude problems," George mutters as the door is closing, "I'm tired of trying to be nice to you."

Medea swings the door back open. "Excuse me?"

"You heard me. You better check that attitude or you gonna be alone the rest of your life . . ." There. After weeks of holding his tongue, George finally let it out.

"What makes you think I want a man, let alone need one? I have a nice home, a good job, an MBA from Wharton's School of Business, and I've lived alone since I was nineteen. I don't *need* a man to take care of me. I am not a cave woman and this certainly isn't the Mesozoic era!"

"The what?"

"Forget it. This discussion is absolute rubbish. I haven't the time or the desire to finish it!" Medea slams the door. George runs a hand across his sweaty face and walks toward his pickup truck. He stops to look at the check. *Might be my last one*, he thinks to himself, placing it in his grass-stained jeans.

George spends the next day driving around looking for new customers. He's not wearing the usual jeans and T-shirt; he's wearing a nice pair of pants, a knit top, and his face is smooth from a fresh shave—he's ready to talk business. Hopefully he can find a good customer or two, because later on he plans on telling Medea to look for a new lawn service. Getting a hefty biweekly check from her is a nice chunk of change to let go, but he refuses to deal with her attitude strictly for the sake of money. Besides, after what happened yesterday afternoon, she'll probably fire him anyway. Figuring out what to do about Medea has been on his mind a lot lately, maybe too much, because he dreamt about her last night. He had a similar dream last week but blew it off. It wasn't that big of a deal. Ever since his girl left him, he's had plenty of dreams about other women. He remembers having a few dreams while he and his girl were still together, but they weren't this intense. Some of these seemed too real. Every single morning without fail, he wakes up with an erection. A couple of times he's slid his hand down his pants to see if he ejaculated in his sleep. His dreams about Medea are sketchy but he does remember this: She's naked. He's naked. And the only thing she ever says is, "May I touch your face?" He never experiences what happens after she does touch his face. He doesn't even know if she touches it at all—he always wakes up prematurely. One thing is for sure: if she were as nice in person as she is in his dreams, he'd be driving to her house to make love, not to drop her as a customer.

He could've done this over the phone, but he prefers doing business face to face, always has. Earlier, he called and asked if he could stop by. She said she would be home at five-thirty. Around six o'clock, George pulls his truck alongside Medea's mailbox. Twice he's run the conversation in his head. As he makes his way to her door, he looks over the yard, admiring his work. He takes a deep breath, knocks, and prepares himself for whatever comments Medea will make. The door opens. When he sees her, he momentarily forgets everything. Her hair is pulled back into a ponytail, making her eyes stand out. He tries ignoring her low-cut blouse and the exotic smelling fragrance she's wearing, but it's hard to focus. Being able to examine every inch, curve, and groove of her body without her knowing turns him on. It's almost like being a Peeping Tom or some kind of voyeur. The only difference is he won't go to jail if he's caught. Finally, he remembers why he came. Without any greetings or salutations, he robotically recites, "I'm sorry, Medea, but I can't do your lawn anym—"

"Would you like something to drink?"

George's lips freeze. "I . . . uh, yeah, sure."

"Come in," she says. George slowly walks into the house, still trying to figure out what's happened to Medea. He thought he was ready for anything she could throw at him, but this caught him by surprise. She seems like a completely different person. "Is lemonade okay?"

" . . . Huh?"

"I said is lemonade—"

"Yeah, yeah, that's fine. Lemonade is fine."

"Have a seat in the dining room, I'll bring it to you."

George cautiously looks around. The opera music playing in the background matches the personality of the house. Fancy decorations are everywhere, expensive ones—things that should be on a home decorating show. *Why would a blind person bother with decorations? That's kinda weird,* George thinks to himself. *Well, she may be blind but she still a woman. Women like that kinda stuff.*

Medea returns. "Here you are."

"Thanks." George takes a sip, "All the times I cut your grass, you never asked me inside for a drink."

"I'm sorry. I just have this thing about people being in my house."

George nods.

"I haven't had any visitors since my last boyfriend."

"How long were y'all together?"

"Two months. For some reason, none of my relationships last longer than three months. And somehow, those three months never include Valentine's Day, my birthday, or Christmas!"

George takes another sip of lemonade. "Why is that?"

"I'm not certain," Medea shrugs, "but each one hurt me. I thought I was over it, but I guess I've yet to fully recover. You were right about what you said yesterday."

Medea's Yorkshire terrier barks.

"Hero, quiet!" she commands.

"I see your dawg is kinda protective, huh?"

"Indeed. That's why I named him Hero—he's my hero."

". . . Can I ask you a question?"

"Let me guess. You want to know what it's like to be blind."

"No." George shifts his weight. "Don't take this the wrong way, but is your . . . condition the reason you mad at the world?"

Medea takes a moment to think before speaking. "I don't have a problem with the *world*. I have problems with the *people* living in it! I'm just tired of them taking pity on me. I never asked to be treated any different from anyone."

"So you just automatically think everybody feel sorry for you?"

"What else could it be? I hear them whispering, I feel them pointing, and staring at me in the same manner you do."

George shakes his head and sighs. "Medea, let me tell you something, I don't stare at you 'cause you blind. I stare at you 'cause . . . I stare at you 'cause I think you're beautiful. I can't help it . . ."

Medea's eyebrows quickly rise as she adjusts her ponytail to soothe her uneasiness. No man besides her father has ever complimented her on her beauty. Unsure about how to reply, she clears her throat. ". . . You pronounced my name correctly," she says, smiling.

"Oh my goodness, look at that! That's the first time I seen you smile."

"Very funny, George."

"Do it again."

Medea turns away to hide an even bigger smile than the first.

George smiles too. "There it is, I see it, I seeee iiiiiittt!"

A soft giggle leaves Medea's lips. "George?"

"Yeah?"

". . . May I touch your face?" George's smile disappears as each word shoots through his ears to his brain. *May I touch your face?* They echo.

He swallows hard even though his mouth is suddenly dry, nothing to swallow. ". . . Y-You wanna touch my face?"

"Well, yes. I have a picture of you in my mind but I would like to—Oh, never mind, it must sound quite silly to you." Medea slouches, dropping her outstretched arms back into her lap.

"No, no, not at all. You can touch my face." Trying to control his breathing, he leans in her direction. She slides closer; her small hands are open and waiting. George exhales a short stream of warmth when she grasps his cheeks. Her hands feel like they belong on his face. They feel like they belong on his body.

As she explores with her fingers, he studies her. At times, it seems like she's looking directly into his eyes; other times she looks slightly past him. Her thin eyebrows twitch every time she touches a new part of his face. His eyes follow a path from her earlobes, down to her smooth slender neck rising from the opening of her blouse. He thinks about all of the enticing treasures waiting underneath it. It takes all of his strength to withstand the urge to touch her. So, he sits still.

"You're so quiet. Am I annoying you?" Medea asks.

"Huh? Oh, no . . ." George closes his eyes as his dreams carousel in his mind. Over his nose, up the side of his face, and across his forehead, Medea's soft fingers continue tracing his features. His gluteus muscles tighten, his manhood stiffens while she strokes his lips, as if daring him to take her fingers into his mouth, lick them, and taste them. His short and quick breaths warm her hands. She slips an index finger between his lips, slowly parting them. George's tongue curls around her finger, pulling it deep into his mouth, taking the middle finger . . . ring finger . . . pinky . . . and thumb, sucking them from knuckle to fingertip.

Hero barks.

George leans toward Medea's lips. He knows she can't see him, but she can feel him coming closer. She waits until his lips meet hers. Their kiss is controlled and precise, full of nervousness.

"Do that again," Medea says, mimicking George's voice.

George smiles and then presses his lips firmly against hers. This time they kiss sloppy and wet. Both of their chairs fall over when they jump to their feet. They continue kissing each other, feeling each other. Reaching under Medea's skirt, George slides a hand slowly from her knee, up between her thighs, and toward her wet center. Up. Up. The closer he gets, the harder Medea breathes. Up. Up. Stop. He purposefully stops just before reaching her gem. Unable to withstand his teasing, she licks the side of his face, her heavy breaths sounding impatient in his ears. She slips out of her blouse; her well-rounded breasts push against her black lace bra. ". . . I want to feel you, I can't wait any longer," she says, tugging at George's pants. "Hurry . . ."

George fumbles at his belt buckle. Soon, the only thing he's wearing are boxer shorts.

The soprano opera singer hits several high notes.

Hero barks again.

George grabs Medea from behind. Lifts her skirt until her plump, round bottom is exposed. He picks up his pants, takes the wallet from the back pocket, and whips out a condom he bought months ago but never used. Like a king cobra being charmed out of a basket, George's manhood pops out of the slit in the front of his boxers, poking against Medea. "Ooooh," she moans, stroking George until his length grows stronger, harder, and so stiff that it burns. The steady tingle radiates from his pelvis to the hot area between his thighs.

"Hurry," Medea says again. This time the "H" sound is deep and airy, full of passionate anticipation. She bends over the dining room table, skirt flipped up over her back. George pulls her saturated panties to the side instead of taking them off. Medea releases a quivering moan as George's thick fingers slide to the center of her thighs. Just the mere thought of his hand massaging her jewel sends a frenzy of lustful sensations throughout her being. It's been a long time since she's been touched, a long time since she's felt the heat of a man. In the last couple of years, the most important things to her were: Work. Food. Sleep. Work. Work. Work. Sleep. If someone had told her she would be stretched across the dining room table getting loved by the yardman, she would've laughed.

"Mmmmmm," George hums, gripping Medea's waist, surfing in her warm ocean, dipping in and out.

". . . Deeper . . ."

George satisfies Medea's request, causing the dining room table to move three inches. The glass of lemonade spills on the floor. Oblivious to the mess, George and Medea move closer to the table in one unified motion.

"Uh huh," she moans, "harder . . ." George moves faster, harder, concentrating on each stroke.

"Like this . . . ?"

"Y-Y-Yes . . . Yes . . . I love the way you feel . . ." Medea braces herself with a hand planted firmly on the table. With the other hand, she unsnaps the front of her bra and begins caressing her breasts. George pulls her hair until the blue scrunchie keeping her ponytail in place falls to the floor.

"Yeah," he grunts with each powerful thrust, causing the dining room table to slide another few inches. Medea begins to tremble from the bursts of pleasure exploding through her body.

The soprano opera singer's voice rises.

Medea's head shakes back and forth, up and down. George grabs her shoulders and pushes deeper inside. She gasps, lifts her head high, and screams at the exact climax of the soprano's solo. With her head bowed between her arms, Medea still trembles, even though George has backed away. As she catches her breath, she places her sweaty hair behind her ears, keeping it from sticking to her face. She turns to George, smiles, but says nothing. He pulls her up by the midsection. Kissing and sucking her breasts, he carefully guides her to the living room, head still buried between the open bra flaps. To his surprise, Medea spins around, takes charge, and guides *him* to the living room. As they walk backwards, she uses her tongue to make wet figure eights up and down his chest. They both share a quick laugh after accidentally bumping into a large antique sofa against the wall. Ice-cold air flows from the vents in the living room, but it will take more than that to cool George and Medea.

"Sit down," she says, reaching out for George's face. He moves her hands to the crown of his head. Using it as a starting point, she slides both hands down his cheeks, to the center of his chest, down between his legs. With a wide grin, she gets on her knees, and rolls George's condom off, throwing it over her shoulder. She squeezes his love rod. It's still solid. It's still hard. With a hand wrapped around its neck, she eases it toward her mouth and pauses, letting her hot breath beat against it. George squirms on the sofa cushions but his eyes stay locked on Medea. She slips out of the bra, allowing it to slide down her arms, into her hands. "Put this over your eyes." Without any questions, George wraps the bra around his head. He ties a makeshift knot in the back to keep it in place while the two C-cups cover his eyes. "Now we're both blind . . ." Medea's voice trails off as she immediately takes George into her mouth. His fists tighten from the sudden wet warmth of Medea's churning lips. She grabs his lower back while flickering her tongue around his thickness. Taking another mouthful, she squeezes her cheeks until the suction makes him beat the sofa cushions with his hand.

". . . Oh gawd . . . ohh . . ." He's imagined her pretty face between his legs, but now he wants to actually see it. He lifts the bra from over his eyes for a sneak peek.

"Are you peeking? No, peeking, Georgey!"

Quickly covering his eyes again, he moans, slamming his head against the back of the sofa. The hungry popping, slurping sounds Medea makes intensifies the moment. George puts a hand on top of her head, takes a deep breath, then another, and another before exhaling. His toes cramp and curl. His legs shake uncontrollably. He feels it. His liquid love boils in his pelvis. It's coming. Medea feels a jerking throb between her cheeks. Massaging George's inner thighs, she keeps coaxing him with her tongue until his love releases.

❖   ❖   ❖

The next morning, George awakes nude and limp, lying in the center of Medea's bed. Aroma of scrambled eggs, bacon, and pancakes floating in the air makes him smile. He shakes his head, amazed at how a blind woman can do everything a sighted woman can do—and maybe even better! He relaxes and begins thinking about last night. Medea is definitely an amazing woman. His thoughts are interrupted when Hero trots into the bedroom. George leans over the side of the bed. "What's up, Hero?"

Hero tilts his head and growls.

"Easy, boy." George yawns, reaching to pet the dog on the head, but Hero launches at George's hand, only missing it by inches. *"Whoa!"*

"*Erfffff. Erff. . . . Grrrrrrrr,*" Hero barks.

"Stay!" George points. "*Stay,* Hero! *Medea, come get this dawg!*"

With a knife in hand, Medea runs into the bedroom, screaming. She stops in the doorway. "Who are you? How did you get in my house? *Get outta my house!*"

"Huh?"

"You better get up outta my house. I ain't scared to use it." She waves the knife in the air.

"It's me. George. Why you talking like that?"

"Errrrrrffff. *Erfff!*"

Medea picks up the phone. "I'm calling the cops. I dunno nobody named no George. You got five seconds to get outta my house . . ."

"What's up with you, Medea?"

"Um, who is Medea? *One . . .*"

"You!" George pleads, "*You!* Remember, Medea from the Greek play, you said—"

"My name ain't no Medea. *Two . . .*"

"Grrrr. *Erfff,* erffff!"

George looks around the room for his clothes. He grabs his pants and shirt sitting at the edge of the bed. "Where my boxers?"

"How should I know?"

" 'Cause we spent the night together, that's how!"

"You think I would spend the night with a fat slob like you? You got me bent—*Three . . .*"

"Look, just help me find my boxers and I'm out of here, all right?"

"Ain't them yo stinky green boxers over there?"

George scratches his head. ". . . H-How do you know they green?"

"*Errf!*"

"I'm looking right at 'em, dummy. *Four!*" she says, pointing the knife at George with one hand, dialing 911 with the other.

". . . But . . . you're blind . . ."

"*Errrrf!* Errrrrfffff!"

"Blind? I see fine. Like them ugly brown pants and faded black shirt you got."

A light-headed feeling seizes George's mind. He looks at the walls, the floor, and the ceiling. *Is the room spinning?* he wonders. So many thoughts enter his head that they clutter his speech. "H-H-How did you know that—?"

Medea pushes the phone to her ear. ". . . Um, yes, hello, there's a naked man in my—"

George uses this opportunity to catch Medea off guard. "Give me that!" He grabs her, taking the knife from her hand.

"Errrrrrrfffff! Erf!"

"I'ma kill you." She swings the phone at George, striking him on the neck, "*I'ma kiiiiil yyyou—!*" He catches her hand before she can swing at his head. She kicks his shin.

"Grrrrr. *Grr.*" Hero bites George's ankle.

"Get off me, mutt!" Medea kicks George again. "*Unghhh!*" He pushes her backwards with all of his strength. She loses balance, trips over the phone cord, and hits her head on the wall. George rubs his sore neck and then quickly finishes getting dressed, as Medea lies unconscious. After gathering his things, he walks to the bedroom door and almost swallows his tongue when he hears, ". . . George? Georgey. Please help me. I seem to have fallen." George clutches the knife tight in his hand and turns around. He sighs in relief when he sees Medea still on the floor in the corner. With her arms out, wildly feeling around in the air, she says, "George, I'm in need of assistance. Are you there? George?" George shakes his head and limps out of the room, out of the house.

# Postscript

**Mitchell Jackson**

She sat alone in a furnished room in the Montgomery Hotel, a cheap accommodation in the city's bustling Midtown area. Nobody knew she was here, for she left her house hurriedly, with a few dresses, some undergarments, three blouses, and an extra pair of shoes. It hurt her to leave but she felt she had no other choice. Marriage had become a noose around her neck, suffocating her, changing her in so many ways, too many ways. For a moment, she looked around the room, at its faded wallpaper, the Gideon Bible on the nightstand, the cracked lamp, the dingy curtains, and the rumpled bed. When she finally calmed herself, she placed a small tablet of white paper on the scarred desk and took out a pen. Words had never been her strong suit. She was better at talking, verbal communication, but this was something that had to be done. If she called him, she might listen to his sweet talk, his seductive words, feel her resolve melt, and go back to him. This was the best way, with a letter, she thought as she began writing slowly with a trembling hand.

*Andrew,*

> *You said if I love you, I would do it. And you were right.*
>
> *You said those words to me, those punishing words, without flinching, not a hint of apology in your eyes. And you knew what they would do. You knew with a little coaxing I would do anything in the world for you—anything. For almost a decade I've given you all that I had. Eight burdensome years I've endured the "Don't worry" and "When I's." "Don't worry, baby, when I finish school, everything will get better." But it took six*

*years for you to finish the four-year degree that you put to no use after you graduated. Don't worry, baby, when I get this job, everything will get better. But you got the job and it never did. Instead, I spent countless nights awake through the morning praying for your safe return. Often you stayed out all night. Don't worry, baby, I won't let it happen again; she didn't mean anything to me. Not she, but they: Lisa, Denise, Collette. I lost track of the names, of the times I sat in the passenger side of your car forced to smell another woman's perfume on your seat belt. Do you remember the early mornings you crept into our bed, with musty underarms and crotch smelling Ivory soap fresh?*

*You think I never knew what was happening? I was under no illusions. I stayed because I love you, not because of the ill-thought concoctions you tried to pawn to me as truth. And not once was I ever unfaithful. No matter what you did, the thought of letting another man touch me was unfathomable, not once entering my mind.*

*And for what? I should have left a long time ago, while I still had a modicum of pride, some semblance of self-respect. Only a fool remains with a man who fathers an out-of-wedlock child. Even though I love Tyler, I was still a fool for staying. So three years later, you could say:*

*If you love me, you'll do it.*

*You have no idea what it felt like to walk into that house and watch you drop our keys in that basket. Carelessly, giving it no more thought than you would dropping a gum wrapper in the trash. You either didn't notice or ignored the way I flinched at the tiny clang they made against the other random sets. How could you notice when you were preoccupied, moving through the room sipping Hennessey, leering at would-be partners like your stare alone could strip them naked. How inconsequential I felt, trailing behind you, head tilted, your invisible indentured wife. You either weren't aware or didn't care the way those men gawked at me—your wife—like I was some stripper, no better than a Vegas ho. The way they shook your hand and stuck their tongues between their fingers at me when you looked away, with a blind eye that would have* gotten you killed on duty. They groped my breast and ass; their breath—full of liquor—turned my stomach, as did their vulgar comments: I'll suck your pussy dry. I'd like to bang you. You sure would be a nice prize. *You didn't hear them, right? You were much too busy with your own groping, catching the ears and glances of women you'd rather lay down with instead of me. But who wants the same old saltines when there's Ritz available?*

*You made no secret about whom you hoped for. And really, who could blame you? She was beautiful. Her taut bronze skin showed no sign of the loose flab that hangs like a rooster's chin from my back arms. No weave or horse mane as you call it; her luxurious jet-black hair fell mid-back. And of course she was tall, like you've always wanted, with the perky breasts of a high school cheerleader. I'm not ashamed to admit I envied her slender frame, a figure similar to the one I'd maintained in my twenties, back when you pretended loving me was still a priority.*

*When you damn near ran out the house with her, I prayed for a change of heart, that your conscience wouldn't allow such a flagrant slap in my face. You'd at least tried to keep it away all these years. Why now involve me? I tried not to imagine what you would do with her. Hoped at the very least you would get a hotel, wouldn't take her to our home, our room, to our bed.*

*If you love me, you'll do it. Those were your words. I believed them.*

*Still, I questioned my sanity, but went along under the assumption that keeping you happy was most important.*

*If you want, you can stop here and save yourself some pain. But no, you'll continue, won't you? You want details. Well, you can have them. But keep in mind, please keep in mind the anguish you sipped for one evening is the grief forced down my throat for years.*

*We left in his Mercedes; with windows tinted limo black, no one saw me slumped in the seat, sitting paralyzed. I hid my trembling hands in my lap; he kept one hand on the wheel, the other on my thigh. His fingers were cold and disgusting, his* knuckles covered with patches of dark hair. He didn't say a word, probed up my skirt, making me squeamish. When he pulled the car up, the sheer size of his home took my breath; it was gated, with a cobblestone driveway that led to a lighted fountain. Inside, we walked through foyers with vaulted ceilings to a dimly lit room where I sat on a beige leather sofa. He fixed drinks—for him Scotch, for me apple martinis. I nervously gulped my first and second. He smiled, kept me refilled, my glass always to the brim.

Tell me about yourself, he asked. Did I read? Yes. Who? Morrison. What kind of music did I like? Soul. Favorite singer? Donnie Hathaway. Did we travel? No. Why not? You traveled alone or with friends. What places did I want to visit? St. Bart, Rio, Cancun. What about my goals, what did I dream about? The inquiry stumped me; you hadn't asked those things in years. Why? Because you thought you knew the answers, or worse, no longer cared to hear them.

Three martinis in an hour eased my tension. I felt warm all over. My head spun; I talked incessantly. He listened, like you'd listened years ago, before I lost our baby. He complimented me. Said I was beautiful, sublime. Said my eyes sang and he loved the lyrics. Soon, his questions grew more intimate. Where did I like to be touched? All over. How did I like to make love? I paused.

He walked to the stereo, started playing a CD of Hathaway, A Song for You. I thought of the first time we made love, in your dorm room, on that tiny twin bunk. I remembered how you covered my mouth to keep me from waking your roommate with my squeals of delight.

He asked to massage my feet, took my silence for agreement, and eased off my heels. The haze of liquor, by then, had warmed his touch. His huge hands felt light, sensuous, and comforting like velvet. I closed my eyes; he swept his tongue between my toes, sucked each one like they were dipped in honey, caressed my calves. If I told you by then I wasn't enjoying it, I would be lying. And please always remember that I've never lied to you. Not once. Ever. He reached under my skirt to *pull down my panties. I fought against him, breathed a sigh of relief when the phone rang, but he ignored the first call, the second, the third, even a fourth.*

*I kept giving myself reasons to fight, but finally gave in, raised my hips off the couch, wriggled my panties down to my ankles. I gulped the last of a fourth martini to dampen my coherence, wanting to ascribe at least partial blame to the alcohol.*

*He put his head under my skirt and licked between my thighs. I still struggled to keep my pleasure quiet, but honestly, when his tongue touched my clit, I couldn't stifle my moans. When the tiny sensations shot up through my body, I silently mourned the pleasures you'd deprived me of for years.*

*What did you have against cunnilingus? Was I not worth it? Was it some twisted sense of masculinity, or more of your selfishness? And still at the drop of a dime, you expected head. He licked, sucked, blew, swirled. It seemed against my volition the way I parted my legs, reached a hand under my blouse to play with my nipples.*

*He led me to the bedroom, which more precisely resembled a hotel's master suite; it was furnished with a sky blue leather couch, a canopy bed, a cherry wood armoire. In the bathroom, he ran water from gold fixtures in a marble jetted tub, slipped off my skirt and blouse. He lit jasmine-scented candles, bathed me in naturally dim light, sponged the breadth of my back, along my neck, and down between my thighs. He toweled me dry, led me to the bed, massaged me with strawberry scented oils as I lay on my stomach.*

*Sex? Yes, we had it—but of that I'll spare you the particulars.*

*You frightened me when you showed up. The way you screamed. The way you drove like a maniac afterward, like you could care less whether we lived or died. Your eyes bloodshot red. Like you'd smoked a joint. Or cried. What I can't understand is how you could act that way when it was something you wanted, that you alone initiated. To share me, share my body with a stranger, all to satisfy some perverse thrill of yours. When you first asked what happened between us, the explanation got lodged in my throat, because I realized then you were hurt. I knew what you wanted to hear—how he kissed me, how he touched me, how his body made me feel. But I could not do that to you. And better to harbor a painful personal truth than inflict it unnecessarily on the one you love. When you asked the second time what I'd done, there was a real ache in your voice, hurt I hadn't heard since you read your mother's eulogy, but by the time we got home, there was only anger. You shouted like you'd break your promise and hit me again.*

*Later, alone in the house, it dawned on me that you cared more about how you felt about what I'd done than about how I felt being pressured to do it. Selfish. You'll never change. You care about nothing but yourself and your own twisted urges.*

*There are many things I want to apologize for. I want to apologize for never giving you the child you wanted. For not being enough woman to satisfy you completely. But most of all, for letting your happiness take precedence over mine. What I won't do is apologize for what happened. I don't regret it. For a few hours last night, a complete stranger made me feel whole again. Alive. A woman. But sadly what he brought to light is our truth: what we had is dead. And because of that so am I. You said if I love you, I would do it. And you were right. I do love you.*

*More than I love myself.*

After an hour-long argument, we finally get to the party. Sheila's wearing her discomfort like rookies wear their badges—boldly, arms folded against her chest, sneering, not saying a word to anyone. After almost a decade together, her flaws stand out like white men did at the Million Man March. Gravity has been playing a cruel joke on her breasts the last three years; ten unneeded pounds wrap her belly like a Michelin tire, and no matter how many *Buns of Steel* tapes she buys, her ass is still flat as a compact disc. But tonight, despite her mood, all I can think about is how good she looks, how her yellow dress picks up the green in her eyes, how her skin glistens, how sensuous her neck looks with her hair pinned up.

Inside, I drop our keys in the basket and head straight for the drinks and buffet snacks stationed on a table so cluttered, it reminds me of Big Mama's on Sundays.

Sticking out like guilty perps in a fixed lineup is a basket full of condoms. There aren't any Magnums, so I grab two ribbed Trojans and nonchalantly throw them in my pocket.

We're here, now loosen up, I chide Sheila, then pour myself a Hennessey. Straight. No ice. No chaser. Sheila doesn't say a word, glares at me like a stern-faced judge. I pour her a glass of white zinfandel, offer it to her like a Catholic peace offering.

Rick, my buddy since the academy, organized the party. Says swapping saved his marriage. In the locker room at the precinct, he brags new pussy has a way of invigorating a man's life, of putting more zest in the old marital bed.

Gather round, everybody. We're about to pick, Rick says, smiling, arms locked with his oval-faced wife, who is simpering at me. There is something in her ass-wiggling that says she would give me a tumble if I asked. But there are new faces and bodies here tonight, all ready for hot action. I rush to the circle; Sheila stays put like a burglar who has tripped a motion sensor during a break-in.

I got my eyes on a piece of the Spanish-looking mami', a señorita with curves that sizzle, across the circle, had them on her since the jump. What I could do to that? Chula's holding hands with a middle-aged disproportioned white guy whose tiny hands and feet don't fit his gangly arms and legs. I'm praying for the switch with them; if new pussy invigorates, new exotic pussy will surely help me get my swagger back. I must have some good karma stored up somewhere because when the keys are picked—I get my wish.

Why don't the new couples take a minute to get to know each other, Rick says, his voice slurred, cupping a glass of Courvoisier. He's leaning on coherence like a weak crutch. Everyone can see he's excited by the tent in his pants.

Andrew, I say, extending my hand first to the husband, then to his trophy wife. I'm already picturing her naked.

Their names are Michael and Maria: she has a thick Spanish accent.

I want to hear her scream "Papi" during sex. I want to feel her mouth on me.

Well, Mike, my wife's over there on the couch. I talk like we're old tennis buddies trading doubles partners. The one with her lips all poked out. I point to Sheila, sitting alone, nursing her wine. Michael's face lights up like a convict getting an early release from an over-crowded jail. I watch him approach her, then lead Maria to a vacant corner. It takes an inordinate amount of control to keep my eyes from staring at the imprint of Maria's hardened nipples through her sleeveless black dress.

Fuck it, I think to myself, then say: I don't mean to stare at your breasts, but they are beautiful. I mean you are *muy bonita*, I say, try-ing to take the edge off my objectification. I must be the luckiest man in the room tonight.

*Gracías.* This is very nice of you, she says.

*¿De donde ere?* I say, thankful for my limited Spanish.

*España.*

*Tu eres muy hermosa.*

Anxious to get her home, I hastily end the conversation and ven-ture to the couch, where Sheila sits like a young widow at her hus-band's funeral. I say bye with a confident smirk and a seductive wink. There's a desperate look in Sheila's eyes; I pretend not to notice.

In the Volvo, Maria and I try our best at conversation. Language keeps getting in the way.

For three years. *Yo lo conoci cuando el estaba de vacaciónes,* she says, when I prod for information on her husband, the white boy with the small appendages. I wonder if all of his appendages are small.

I'm green; this is my first key party, I confide. My wife was wary.

Wary?

Yes, scared and *muy* hesitant, I say.

We attend many in one year, she says, No worries. Your wife will be fine. *Mi esposo es un amante maravilloso.*

Great lover, I repeat quietly in English, grinning slyly. No way Sheila will be able to follow through; her conscience won't let her.

To discourage more forced conversation, I raise the volume on my favorite jazz station, and it's successful: we don't speak the rest of the way to the house.

In our forced silence, I try to image the conversation, if any, be-tween Sheila and Michael.

At home, I lead Maria straight to our bedroom; it's pitch black save for a tiny light creeping in from the hallway. Talk is cheap and by now I'm short on it. Maria, apparently not much for meaningless conversation, wriggles out of her dress. I watch from the edge of the bed, enthralled, like staking out a beautiful prostitute—four-inch stilettos, canyon cleavage, hiked skirt—on the stroll. She stands half-naked in black silk panties, high-heeled sandals. Her breasts are just as I'd imagined; her black hair is strewn over her eyes. My eyes drift to the nightstand. I turn face down a wedding picture of Sheila and me.

Maria kneels, unbuckles my pants, pulls out my dick, teases the head with her tongue. She doesn't suck right away, but instead takes my swollen cock in her hand and coaxes me to near eruption. Partial to eye contact, I glance down. But what I see makes me wish I wouldn't have looked. Maria's right thumb is green and covered with a fungus of some sort. This unsightly imperfection instantly softens my erection. Sensing it, she finally puts me in her mouth. She swirls her tongue, takes the head of my dick to the back of her throat like she's got a false bottom there, then sucks my balls like jaw breakers.

You like? she asks, holding my penis—throbbing, spouting drops of cum—in her hand. My semen shines her lips like gloss.

I want you to come in my mouth, she says when she starts again. Usually that phrase triggers emotions of grandeur, but my mind is occupied with thoughts of Sheila and Michael. I see them making out on the carpeted floor, against the wall, in the doorway, and on the kitchen sink with her ass backed up against him. Disgusting images are seizing me like clips from bad porn: Sheila bent over doggie style cupping a hand to her mouth, or worse sucking Michael's pink dick. I keep busy to purge my imagination, guide Maria's head with my hand.

I'm sure she can sense my moan is contrived. Ahh, you feel so good, I whisper, like I'm reading a bad script. The rotten fingernail is steadily softening my erection like a good broken-in baseball mitt.

When she finishes, she stands to kiss me. Her breath is the acrid combination of dick and alcohol. I kiss back, reluctantly, no tongue.

I wonder if Sheila will kiss him; then I dismiss my worry as silly. Maria pulls off my shirt, sucks my nipples, kisses my neck, the insides of my elbows. But by now, the kisses are cold and wet on my skin—unpleasant. She moans like actresses do on daytime soaps. Fake passion.

Condom, she says, and leans me back on the bed. And I feel weak. Like I've lost control of the situation. Like a woman.

In my pants, I say, my voice scarred with treble.

Maria pulls the gold Trojan package out of my pocket, opens it, places it between her teeth. She blows the tip and rolls it down my shaft with her mouth. She wastes no time mounting me, rolling and rocking her hips wantonly. After just a few seconds, her wet cunt laces the room with a fishy stench. I almost lose what's left of my hard-on. Not to mention, I smell Sheila in our pillows. That only makes matters worse.

I make you feel good? Maria asks, using her hands to guide my dick in her catfish depths, as if my half-hard dick could do any real damage. The fingernail stares up at me like a third eye.

I don't pump, don't raise my hips, don't concentrate on anything that will help my erection return. I take two deep breaths then say: No.

She keeps riding, swinging her hair around, like maybe there's cameras in the room. Almost like she's playing to an unseen audience.

Stop, I say.

She doesn't.

I said stop, I repeat, and push against her chest for emphasis.

Call your house. Get my wife on the phone, I order harshly, like I would a fleeing suspect to stop.

Maria has a stunned expression that lasts a full ten seconds. She dials three separate times and gets no answer. It rings, rings, and rings.

We dress and leave quickly.

Maria leaves a tiny fist-sized bloodstain on the comforter.

I drive to Maria's house like I'm on a high-speed chase. The beauty I couldn't get enough of hours earlier is bewildered; lipstick sucked away, hair strewn, breath sexed. There is claustrophobic silence inside the Volvo as we blaze for her house. In minutes, we pull outside the gates. My anger steals what would normally be awe at the sheer elegance and grandeur of their crib. It's a damn palace. Maria types a code that opens the gates; we take the winding driveway to the front door just as Sheila steps out; Michael is a second behind, pulling the door shut.

Get in the car, I scream, with the heavy baritone I'd misplaced not more than an hour ago. She's smart enough not to argue, gets in the car without so much as a glance in Michael's direction.

On the highway, windows lowered, the wind whistles through. Neither of us utters a word for what feels like an eternity. I want to question her, but fear the truth might break me.

Please tell me you didn't do anything, I say, after a few minutes. My grip is tight on the steering wheel, bracing for bad news.

She pauses.

No, the fuck you didn't, I say with my eyes darting between Sheila and the road.

Sheila stares blankly out the window, folds her fidgeting hands in her lap.

We drive the rest of the way in excruciating quiet.

Tell me what the fuck happened. I slam on the brakes; we peel into the driveway. Sheila flinches.

When she turns to me, my heart thunders like I've been fired on by a murder suspect. Her hands tremble. I want her to say it, make it real for me.

You fucked him! I slam my fist into the steering wheel, shake the whole dash. I can't fucking believe you!

You asked me to do it, she says it timidly, like she's still scared I might go upside her head. At that moment, I damn sure want to slug the bitch.

Get—the fuck—out! I yell it at the top of my lungs. Screaming.

Andrew—

I lean over her, yank the handle, push it open.

Get out—now. I'll be back in the morning to get my shit.

I start the car and race out along the highway, going miles away at top speed. My eyes are heavy. How could she betray me like that? What was she thinking? How could she fuck him? A damn stranger. Hell, she's probably been fucking everything in pants whenever I leave the house. Anger keeps me awake. I pull into a rest stop. Stars are bright in the moonless sky. I pull down the visor and a 3 × 7 picture of Tyler floats down. I turn on the cabin light and inspect it.

She's smiling at me, gapped teeth, hair braided in two pigtails. Innocent. Innocence I want to protect, but from what? From guys who think and behave like me? I recall the picture that sits on the den bookshelf, of Sheila at age five. Her smile showing no hint of the pain I've inflicted on her most of her adult life. I think about the humiliation she's endured, Tyler being a part of it. My stomach turns sour and heavy. When I close my eyes, the seven glasses of Hennessey spin my head, saying horrible things in my thoughts about my tramp wife, our shattered marriage.

It's taken strength I will never know for her to endure years of such blatant unfaithfulness, to love Tyler, a living relic of my infidelity. And now I feel lower than I've felt in years, worse than when I was young and snatched the pocketbook of an elderly lady who only wanted help across the street. Selfish. Callous.

I sit cramped in the Volvo till sunrise.

Morning, I return. The house is dead silent. I trudge to the living room, slump on the couch, stand up a picture of Sheila and me that lays face down on the coffee table. The glass in the frame is cracked. I close my eyes, cup my face in my hands like a teen sentenced to adult time. Pain in my lower back throbs up my spine. I rub it gingerly, wince, walk to the hallway bathroom. I pour four Advil in my hand, swallow them with faucet water, while trying not to look at my bloodshot eyes in the medicine cabinet mirror.

Down the hall from the bedroom, the alarm clock sounds. I splash my face awake, towel dry. Beep, beep, beep—it rings steady, loud, piercing, like it's screaming at me.

Sheila.

No answer.

Sheila, I call a second time.

I walk to the bedroom; the door is flung wide open, and I stand for a moment on the threshold, hesitant, petrified, like arriving first at an unsecured murder scene. A cool morning breeze flaps our thin curtains. My pistol weights a single sheet of ruled paper on the comforter; from my vantage, I notice Sheila's scrawled handwriting. She had a tough time writing this, I could tell that. I look left; the closet door is slid open, all her clothes are emptied. Her shoe boxes are scattered about the floor, and all dresser drawers are cleaned out. I trudge to the bed, legs like a teenage son asked to carry his mother's casket—weak. I pick the pistol up, hold it in my left hand; with my right I pick up the letter.

It covers Maria's fist-sized bloodstain.
I read the first page; the back page begins:

*P.S.*

*For years I've been deceiving myself that you loved me, that you cared about me, fooling myself. You care about you. Always have. Always will. And to think I put a gun to my head, thought my life would be meaningless without you. No! What I learned more than anything tonight is that my life will be nothing with you.*

# An Act of Faith

**David Anthony Durham**

Joyce had just turned twenty-one when she first met Calvin, in the fall of 1967. It was a fair day at an outdoor shopping center, where she worked in a flower shop. She stood behind the counter, her concentration focused on the cash register, whose jammed drawer she was trying to pry open with a screwdriver. She moved gently, eyebrows close together in concentration, scared of scratching the paint and yet angry because the stupid thing was always messing with her.

Business had been light all day. Perhaps that was why her head snapped up so forcefully when he strode through the entrance, bringing with him a gust of air that ruffled the leaves of the plants around the door. He held a clipboard in one hand, a small package under his arm. A pencil stuck out from behind his ear. He was a slim, dark-skinned brother in his early twenties, with an athletic body like a mid-range sprinter. His tight-fitting brown slacks hugged the muscles of his legs and outlined the firm shape of his behind. Joyce took him in with one quick glance, and then shoved the screwdriver under the counter.

He skipped-slid toward her and handed her the package. "Hey, girl, you working here or tossing the joint?"

"It's just jammed," Joyce answered. "Should I sign?"

Their hands touched briefly as he handed her the clipboard. Though Joyce was shy by nature and circumstance, she found her gaze lingering on his for a few long moments. His eyes pressed heavy on his lower lids, but instead of looking tired they gave off a bemused sensuality, as if he were watching her from under the bedsheets, contemplating her after a moment of intimacy sprung on her by surprise. Joyce suddenly remembered that she hadn't brushed her

teeth after lunch. She feared that a bit of lettuce was wedged between her lower front teeth. With her lips shut tight, she looked
down to sign for the package. She could feel his eyes watching her,
almost like a physical touch that slid down her arm and focused on
the bones of her wrist. Her fingers tingled, and her signature came
out in jerky letters quite unusual for her.

Joyce handed the pad back to him. "I have something I'm supposed to mail out with you all. I just need to find the address." She
searched through an address book below the counter, then began filling out the tab. She again felt the touch of his eyes on her. She
couldn't fight the urge her eyes seemed to feel to look up. When she
did so—just for a moment—he was indeed gazing back at her, with
the oddest look of enchantment in his eyes.

A moment later, he said, "I'm having the strangest feeling watching you. It's like . . . I mean, it makes me think . . . I just might fall in
love with you." He waited, as if he knew Joyce would need a moment
to weigh the full import of the statement. "I don't know if you'll believe me on this, but I have this sort of sixth sense. My grandmother
used to call it 'the touch.' It means that I always know my destiny. All
I have to do is keep my eyes open, and if I do, sometimes I can see
my future clear as day."

Joyce cast her voice dry and humorless. "You're telling me you're
touched, are you?"

"I'm saying something just hit me like a flash, just when I was
watching you." He eyed her for a moment, ran his fingers over his
chin, and seemed to consider his words carefully. "When I look at
you a bunch of different things pop up in my head. I see us getting
old together. I see me scraping the bunions off your toes. I see a
whole mess of grandchildren around us, and a big ole dog sitting at
our feet as we watch the sunset, thinking about how fabulous our life
has been, and how glad we are that we didn't let the love slip through
our fingers back in sixty-seven when we met straight out of the blue.
Same thing didn't occur to you?"

Joyce finished writing and handed him the envelope and mail
form. "What makes you think I have bunions?"

"Okay, I'm not sure about the bunion thing, but . . . do you like
dogs?"

"Allergic. One whiff and I'm spitting and hissing."

He smiled thinly and acknowledged his tactical error with a shrug. He reached out a finger as if to touch her chin. He didn't do so, but motioned as if he were lifting her face up toward his. Which, in fact, was just what happened.

"Listen, I don't know your name or anything about you, but I'm not hustling you. My name is Calvin Carter. I'd like to know you better. That's all. People gotta connect in this world and sometimes it takes a little faith to let that happen. Sometimes you gotta pull out a couple blocks in that wall and let some air through and look a brother in the face and just give him a moment. That's all I'm talking about. I could tell you my life story; you could tell me yours; then we could see what comes of it. That's all, just some time to talk. Think we could do that?"

Joyce, as if she heard this question regularly, said, "Let me think about it." And, despite the fact that she told herself Calvin could only be another young hustler doing what young hustlers do, and despite the fact that his invocation of the word 'love' was as subtle as knocking on a door with a battering ram, and despite the fact that her common sense told her she should handle him with the curt, cold civility that she usually reserved for religious fanatics carrying clipboards . . . Despite all this, think about it was just what she did.

For each of the next five days Calvin waited for Joyce after work. He would rush into the store breathless, still in his work uniform, pluck a flower from one of the bouquets by the door, and present it to her with courtly formality. The first time she charged him for the flower and refused to let him walk her home. The second, she allowed him to walk with her, but wouldn't let him touch her bags. The third, she told him he was getting on her nerves. The fourth, she asked him if he knew what he was getting into. And this day, the fifth day of his assault, she allowed herself to laugh out loud and look, for long periods, straight in his eyes. They were the kind of eyes that had a certain glint to them, as if the light was always catching them just right.

A few hundred yards from her apartment building Joyce stopped walking. "Where did you get eyes like that?" she asked.

He grinned. "Eyes like what?"

"Eyes like . . . I don't know like what. That's why I asked."

He stepped closer, shifting the grocery bags that he carried tucked under his arm. "Why don't you describe them to me? Maybe we can figure it out."

Joyce opened her mouth as if to say something, but then shifted her jaw a little to the left and resumed walking. "You are vain. Get something a little good and it goes straight to a black man's head."

Calvin kept up with her. "They come from my momma if you want to know the truth. People say she was part Indian."

"Where was she from?"

"South Hill, Virginia. Tobacco country."

"You're a country boy?"

"Born and raised. Most of my family still lives down there. That's where I'd be if I hadn't come up here to find you." He flashed his smile again, but Joyce just pursed her lips.

When they reached the steps to Joyce's row house, she took one step up and paused. Calvin glanced up at the large structure behind her. The house sat on the corner and was shaped in a strange, triangular design, like a wedge cut out of a cake of red brick. He stepped up as if to look into the lower windows.

"You live here? You share it with someone?"

"It's my parents' house," Joyce said, her businesslike tone returning.

"Uh-oh, you still live with your folks? I guess that makes you one of them wholesome type girls. That's the kind I like. You gonna let me meet them? I got a way with parents."

Instead of answering, Joyce reached out for her bags. "Let's not worry about that. Now, I suppose I should tell you that I don't work tomorrow. So don't go showing up there worrying Mrs. Goldstein with your crazy self. She will call security on you."

Calvin shifted both bags to one arm and stepped forward. With his free hand he gently reached up and touched the chilled skin of her cheek. "I'm not crazy," he said. "I like to joke and all, but about some things I'm right serious. Like I'm serious that your face may be the only face I'll ever need. It's that beautiful."

Joyce's lips crinkled into a crooked smile, defensive even though her words were plainspoken. "How can you be so sure? I can't see things beyond tomorrow."

"Faith, baby. You need to open yourself up and let what has to happen happen. How about this? From now on you don't have to be sure. I'll be sure enough for both of us. Okay? All you have to do is do what you know you want to, and I'll take care that everything else is all right. Okay?"

Her head moved in the tiniest indication of a nod. "Maybe we should start getting to know each other."

Calvin straightened up and inhaled the cool evening air through his nose. "Yeah. That's what I'm talking about."

After parting a few moments later, Joyce stood alone inside the house. She leaned her back against the door and listened to the uneasy silence around her, hearing the fading tones of Calvin's voice. When Joyce said that she lived in her parents' home, she spoke the truth, but a somewhat incomplete truth. She lived in her parents' house, but the old couple had passed into the next world some nine months before. Robert and Caroline Johnston had had their daughter late in life. They raised her in that drafty, old row house that they had correctly prophesied they would live in until they passed on. They had aged into one of those old couples we might all wish to emulate, so used to each other that they seemed to speak from different regions of the same mind, move with different limbs of the same body, and look upon each other with the casual acceptance with which one looks upon one's own reflection. They dealt with life's trials with a resigned reliance on each other, on their daughter, and on God. If there was any irony to their lives, it was that they produced a daughter that seemed incapable of inheriting any such trust.

For Joyce, her faith in most things ended one breezy winter night. The house's rattling windows had been sealed with plastic and the doors stuffed with old rags. These were their customary insulations, and that fateful night they worked so well that the old couple slept their way into death, quietly asphyxiated by a carbon monoxide leak. Joyce had stayed the night at her friend's, and would never truly come to terms with why her life was saved by something as frivolous as a sorority dance. Guilt gnawed hard at her, the unshakable belief that she could have saved them had she been home. Indeed, for many nights she dreamt of waking to the smell of gas, rushing through the house crying warnings and throwing open the windows, finding her parents sound asleep and shaking them, shaking them, shaking them . . .

Upon waking from these dreams, she often wished that she had been allowed to die with her parents, instead of being left alone in this empty house, with all her memories, with the vague, nagging fear that the world was a creature not to be trusted, and that love was a burden too heavy to bear. Thoughts such as these were just a few of the many things held trapped inside her, the bits and pieces of the real her, the things she wished desperately to get beyond, but which she could never imagine sharing with another living person.

Joyce walked alongside Calvin through the damp air of the Capitol Mall. She wore a light blue, knee-length coat, whose large collar spread across her shoulders. Her face was carefully made up, her straightened hair wrapped tight around the top of her head and pinned in the back with a seashell brooch. Her eyes studied the Washington Monument as they approached it, several hundred yards ahead of them. It was near sundown, the sky dim and overcast. All day long it had threatened to rain, but they decided to walk anyway, as the streets were less crowded than usual. The air had a moist taste to it that was almost sweet to inhale. As usual, Calvin talked.

"I was over at my buddy's house yesterday watching the Jets game. One of the hardest things for me to do is watch a football game these days. I should be out there myself."

"Out there yourself doing what?"

"Playing ball! I was good enough. I was better than good enough. I played varsity from the time I was a freshman. Had the fastest hundred yards in the county—would have been a state record, but they didn't recognize my time 'cause they said it wasn't official. I even had some colleges coming out to look me over. Can you imagine that? Coming all the way out to South Hill?"

"So, what happened?"

"My knee blew."

"That's all?"

"What do you mean, 'that's all'? That's enough. Some fool slammed into me from the side." Calvin indicated the blow with a chop to his left knee. "And that was that. Just ripped the joint apart, tore up the cartilage, just did a job on it. You can't mess with a knee, not when you're talking about going pro. Man . . . It's a shame too. When I was on my game, wasn't nobody that could touch me. It was like I was moving at a different speed than everybody else, always a step ahead."

For a moment, Calvin hunkered down into a running position. One hand came up before him, and his body indicated slight, subtle weight shifts, as if the walkway before them was full of invisible opponents. He dropped the stance when he noticed Joyce smiling at him. "But I guess that's payback, or something. That's the way the world comes back at you for your sins."

"What did you ever do that was so bad?" Joyce asked. "You act like you did something unmentionable."

Calvin looked down at the ground. "As far as my momma's concerned, I did. I left South Hill. That was all I had to do to hurt her. I ran away, like a thief in the night. When my oldest brother, Marshall, was alive, everyone figured that he and Jefferson would take care of the farm, and I might be the first one to get out and travel or go to school or something. There's some beautiful things about living at South Hill, but it feels so far from the world. Nothing's happening there but small things, close-in-on-you things."

They had reached a cross street and stood waiting for the light to change. Calvin shoved his hands deep into the pockets of his jacket. "I haven't told you about Marshall, have I?"

"No."

"He got killed."

"Murdered?"

"That's the word. Murdered the old-fashioned way—out in a field at night, a good, honest Southern lynching. After that everybody just knew that I was supposed to stay, help Jefferson and run the farm and get married and that would be my life. But shit . . ." The light changed and they started walking. "I mean, when I was little we had gotten *National Geographic.* I used to read that magazine from cover to cover. All those animals, and countries, and naked little African girls. I spent all that time reading that stuff and just waiting to get out and see it all, and then Momma just expected me to forget about it. How was I supposed to forget? It just never felt like farming was supposed to be my life. So I packed up a handful of stuff and snuck out one night, caught a bus up to D.C., and I've been here ever since. I guess I didn't get that far, really."

A moment before, when she'd named the method of Marshall's death, Joyce had felt a quick tingle in her lower back, the fear that this was where the truth began to come out, the secrets that might begin to chip away at the image she'd built of Calvin. She'd never been as near to crime as she was with his casual mention of a killing. But a few sentences later he'd moved the conversation along and she'd followed. This was not a man to be afraid of. He'd done nothing to others, and yet the world had done violence to those close to him. She felt her shoulder brush his and had a sudden desire to slip her arms inside his coat and press herself against the heat of him and tilt her head and open her mouth to his, to break through that wall he mentioned and to start consuming and being consumed.

Instead, she said, "That's not that bad, Calvin. You have to live your own life."

"That's not the way Momma sees it. I started writing her letters as soon as I got a place to stay, trying to explain to her and tell her about all the things that were going on around here, the Movement and all, being in the center of everything. She never wrote me back, not once. I don't even know if she read them." He stopped walking and looked Joyce in the face. "It's been three years. Three years. And it feels like it'll be forever. Like I can't go back there and she'll never come to me here. That gets to me more and more. People got to have connections, don't they?" He reached out, took Joyce's hand, and held it loosely in his. "What do we have without connections? Sometimes I know I had to leave, other times I feel unhinged from everything that made me who I am. You ever feel that way?"

Joyce didn't answer. She looked down at his hand, and then intertwined his fingers with hers. "Come," she said, and pulled him on.


Calvin and Joyce's next date began well enough. They ate dinner near Dupont Circle, in a restaurant that specialized in tomato dishes. Afterward, they walked to a movie theater and caught a cheap showing of *Doctor Zhivago*. Calvin enjoyed the film more than Joyce. He liked its grand scale and its focus on one man moving through large historical forces. And he liked the fact that—despite everything else—it was still just a love story.

Joyce nodded as he spoke, agreeing mutely with his enthusiasm. She wasn't actually thinking much about the movie. Rather, she found herself wondering who this man was, where he came from, and why she so enjoyed listening to his voice, why her eyes so liked to wander over his backside, and why she felt that his hand fit so naturally into the small of her back. She recognized in him many of the same traits that so turned her off in others. It was obvious he liked to hear himself talk. He had a certain vanity that he showed when he smiled. And he, like so many men, looked at the world with a boyish naïveté that he both disguised and betrayed by his musical flow of words.

But with Calvin each of these traits struck her as endearing. Not only did she tolerate them; she actually welcomed them. She found herself questioning her own pessimism. The more she questioned, the more she felt herself to be pale next to his color, tired where he was energized, dull while he was inspired. She began to wonder why he liked her, and if he would continue to. Each passing moment made the evening more difficult for her.

After the movie they went to a nightclub nearby. Once settled at the bar, Calvin turned to Joyce and smiled. The blue light that lit up the back of the bar reflected off his teeth and sparkled in the liquid of his eyes, tainting the whites with a warm indigo. Joyce realized she didn't know the exact color of his eyes, even though she spent so long looking at them.

"I don't know why people complained about the movie being too drab," Calvin said. "I mean, it's kind of gray, but then when there is color it's like, bam! The whole world just burst out in flowers. I like that. I like it when things hit you by surprise. I do fault the man for cheating on his wife, though. I understand what it means to have passion, but you gotta do right by the ones you commit to." He paused and studied Joyce for a moment.

She knew he was waiting for her to say something. "So you're claiming your eye doesn't wander?"

"Well . . . You can't tell where an eye may move, but it's not the eye that matters. It's the heart. You know? It's the body as it betrays the strengths or weakness of the heart. An eye just looks at the world. It's the person behind it that has to decide what to do with what it sees. On that you can always trust me."

"How do you know you can always trust me?"

Calvin grinned. "Girl, once you've swum in this sea you won't want to go anyplace else. This here's deep water, and you're fish that likes to swim." Joyce began to laugh. "I'm serious. I am, even if it's a fucked-up line. Don't laugh. Joyce . . . Can't you see a brother's trying? But, anyway, I'm talking too much. Now it's your turn. This is what I've been waiting for. Let's have the full history of Joyce Carter, starting with day one. Gimme all of it."

Joyce looked over and nodded at the bartender, who was strolling toward them. "How about we get a drink first?"

For the rest of the evening, Calvin continued asking questions, and Joyce kept deflecting them. As they talked, Joyce steadily put down drink after drink. She drank hoping that alcohol would relieve her nervousness and allow her to loosen up. She actually wanted to be as honest with him about the pain in her past, wanted to explain herself to him. But before long she lost—along with her nervousness—most of her inhibitions, her motor functions, and eventually, a chunk of the evening's memories.

A few hours later, she awoke from a rambling, fluid dream of twirling ceilings. She opened her eyes and realized that she was lying stretched across her couch, with a towel tucked under her chin, a slow stream of tomato-based drool dribbling from the corner of her mouth. Calvin sat at her side, wiping her vomit clean with his handkerchief.

"Hey, baby" he said, with a familiarity she had not heard before. "How about that? We've gone and spent the night together."

"What?" was all Joyce managed to say.

Calvin leaned in and whispered, as if sharing a secret, "Well, I guess you had a little too much to drink. I walked you home. I helped you change your clothes. And then I just took care of you. I just sat here and memorized your face."

Joyce closed her eyes and covered her face with her hands. Her head still swam and sloshed as if it were full of liquid. She could only half put meaning to his words, but she understood enough to feel shame creeping into her crowded thoughts. "I just wanted to talk," she mumbled.

Calvin smiled. "Of course you did. You did talk, Joyce. You told me everything. We've got no secrets anymore. You even convinced me to go home and introduce you to Momma."

It took a few moments for Joyce to respond. She cautiously pulled her hands away from her face. Calvin's smile was still there, his teeth as bright as ever, and his face still held that childish enthusiasm. But it seemed to Joyce that something about him looked different. She couldn't be sure whether the expression on his face had changed, or whether the way she looked at it had changed, but she did know without a doubt that he had seen her at her worst, must have heard the things that pained her, must have pushed her limbs through the motions of life—all this, and still he looked upon her and smiled. He never told her exactly what she said that evening, but he also never spoke of it with anything but fondness. This—as pathetic and nauseating as it was—was the moment she felt herself falling for him.

The following evening Joyce accepted this man into her bed. She wouldn't remember later just how it happened. She didn't know which of them initiated it, whether they spoke about it first or if they acted without words. But none of this mattered. Once they were together, it felt to her that it had always been this way. He had always been there above her, inside her. She knew every portion of his body, every swell and depression, the curve of his muscles and the softness of his backside. With her arms cinched around his back, she took in the whole of him. She felt each contour of his penis inside her, gripped so tightly she committed it to memory in the very first moments. She pressed her palms against his sweaty skin and brushed her lips across his shoulders, tasting the salt scent of him, knowing in those moments no sweeter scent, nothing more right.

She had a strange thought then. She remembered reading once that by comparison to the possible variety of organisms in the universe, all of the earth's living creatures were quite similar, made of the same simple elements. She'd never given this much thought before because the world seemed so full of difference. But with his flesh gripped between her teeth she knew that on this one thing science was right. The two of them were of the same material.

And Lord it was good to finally realize it.

"Jesus . . . ," Joyce said. "How far back here do you all live?"

"It's not far now," Calvin said. "It's just starting to look like home."

They had been driving for the past four hours. First down the interstate, then on to increasingly smaller and smaller roads. For the last several miles their rental car bounced along a dirt road, beneath great, bare trees, through a countryside of farms and rolling hills. They hadn't actually needed to come down this road, but Calvin chose it for scenic value, what he called "the complete country-fide experience." He spoke almost nonstop throughout the trip, recounting his youth in the country. He tended to exaggerate the backwardness of country people. He claimed that none of them had figured out how to keep their teeth, and urged Joyce to pretend she didn't notice. He argued the virtues of inbred marriages, focusing on how simple it made inheritance. And he told the tale of some local man who, in old age, took to exposing his erect penis in public, apparently proud that the years had not weakened the flow of blood to this vital organ.

He joked, but often Joyce caught a deeper tone to his voice, some pain in his remembrances that his laughter couldn't disguise. This was his first trip home since he ran away three years before, and she could tell that the call, and the cries, of home weighed more heavily on him with each passing mile. She began to wonder why they were here. Hadn't this trip been her idea? Hadn't she proposed that she meet his family? The idea had seemed novel, almost brave, in the safety of her apartment. Now she felt her fear growing at this endless list of names that Calvin produced, the strangeness of his stories, the tone of his voice, and the image she had conjured up of his mother, a woman who seemed as hard and cold as steel, who towered, in Joyce's mind, like the great trees they drove under.

Joyce grimaced with each jolt of the car. "How hard is it to pave a road?"

"No harder than plucking a chicken," Calvin said, grinning.

Joyce looked askance at him. "What does that mean?"

"Nothing." Calvin shrugged. "Just, you ever pluck a chicken?"

"No, I never plucked a chicken."

"Well, plucking a chicken ain't easy. Matter of fact the whole chicken killing thing'll mess you up. Grams only tried to make me kill a chicken once. I must have been about seven . . ."

"Seven?"

"Yeah." Calvin glanced over at her. "That's old enough to kill a chicken, if you have the stomach for it. We always used a hatchet. Just lay its little neck across the chopping block and . . ." He chopped precisely at the dashboard. "Thing is it scared me to death because sometimes the chicken would get up and run around the yard headless. And there was this one rooster, Mr. Charlie, that I used to have nightmares about. We called him Mr. Charlie 'cause he was so evil. Fact is that Mr. Charlie spent too long watching us kill his hens. That would have to get on your nerves, all them plump thighs . . ."

Calvin glanced over at Joyce. For a moment he studied her profile seriously. "Anyway, I didn't do it. I broke down crying. Grams had to take the hatchet from me and do it herself. I just knew that if I did it I'd never stop dreaming that Mr. Charlie and a flock of headless hens were coming after me."

They eventually stopped on a hill overlooking the valley that the Carter family owned. They walked a short distance through the tall grass and climbed up onto the stump of a large tree. The valley that spread out before them seemed as dry and barren as the winter air. The hills rolled off as far as the eye could see, cut up into geometric plots, with different shadings of brown, yellow, and gray. One dirt road carved its way hesitantly through the valley. A lone hawk floated high above.

"You should see it in the spring," Calvin said. He wrapped his arms around Joyce from behind. "It's so green you wouldn't believe it. Imagine all those trees in full bloom, and the fields bursting with little shoots. Look there, I think that's my Uncle Pete's place." Joyce followed Calvin's finger to where a thin stream of smoke trailed up. She could just make out the roof of the house through the trees. "We'll need to stop there on the way in. That's the way people always did it when they visited—stopped first at Uncle Pete's, then Uncle Levert's, and on down the line to my momma's house. By the time they got there, word had already been sent down and Momma would be out in the yard waiting. I suppose that might happen today. It's hard to sneak up on my mother."

"Calvin, you make it sound so . . . nice, I guess. All that family. All those stories. I don't really know why you left. I mean, you told me, but . . . I don't know."

Calvin ran his tongue across his teeth and thought for a few moments. "It was just too small a world, with too much in it. Everything that happened seemed right up in your face, cramping you. I saw my father just a couple hours before . . ." He drew his shoulders together like he was shivering, then relaxed them and looked out over the valley. His eyes settled on the hawk. "Do you know sometimes I used to wish him dead? When I was young I used to think how different it would have been if he were gone. He wouldn't be around to get at us the way he did, and Momma would be different. She had to carry so much because of him. He lost half the land she owned, gambling, I guess. Things just went through his fingers."

The hawk suddenly dipped and dropped downward for several seconds, only to check and slowly rise again.

"It was a Saturday night, late in the summer. Me and some friends had gone into town, to one of the little joints they had. I walked in there all ready for a night out and guess who I see? My father, acting like a man half his age, with his mouth all over some woman that sure as hell was not my mother. I froze dead in the doorway. Everybody in the place stopped and stared at me, hoping there'd be some sort of scene. I just stared at him. I could see he was stumbling drunk. I can still picture it now: the grin across his face, the way his hands were groping over her, all of it. I just had to turn around and leave. I remember my friend James said I should go in there and grab him and take him home so he didn't end up driving like that, but I didn't care. Right then he could drive himself straight off a cliff for all I cared. And that's just about what he did. Just what he did . . ."

Joyce turned and slid one arm inside his jacket. She laid her cheek against his chest.

"They found him the next morning, about a half mile from the house. There's this turn in the road . . . Always was a treacherous turn. He drove straight off into the field and drove the car up the base of a big old tree. It looked like he was trying to ride over it, like he thought, 'I'll just take a shortcut over this tree here . . . ' So then there's that to mess around in my head as well. And then Marshall gets killed the way he does. All that stuff just starts crowding you. Like the hills keep it in, like family never really leaves. Either dead or alive, they're all here, buried over on that hill, rambling around in this valley. How could I stay when I had to see that tree every day and wonder why God had given me the choice to save his life. It felt like James had whispered right into my ear. He said, 'You shouldn't let him drive like that.' But I did. I sure enough did." He sniffled and stroked Joyce's hair. "Anyway, I had to leave to find you. That's all I really wanted."

Joyce thought, "God, forgive me, but that's good to hear!" She'd listened to his story and recognized the pain that it caused him and wished it wasn't so. But still—selfishly, hungrily—she wanted nothing else at that moment but for him to truly find her. She understood that you never know a person completely at any one moment. She didn't need to have all of him at once, and she didn't have to tell him everything from her own life today, or tomorrow, or at any specific moment. The sharing between two people could go on always, evolving each day as the world pressed against you with different currents, as they grew more confident with each other, as their eyes learned to look ever deeper into each other. She believed that she'd finally found the other person in front of whom she could slowly strip piece by painful piece of her facade away. She would one day stand naked before this man, her true self exposed; as he would before her.

At that moment, feeling the chill rushing up from the valley of South Hill, hearing the whispers of the ghosts that haunted Calvin, Joyce signed her name on some imaginary dotted line. She agreed to take a journey, to accept the slow revelations that, hopefully, would stretch into two long lifetimes. It was a gesture as great as if she'd lifted her arms and threw herself into flight like that hawk. An act of faith.

Outwardly, she said only, "Then let's go home." She whispered it, softly, into the collar of his coat.

Calvin stood silent. His nose was running, but for a few moments he stopped sniffling. As if he were a child out too long in the snow, a little trickle of moisture hung at the rim of his nostril. Joyce kept her cheek pressed to his chest. A truck passed on the road behind them. Something rustled in the grass.

"Okay," Calvin said, and without another word they drove the five hours back to the District.

# Lust Enraptured

**Robert Scott Adams**

Cheating. Infidelity. Betrayal. Tryst. They never considered what they were doing to have anything to do with any of these things. They were meant to be together. It wasn't a matter of their partners not taking care of business, or neglecting them in any way, or failing to do what was needed. They just enjoyed each other's company. They just enjoyed each other's passion, each other's body, each other's desires.

They needed each other. She needed the time away from the responsibility of marriage, needed the time away from children, obligations, routine, and morality. He needed time away from his clinging girlfriend, the sister who was pressuring him for a trip to the altar. Her biological clock was ticking, as she loved to remind him. She was thirty-two going on fifty-two, in her head. To hell with what was right or wrong. To hell with consequences.

Now they were together again. No more lies. No more deception. It was their time. Everything came to a halt as they made love on the steps of Miguel's house in the country. His girlfriend was away, visiting a sorority sister on Martha's Vineyard. Carlotta had used the excuse of coming east on business, one of her countless trips back into his arms. Someone once told her husband that she had another lover, but he didn't care.

Or at least he didn't make a fuss about it. She was free to do what she wanted to do. Not that they had an open marriage, but as long as she kept her affairs out of his face, everything was cool.

Carlotta had made one of her rare cross-country trips to see Miguel. They were making up for lost time. They had spent five glorious days together making love, eating, shopping, going to clubs, and making love. Oh yes, and then there was always fucking, which was what they were doing now.

Carlotta's dress was bunched up around her waist. Her ass was on the edge of the carpeted stairs that led down from the living room to the doorway. They were supposed to go to the airport, so that Carlotta could return home. She'd talked to her husband the night before on her cell phone, assuring him that her meetings were all going well and that her flight home was scheduled to get in around nine that following night. The kids seemed especially glad to talk to her, with her oldest boy jabbering away about some new video game purchased for him by his father.

Now they had a little extra time. But after an all-night session of fucking, who would have thought they would be at it again? Driven by their unrelenting passion, they were like teenagers discovering the joys of sex for the very first time. This was so different than the muted feelings they felt during the regimented couplings with their respective partners. Carlotta's shapely legs were straight up in the air, her ankles together across his glistening back, her pelvis lifted to receive him full force. Miguel didn't disappoint her. He held her legs tightly as he vigorously pumped his hardness deeper into her body, savoring her wetness, and the tightness of her hungry sex. Then he shifted her ankles so they rested on his shoulders, enabling him to play with her taut nipples while he kept rotating his hips. Moaning, she gripped him firmly, her fingers making marks on his arms, trying to match him stroke for stroke.

"Goddamn, fuck me harder, Miguel!" Carlotta uttered her urgings between pants and moans.

He lightly pinched her nipples while maintaining his steady rhythm. Occasionally, he moved his mouth to her big toe and sucked it like a newborn sucks its mother's breast. The fierce intensity of their lovemaking increased as they both entered that fevered zone where they lost track of time. Two of Miguel's fingers found their way to her delectable mouth, tracing her lips gently before slipping between them, and she sucked his fingers as if they were a cock, his cock. She knew how much it turned him on when she slurped and drooled in this second form of carnal entry. Double penetration.

At the same time, she could feel the sexual heat overtaking him, could feel his hips start to pound harder against her. God, if only her husband could match this!

Miguel looked deep into her eyes. "Shit baby, I'm gonna come. Where do you want it? On your titties? You want to swallow it? Or do you want it deep inside that hot pussy?"

He knew Carlotta loved for him to talk like this. It made her hot as hell. He felt her make the sweet, soft walls of her pussy clamp down on his throbbing meat even more.

"I'm right there, baby," he whispered softly to her, sensing that his orgasm was close, very close. "You know how close I am to coming, don't you? Here, let me show you."

He quickly yanked himself out of her with her legs still resting on his shoulders. She moaned once again, letting him remove his fingers from her mouth, before taking his hard dick in her hand. She milked it ever so slightly, until a little bit of cum seeped out of the head.

"See?" He took his finger and caught the little drop of nectar on its tip, smiling. "Do you want to taste it?"

She said nothing; instead she tightened her grip on him and brought his engorged penis to her open mouth. The memory of swallowing his juices earlier came back to her suddenly and her throat contracted involuntarily in reflex, recalling the descent of his cum two hours before. Hungrily, she caught what gushed forth and grinned, wanting more.

Still, she was dissatisfied. "You know what I want. I want you to choke me with that dick, make me gag with it, and let me drink it all. I promise I'll drink every drop."

With that urging, he began to jack himself off, slowly at first, then harder and harder until he was ready again, on the verge. His balls ached slightly, then pulsed. Then his entire body convulsed, his orgasm twisting his spine and sending a spasm through his legs. He pumped into her mouth, completely caught up in the surge of savage feeling, until it was all out of him. Afterward, sprawled back on the steps, he smeared it all around her mouth. Giggling, she ran her tongue around her lips, savoring the taste before making it disappear.

As she slowly took him from her mouth, she let her tongue circle around the large purple head of his manhood, making sure she got every drop of his sap. They looked at each other. She then glanced at her watch and made a sad face.

"Well, I see why we gave ourselves some extra time," she said. "God, I love the way you make me feel. You have no idea how much I miss this when I'm out there away from you. Nothing beats it."

He watched her face, the deep blush of a satisfied woman. "Do you ever feel guilty about your trips?"

She sat up, balancing herself on an elbow. "No, this is separate from what I have with my husband. That is one thing; this is something else. I never confuse the two."

"Do you think he has ever suspected anything?" he asked, wondering where his cigarettes were. "I called you once a few months ago and I thought I heard something edgy in his voice. Like he suspected something."

"He knows we talk," she said matter-of-factly. "I don't keep that from him. He used to bug me about you, but I informed him that I never even thought about you that way. That you were just someone I knew from back in the day."

He sucked his teeth. "I can't believe that he is not jealous."

"I didn't say he was not, but I work hard to keep his trust," she said. "I used to be careful when I'd talked to you on the computer from home. I caught him watching me one night about a year ago. But, thank God, he's almost blind or I would have been busted. Now I just talk to you from work."

"That's safe," Miguel admitted, getting up to locate a pack of the killer weed.

"No, he trusts me. I give him no reason not to trust me."

He came back from an upstairs room, carrying the cigarettes and a plastic lighter. His dick was still hard, which immediately caught her attention. "Do you have other lovers, Carlotta?"

Her face was emotionless, not a twitch of anything that would give her away. "Why ruin the moment with questions like that?" She was annoyed but held it in check.

"I just wondered . . ." He didn't want to imagine her doing the same things she did with him with someone else. Just the thought of that made his hardness wilt.

"All I want to do is to enjoy the moment, to enjoy you with nothing to spoil the magic of it," she said, putting a finger near her lips suggestively. "If you notice, I never ask you anything about what happens with you when I'm not here. I don't ask because I don't want to know. That's your business, what you do when I'm not here. I don't need to know."

He wondered how many married couples did what they were doing, had an agreement like theirs, a secret life apart from their mates. How many couples met secretly on the sly to break the monotony of their daily lives? To bring some excitement into their regimented existence? He wondered how they felt when they left those rooms to return to the marital beds, to the same old kisses and caresses. Everybody acts as if monogamy is the norm, but it isn't. Almost everyone he knew cheated. Everybody felt jealous or guilty at some time or another, but most would cheat if the opportunity presented itself. All around him, it seemed the norm to be promiscuous when there was so much free dick and pussy to be had. Everywhere you turned, someone was offering you some, often with no strings attached.

This was a life where the successful lie was frequently rewarded with unlimited pleasure, and honesty and kindness only got you a kick in the ass. Or humiliation, pain, loneliness and a blow to the heart. The fact is that we betray the ones we love and let them down in so many ways. We thrive on cheating because it allows us to see ourselves in new ways, in new situations that have nothing to do with the people we love. Each new sexual partner is an opportunity for change, to explore, to forget the limitations of the man or woman at home who has grown old, stale, routine.

There is no one without secrets, hidden lives, the clandestine sex done on the sly. In the end, you wonder what makes people stay together. What keeps them together as a couple when there are so many other bodies, so many hearts out there to be sampled?

Sometimes it was hard to deceive yourself into remaining faithful with a body that you knew all too well. As someone once said, familiarity did breed contempt. Or a couple is a conspiracy in search of a crime. Or maybe another bed to occupy.

Just before they left, Carlotta said two things that surprised him. Two things that stopped him in his tracks. But then that was one of the things he loved about her: her brazen honesty and her startling unpredictability.

"Miguel, I've always wondered what it would be like to have a dick," she said with a chuckle. "To pee standing up. I think most women wonder about that."

"Huh?" That was the only response he could muster.

But she was not finished. In a few seconds, she could say things that could turn anyone's head and leave them struggling for a reply.

He was floored again when she said the following with a perfectly straight face: "You know, I had a bad moment of crisis in my marriage about three years ago. I thought about leaving my husband, children and marriage for you. I was obsessed with the idea for almost two weeks. I couldn't get it out of my mind. Just as I was home packing my suitcases, my mother calls and asks if I was bringing the kids out for Thanksgiving. I don't know why but that snapped me out of it."

He didn't know what to say at first. The silence grew in the room like a well-tended mushroom.

"Do you ever imagine what it would have been like if you had married me instead of him?" He asked the question, not really wanting to hear the answer.

"Sure I have, but then it may not have worked," she said sadly. "Who knows, probably this is the best situation for us. You know I love you. Very much."

Neither of them said anything else about that conversation on the way to the airport. The drive to the airport was always a special occasion. It was either Miguel fingering her swollen sex lips under her short skirt or Carlotta playing with his dick, getting him thick and pulsing before she covered him with her lips. Regardless of how often she gave him head while driving, he never got used to it, constantly afraid that he would lose focus and cross into oncoming traffic or speed up into a rushing tractor trailer. With explosions of heat and sensation going off throughout him, he struggled to keep his mind on the road, to keep the car between the lines, to keep from crashing into the trees.

As the car approached the airport, the familiar feeling of loss began to infiltrate both of their souls, moving gradually but steadily like a slow poison through their bodies. They both dreaded goodbyes. But it had to happen. They each had a life separate from the other, an entire world, and their time was up. Due to the recent security measures at all airports in the wake of the 9/11 terrorist attacks, he was forced to leave her at the front of the terminal, which annoyed him, for he wanted to stretch out their final moments together.

He walked around to open the door for her. As she got up to exit, she threw her arms around him, tears in her lovely eyes, and they kissed as passionately as they had when they first met. Their lips crushed against each other as they held their tight embrace for another lingering second.

When they stepped back to part, he mumbled a farewell and watched her walk away. He felt so empty as his eyes followed her through the electronic doors into the terminal, shadowing her until she moved beyond his view. They would see each other in a couple of weeks, and the thought of that meeting ultimately comforted them. As far as he was concerned, they should be together and these painful separations, this constant parting and reuniting, should end.

Nevertheless he accepted the fact that she was married and had children, and for whatever reason, she was not about to break up her family to be with him. It was illogical to expect her to toss all that aside for him. Still, he felt he was being rejected in some way. But that was the price he had to pay for their illicit affair. He just had to deal with it and wait for their next time together. Brooding about it didn't help.

Still dejected, he started the car and pulled out into traffic. Close to the exit going to the expressway, he noticed there was a line of halted cars ahead, moving slowly around a stalled automobile that was halfway on the shoulder of the ramp. The sky was overcast with dark clouds, suggesting the possibility of rain.

Finally, the cars started moving at near-regular speed, and his vehicle fell into line with the others, easing past the cause of the bottleneck. As he approached the ramp, he spotted a woman struggling to get out of the stalled car, twisting her body to avoid getting hit by the passing parade of impatient drivers. She frantically tried to wave down someone to give her a bit of assistance. The skies opened and the rain began to pour down. She wasn't wearing any protective rain gear. She was a large, rather shapely white woman with blonde, crinkly hair. She wore a short flowery dress that was getting soaked as the rain continued to come down into drenching, wind-whipped waves. The cars began to speed a little.

He could see how upset she was. It was at that point he decided to assist her. He pulled his vehicle behind hers and blew his horn twice before motioning to her to come to the window on the passenger's side. As she ran over to him, he couldn't help but notice how full and plump her body was, and particularly attractive to him was the way her huge breasts bounced while she ran the short distance to him.

He pressed the button to lower the window close to her. She had a faint smile on her face when she looked in at him, glad that someone had finally stopped to help her. Their eyes met. She noticed he was black, but at that moment she was soaked and didn't care.

"Thanks for stopping." She stood outside of his car, still getting drenched.

"I think you'd better get in before you get any wetter," he said.

As she entered, he noticed how her wet dress clung to her ample hips, thighs and breasts. The dress was short to begin with, but it rose even higher up her thighs as she got into the car.

"Thank you so much for stopping," she repeated. "I didn't think anyone was going to help me."

"What happened?" he asked, trying to not to gawk at the shape of her body now on display through the wet fabric. "That's a relatively new car. It shouldn't be breaking down."

"I don't know," she explained, wringing her moist hands in her lap. "You're right. I was sitting behind a car getting ready to get on the freeway and it stalled. I haven't been able to get it to start. I usually have a cell phone but I was in a hurry this morning and left it home."

"I'm sorry," he said, extending his hand. "My name is Miguel."

"I'm Shana." She shook his hand. He looked black but he had a Spanish name, maybe Puerto Rican or something like that. That didn't matter to her right now. She just wanted to get home.

Before she could say another word, he reached over the backseat and pulled out a towel. He gave it to her. "Here, you can use this. It's clean. Now, how can I help?"

She stopped drying her arms and hands. "Well, if you have a phone, I can try and call my husband. He can come and get me."

"Were you dropping somebody off at the airport?"

"Yes, my sister. She came in for my aunt's funeral. Aunt Evie."

He reached down on the seat and handed his phone to her. "Here. While you call him, give me your keys and I'll see if I can start your car. I'm no mechanic but hopefully it's something simple."

"Look, I really appreciate this," she said with a pleasant smile, then she started to dial up her husband. She gave him the keys.

Disarmed by her smile, he got in her car, opened her glove box and settled back in the seat. He put the key in the ignition and turned it over. The motor made a futile attempt to start, coughed some and fell silent. He tried again but it didn't even stir. Once more he attempted to get it going but it didn't even groan.

As he came back to the car, he noticed the woman was having a rather animated discussion. He didn't know if he should interrupt such a heated exchange. But he couldn't remain out in the rain, getting soaked and possibly catch a cold.

"Well, fuck you too, you no-good bastard!" She was screaming that when he got in the car. She broke into tears, her mouth trembling.

"Is everything all right?" He was no fan of crying, hysterical women. Yet being a somewhat sensitive soul, he sat there while she wailed away.

She held her face in her hands, her skin turning a beet red, and cursed between sobs. After a bit, he reached over, pulled her hands gently away and asked her what was wrong.

"It's my fucking husband!" she shrieked. "I called him to ask what to do and he fucking blew me off. He said he was in the middle of some meeting and couldn't be disturbed. I demanded that he talk to me. He took the phone and cursed at me. He said I was a stupid spoiled bitch. I should figure it all out on my own and leave him alone."

"So what now?" He didn't want to get involved in any drama.

She was still in a state of fury. "What a prick! He thinks he fucking owns me because he bought me this car. Shit, he bought it trying to make up for me catching him screwing my niece a few months ago."

He just wanted to go home and revel in the sensual glow of the last few days. He didn't need this, any of it.

Suddenly, Shana looked at him with supreme embarrassment on her face. She wore the expression of someone who was telling too much. "I'm sorry. I didn't mean to say all that. But I'm just so upset. Now I really don't know what to do."

Their eyes met again. There was a little something extra in her look this time. The old feminine wiles. A promise of something more than a handshake. That worried him.

"Look, I have the number to call for roadside assistance," he stammered, the car suddenly feeling smaller than before. "We'll call them. Have them tow the car to your house or the dealer. How does that sound?"

She was still sobbing a little. "But how am I going to get home? I live on the other side of town, past Springfield."

"Don't worry. We'll work that out after we talk to the car dealership. Just relax and it'll be OK." He was taking control of the situation, wanting to get this over and go home.

When he turned to look at her, she was wearing that same smoldering look. "Thank you so much," she said, moving a little closer to him, placing her hand on his as it lay on the seat between them. "I should apologize for being so damn neurotic and dramatic. You'll never know how grateful I am for all you've done."

Suddenly, there was the squeal of a police siren and the flash of red lights. She exited as fast as she could, pulling down her wet skirt. Her arm waved furiously as the cop car stopped on Miguel's side and two white officers got out, one walking around the front of their vehicle and the other coming up from the rear. Both had their hands resting quietly on their holsters.

The officer in front glanced at the white woman, then at Miguel. "Sir, can you step out of the car, please?"

He did as he was told, glancing at the officer behind him, then at the one who spoke. His hands were shaking and words were not coming out coherently. Careful, buddy, this could get real strange, he told himself. He made no sudden moves.

"What's the problem here?" the first officer asked, looking at Shana. "Are you OK, ma'am?"

"Do you have some identification, sir?" the other officer asked Miguel, holding out his hand. They were going to run a check on him to see if he had any warrants against him.

For three beats, she was silent, her eyes locking on the terrified black man. Whatever might have happened next was never going to happen, she thought. She quickly returned her gaze to the officer questioning her, smiling to let him know all was well. The officer to the rear motioned for Miguel to walk back and get into the backseat of the police cruiser while the other two chatted near her stalled car. Miguel eased onto the seat and the officer closed the door, still watching him with the hand on the holster. He watched the whites, the cops and the woman, chatting among themselves, with her becoming animated and pointing back at him. One cop got on his radio and was talking while the other talked with Shana and occasionally looked back at him.

Oh shit, Miguel thought. He closed his eyes and tried to put his mind somewhere else. The image of him with his head between Carlotta's smooth thighs flashed into his head, his tongue on the moist button of her clitoris, around the edge of her labia, face buried in it, her voice screaming yes yes yes right there, keep it right there. He shifted on the seat and peeked at the trio, all looking under the hood of her car. Then his eyes closed again. Carlotta's mouth open now in a silent scream, his fingers in her, two of them, and his tongue replacing them with her shouting in yelps before she began arching her back and twitching, her shimmering legs outstretched as far as possible.

Then there was a knock on the door and the officer yanked it open. "Everything checks," he said in an official voice. "You can go."

Miguel had a huge erection, the by-product of his fantasy, and it showed when he stepped out of the cruiser. The white officer glanced quickly at it, his blue eyes narrowing, and then glared at the black man, his hand still on the holster. You could see he was trying to figure out what was on this man's mind. Was he a pervert? Was this boner due to the white woman? What was the deal?

"Step closer, sir," the officer finally said. "Open your mouth. Exhale."

Miguel was dumbfounded by the request. He had not been drinking. All he'd done was to stop to help out a white woman in distress, nothing more, nothing less.

Good deeds, my ass. Do as the man says and get the hell out of here, he concluded.

"OK, everything's fine," the officer said, waving him on. "Get in your car. You may leave. We'll take care of this situation."

He walked back to his car, got in and started the engine. The woman waved at him, smiling but he didn't wave back. He looked down. All of the starch was gone from his dick and a shriveled weenie was there in its place. What a day! It continued to rain, hard and fast as he switched on the windshield wipers. He felt like crying but didn't, fighting back the tears with a repeated mantra, "they can't take that away from me, they can't take that away from me." The joy and bliss of his time spent with Carlotta. He chanted that all the way home, through dinner and the news, his phone call with his girlfriend in Vegas, and before bedtime. It really didn't make him feel any better. It only provided temporary relief. But when he held the sex-soaked sheets to his nose, the glow of the joy came out in his head and heart and all was right again with the world.

# Male and Females

**Cole Riley**

His head was reeling from the previous night's bachelor party—
the booze, the stags on a rampage, and the strippers who said
they would do anything and everything for the right amount, then
delivered on their promise. Both had been handpicked, for the boys
knew he was an ass-man. Loved the booty. The tall one, dark sister
from Barbados, proved to be a marvel, gifted with hands, mouth, and
other parts of her. She was the most popular for she took on the
brothers two and three at a time. And wore them all out! But it was
the shorter one that caught his eye, sporting incredibly perky
breasts, thin waist, and a butt that put J. Lo to shame. The rear view
of her assets was sensational, causing him to think more about the
posterior of his bride-to-be, Olivia, who was gifted in this area but
somehow paled next to the booty on this copper-colored woman.

"Ever seen anything like that?" asked Calvin, who was an expert
in the field, known for his private collection of shapely butt picture
scrapbooks. A computer geek, he frequently made trips to Rio during Carnaval just to take ass shots of the fabulous beauties who
danced in endless samba lines along the city's thoroughfares.

"Damn! What a boo-tay!" yelled Howard, another professional
butt watcher, who considered the close scrutiny of a finely curved
backside a matter of Zen contemplation.

Marvin was more hands-on than most. Being a dentist, nothing
could prevent him from sampling a woman God had put together so
exquisitely. His digital examinations of the female caboose and
follow-up analysis of his work would have inspired Sir Mix-A-Lot to
pen a second righteous ode to the smoothness and curves of one of a

black woman's most alluring body parts. His marriage didn't keep him from visiting strip clubs, buying porn DVDs with rear action, or going to private shows with exotic dancers who loved to push their high bubble bums into the excited faces of their male onlookers.

"Got to get some of that before I leave here," Marvin whispered. "What you gone do, Mr. Man? This is your last night of freedom before you fall victim to the old ball-and-chain. If you pass this up, you're a fool. Better hit it while you can."

He didn't answer his friend immediately, instead he watched as Calvin sucked one of the woman's breasts, then the other. Another of their pals, Frank, was rubbing that ass while he pumped viciously into her from behind. He kept his eyes on them until Frank finally got his fill, trembled like a man electrocuted, and dropped to his knees. The cute one with the stunning rear end reached around and palmed her lover's still-stiff cock, smiling.

"Like that?" she asked the groom-to-be with larceny in her eyes. "You're next. I've got something special in mind for you. Step up and get your wedding gift."

The boom box was playing an oldie, "Stay In My Corner" by the Dells, a record he'd slow-danced and grinded to with many girls during his hormone-drenched adolescence. All of his eight male buddies, his crew, were getting busy throughout the hotel room—on the floor, against the walls, in the doorways, on the sofa, and even on the windowsills. If their wives could see them now, there would be hell to pay, especially with the fragile state of some of the marriages. A few of these guys had a history for shattering their wedding vows, heeding the call of their roving eyes and unquiet dicks.

"No, thanks, I think I'll pass tonight," the groom-to-be replied, a hand shielding his excitement from the other guys.

There was a collective moan and taunting from the fellas throughout the room. But he didn't mind. In his thirty-nine years, he'd sampled more pussy than most of them had seen in their lives, real foxes, plowing through it all, and then there was his sorry record as a husband. But now he was a retired satyr. Three times he'd been to the altar and said the magic words. Three times he'd screwed it up. For once, he wanted to do everything right, to do his part as a good man and husband. He loved Olivia, his dark beauty, a woman who was the epitome of common sense, thrift, fidelity, and sensuality. She was a real catch. She was twenty-five, in school for advertising, and a looker that often turned heads when they were out on the street.

"I don't get it, Andy," Frank said, kneeling close to him. "All of this pussy here and you acting like a priest. You can bet those hens got your lady at her party doing all kinds of nasty shit to those hunky stripper boys. I know my wife."

He wasn't hearing it. This time he would play it straight. No secrets. He remembered his first wife, Debbie, an exotic dancer she called herself. A group of them went to a downtown club where she was performing, spinning around the pole under the bright lights, doing things with various toys, letting the leering men place dollar bills into her G-string. Then their eyes met and afterward he asked her to join him for a drink, which she did.

"You're not too bad," Debbie, also known as Spice, told him after they had sex in her antique Mustang convertible. He later learned it belonged to her boss, who she was also screwing on occasion. "What you lack in technique, you made up in zeal. You got a lot of energy and I love the way you kiss."

But he was eighteen, and the future, kids, a house and responsibility were the last things on his mind. Still, he was horny as hell most of the time. Before Spice, he'd had sex with only three girls, all disasters, since they were squeamish and inexperienced. It pissed him off when they yelled it hurt, pull it out. Sometimes he went home with a case of aching blue balls and relieved himself manually, spraying his DNA into a pillow tucked between his legs. That all changed with Spice and her hourglass body in the picture. It was her idea to pick up a couple bottles of wine, some herb, and go to a motel. He did it just to see what it would be like, and man, they spent the night, sexing for hours and hours.

She loved kissing him everywhere. It was obvious she was into it and not just doing it like her routine at the club. Touching him all over, totally comfortable with her body, unlike the girls from before. Once he got her dress and panties off, they fell into bed or on the floor for some slow, steady fucking. Mostly with her on top, her soft hands stroking his hairless chest, as she slid up and down his dick. Sometimes he asked her to turn around so he could watch her tight, perfect ass while he thrust deeply inside her agile, young body. They had sex every time they saw each other, three times a week, and several times a night. You can do that when you're eighteen and your machinery is still in mint condition. But most of all, he loved that Spice talked to him, like a grown-up, like a friend, cozy and open like an old couple with some years behind them.

"How old do you think I am?" Spice asked after a particularly satisfying session. There was sweat dripping from her face. He felt one of her legs shaking underneath his.

"I dunno. Twenty-six?" His guess was based on his thought that she was too flexible in the sack to be thirty or older. That would be like seeing his mother in bed with the old man.

"Thirty-five," she said, hoisting a well-muscled leg straight into the air.

He was shocked—damn she was in good shape. "You go to the gym a lot, right?"

"Whenever I can," she replied. "I've had a lot of guys. Guess why I like making love to you, Andrew? And I've had guys with huge equipment, guys with stamina where they could pound all night, guys with a deep knowledge of endless positions. Guess why I chose you?"

He had no idea. He lifted her hair to nuzzle the soft curve of her neck, played with the small soft lobe of her ear before planting a light buss behind it. She trembled and smiled. "Hell if I know," he answered quietly.

"I love how you kiss," Spice said. "Most black men don't know how to kiss, unfortunately. But you do. You know what to do with your mouth. Your kisses are warm, soft, and passionate. You're tender and gentle. Most men grind their mouths against yours, no sense of sensitivity or emotion, just flesh to flesh. I love it when you do it because your kisses fill my thoughts, heighten you being in me, and make the whole thing more personal. In fact, I love when you kiss all of my lips, you know what I mean?"

They laughed together while she continued to stroke his penis, all the while looking deeply into his eyes. During that session and others that followed, he learned a lot about her: her two failed marriages, the death of her only baby from SIDS, the death of her abusive second husband in a head-on crash with a drunk driver, her battle with drugs, and her dream to save enough money to open a beauty salon.

"Black women love to get their hair done," she laughingly told him. "It's a ritual with them."

One Saturday afternoon, they drove the Mustang to Vegas after she got off work, found a wedding chapel, and let an Elvis clone marry them. One of the witnesses was on something, eyes rolling around in his head, started singing the King's classic, "Love Me Tender," to a polka beat before the chapel's owner threw him the hell out. That should have be an omen, for once they moved in together, him with her, the troubles started. If you want to find out the darkest secret about your mate, come home unannounced, which was what he did. Tiptoeing quietly, he moved through the house, stopping to observe a pile of clothes, thrown off hurriedly it seemed, on the floor near the coffee table. His heart pounded with each step, each footfall toward the half-opened door of their bedroom. He heard them before he saw them. Spice, his wife, was straddling a young woman, Jean, the Dominican chick from her job, bent over locking tongues with her while her other hand ran a vibrator in expert circles over her lover's damp sex. Endless buzzing and moans. The shock of the unbelievable sight was mesmerizing and nailed him to the spot. He only moved when they shifted positions, locking their legs in a V, joined at the pelvis, rolling like restless sea waves against each other until the Latin girl cried out: "*Mi vida,* eat my *chucha*! I want to feel your tongue in me, *por favor.*"

That night, he collected his belongings, listened to her plead that she would never do it again, that she was bisexual but that she would hold it in check for the sake of their marriage, then packed his bags and drove off to a motel. The phone rang several times, relentlessly, all through the night, but he never answered it. He got a divorce shortly after that and ended a period where he avoided women, no matter how much ass they had.

The phone was ringing now. Melvin trotted to pick it up, spoke into it, and then held it out to Andy. "It's for you, chief," he said, laughing.

It was his wife-to-be, Olivia. "Hey, baby, you having a good time?" she asked. "Didn't mean to bother you. Yes, I did, just checking on you. You behaving yourself?"

"Yes, dear." He grinned, trying to sound like a henpecked husband.

"I hope you're leaving those skanky wenches alone," she joked, not really joking. "Don't mess up and pick up something you bring to our marital bed."

"You don't trust me?" he asked, watching Melvin pushing into the sex of the tall woman at the sofa, her legs spread to allow him deeper into her.

"Sure, I do," Olivia replied. "I just want you to be a good l'il boy."

"Don't worry," he said in an assuring tone. "It's you I want."

"Good, that's all I wanted to know," she said firmly, trying to talk over the noises and whistles in the background. The muscle boys must have been putting on quite a show. "I'll have something for you after we say the words that you'll never forget. Believe that, sweetie. Well, I gotta go."

No sooner than Olivia hung up, Frank got all into his business, teasing him about how being soft, about letting his wife-to-be keep tabs on him, about how she was going to keep him on a short leash. This really didn't bother him. His second wife, Audrey, taught him all about jealousy, mistrust, and short leashes. Orphaned at eight, she had been raised in a religious home for abandoned and abused youngsters, a strict and moral institution that preached the evil of sin and the impurity of sex in all its incarnations. Stung by the failure of his first marriage, he considered Audrey and her attitudes of no sex outside of marriage a pleasant change of pace when compared to the wanton desires of Spice and her no-holds-barred view of carnal acts. Average height, with sweet girlish features and a stacked body that seemed at odds with her sacred beliefs, Audrey told him on their first date that she never touched herself and considered too much thought of the flesh to be harmful to the salvation of one's soul. He figured that he would turn her out once they got married, like many brothers did with the Catholic girls who were pent up and starved to break free sexually once they got the chance. His boy, Paul, was married to one and she was a real vixen, causing him to suffer a severe fracture of the penis after one of their heated nightly sessions. To look at her, you would not think she held those possibilities, but once the lights were low, look out! The woman was a smoldering tigress, all desire barely confined under a veil of piety, and that was what he felt about Audrey, just waiting to get her freak on. Her body, in all its splendor, cried out for some good, strong loving. They got married at her church after a chaste three-year courtship with only closed-mouthed kissing and light petting allowed, always clothed.

"I know sex is important to you, Andy," she said on their honeymoon night. "But understand this, I think it should be mainly for making babies and little else. I wouldn't deny you that."

"Are you saying you won't perform your duties as a wife?"

"I never said that," she replied sternly. "I'm just saying I will *not* be your sex toy. Simple as that. I will not let Satan into our bedroom. Is that understood?"

"I guess," he said, thinking on what she meant. "But what does that mean?"

"You should not try to make me do anything that could lead to my damnation," she quickly said, her eyes flashing with seriousness. "I think you know what I mean by that. I've seen some of those dirty magazines at the newsstand. Disgusting. And not even sanitary. So do I make myself understood?"

Three nights after their honeymoon, he went for broke, deciding to test her resolve. During the day, he'd tried to give her a little peck and she turned her head, forcing him to miss. Then she proceeded to lecture him on why women should not be sexually aggressive, "forward" as she put it, and doing whatever the Devil put in their heads. No, sir. No perversion. He smoked a cigarette, which was a rarity for him, only because it opened the door for another pious lecture on the sins of tobacco and physical dissipation. Following some coaxing, he launched a full assault on her senses, using words, kisses, caresses, everything in his bag of seducer's tricks. It was his firestorm of kisses, passionate but passive, that lowered her guard and brought forth a small, submissive moan. For the first time in her young life, she felt hot surges of excitement coursing like powerful voltage through her supple body to that nexus between her soft thighs. He saw her smile in a way he couldn't have imagined, a wide serene smile, a smile that said she loved him. She trusted him.

"Is that better, darling?" he asked, kissing her closed eyes lightly.

"Yes, Andy, I've never felt like this before," she murmured, kneeling before him to stroke the front of his pants, surprised at the heft of him under the fabric. Slowly her fingers engaged the zipper and drew it down, revealing his iron tumescence.

"See, it won't bite," he teased, watching her stand, then shed her clothes to lay before him on the bed. A magnificent vision of toffee-colored flesh, waiting for his touch. She parted her legs so he could witness that she was sopping wet, before throwing her panties at him. When he caught them, he recognized that they were soaked in the crotch and sniffed them once, inhaling her near-virginal scent. Soon his kisses were trailing up her perfectly formed legs, but his eyes remained on the increasing turbulent heaving of the woman's full breasts. His breath quickened when he saw the triangle of curly black hair between those legs, causing him to separate them even more. Eventually, he lowered his head onto her lower lips, lightly licking, tasting, stroking, until her body arched off of the bed, leading her to scream more than once. She was trying to scoot away, when the waves of orgasmic bliss got the better of her, short-circuiting all of her reason and control. Her hands clamped his face into the center of her, while she repeatedly climaxed, giving off hoarse shouts and bucking wildly into his mouth.

Between pants, she asked him earnestly, "Andy . . . you aren't the Devil, are you?"

He lifted his head slightly, catching a breath before going back under. "No, darling, I'm not. Trust me."

"It feels too good, Andy, it feels so good," she mumbled. "This must be wrong, feels too good."

"No, baby, everything's OK." Another series of licks under the clitoris made her wrap her legs around his head, then she yelled something almost biblical and tried to snap his neck in her trap of flesh. Suddenly she sat up and pushed him back, before seizing his thick meat in her grip and marveling at how it twitched and pulsed in her hand like a trapped wild animal.

It was a low growl that she emitted from her lips. "I want this, now." A demand. It was if she was possessed, by him, by his lust for her, by his thing that was now benignly in her fist.

He needed to hear those words. He mounted her, placing her legs up over his shoulders, teasing her tingling pussy lips with the tip of his dick until she whimpered, disappearing gently inside her while she fought to breathe, and then he started moving, an accelerating rhythm, fast, faster, faster. She gave out a tortured yelp and bumped hard back against him in her sanctified version of his sex dance, holding fast to his arms. Twice he thought his back might give out, but he didn't let up, not even when she yelled for him to take it all, not even when she garbled out a warning of her impending death. She began hollering again as he slammed it all the way in and pulled it out suddenly. Something snapped in her, and she crammed it back inside, riding him until finally she screamed at the top of her lungs, a crazed banshee wail.

Before he knew it, she leaped from the bed, then slapped him cruelly across the face, "Damn you! You are the Devil's spawn." He saw stars, heard her pad in bare feet to the bathroom.

She remained in there for several hours, with him knocking and pleading for her to come out. There was not a sound coming from inside. He was worried. He thought she could be doing something to herself. His pleas were totally ineffective. Finally, he put his shoulder to the door, ramming into it with all of his strength, and soon it gave way. When he saw her squatting on the bathroom floor, it startled him to watch her laughing and crying, her face twisted, her eyes large and desperate. Something had broken inside her. Whatever it was had scared the hell out of her. She kept mumbling that he was Satan, that he had won over her body with diabolically evil tricks, that she would be doomed to eternal damnation. Nothing could move her from her refuge. She was still in there when he went out for juice, eggs, and wheat bread the next day. But upon his return, all of her things were gone and a divorce notice appeared three months later. He never saw Audrey again.

Someone shook him, snapping him out of his reverie. The phone was once more held before his face. "It's your beloved again," Frank intoned snidely, shaking his head.

"Yes, baby, what's up?" He was wondering if she was having any fun at her party.

"Bored," she said without any spunk. "These women have lost their damn minds, We may have to call the police to get these guys out of here alive. They got one guy holed up in the bathroom and the other is threatening to leave if they don't get their act together. I believe he's really scared. You've never seen estrogen when it's out of control. It's not a pretty sight."

"What are you doing?" He didn't really want to know.

"Watching them act a fool," she said. "Are you behaving yourself?"

"Yeah, all I got was a itty-bitty blow-job, just to tide me over." He chuckled, but the joke didn't go down well.

She took a deep breath. "If I even thought . . . Don't make me have to come over there. I'll Bobbitt you in a minute. Hear me?" There was something in her tone that said she was capable of doing a trim on him without a second thought. He was already her property.

"Just joking . . ."

"Well, I don't play that, not at all." She hung up.

Frank and Melvin were on him this time. "Man, she sounds like trouble. Maybe you need to give this thing some second thoughts. She sounds totally paranoid." They were both speaking at the same time. He couldn't figure who was saying what.

Paranoid. They didn't know the meaning of paranoid. Kathy equals paranoid. Kathy equals crazy. Kathy equals the finest time he'd ever had in bed. Who was Kathy? The first time he met Kathy was four years ago, while hitchhiking along the interstate in New Jersey, his car, a new Chrysler having died on the side of the road. It was dark and cold. The snow, whipped by the strong winds, stung his face, but he kept trudging along, waiting for someone to stop. Kathy did. She was driving her aged mother out to get a *TV Guide* in the middle of one of the worst winter storms in decades, semi trucks turned over on the side, cars huddled in multivehicle smashups or abandoned. It was madness to be driving in such a storm.

"Thank you for stopping," he said after getting in the car. Kathy smiled and introduced herself and her mother, who kept quiet, watching him with a lethal evil eye. With her long gray hair and wrinkled face, she looked like a witch on the prowl for souls. She said nothing for much of the trip, while he and Kathy exchanged chitchat and information about their jobs, backgrounds, the winter, the basketball playoffs, and the Gulf War.

"Were you in the Service?" she asked.

"No, bad knee." He replied. "They didn't take me."

Her mother interjected with a grunt and smirk. "Looks like a convict. He smiles too damn much. Never trust a Negro that shows his teeth too often."

"How far are you going?" she asked. "Where can I drop you?"

"Just beyond the bridge. I can get a tow truck to get me off the highway. You don't know how happy I am you stopped for me. Thanks a lot."

At the gas station, Kathy, with her impish face, bee-stung breasts, and wide bottom, apologized for her mother and gave him her number. Later in the week, he called her and began a phone chat that lasted for another two months before they hooked up that first time. They went to a movie in the city, dinner, drinks, and bowling where she almost killed a white guy in the next lane with a ball that sailed out of her hands. It hit him in the chest and he went down. His friends ran over to him. Kathy was laughing so hard that she had to run to the john to keep from wetting herself. That was the first clue.

They put off making love for the longest time. He was afraid of his bad luck streak. A history of misfits and mishaps. Marco, a gay guy at his sales job, said he should switch, try the big boys and find out what real satisfaction was all about. Weenies and buns. He added that men are always so much more predictable, pivoting to shake his booty. He laughed at Marco. And on that fifteenth date, he and Kathy got down to business—their lips met, their tongues tangoed, and it was on. On the way home from a late snack, she shoved him into a dark alley and pushed him against a brick wall, quickly shoving her hand down into his pants. His hands could feel the steam rising from beneath her panties. When he twisted her panties around and explored her sex, his fingers immediately touched wet, matted pubic hair and then moved on to caress the smooth cheeks of her ass, taut and firm. She purred to his touch and grabbed his hands, separated three fingers and filled herself with them. Grinding her pelvic bone against his fingers, she climbed him like a cedar tree, rolled her hips against him, trapping his hand deep inside her wetness.

"Do you have a place?" she asked.

"Yes, twenty minutes from here," he said. "Wanna go there?"

Sometimes a man cannot seem to shake a run of bad luck— especially with women, with matters of the heart—that can run on for years, gobbling up one's youth, potency, and hopes. Kathy was the worst kind of trap, a velvet trap, a siren with a wicked body and the wisdom of how to use it. A few of the old-timers have said that passion and fantasy makes for the best lovemaking, over and above technique, fancy tongue work, tricky fingers, and unfettered perversity; going all out, unafraid, pushing the body to the limit.

But Kathy had that gift and more. Having sex with her was like screwing an insane person, someone with no barriers or boundaries, someone who believed in putting all of herself into it each time. She brought no fear or apprehension to sex. He loved to look at her ass, breasts, and the way her curves fell into place, but it was her clit that fascinated him, for it was unusually big. After they married, there was no stopping her. She would rub her clit, that familiar circular motion, while she waited for him to rest, then it was on again. With foreplay, fondling, and relentless penetration, she probably came about ninety percent of the time, often ejaculating like a man, shooting off an arc of clear fluid from her hairless pussy. Frequently, he got on hands and knees, watching and waiting for her to climax, secretly hoping that it would tire her out and put a close to the night's frolic.

No dice. She would be still turned on, even after four, five, six rounds of serious boning. Her mouth would cover his dick, sucking, slurping, urging him to get it up one last time. Finally his dick would stir, sore and tender to the touch, yet ready for another round. Her fingers massaged his balls, stroked his shaft, testing its firmness, and at last she'd sit astride him with her thighs bent back, rocking and rolling, her eyes closed to the smacking sound of her buttocks slapping against him. Swaying her bottom, she'd move hard and strong on him, her knees up now, her breasts bouncing to the clave beat. He kept up with her, trying to hit the core of her before the explosions came, one after another, draining him even more. Sometimes she ripped his penis from its hiding place to see the jets of milky fluid shoot off into the air, caught them either in her hand or mouth.

She was killing him. He was thirty-five, in his second prime, but felt sixty, or maybe seventy.

"Andy, do you know anything about the different types of orgasm?" Kathy asked him one day as they fooled around in the shower. "They're not the same, you know."

He shrugged his shoulders, putting his face directly under the jet of lukewarm water. He didn't know. In fact, most men probably did not know.

"The vaginal orgasm is best, total, more full and complete," she explained. "It comes in waves, one after another until the body is swallowed up. That is why I love having you in me so much. And your dick is just the right size. It's not too big and not too small. It fits just right. The clitoral one, when you put your mouth on me, is more intense, sharper, stronger in a way. It's much more predictable than the other one. With you inside me, it can be faint, gentle, or powerful and concentrated. You never know. That's the fun of it."

He no longer cared to know. She was killing him, fucking him to the grave. No rest. No timeouts. Every night, full out, until his heart felt as if it was going to explode. He began to pee blood and get cramps, blisters on his weenie, and even bruising and puffiness. His doctor told him to go easy or he'd be worn out by the time he was forty. She gave him pills, vitamins, herbs, elixirs to keep his strength up and his jimmy hard. But the doc told him to go easy. So that was what he did, went easy and quiet, packed once more and left after a back-breaking, lung-burning all-nighter that left him with a splint on his Johnson, a heart murmur, and a big bottle of painkillers.

Three marriages, three tries, three failures. What had he, as a man, learned from all of his trouble? Maybe that he had been a dumb cockhound, a booty worshipper, and not mindful of his women's other needs. The only emotions he seemed to feel on a general basis were rage, resentment, and regret: the three R's. He hated the way he'd lived his life, the wasted years, the missed opportunities, the poor choices, the quest for the perfect ass and the best sex. Even though men were supposed to be in charge, make the rules, they damn sure didn't seem to know what the hell they were doing. Most of them bumbled along like he had, believing women were weaker, dumber, emotion-driven, and unpredictable. And yes, unreliable too. When the real fact was that women understood men much better than men understood them. Maybe women, especially black women, were the only ones to really evolve beyond the mammal stage, beyond their base urges and desires, whereas men seemed to have a long way to go.

The next day, he sat there in a back office of the cathedral where the wedding was to take place, his mind full of doubts, not about her but about himself. Was this marriage another mistake? Would his problems be solved by a happy marriage? Could he make her happy? Or would this be mistake number four? Was he doing it again anyway? Were all of his marriages alike in some way if you looked closely at them? How were they the same? How were they different? What if they can't talk? What if they're not sexually compatible? What if she isn't "the one"? Is it too late to back out?

But Olivia loved him, in a complete way, in a mature way. Theirs was a relationship built on more than sex, orgasms, and thrills. There was a common trust, respect, communication, values, and she was not going to put up with any of his foolishness. That was a good thing. Plus he loved her, fully, deeply, and totally, in a manner that had eluded him with his previous wives. They had a chance, a real chance, to maybe last and grow old together with their grandchildren around them. Just maybe.

Suddenly, there was a knock on the door. It was Deacon Lipscomb, head of the church's Deacon Board and the man who had the reverend's ear. The fat man was in all white, wearing his customary smile and smelling of Old Spice.

The deacon took one look at his face, frowned, and asked if he was all right. "Boy, there's nothing to it," he said, waving him on. "You been down this road before. Take a deep breath and it'll be over before you know it. Come on now."

With that, Andy sighed, listened to the bass tones of the organ playing the Wedding March, the murmur of the guests, and followed the deacon out to his fate. The man was right. He had done this all before. Like riding a bike, getting a molar yanked, or watching a pretty ass move sweetly down the street. Nothing to it but to do it.

# Coming of Age

## C. Kelly Robinson

Pressing the accelerator, Maxwell Jordan whipped past another block of mushrooming shops and restaurants. The roaring of his red Mustang's engine was now a tinny whine, filling his ears as he passed Tri-County Mall and neared his destination. His heartbeat jerked and pitched with the rhythm of the engine's pleadings, as he recalled Andre's desperate appeals. He and his son had finished arguing hours earlier, but for Max the encounter still smelled like freshly baked bread.

Andre's pleas bounced around his brain as he hurtled into the emptying parking lot of Zulu's restaurant. "Swear to God, Pop! I swear to God I ain't poke that girl without coverin' up!"

As the realization he might soon be a thirty-two-year-old grand-father settled in, Max's mind had filled with temperature-cooling thoughts. *Stay cool. He's no different from you at that age.* He had gathered himself, crossing his arms and flexing a fist before respond-ing. "You stupid son of a bitch," erupted from his mouth, though the words flowed with emotionless precision. If he let feelings reign, he'd lose control of his lips, teeth, and tongue. His stutter insisted on patience; either speak at the cadence of a robot or go the way of Porky Pig.

He had stood from his low, scarred kitchen table and reared back then, ready to cut his mouthy child down to size. Andre had three inches of height on him, but there was little meat on his bones.

The boy's cringing was what saved him. The sight of Andre flinch-ing, as he stepped back and lowered his eyes, drained the violent anger from Max's soul. Feeling himself cool, he dropped his fists and leaned against the table. "D-Do you realize the position this puts me in, Andre?"

The boy glared at him with wounded eyes. "I ain't know who her mother was."

"Never mind that, that's on me," he responded, his voice growing husky. "The point is, you don't need no baby." He grabbed a patch of his long, twisty locks and left his hand there. "Wouldn't have the first clue how to raise one, that's for damn sure."

Andre took a cautious step toward him, his gangly arms at his sides now. "Why don't you tell her mom that, then?"

"W-Why didn't you tell me about this as soon as you knew?"

"I thought I could talk her down, Pop. She knows I don't love her. She don't even want no kid. Her mother's the problem."

The mother, that's who was on Max's mind as he stepped from his car onto Zulu's paved lot. Dynah Thompson was her name, and she owned this restaurant along with her husband Kenneth. They had been married for roughly ten years, if Max's math was correct. If you had strapped him to a lie detector, he might have failed the test, but in his heart Max didn't believe he still loved Dynah. That didn't mean she wouldn't always be with him, in her own way.

It was just after ten this Wednesday night, so the restaurant had just closed. Max took tentative steps toward the main entrance, a pair of tall doors wrapped in what looked like tree bark. When neither door gave, he looked in vain for a ringer before pulling his cell phone off his hip. "I'm out here," he said when she answered.

It had been more than a decade since he had seen Dynah, so he fought pleasant surprise when she opened the doors and stood before him. At five foot ten, Dynah was nearly his equal in height, and from what he could glimpse in the dim light of the restaurant foyer, she still possessed a voluptuous figure free of excess fat. Her hair was plaited in short waves, framing an oval face with strong cheekbones and narrow eyes covered by round black-framed glasses. Time had been kind to her, but with the glasses and the conservative black business suit, Dynah looked much older than Max felt.

Only when he caught himself admiring the bulbous shape of her hips did he realize she had turned her back to him, doing away with social niceties. *Look at you, Maxwell Jordan. All these years pass and you still look like a kid. I like the beard, though. Never thought you could grow facial hair back in the day.* . . . Given the circumstances, maybe that was asking too much.

"Let's talk in my business office," she said over her shoulder, keeping her pace brisk as they crossed a cherry-wood floor and dodged busboys and janitors with mops, brooms, and wet rags in hand. Max glanced over at the sunken bar to his right and looked overhead, trying to figure how high the cavernous ceiling was. A mural was painted across it, filled with imagery Max recognized from years touring with his family in the early nineties: Ghanaian foliage, Senegalese countryside, South African seaside views. His nostrils filling with the smell of incense, he felt himself relax. "You've done a nice job here. Been hearing about this place since you opened."

"I'm up here," Dynah said, ignoring his tepid compliment and stopping in front of the noisy kitchen. She pulled back a curtain and pointed up a set of steps.

When they reached the upper floor, she pointed him to a maroon leather couch opposite her desk of black lacquered wood. Realizing she had no interest in small talk, Max took his seat. He waited patiently as she flipped through a stack of invoices sitting in her chair, then removed her jacket.

"Well, you may as well say what you have to say," Dynah said finally, rolling up her sleeves and taking a seat. "I couldn't finish this conversation over the phone. This is too important."

"I d-don't mind stopping by," Max said, trying to keep his pace slow and lowering his eyes from the sight of her toned, muscular arms. "You may recall I'm not much of a phone person anyway."

"Hmm, yeah." The sight of Dynah's pearly white teeth startled him as she smiled for the first time. "Took me forever to figure out why you never returned my phone calls."

"I never returned any girl's calls back then, least not any girl I wanted to like me."

"You preferred being a man of action, huh?" The curve of her lips, the way her tongue peeked from between her teeth, took him back. That was exactly what she'd done that first day in the pool house, when she had started his education . . .

He pinched himself back to present day. Let the past stay exactly where it was. "I d-don't want to waste your time, Dynah." He took an anxious glance around the small office, let his eyes rest on a family portrait near the edge of her desk. There she was, flanked by Marquita, Kenneth, and the two youngsters they'd had together. "Will your husband be joining us?"

"He doesn't know about this yet," she said, her voice firm but low. "Now, what did you want to say?"

*He didn't know.* Kenneth's ignorance wasn't hard to understand, based on what Max had heard about the brother's temper. Everything was secondhand, of course, but between folks from Dynah's church and Max's brother-in-law, who worked as a desk sergeant downtown, there had to be a few droppings of truth.

Shooing away stuff that wasn't his business, Max felt his chest tighten. He knew he was about to butcher his point, but he plowed forward. "I-I'm willing—" He held up a finger, signaling for her patience. "I-I'm w-willing to help with any expense, Dynah. Our children don't love each other."

"So you'll pay for her to kill the baby, that's your offer?"

"Look," he replied, feeling his way more confidently now, "you don't know my son. I love him, but he's as jacked up as I was at that age."

Dynah's eyes softened suddenly, though her back remained high and tight. "You weren't that bad. You were a class act compared with Marcus."

He nodded, recalling in an instant the trials Marquita's father had put her through. "Andre is not a carbon copy of me, understand. For one, he can talk pretty goddamn well. For two, he's a-arrogant as hell. P-Picture my brother Jamie without the wealth and fame."

Dynah's eyes darkened as she glanced at the desk. "Marquita's told me enough, I realize he's no saint. That's beside the point. As Christians, Kenneth and I believe that any life God allows is precious. We would never consider what you're suggesting."

"I'm speaking from experience," Max retorted, "a-and so should you. I have three children by three different mothers, in case you hadn't heard. Life ain't been no crystal stair just 'cause I allowed them to be born."

"I've done my share of dirt, Max, but that doesn't mean I haven't grown. Don't think Marquita wound up pregnant at sixteen for lack of home training. I taught her to be abstinent, save herself. Not to mention, I modeled responsibility for that girl. You think I married Kenneth for pure love? I was carrying little Kenny the day of our ceremony. So don't talk like I don't know the real world."

"Y-You know what," Max said, rising from his chair, "this is between you and your family. I can't handle this." He stood there in front of her, his fists balled, as he reflected on his life. He hadn't sold a song to a viable artist in three years, was relegated to playing in clubs he wouldn't have stepped foot in a decade ago, and had moved back to Cincinnati as a last resort, both to settle child support issues and to get back on his feet financially. He had raised Andre on his own for years now, and after plenty of other dramas there was no room on his plate for this one. He told Dynah to call him if she wanted money for the procedure, and let himself out of Zulu's.

The Quiet Storm was on the radio and he let that accompany his drive home. Smoldering, he laughed out loud at the irony of Dynah's pious words. This from the woman who first snared him in the thicket of his healthy loins. There was an argument to be made that Dynah Thompson's body had erased Max's hope of ever being the steadfast, monogamous husband her Bible spoke about.

She was sensuality personified the day she walked into his homeroom, sophomore year at North Central. Taller than him at the time, and blessed with the piercing eyes of Jayne Kennedy, the bosom of Pam Grier, and the toned thighs of the "Pleasure Principle" Janet Jackson. New to the public school system and suddenly weighted with a more insistent stutter, Max had tried to blend into his surroundings, anything to keep people from making him talk or trying to compare him to his famous family members.

Dynah and a short, plump girlfriend, Ronnie, sat at the homeroom table across from his each morning. Joined at the hip, the two cracked on other girls' physical flaws, ran down their most despised teachers, and slyly sang the sexual praises of their latest boyfriends. Max had drawn their attention the first few days—Ronnie had said something like *you too cute to be so quiet*—but he had quickly lost their interest. The latest sexual slang flew over his head, his jokes were too innocent, and he had nothing to share in the arena of "afternoon delights," the common after-school rush home, where teen lusts were indulged and babies made babies before Mama arrived home from first shift.

It took *Right On!* magazine to get him back on Dynah's radar. She and Ronnie were flipping through an issue one morning, when they paused at a full-page poster of his older brother with his music group, Family Ties. Ronnie was oohing and ahhing over it when she rooted her gaze to Max, willing his eyes to meet hers. "Anybody ever say you favor Jamie Jordan? They from Cincy, right? I think y'all were separated at birth."

He had played stupid, but that night they had gone home, reread liner notes on their CDs, and put two and two together. The rest of the semester, Ronnie and Dynah had taken him into their circle, trying to fix him up with girls who thought he was cute. He knew they were just using him to eventually meet Jamie, but by then Dynah had taken him over, in a way that he alone was privy to.

The more time he spent walking the halls with Dynah, hearing her and Ronnie's veiled tales of sexual conquest, the more addicted he became. Her sharp, sweet perfume, her smooth cardboard brown skin, her full woman's body—these sensations and more rocked him to sleep each night, as he turned up his stereo and pictured Dynah hopping up and down on his erect penis, over and over until his DNA was splattered across his bedsheets. All that, yet he dared not approach her with his feelings. She was seeing grown men, dudes who were college age in some cases. He kept to himself, literally, sheltering his passion close to the chest.

These and other resurrected images still haunted him a week later, as he sat before the piano at Club Rebirth. He tried to suppress them for the good of the crowd as he completed his rendition of Brian McKnight's "Anytime." Time was when these places wanted to hear his compositions; now he was just a conduit for the talents of others. His most recent solo CD was six years old, and no major label wanted a thirty-something has-been. This was his life. Marvin Gaye, Sam Cooke, Musiq, or Babyface: if he could hit the notes, he'd become whomever you wanted, long as you paid his ass.

As he pushed back from the piano, the club's hushed atmosphere hummed with polite applause. Max stroked his goatee and lingered a moment, mindful of his responsibilities. The owners insisted he wait around for the occasional fan who wandered in. No matter how far you fell, there was always some nostalgic soul who remembered you at your best.

The air filled with canned jazz and Max relaxed, figuring there would be no pseudo-fans tonight. He reached into his pocket for his cell phone, considered calling Andre to see whether he'd heard anything new from Marquita. The boy had spent last night at his mother's and hadn't called since leaving.

"Hello." The sudden greeting startled him. He arched his back and looked up into Dynah's eyes.

"Damn, you always were sneaky." He hoped his eyes evoked the smile he couldn't bring himself to form. "You could have just called me."

Her arms crossed over her navy business suit, Dynah spoke forcefully but seemed to be looking over his shoulder. "Buy me a drink?"

"Didn't Paul say something about forsaking wine?"

She smacked him on the shoulder. "I didn't say what *kind* of drink."

He grabbed his tuxedo jacket and rose, guiding her toward a table near the back. "D-Didn't Paul also say something about using the word fool?"

"If this is your way of lightening the mood," Dynah said, taking a seat, "consider your work done. I wanted you to know where things are headed."

Max began to scoot his chair closer to hers but corrected himself. "Okay, shoot."

"Kenneth and I are unable to agree," she said suddenly. She looked at the flaming gold tablecloth and began twisting her sparkling wedding ring. "The more I talk with Quita, the more I see she won't be a fit mother. She doesn't want a baby right now; she's insistent."

Max looked at the floor, then waved a waiter over. They ordered their drinks, and he nodded back in Dynah's direction. "Go ahead."

"Maybe I did too good of a job. She said she doesn't want to end up like me, can you believe that?"

Max blinked in response.

"I mean, she knows I wanted to open up a restaurant years ago, but held off because I had my hands full with her, not to mention that once I married Kenneth he thought the idea was too risky."

"He supports you now, doesn't he?"

Dynah's expression hardened. "As long as we keep making money, yeah. The minute that stops he's already told me we have to cut our losses."

Max sucked his teeth, trying to figure out how this was his problem. He had known just enough about Marquita, *before* learning whose child she was, to know that she was a varsity cheerleader and top student. He couldn't blame her for having ambitions. Matter of fact, if she already knew Andre had no intentions of being a real father, she had brains to match. It seemed Dynah was learning the unavoidable truth on her own.

"Quita's determined," she continued, her head down as the waiter brought their drinks, a Scotch for Max and a diet Coke for her. "She refuses to be knocked off course for college and med school. I'm trying to be the middle ground, saying she should have the baby and we'll put it up for adoption. But Kenneth won't have it. He says she must have it and accept our help raising it."

Max took a slow sip of his Scotch, wiped his eyes. "You realize you've got a split jury. Sounds like the k-kids are the only ones on the same page."

"But they're wrong," she said, leaning forward and stretching her hands toward him. "Aren't they, Max? What would be so wrong with just having the baby, and giving it to a loving home?"

Max stared at Dynah's outstretched hands. Etched with faint lines, they showed more age than the rest of her, but were still rich in color and smooth to the touch. As he gripped them, he entered another time and place.


Sophomore year again, an early spring field trip to a community pool. The pool and park grounds had been reserved for their class that day. Max had spent most of the day bullshitting with new friends, a cross-section of fellow basketball jocks and a few proven hoodlums who'd long since succumbed to the call of the streets. Though still a virgin, he was slowly emerging from his shell, cautiously taking part in games of "the dozens" and other bonding talk with the boys. He flirted increasingly with the girls, all of whom knew of his famous family and ranked him as "fine" in his own right.

He was becoming a man of mystery as well: not even the cutest girls could claim that Max had used their phone numbers, no matter how creatively they had slipped them to him. Though he knew he might eventually have his manhood questioned, his fear of tripping over words fueled a stubborn resolve: *better to let them think I can't talk than to call them and remove all doubt.*

He had been on his way into the boys' pool room, just before the lunch break, when Ronnie and Dynah called him out. He couldn't tell you what Ronnie had worn if you tortured him, but he still recalled the snug fit of Dynah's bright orange two-piece swimsuit. "Max," Ronnie had shouted from their perch fifty feet away, outside the girls' room, "Dynah said you got nothing but a pencil and two pebbles under those trunks."

Still smarting from having lost a game of dozens earlier, he waved them off. "A-All you two do is talk shit. D-Dynah just talks mess 'cause she know she couldn't handle this."

Ronnie brayed like a mule, but it was Dynah's response that made Max's pebbles flex. "Why don't you come over here after you clean up?" she said, smiling and sliding her tongue at him, "maybe I'll see what you're working with."

His insides juiced, he raced into the boys' room, jogged under a spigot in the community shower, and toweled himself dry. Grabbing his Jams shorts and a T-shirt, he dressed in a blur, blind and deaf to the antics of the other boys surrounding him. He waited until they were done wrestling and passing two joints among them, then watched them run back into the park. His heart hammering, he tried to mentally suppress the growing bulge in his shorts.

When he peeked his head inside the entrance to the girls' room, it was empty. He chewed his lower lip and looked forlornly at the pitted concrete floor. An overheated dick had frozen his brain, blinding him to the possibility he'd been set up.

Warm hands melted into his shoulder blades. "What's up?"

Max turned and faced Dynah, who grabbed his hips and nudged him backward. As he fumbled his hands around her taut waist, they crashed against the metal lockers.

* * *

He tried to stop his mental tape there as he considered Dynah's urgent question. "I can't tell you the right way to go," he said, clearing his throat but holding to her wrists. "I-I've told you what Andre and I are prepared to do."

"You wouldn't help care for the baby if we helped Quita raise it?"

Max's eyes ran from the pain in her voice. "We'd deal with it somehow. I know how a real, live baby changes things. I wouldn't let Andre disown his child, if that's what you're asking. But we don't have any money to speak of. I-I hope Marquita didn't think she was landing music royalty by hooking my son."

"This is payback, isn't it?" He could feel her temperature rise, saw new muscles pop out on her neck. "How else did my baby wind up with yours?"

Max felt himself flinch, hearing Dynah speak words that had danced around his mind as a question.

"I was wrong," she sighed, her shoulders shuddering. "I teased you, didn't I?"

It was her fault this time. He was sucked back into the pool room, as they huddled against the locker. Dynah placed his hands onto her firm round breasts first, whispering how he should circle them with his palms. When her nipples popped out and hardened, she eased her top down and drew his head to them, continuing the coaching. *Slow down, we got time. Lick around the edges, then suck, okay?* A patient, intent student, he followed instructions, feeling his knees buckle as he tasted her sweet, salty skin and inhaled her rosy perfume. Nearly on his knees, with his hands massaging her lower back, he licked and sucked away but fought the surge of semen coursing up the shaft of his steely, lengthening tool. That task became nearly impossible when she grabbed his right hand and inserted it into the soft, balmy folds between her thighs. What had Jamie said, the way he kept from coming too quick with new groupies, to keep his reputation intact? *Think about the least sexy thang you can, man: the ugliest girl in your class, the nastiest food you've ever hated, anything.*

The advice had served him fine, until Dynah sat him on the bench, tugged his shorts down, and began rubbing him in ways he'd never perfected on himself. "More than a pencil," she'd cooed over and over, until he gave up the ghost and sprayed the lockers with three leaping, pungent shots. Technically, he had been a two-minute brother, but she'd been only slightly amused. She had kissed him before asking, "This was your first time, right?"

"I-I'm still a v-virgin, if that's what you mean."

"Don't worry," she whispered as she tongued him and helped yank his shorts back on, "we'll fix that later."

"You didn't tease me, Dynah." They were outside the club, standing in front of her Grand Prix. He imagined he should be careful with his body language, just in case some friend of Kenneth's was lurking in the shadows, but that wasn't his problem, was it? She shouldn't be having this conversation alone in the first place. He took her hands in his again. "We weren't much more than children. You didn't earn any bad karma by dissing me, if that's what you're worried about."

"I played you," she said, shaking her head and looking at the asphalt. "I was wrong to promise I'd take things to the next level. It would've been the wrong way to learn the facts of life anyway. I didn't know anything about love."

Max tightened his grip on her hands but looked away. "Love wasn't exactly on my mind then. Not to mention the fact that the girl who broke my fall—Andre's mother—made you look like Mother Teresa."

"You're too kind. I really liked you, Max. Everyone thought you were cute, and obviously we wanted to meet some of your family too. But you were so shy—so quiet—I could never have been your girlfriend, not back then. It wouldn't have fit with what everyone expected of me."

Max smiled grimly, her words a simple confirmation of conclusions drawn years ago. "No hard feelings," he said, placing an index finger on her smooth, glossy lips. "Might have been nice if you'd broken me off all the way, but you got me started. I might still be a virgin if you hadn't stepped in."

In the dark night, Dynah's eyes gleamed bright, flashing in time with her words. "Maybe if I'd been smarter then, both our lives would be simpler today. Good night." She stroked his cheek before placing a kiss there.

"M-Maybe you should have Kenneth call me when you two work

this out with Marquita," he said softly as he held her door. She didn't answer, just let him close it as she started the ignition.

A side of him wanted to speak to Kenneth, a side that nearly drove to Zulu's the next night, after Max called to confirm Kenneth was manning the restaurant for the evening. Based on round-the-way chatter, Kenneth was no better a husband to Dynah than Max had been to the mother of his second child. The brother's righteousness about Marquita's situation would have been comical, except that it was tormenting a woman who had reentered Max's universe.

He chewed on his feelings but decided not to chase, instead focusing for the next two days on Andre. The boy had failed his latest proficiency test and needed to step it up. Max pulled him from the basketball team and sat down with him in the evenings, shortly after completing his weekday job at the warehouse. In between academic coaching, he tried slyly to prepare the boy for the possibilities of fatherhood.

He was reclined in his easy chair the next night, trying to stay awake through the evening's newscast, when the phone rang. Andre hadn't come home yet, but Max figured the boy was cooling his heels at his mother's, probably freaked out over Marquita's silence about her plans. As he raised the receiver, he steeled his spine, ready for another argument. "Andre, get your ass over—"

He knew who it was immediately. "It's not Andre."

He sat forward in his chair, grabbing an armrest with his free hand. "Hello. What's up?"

"You may as well know," Dynah said, her voice quivering like Jell-O, "Andre and Quita came by."

"I-I don't understand."

"They took matters into their own hands."

"Oh." He bent over, pulled at his hair anxiously. "I-I'm sorry. I know this is the last thing you wanted."

He could hear sobs building in her throat. "I need you, Max."

"I-I'll handle Andre, Dynah. If he p-pressured her, I'll kick his ass good."

"No," she said, her voice dropping to a whisper. "I want to come there. Kenneth won't look for me at your house. He went crazy when they told him what they'd done, chased them out of here and left a few minutes later, determined to track them down."

"You don't think they're headed here?"

"Andre said they were going away for a few days, to decide what this means for their relationship."

"Oh, they're in love now?" He knew his son was a bullshit artist, but this was news even to him. "Look, if coming here makes you feel better until we figure out what's going on, I'll leave a light on."

"Thank you."

Dynah wore no glasses when she showed up on the wooden porch of Max's shotgun house. He opened the door and watched the stride of her legs beneath her red skirt and matching silk blouse. She took an uninvited seat on his plaid couch and began to weep.

Unafraid of where it might lead, Max took a seat next to her. Gingerly, he raised her chin until their eyes met, then kissed her gently. She responded by wrapping his tongue in hers and drawing him close. His heartbeat pounding in his ears, he pulled away momentarily.

"You don't owe me, Dynah. What you did, that was no tease. It freed me." It was true; being with Dynah had instilled him with sexual confidence, opened the window to a world of expression that required no fluency, no expertise at articulation. The tools most important to communicating physical desire—his sex, his hands, even his tongue—had proven themselves perfectly reliable. He had sought in vain for an end to his stuttering; the world Dynah introduced him to required no such struggle.

He drew her closer, fearing his forgiving words might drive her away. "You have a clean slate with me, understand?"

"I understand," she said, her breath quickening as she began loosening the buttons on his shirt.

Relief flooded him as Dynah rolled his shirt down his arms. He removed her blouse and skirt with a blur of careful movements and pulled her onto his lap. She had worn no bra, so he rediscovered her nipples before deftly probing the damp space between her legs. As he let her rest her still-firm breasts against his chest and felt her envelop him, Max prayed to Dynah's God for grace. She had not owed him anything, but as they merged suddenly with a reverent, coordinated thrust, he felt an undeniable sense of peace. He had no silver tongue, but in this moment his body whispered every assurance she needed.

# A Fan's Love

(From the novel
*Days Without Weather*)

## Cecil Brown

That night on stage I was still too afraid to leave my routine, but I managed to get across some of my "message." I could not betray Lindsey. ". . . I once tried *not* to be a comic," I told them, "but I didn't have the willpower *not* to expose these impostors and hypocrites! They're everywhere. Things have gotten so bad that a friend of mine decided to sell his soul to the Devil. He called the operator to get the area code to Hell . . . The operator asked him, 'Where are you callin' from?' He said: 'Hollywood.' She said, 'That's a local number.' "

They knew what I was talking about and gave me a big hand. ". . . This town reminds me of my own home town back in the Deep South. Mr. Mose Tucker had him a nice business selling ice in the community. But this one sister kept buying her ice from the white man. One day somebody asked her why she kept buying her ice from the white man when Mr. Mose Tucker was selling it. The lady said, 'Well, I tell yo' the truf'—I tried 'em both and, you know, that white man's ice is just colder than that nigger's ice . . .' "

Somebody way in the back laughed with me. What I decided to do, then, was slip one more about the South.

". . . Sort of reminds me of my Uncle Lindsey. My Uncle Lindsey was lazy . . . I ain't bullshitting you . . . He was the original lazy nigger that we've all been trying to get away from . . . right?"

A black bourgeois couple were sitting in the second row so I directed the joke to them.

". . . Lindsey was sleeping under a tree one day and this white man from the North came up to him. 'Say, my good fellow, what're you doin'?' Lindsey said, 'Restin'.' The white man said, 'Why don't you get busy and develop your fields?' Lindsey said, 'Why?' 'So you can make a lot of money.' Lindsey said, 'What good is money?' The white man said, 'Money will bring you leisure.' Lindsey said, 'What'll I do with leisure?' White man said, 'Then you can rest.' 'But why do all that,' Lindsey wanted to know, 'when I'm restin' now.'

"My Uncle Lindsey was a very groovy guy—way ahead of his time. He was so hip that he had me believing that Jesus was a black woman with big tits and a big, well-stacked ass . . . that's right! Every time he saw a fine black woman he'd look at her and go, 'JEEZ-*US!*'"

The house got really happy and gave me a big hand. "Thank you. G'night!"

I was still standing right there on stage feeling like a cork bubbling up on one of them ocean waves. I knew I wasn't gonna get another big laugh as big as the one I done got, so decided to let it go. By now the people were clapping their hands big and loud enough to wake the dead. I saw a dude down in the front row put his fingers in his mouth and whistle a catcall. Right in the front row, all of them—the girl in the Midwestern scoop-up hairdo, the joker in the green polyester double knit, the two gays from West Santa Monica with short crew-cut hairdos—can't quite get those long, broad smiles off their faces.

Placing the mike back in the stand, I said, "Thank you. G'night!" What'd I do that for? They started clapping louder than before now. Was I really funny? A couple guys were standing up in the back.

Now, as I'm coming off the stage through the path of tables and chairs and laughing people, they were gleaming up at me like I'm some kind of imperial chieftain. A hand reached out and grabbed mine, its owner saying, "Thank you, man!" Long after he let my hand go, I still felt the encouragement in his grip. By that gesture he'd laid an accolade on me, given me an award for my courageous feat, like I'd been out on the basketball court—Dr. Magic Johnson or somebody. I hit the end of the aisle where a lot of people were waiting for me. Dap was already on stage, and over my shoulders I heard him—"Ladies and gentlemen, I've decided to give up part of my sex life. I'm trying to decide which half to give up: thinking about it or talking about it!"—but I'm still movin' very fast toward the broom closet.

I wasn't swift enough, though. A girl threw her arms around me as I hit the top steps to the dressing area and busted me on the lips with one of them big, juicy kisses that girls can give and nobody, not even faggots, can resist.

"You were *in-cread-dee-bull*!" she shouted and kissed me again. "I could NOT buleeeeve it!" turning to nobody in particular and going, "Do you believe this guy?" and then: "He's unbelievable! I mean, you were unbelievable! You really were!"

I looked at her—she looked like Jane Fonda and Catherine Deneuve rolled into one.

"What's your name?" I asked. I couldn't really think of anything else to ask. I was still pretty excited and everything. "Cheryl," she said.

That was funny, though, because practically every night I do my act I meet some chick and her name is always something like Cheryl. I just can't seem to get away from that type. Big titties. Shapely body. Blonde. Just ready to screw a comedian. Like me.

She leaned closer to me again. "Would you like a toot of coke?"

"Sure," I said, "but not here." We went over to her car—a nice little Porsche. When I really looked at her, she was quite a fine lady.

Inside, she unfolded the white package of coke while I rolled a dollar bill into a tube.

"Did I ever tell you the one about the man with the small head?" I asked.

She threw her head back and laughed. "Oh, you don't know how much I love comedy. I got sexually aroused when I saw you on stage! I really did."

"A couple went into this restaurant and there was a good-looking guy sitting across them. He was a very handsome dude but he had a very small head. So the girl said to her date, 'That's a very handsome dude, but what a small head,' and the guy she was with said, 'Oh, don't you know the story about him?' And she said, 'No, tell it to me.' Well, it seems that a long time ago this guy ended up on an island where he found this bottle in the sand. He opened the cork and a genie came out. The genie thanked him for saving her life and offered as his reward to grant any wish he might have. The genie was a real knockout, so the guy said, 'I'd like to sleep with you.' The genie said, 'I can't, I'm on my period.' And the guy said, 'Well, how about a little head!'"

Cheryl laughed so hard that I got a good glimpse at her full breasts without her noticing. I figured that if I kept telling jokes I'd end up in her pants.

She looked like a million girls you've seen before in *Playboy*. She was a modern goddess, an icon of our film age. Perfume exuded from her body and I wanted to kiss her red, full, smiling lips.

"I'd like to talk to you," I said, "but I'm not feeling well."

"Why? What's wrong," she asked, still smiling.

"I gotta lay down somewhere. Can we go to your house?" I was acting of course.

"Sure," she said, and turned the key in the Porsche. "Just tell me some more jokes."

I was acting, playing my favorite character, Mr. Jiveass Nigger, me. As the car swerved out into the street, a couple white boys walked around the car. They sneered at me, the very picture of an arrogant nigger with a pretty white woman, but sneer all you want, I thought.

"The lady who owns the club thinks I hate white people," I said to her. Thalia didn't think that, but I wanted to put Cheryl on. It was more fun when you put people on.

"You hate white people?" She laughed. "You're the kindest, the gentlest person I've ever met!"

"Well, that's what she told me," I said. "But I thank you for the kind words."

"They're crazy," she said, caressing the side of my face with her free hand. "I've never met anybody as friendly as you."

"Well, that's what she told me," I said. "I really appreciate that."

"Oh, it's no problem, believe me!" Cheryl said. "I'm just so happy to do anything for you. Know any more good jokes? I'm really getting turned on."

"A soul brother, from Midnight, Mississippi, died," I said, ". . . and . . ."

"Oh good!" Cheryl said. "Tell it . . ."

". . . died and went to heaven. When he got there he saw a door with 'White Only' on it and another one that said 'Colored.' When he went to St. Peter to complain, St. Peter said, 'Boy, whar yo' from?' Very proudly, the soul brother said, 'I'se from Mississippi, and I have you know, Brother St. Peter, that Mississippi's now *integrated*. Why, the colored goes to eat wid da whites in the restaurants. Dey goes to

school wit' 'em. And as a matter of fact, just five minutes ago when I
was alive, I was goin' into a white church to be *married* to a white
woman!' Then the soul brother paused and started to scratch his
head. 'What's the matter?' St. Peter asked him. 'Well, as a matter of
fack, dat wus the las' thing I remember!'"

She laughed. "You're very funny—not just on the stage."

"Jewish humor is very funny," I said, "because Jews went through
a lot just like we black people did."

"That's true." Cheryl giggled.

"The only thing is, though," I said, "we went through it and then
Jews went through it and we are still going through it! This Jewish
guy once walked around this corner and ran into Hitler. Hitler said,
'See that pile of shit over there, Jew? Eat it!' So the Jew is eating the
shit and Hitler starts laughing so hard that he drops the gun. The Jew
grabs the gun and makes Hitler eat the shit. When he went home
that night his wife said, 'So how was your day?' The Jew said, 'Dar-
lin', you won't believe who I had lunch with today.'"

She lived in West Los Angeles, south of Westwood, west of the
Santa Monica freeway, near the Nu-Art Theater, in a nonglamorous
neighborhood that was so safe, she said, as we came into the apartment, "that I can empty the garbage in my bathrobe."

It was an apartment with hanging ferns and stained-glass windows, very chic.

"Make yourself comfortable," she said, "and I'll get us a cognac."

When she returned, I asked her if I were right about her coming
from the Midwest.

"No," she said, "I'm not from the Midwest. I'm from Pasadena. It
is true that I'm an actress."

"Oh?"

"I'm on *General Hospital*," she said, handing me my drink.

"What part do you play?"

"I'm a nurse," she said, "but I don't have more than a few lines."

She looked like the straightest Miss America. "Would you like to
listen to some music?" she asked.

"What kind of music do you have?" I asked, expecting her to say
the name of some country western singer whose name I would
vaguely know and whose music I would tolerate.

"Early Coltrane," she said.

I laughed.

She looked at me and smiled. "I told you that my straight look is very deceiving," she said. "I've loved jazz since college and I get turned on with black humor."

"What do you mean?" I asked her.

She leaned over and kissed me lightly and teasingly on the lips. "I mean that you made me hot when you were on stage," she said, getting up and going over to the record collection.

I watched her as she took out a Coltrane album and put it on the turntable.

"Is that why you wanted to get on stage?" I asked, watching her legs and thighs from behind.

She turned around when the sound of the soothing jazz exuded from the speakers. "I'm an exhibitionist," she said. "Haven't you picked that up yet?"

She sat down beside me on the sofa again. "I'm very horny tonight," she said.

"And so am I," I said.

"Was it true," she asked, "about how you got started in comedy?"

"Yes, you mean about Gramma Connie?"

"Yes?"

"Everything is true that I say on stage. The one thing that I didn't tell was about how Lindsey was killed. His death will always make me bitter. But not bitter about white people, but about life. That's why I like to perform. It takes away the bitter experiences."

Spreading her legs wider apart so that I could not miss the view of her panties, she smiled at me and licked her lips.

Trying to avoid the obvious, I went on to another joke. "A white man went to a black man. Said, 'When I fuck, my babies come out white, but when you fuck, they come out black. I want you to teach me how to make them come out black.' The black man said, 'I'll tell you how. When you make love with your wife, drink plenty of wine.' So the white man thanked him and went home and got drunk on wine, but when his wife had the baby it was still white. So he goes back to the black man and tells him. The black man said, 'Well, the next time you make love to her, put some grease on your dipstick.' So the white man came back and said he'd put grease on his dipstick but his children still came out white. 'Well, tell me this. What kind of dipstick you using?' In a whiney, femme, West Santa Monica, faggot's delivery: 'Jes my regular . . . old . . . dipstick.' 'Did you use a fourteen-inch dipstick?' 'No, why?' 'Was it four inches thick?' 'N . . . no.' 'Well, see that's your problem right there.' 'What?' *'YOU LETTING TOO MUCH LIGHT GET UP IN THERE!'* "

Watching her throw her head back and laugh, I felt power over her body as I laid my hand on her hot thigh. I kissed her, and suddenly forgot all of the anger I'd felt a few minutes before.

I sucked her delicious tongue in my mouth and cupped her swelling breasts in my hands, gently rubbing the hardening nipples between my fingers. I heard her moan as I pulled her closer into my embrace. Pushing my hand up her dress, I felt her smooth sun-baked thigh. With the tip of my fingers I caressed the moisture through her pubic hair until I had my fingers as deep as they could go inside her pussy. She was so hot she got up and led me to the bedroom without a word. She clicked on a light, displaying a bed with a mirror. She pulled her dress over her head, revealing a long, thin body in panties and bra which she quickly slipped out of as I watched. She laid down on the bed with her legs open and her eyes closed. I thought of all the white motherfuckers I could get revenge on as I bent my head down on her wet throbbing pulsating vagina. I took the clitoris between my lips and flicked it with my tongue at the beat of a congo drum, running her mad with pleasure. When I penetrated her, I stood back and held my dick, thinking, *If those white motherfuckers could see me now they'd blow their own brains out!* I eased down between her long, creamy thighs and sank in. She gave a moan and started screaming loud every time I pushed in and out.

"Tell me a joke," Cheryl said suddenly.

"What? Are you kidding? Right now?"

"Yes! Just when I'm about to come! Tell me a joke! Be funny!"

I was pumping away at her firm white ass. "I can't be funny now! I'm *fucking* you!"

She grabbed my shoulder so tight that I felt her nails tearing into my skin. "I'm gonna come! Tell me a joke," she screamed. I could feel her orgasm coming on like a thousand bulls.

"Be FUNNY!" she bellowed. "I'M GONNA COME!"

"I can't think of a joke right now," I whispered. I couldn't. I couldn't think of anything.

"Tell me a joke. I want to laugh and come TOGETHER!" She was begging me.

"Once . . ." I banged my nuts against her raised, tight white ass. "Once . . . there . . . was a . . ."

"Oh, please go on . . ." she moaned. ". . . Oh, you making me COME!"

". . . A Jew! . . ."

". . . Squirt your come in the bottom of my pussy, baby!"

". . . And a black man . . . !"

". . . Fuck my pussy, Drum . . ."

". . . And a white man . . ."

". . . Come in my cunt . . . !"

". . . They all went to heaven . . ."

". . . I am in HEAVEN TOO! I'M COMING! Oh, MY GOD, I'm coming!"

". . . Can you wait for the punch line?"

". . . I CAN'T WAIT! HA, HA, HA! You are FUNNNNNYYY AND I'M COMING!"

She came for about three minutes. When she was finished, I asked her why she wanted me to tell jokes while she had an orgasm.

"I always wanted to have a comic orgasm, you know," she said, "come while I was being balled by a comedian."

"And you picked me?"

"WELL, you're funny, aren't you?"

# In the Wee Hours
# of the Morning

## Kenji Jasper

*For Konata, Salae, Mill, Judy, Iva Sabina, and Baba Steve*

"What do you really want?" her voice whispers. Every night it is a different question, a different tongue easing across a different erogenous zone. Her costumes take on many permutations, each thoroughly exposing the elements and assets that make me love the opposite sex far more than my own. Tonight, it is a silver bikini top covered in sequins, exposing the chocolate cleavage of breasts the size of mangoes. Tight leather reveals an ass that only God could have designed. But the menu always changes.

The night before she was tall and slender, peanut-colored flesh with a runner's calves and long curly hair draped down her spine. She wore a purple lace bustier with matching garters and heels, her palms slick with scented oils of sandalwood and jasmine. She once had green eyes on a burnt sienna face. Her nonexistent breasts sprouted nipples tailor-made for my lips, lips aching to bathe themselves in boiled-over passion.

Every night my lean and muscled frame flexes as I lean against the leather cushioning of my fully loaded E-class limousine. A white towel hangs loosely from my skull like the cloth on a restaurant table. The perspiration gradually slows as I begin to relax. Another show, another lady, another night of comfort from creatures superior.

The best of The City is the two-way tint on the windows. The air is clean and cool, raising gooseflesh on my thighs as it squeezes through the opening in the driver's window. I sip Betancourt and grapefruit, eagerly awaiting what is to come, once I reach my destination. This has been a long time coming, the just reward for years of nine-to-fiving, for tolerating females with picks and shovels, waiting for the day they'll don the platinum circle that signifies commitment, a yoke around the neck of unjustly enslaved "players for life."

But I have survived. Yes, I have survived. I am living the lie that holds the most truth. They do what I want when I want it, taking me into their mouths until I touch the backs of their skirts, and pulling panties to the side in reverence to a young black man who deserves all they have to offer. I am the cream of the crop. I am the deciding factor as to whether they ever get to "exhale."

Even in absence, I still feel her, hot breath against my ear as she calls for me: Baby, honey, papi, Daddy, sweetie, or just my name. Oh, how I love to hear her say my name, for her to submit to it without question, a verbal admission of what I do to her, and for her, and with her, each and every time it all goes down. She is everything I've always wanted, and nothing that works my nerve.

Her hands know how to push and pull, how to stroke me into submission at the moment that most matters. She knows that light-headed rush that goes through me when she does her thing, one that leaves me temporarily helpless, a victim of her wiles and ways.

My limousine creeps at a snail's pace. I can hear the thousands of feminine whispers just beyond the tinted glass. They don't need to see my face. The brand and make of the car tells them all that they need to know. Their feminine fingers beat against the dark glass that reflects their anonymous faces, as they hope to get a glimpse of an idol God on their way back to their various homes, accepting me whom they love with their fists, and credit cards, men who live in the hovels of their own insecurities.

And for a splinter of a moment, I remember the hovel where I once lived. I remember the search for love in hearts that no longer believed in it. I remember melding tongues with single mothers in apartment hallways while their children looked on, cursed with looking exactly like their absent fathers. I remember passion that stretched into the early hours, thrusts and friction slick with perspiration performed in hopes of filling the massive void within her where trust used to be.

I had tried to save them all, only to find myself drowning in disbelief from their various betrayals. But the memories are remote fragments, fading like photographs in the summer sunlight, until I don't remember them at all. Where I am now, the present is your only past. And in the present, I only have the "Shes" to worry about. This is always the moment when the limo stops.

"Could you be the one?" She always whispers this question in my ear as she straddles me, her interchangeable thighs clapping around my waist in greeting. The door is open and a crowd stands on a red tongue that leads into the building.

"Maybe," I say playfully. "But you need to show me what you've got to offer."

She exits the way she has just entered, and leads me down the plush red carpet into a hotel of Hype Williams music video proportions. Her fingers fondle my behind as we saunter in. Her voice crawls through my ears as she utters things that even I am too shy to repeat.

Our lips meet in the elevator. My finger circles her clitoris through layers of clothing. I can feel her staining herself with each stroke. And I want to taste the mess that I've made. But I'll only have to wait a little longer.

The corridor that leads to my suite is made of the finest velvet. The material is so soft that it cushions my feet through the thousand-dollar shoes. And when I get to the door, I don't need a key. It swings right open, just as she removes the fabric between her cheeks and crosses the threshold, of her own accord.

She pulls me through the door after her and we tumble to the carpeted floor. The décor shifts and swirls depending on the night and room number. The night before last, it had a Japanese theme, a platform bed and paper lanterns accompanied by two powder-faced geisha girls trained from birth in the art of deep tissue message. Last night, I was in an Italian villa with a fountain in the bathroom and two olive trees that cast a shade over the mattress as she fed me bites of tiramisu, and I licked the pool of Pinot Grigio from her navel.

But tonight they have me in a *Thomas Crown Affair* sort of thing, with seven different types of pillows on the raised bed and a half fridge with all kinds of chocolate and candied goodies, that start at $50 a bite. I lay my spine against the softness of the bed as she slithers toward me, on well-manicured hands, and knees emitting the breathy exhales of a woman obsessed, with me.

She is always perfection, in that MTV sense, hair straight and shiny, body the product of thousands of hours at the nearest fitness center. She runs her pink tongue over lips smothered in Lancôme.

She breathes on my crotch and it stiffens, painfully seeking room in pants that have no more to give. She bites a button away from the front of my shirt and spits it in my face. Her lips approach mine once more. This is the moment I wait for every night.

We almost kiss again. Her nails claw at my chest, as if there's something priceless underneath. My zipper is still in the up position as she climbs on top, again. She moves up and down, finding her own rhythm in the hills and valleys of mock intercourse. I should be on the verge of spontaneous combustion. But instead . . . I feel nothing.

Her touch is empty. Her words are soap bubbles on a summer day, bursting too soon to be remembered or forgotten. She is a passing behind during the lunch rush, a pretty young thing whose beauty only exists in the moments when I cannot have her. She is nothing but a reflection of all that is meaningless, chemical impulses in a mind that far too often functions like that of an animal.

"All I want is one night," she pleads. "All I want is you inside me."

The lights have been dimmed by the remote in my well-moisturized hand. Our clothes are gone. Her breasts heave with droplets of sweat brought forth by her own burning desire. And this is when it all begins to come apart.

Because at this point I know that I am not Superman or Denzel, or foot-long porn legend Sean Michaels. So there has to be a catch. And I always know what it is.

My eyelids separate to reveal the rays of a new morning. They stream in through the broken shutters that surround our corner-of-an-apartment's two little windows. The space around our full-sized mattress is more than cramped. The creaky and uneven floor is cluttered with dirty clothes and cracked CD cases. Books bought years before are still in boxes, and the pile of bills on the nightstand is on the verge of avalanche.

Outside police sirens sound as two raggedy crackheads slug it out for the rock of cocaine that two dealers offer up as the purse. This is not my own private paradise. This is the choice we've made.

The dream comes every once in awhile, creeping in through a back door in the cortex. I can't save my own life. I took a vow for forever and the clock ticks so slowly. I feel as if I know everything there is to know, that life has all become routine, that I am trapped in a cage of commitment and will never escape, because I don't want to.

The dream isn't about me not being happy. Nor is it about what I'm not getting at home. It's about letting go, accepting the hard, cold fact that those platinum circles of commitment change it all in a heartbeat. I becomes we, which means he and she, which means that I'm not alone anymore, except in my dreams, where I'm still hashing out the scariest thing of all: that I am finally safe.

She has no agenda. She has no need of men with fortune or fame. No thirst for power, no fantasy of owning the latest model car equipped with all the features, or at least not in comparison with her heart and my heart, the thing we share and know through and through.

My torso rolls to the right, and I feel her morning breath scorch the back of my neck. It gives me an inner-warmth that defies description. But the rest of me is ice cold, because she's pulled both blankets over to her side during the night.

That's right. I am no longer living the average man's wet dream. I am not trapped in fantasies of femme fatales who slither and seduce because they'll never make it as real actresses. I don't have to be a star to know what it is to shine. And in the midst of thought, knowing that dinner will be rarely waiting for me, knowing that her stomach will swell and never flatten the same way again, I can turn the channel to the latest X-rated flick, and cut one more selfish frame from our life's reel.

She grins in her sleep and I lightly kiss her neck. And mumbles that she loves me. Then her fudge-colored lids part to show me the eyes that I always get lost in. There is dried saliva on her cheek. Her tight coils of short brown hair are flattened against her head. And yet she is still the most beautiful thing I have ever seen.

"What did you dream about?"

I think for a moment, weighing the implications of my answer. Then I run all that I remember of it through my mind. The pictures are so vivid that I can draw them.

"It wasn't a dream," I say before a small kiss. "It was a nightmare."

# Private Domain

(From the short fiction collection
*Hue and Cry*)

## James Alan McPherson

### I

Rodney finished his beer in slow, deliberate swallows, peering over the rim of his mug at the other black who, having polished off three previous mugs of draft, now sat watching Rodney expectantly, being quite obvious with his eyes that he held no doubt that more beer was forthcoming. Rodney ignored his eyes. He licked his lips. He tabled the empty mug. "Now give it to me again," he said to the heavily bearded beer-hungry black still eyeing him, now demandingly, from across the small booth. "Let me see if I have it all down."

"How 'bout throwing some more suds on me?" said the black.

"In a minute," said Rodney.

The black considered. "I'm dry again. Another taste."

Rodney sighed, considered his position from behind the sigh, made himself look annoyed and then grudgingly raised his hand until the cigar-chewing bartender noticed, stopped his stooped glass-washing dance behind the counter, and nodded to the waitress, sitting on a stool at the bar, to replenish them. She was slow about getting up. It was a lazy day: the two men in the booth were the only customers.

"Now," said Rodney. "Give it to me again."

The other man smiled. He had won again. "It's this way," he said to Rodney.

Rodney ignored the waitress as she pushed the two fresh mugs onto the table while his companion paused to consider her ass bouncing beneath the cloth of her blue dress. Lighting another cigarette, Rodney observed that the waitress wore no stockings and felt himself getting uncomfortable.

"Well?" he said.

"It's this way," his companion said again. "Your *bag* is where you keep whatever you do best. Whatever is in your bag is your *thing*. Some cats call it your *stick*, but it means the same. Now, when you know you got your thing going all right, you say 'I got myself together' or 'I got my game together.'"

"All right, all right," said Rodney. "I've got it down now." He was growing very irritated at the other man, who smiled all the time in a superior way and let the beer wet his gold tooth before he swallowed, as if expecting Rodney to be impressed with its gleam. Rodney was not impressed. He disliked condescension, especially from Willie, whom he regarded in most respects as his inferior.

"Anything else I should know?" Rodney snapped.

"Yeah, baby-boy," Willie said slow and matter-of-factly, implying, in his accents, a whole world of essential instruction being overlooked for want of beer and money and mind and other necessities forever beyond Rodney's reach. "There's lots. There's lots and lots."

"Like what?"

Willie drained his mug. "You know about the big 'I Remember Rock 'n' Roll' Memorial in Cleveland last week?"

"No." Rodney was excited. "Who was there?"

"All the cats from the old groups."

"Anything special happen?"

"Hell yes!" Willie smiled again and looked very pleased with himself. "Fatso Checkers didn't show. The cats would have tore the place down, but Dirty Rivers filled in for him. He made up a song right on stage. Man, the cats dug it, they went wild they dug it so."

"What's the song?"

"I donno."

"Is it on record?"

"Not yet. He just made it up."

"There's no place I can check it out?"

Again Willie smiled. "You can follow the other squares and check out this week's issue of *Soul*. They might have a piece on it."

"I don't have *time*," Rodney said. "I've got my studies to do."

"You don't have to, then; just be cool."

Rodney got up. "That's it," he said to Willie. "I'll check you out later." He put two dollars down on the table and turned to go. Willie reached over and picked up the bills. "That's for the beer," Rodney cautioned him.

"Sure," said Willie.

Rodney walked toward the door. "Be cool," he heard Willie say from behind him. He did not look back. He knew that Willie and possibly the waitress and even the bartender would be smiling.

Although he felt uncomfortable in that area of the city, Rodney decided to walk around and digest all that he had been told before driving back to the University. He had parked and locked his car on a small side street and felt relatively protected from the rows and rows of aimless men who lined the stoops of houses and posts and garbage cans on either side of the street, their eyes seemingly shifty, their faces dishonest, their broad black noses alert and sniffing, feeling the air for the source of the smell which Rodney half believed rose from the watch and the wallet and the valuables stored in his pocket. He walked faster. Her felt their eyes on his back and he was very uncomfortable being there, in the rising heat from the sidewalk, amid the smells of old food and wine and urine which rose with the heat.

He passed two boys with gray-black, ashy faces and running noses who laughed as they chased a little black girl up and down the steps of a tenement. "Little Tommy Tucker was a bad motherfucker," one of the boys half sang, half spoke, and they all laughed. Rodney thought it obscene and a violation of a protective and sacred barrier between two distinctively different age groups. But after a few more steps he began to think that it was very clever. He stopped. He looked back. He began to memorize it. Then he began to walk back toward them, still at play on the steps, having already forgotten the inventiveness of a moment before. Rodney was about to call to them to repeat the whole verse when a robust and short-haired dark woman in a tight black dress that was open at the side came out of the tenement and down the stairs and began to undulate her way, sensually, toward him. The three children followed her, laughing as they attempted to imitate her walk. Just when he was about to pass her, a light blue Ford pulled over to the curb next to her and a bald-headed white man leaned, questioningly, out of the driver's window toward the big woman. She stopped, and looking the man directly in the eye with a hint of professional irritation on her round, hard face, asked, "How much?"

"Ten," the man said.

"Hell no," she said turning to go in a way that, while sharp and decisive, also suggested that there was a happy chance that, upon the occurrence of certain conditions, as yet unnamed, she might not go at all.

"Twelve," said the man.

The woman looked at Rodney for a moment; then she looked the leaning man full in the face with fierce eyes. "Fuck you!" she said matter-of-factly.

"Well, damn if you're worth more than that," the man said, ignoring Rodney and the children.

"Get the hell on," said the woman, and began to walk slowly and sensually in the direction in which the car was pointed.

"She ain't got no drawers on," exclaimed one of the children.

"Can you see her cunt?"

"Yeah" was the answer. They all ran after her and the car, which was now trailing her, leaving Rodney alone on that part of the hot sidewalk. But he was not minding the heat now, or the smells, or the lounging men, or even Willie's condescension; he only minded that he had not thought to bring a notebook because he was having difficulty arranging all this in his head for memorization.

Returning to his car at last, Rodney paused amid afternoon traffic to purchase a copy of *Muhammad Speaks* from a conservatively dressed, cocoa-brown Muslim on a street corner. Rodney tried to be very conspicuous about the transaction, doing his absolute best to engage the fellow in conversation while the homebound cars, full of black and white workers, passed them. "What made you join?" he asked the Muslim, a striking fellow who still retained the red eyes of an alcoholic or drug addict.

"Come to see us and find out for yourself," said the fellow, his eyes not on Rodney but on the moving traffic lest he should miss the possibility of a sale.

"Are you happy being a Muslim?" asked Rodney.

"Come to our mosque, brother, and find out."

"I should think you'd get tired of selling papers all the time."

The Muslim, not wanting to insult Rodney and lose a possible conversion and at the same time more than slightly irritated, struck a compromise with himself, hitched his papers under his arms and moved out into the street between the two lanes of traffic. "Come to our mosque, brother, and gain all knowledge from the lips of the Messenger," he called back to Rodney. Rodney turned away and walked to his car. It was safe; the residents had not found it yet. Still, he inspected the doors and windows and keyholes for jimmy marks, just to feel secure.

## II

"Where have you been?" Lynn asked as he opened the door to his apartment. She was sitting on the floor, her legs crossed, her panties showing—her favorite position, which always embarrassed Rodney when they relaxed with other people. He suspected that she did it on purpose. He had developed the habit of glancing at all the other fellows in a room, whenever she did it, until they saw him watching them discovering her and directed their eyes elsewhere in silent respect for his unexpressed wish. This always made Rodney feel superior and polished.

"Put your legs down," he told her.

"For what?" she said.

"You'll catch cold."

"Nobody's looking. Where you been?"

Rodney stood over her and looked down. He looked severe. He could not stand irritation at home too. "Go sit on the sofa," he ordered her. "Only white girls expose themselves in public."

"You prude," she said. "This isn't public." But she got up anyway and reclined on the sofa.

"That's better," said Rodney, pulling off his coat. "If sitting like that is your thing, you should put it in a separate bag and bury it someplace."

"What do you know about *my thing*?" Lynn said.

Rodney did not answer her.

"Where you been, *bay-bee*?"

Rodney said nothing. He hated her when she called him that in private.

"We're going to be late for dinner, *bay-bee*," she said again.

"I've been out studying," Rodney finally said.

"What?"

"Things."

"Today's Saturday."

"So? God made Saturday for students."

"Crap," she said. Then she added: "*Bay-bee!*"

"Oh, shut up," said Rodney.

"You can give me orders when we're married," said Lynn.

"That'll be the day," Rodney muttered.

"Yeah," Lynn repeated. "That'll be the day."

Rodney looked at her, legs miniskirted but sufficiently covered, hair natural but just a little too straight to be that way, skin nut-brown and smooth and soft to touch and feel against his mouth and arms and legs, body well built and filled, very noticeable breasts and hips, also good to touch and feel against his body at night. Rodney liked to make love at night, in the dark. He especially did not like to make sounds while making love, although he felt uneasy if the girl did not make any. He was considering whether or not it was dark enough in the room to make love when the telephone rang. Lynn did not move on the sofa so he answered it himself. It was Charlie Pratt.

"What's happening, baby?" said Rodney.

"Not much," said Charlie. "Listen, can you make dinner around seven? We got some other cats coming over at nine we don't want to feed nothin' but beer."

"Cool," said Rodney. He looked at his watch. "We can make it as soon as Lynn gets herself together." He glanced over at Lynn still stretched out on the sofa.

"Great," said Charlie Pratt. "Later."

Rodney hung up. "What do you have to do to get ready?" he asked Lynn.

"Nothing."

"You *could* put on another skirt."

"Go to hell," she said, not lifting her head from the sofa. "This skirt's fine."

"You could at least comb your hair or something."

Lynn ignored him. Rodney began to reconsider the sufficiency of the darkness in the room. Then he thought better of the idea. Instead, he went out of the room to shave and take a bath.

These days Rodney found himself coming close to hating everyone. Still, he never allowed himself to recognize it, or call what he felt toward certain people genuine hate. He preferred to call it differing degrees of dislike, an emotion with two sides like a coin, which was constantly spinning in his mind. Sometimes it landed, in his brain, heads up, signifying a certain affinity; sometimes it landed tails up, signifying a slight distaste or perhaps a major objection to a single person and his attitudes. He refused to dislike absolutely because, he felt, dislike was uncomfortably close to bigotry and Rodney knew too many different people to be a practicing bigot. Sometimes, very frequently in fact, he disliked Willie immensely. On the other hand, he sometimes felt a bit of admiration for the fellow and, occasionally, footnoted that admiration by purchasing an extra beer for him. This gesture served to stamp those rare moments onto his memory, a reminder that, because he had done this on enough occasions in the past, there would always be a rather thick prophylactic between how he really felt and how Willie assumed he felt.

Talking to Willie was informative and amusing to Rodney up to the point when Willie began to smile and to seem to know that what he was telling Rodney had some value. After he could see when that point was reached in Willie's face, Rodney was not amused anymore. Sometimes he was annoyed, and sometimes, when Willie smiled confidently and knowledgeably and condescendingly, Rodney began to almost hate him. He felt the same about Lynn and her panties and her *bay-bee* and the loose ways she had, Rodney assumed, picked up from living among many whites for too long. Sometimes she made him feel really uncomfortable and scared. He began to say *bay-bee, bay-bee* to himself in the shower. Thinking about it, he suddenly realized that he felt exactly the same way about Charlie Pratt.

Pratt made Rodney feel uncomfortable because he did not fit either side of the coin. The fellow had well over two thousand records: some rhythm and blues, some jazz, some folk, some gospels, but all black. And Charles Pratt was not. He knew the language and was proud to use the vocabulary Rodney had been trying to forget all his life. He was pleasantly chubby, with dark blond hair and a fuzzy Genghis Khan moustache which hung down on either side of his chin. Sometimes the ends dangled when he moved. And sometimes Pratt dangled when he moved. Sometimes Charlie Pratt, his belly hanging over his belt and his chin going up and down in talk, dangled when he did not move. Drying his legs with a towel, Rodney thought of himself and Charlie locked in mortal combat. Rodney had no doubt that he would win; he was slim and wiry, he was quick, he had a history of natural selection in his ancestry. Besides, Charlie was fat. He never used his body. Thinking about him, Rodney realized that he had never seen Charlie dance or move to the rhythm of any of his two thousand records. He had never seen him snap his fingers once, or voluntarily move any part of his body besides his arms and legs; and even those movements were not rhythmic but something close to an unnatural shuffle.

Rodney did a quick step with his feet as he brushed his teeth in front of the mirror. He moved back from the mirror in order to see his feet. He did the step again, grinning at himself and at the white-foamed toothbrush hanging loosely from his mouth. The foam covered his lips and made him white, and, remembering a fast song in his head, Rodney snapped his fingers and did the step again. And again.

## III

"When you finish," said Charlie Pratt in between chews on a pork-chop bone, "I'll let you hear some of the stuff I picked up yesterday."

Rodney wiped his mouth carefully before answering. "What'd you get this time?" he asked, knowing what to expect.

"Some vintage Roscoe and Shirley stuff," said Charlie. "We found it in Markfield's back room. It was just lying there under a stack of oldies full of dust. We figure it must be their only LP. Jesus, what a find!" Both Charlie and his wife smiled pridefully.

"How about that," said Rodney. But he did not say it with enthusiasm.

Charlie stood up from the table and began to shift his bulk from foot to foot, a sort of safe dance, but more like the movements of someone who wants desperately to go to the bathroom.

"Whatever happened to them?" asked Lynn.

Both the Pratts smiled together. "They broke up in '52 because the girl was a lesbian," his wife said. She had gone to Vassar, and Rodney always noticed how small and tight her mouth became whenever she took the initiative from her husband, which was, Rodney had noticed over a period of several dinners and many beer parties with them, very, very often. She was aggressive, in keeping with the Vassar tradition, and seemed to play a very intense, continuous game of one-upmanship with her husband.

"That's not what happened at all," her husband said. "After they hit the big time with 'I Want to Do It,' it was in '53, Roscoe started sleeping around. One night she caught him in a hotel room with a chick and razored his face. His face was so cut up he couldn't go on-stage anymore. I saw him in Newark in '64 when he was trying to make a comeback. He still looked razored. He looked bad."

Rodney felt tight inside, remembering that in '64 he had been trying desperately to make up for a lifetime of not knowing anything about Baroque. Now he knew all about it and he had never heard of Roscoe and Shirley. "There was an 'I Remember Rock 'n' Roll' Memorial in Cleveland last week," he said.

"Yeah," said Charlie. "Too bad Fatso couldn't make it. But there was one hell of a song Dirty Rivers made up. Jesus, right on the spot too! Jesus, right on the stage! He sang for almost two hours. Christ! I was lucky to get it taped; the cats went wild. They almost overran the stage."

"How did you get the tape?" asked Rodney, now vaguely disgusted.

"We knew about the show for months," Peggy Pratt broke in. "We planned to go but there was an Ashy Williamson Revue in the Village that same night. We couldn't make both so we called up this guy in Cleveland and got him to tape the show for us." She paused. "Want to hear it?"

"No," said Rodney, somewhat flatly. Then he added: "Not right now."

"Want to hear the Roscoe and Shirley?"

"No."

"I got a new Baptist group," said Charlie Pratt. "Some new freedom songs. Lots of finger-poppin' and hand jive."

"That's not my stick," said Rodney.

"You mean that ain't your *thing*," said Charlie.

"Yeah," said Rodney. "That's what I mean."

## IV

They were drinking beer and listening to the Dirty Rivers tape when the other people came in. Rodney had been sitting on the sofa, quietly, too heavy to keep time with his feet and too tight inside to care if the Pratts did. Lynn was in her best position, on the floor, cross-legged. The two girls with names he did not catch sat in chairs and crossed their legs, keeping time to the music and smoking. Looking at Lynn on the floor and looking at them on the chairs made Rodney mad. Listening to the Pratts recount, to the two white fellows, how they got the Cleveland tape made Rodney mad too. He drained his beer can and then began to beat time to the music with his foot and both hands on the arm of the sofa with a heavy, controlled deliberation that was really off the beat. Still, he knew that, since he was the only black male in the room, the others would assume that he alone knew the proper beat, even if it was out of time with their own perception of it, and would follow him. The two bearded fellows did just that when they sat down on the floor with Lynn; but the two girls maintained their original perception of the beat. Nevertheless, watching the fellows, Rodney felt the return of some sense of power.

"Some more suds," he said to Peggy Pratt.

She went out of the room.

"You've had enough," said Lynn.

Rodney looked at her spitefully. "Just be cool," he told her. "You just play your own game and stay cool."

The two girls looked at him and smiled. Their dates looked at Lynn. They did not smile. Dirty Rivers was moaning, *"Help me! Help me! Help me!"* now, and Rodney felt that he had to feel more from the music than any of them. *"Mercy! mercy! mercy!"* he exclaimed as Peggy Pratt handed him another can of beer. "This cat is *together!*"

The girls agreed and smiled again. One of them even reconciled her beat to Rodney's. Lynn just looked at him.

"He's just a beautiful man," the reconciled girl said.

"He's got more soul than anybody," said Rodney. "Nobody can touch him." He got up from the sofa, put his hands in his pockets and began to exercise a slow, heavy grind to the music without moving his feet. Charlie, who had been standing by the recorder all this time with his hands locked together, smiled his Genghis Khan smile.

"Actually," he said rather slowly, "I think Ashy Williamson is better."

"You jivetime cat," said Rodney. "Williamson couldn't touch Dirty Rivers with a stick."

"Rivers couldn't adapt," said Charlie.

"What do you mean?"

"He's just an old man now, playing the toilets, doing his same thing. Williamson's got class. He's got a new sound everybody digs. Even the squares."

"What do you know?" said Rodney.

Charlie Pratt smiled. "Plenty," he said.

After more beer and argument all around, and after playing Williamson's oldest and latest LPs by way of proof, it was decided that they should put it to a vote. Both the Pratts were of the same mind: Ashy Williamson was better than Dirty Rivers. The two fellows on the floor agreed with them. And also one of the girls. The other girl, however, the skinny brunette who had reconciled her beat to Rodney's, observed that she had been raised on Rivers and felt, absolutely, that he had had in the past, and still had now, a very good thing going for him. But Rodney was not impressed. She had crooked teeth and was obviously out to flatter her date with her maintenance of an independent mind in spite of her looks. Rodney turned to Lynn, still sitting cross-legged and exposed on the floor, but saving Rodney from utilizing his cautioning eye by having the beer can conveniently placed between her open legs. "Well, what do you say?" he asked, standing over her in his usual way.

She looked up at him. Casually sipping her beer, she considered for a long moment. The room was now now very quiet, the last cut having been played on the Williamson record. The only sound was Lynn sipping her beer. It grated in Rodney's mind. The only movement was Charlie Pratt doing his rubber shift from foot to foot. That also irritated Rodney. "Well?" he said.

Lynn placed the can between her legs again, very carefully and neatly. "Dirty Rivers is an old man," she said.

"What the hell does that mean?"

"He's got nothing new going for him, *bay-bee*," she said in a way that told Rodney she had made up her mind about it long before her opinion had been asked. She looked up at Rodney, her face resolved and, it seemed to him, slightly victorious.

"There you go, mother," Charlie said.

Rodney could see them all smiling at him, even Lynn, even the ugly brunette who had reconciled. He sat down on the sofa and said nothing.

"Now I'll play my new Roscoe and Shirley for you," Charlie told the others.

"Wasn't she a lesbian?" one of the fellows asked.

"Absolutely not!" said Charlie Pratt.

Rodney was flipping the coin in his mind again now. He flipped it faster and faster. After a while it was spinning against Willie and the cigar-chewing bartender and Lynn and especially the Pratts. Finishing the beer, Rodney found that the coin had stopped spinning; and from where his mind hung on the bad side of it, somewhere close to the place where he kept his bigotry almost locked away, he could hear the Pratts battling back and forth for the right to tell the others about a famous movie star who sued her parents when she found out that she was a mulatto. He got to his feet and walked over to the stacks and stacks of records that lined the wall. Aimlessly going through them, he considered all the black faces on their covers and all the slick, praising language by white disc jockeys and white experts and white managers on their backs. Then he commenced to stare at the brunette who had agreed with him. She avoided his eyes. He stared at Lynn too; but she was looking at Charlie Pratt, very intentionally. Only once did she glance up at him and smiled in a way that said *"bay-bee."* And then she looked away again.

Rodney leaned against the wall of records, put his hands in his pockets and wet his lips. Then she said: "Little Tommy Tucker was a *bad* motherfucker!"

They all looked at him.

"What?" said Peggy Pratt, smiling.

He repeated it.

## V

Driving home, Rodney went slower than required and obeyed traffic signals on very quiet, very empty streets. Lynn sat against the door, away from him. She had her legs crossed.

"You were pretty good tonight," she said at last.

Rodney was looking at a traffic light changing back to red.

"You were the life of the party."

Rodney inspected a white line of bird shit running down the top of the window, between him and the red light. It would have to come off in the morning.

"I knew you would let that color through if you had enough beer," Lynn said.

"Oh shut the hell up!" said Rodney. He was not mad. She had just interrupted his thinking. He was thinking of going over to buy some more beer for Willie and talk some more before the usual Saturday time. He was thinking about building up his collection of Ashy Williamson LPs. He was thinking about driving Lynn directly home and not going up with her to make love to her in her bed, which was much wider than his own, no matter how much she apologized later and no matter how dark and safe and inviting her room would be.

# Forty-five Is Not So Old

## Kalamu ya Salaam

It was 1:30 in the morning. Lucinda was half a jigger away from inebriated as she held a double shot of Seagram's and 7-Up poised before her glossy, hot-pink painted lips. Precisely at that moment, Lucinda made up her mind *since I'm going to die eventually, I might as well live tonight* which meant she didn't want to go home alone tonight. In fact, she hoped she wasn't going home at all, at least not to her own home.

Billy must have thought she was a fool. "Away on business" or so he had said with feinted casualness. Lucinda knew. Even as she had allowed herself to act like she believed him when he said he had to go to Portland for four days, she knew. Maybe he really did have some business to do there, but for sure he was sleeping with Sandra with her little narrow ass. It didn't matter that Billy Jo had left Thursday during the day and that Sandra was at work on Friday, answering the phone when Lucinda called on some pretense or the other. "I know something is up," Lucinda mouthed right before the cool liquor crossed her lips.

Lucinda was a public relations specialist; she knew how to make things look like what they weren't. Who had said life was just an illusion? Wasn't it true that illusions were part of life? The only question was do you believe? Do you believe in what's not there? Damn, this liquor makes you think some funny thoughts. But no, Billy Jo's disinterest was no illusion. Nor was Sandra an illusion.

Just thinking of that little ninety-six-and-three-quarter-pound strumpet made Lucinda angry because invariably it made Lucinda think of when she weighed 115 pounds and was good to go, but that was at least eight years ago. Her eyes growing increasingly glassy,

Lucinda silently surveyed herself in the large mirror behind the bar. One hundred fifty-five pounds really wasn't that heavy, *besides I'm tall and have big breasts. How is it these little skinny wenches can get men so excited, what's to it?*

*Furthermore, the slut has buck teeth. What in the world could skinny Sandra possibly do for William James Brown that he likes better than what I do for him?* Lucinda wondered as she took another slow sip of her mixed drink. "I don't look bad—for my age. Hell, in fact, it's not really age. It's experience. I look good to say I'm as experienced as I am."

Lucinda smirked as she thought about how Sandra couldn't massage Billy Jo's feet like she did, then wash them in a little antique porcelain washbasin—*I bet she doesn't even own any antiques*—dry them with an ultra-fluffy, teal-colored towel, and then slowly suck his toes as her flawlessly lacquered fingernails crawled up and down the soles of his size-eleven feet. And for sure, Sandra had no clue of some of the more stimulating thrills Billy Jo's big toe could arouse. Like when Lucinda felt really risqué, really felt like lighting up Billy Jo's little firecracker in her sexy night sky, after cutting his toenails with a clipper and gently buffing the edges to a smooth evenness with an emery board, after washing them in warm water with a scented soap, after tenderly drying them and then sucking them as he lay back on their bed, and after massaging his feet with baby oil, and as it got good to him, after all of that, Lucinda would climb up on the bed and slowly stroke her pussy with his big toe, stroke it until she was wet. God, a woman didn't know what she was missing if she had never reached a climax with her lover's toe tapping on her clitoris. What did that inexperienced child know about sophisticated lovemaking? Lucinda took a long sip of her drink.

Lucinda recalled how pleasantly surprised Billy Jo always seemed whenever she dropped in on him at work. With a toss of her luxuriously coiffured hair, which had been crafted into a gleaming and glistening, jet black, lengthy, chemically treated mane that languidly lay across her shoulders, Lucinda smiled slyly as she reminisced about how it had been, the last time she turned Billy Jo on at his office.

"Billy, I was in the neighborhood, on my way to that little boutique I discovered, you know the one I told you specializes in silk batiks, and as I crossed Poydras I felt this twinge like a little spark of lightning." He had looked at her partially annoyed but also partially pleased as she stroked his male ego. "I couldn't wait. So . . ." she slid seductively around his desk, "I decided to stop here."

Lucinda reached down and slightly opened Billy Jo's bottom desk drawer. She propped her leg up on the edge of the drawer as she took his right hand and cunningly glided it beneath her skirt and up her thigh. Lucinda shuddered involuntarily as she expertly guided his fingers into the curly mass of pubic hair and the moist flesh of her mound. She tensed her thigh muscles when his fingers reached her clit. "Yes, yes, I needed that," she salaciously whimpered while throwing her head back and squeezing her eyes closed with the same intensity as the forceful contractions caused by Billy Jo's fingertips tap dancing on the head of her clitoris. Lucinda savored the first trickles of what would soon become a flow. And then his phone rang. It was intrusive Sandra reminding "Mr. Brown" he had an appointment in ten minutes.

"That's enough," Lucinda said, pulling his hand away, "for now." And then she remembered his astonishment as she bent over to slowly suck her moisture off of his fingers. "We can't have you smelling like pussy when you shake hands with the movers and shakers of industry."

When Lucinda completed tongue washing each finger, she reached into her mauve silk purse which hung by a silver metal shoulder strap dangling off her left hip. Moving aside her black satin panties which she had removed in the parking garage, she withdrew a pink linen handkerchief that was embroidered with her initials. Before she finished drying his fingers, there was a knock at the door.

"Come in."

As Sandra entered, Lucinda ostentatiously finished her task with a flourish, waving the handkerchief. "There, all clean, all dry."

After daintily refolding her handkerchief and replacing it in her brightly beaded pouch, Lucinda slowly kissed her husband on his clean-shaven cheek, paused to close the bottom desk drawer, and cheerfully called out to him over her shoulder as she sashayed past Sandra, "Have a good meeting, honey. We'll finish ours tonight."

Pausing at the doorway, Lucinda pirouetted coyly. "And, Sandra, you have a nice day. OK." That little narrow-ass secretary didn't know anything about how to administer sexual quickies, didn't know that men liked sexually aggressive women who were otherwise the model of ladyhood.

While she was lost in the reverie of remembering the sexual games she often played with Billy Jo, an impeccably dressed young man sat on a stool one removed from Lucinda. Attracted by the resonance of his masculine baritone ordering a cognac, Lucinda turned to look directly at his massive profile. She sniffed and caught the faint whiff of an expensive cologne. He was ruggedly handsome.

"Hi," she smiled at him.

He looked at her, briefly. Lucinda saw the almost imperceptible survey flicker as his eyes started at her face, moved quickly down her body, strayed briefly to her behind—she sat up straight and slightly arched her back—and down her legs, and . . . and, nothing. He turned away without even responding.

She wanted to throw her drink at him. Instead she decided to annoy him. "I said, hello."

He grunted, turned his head, and pretended he was ignoring her. Lucinda hated to be ignored.

She got up, slid onto the stool next to him, and ignored his ignoring her. "My name is Lucinda."

"OK."

"And your name is?"

"Jawon."

*Oh god, what a common name*, Lucinda thought. *He probably doesn't even have a college degree.* Lucinda's liquor continued the conversation. "Jawon, that's nice." Pushing her purse aside, Lucinda leaned forward on the bar's leather lining. "Jawon, I'm conducting a survey. Would you mind if I asked you a couple of opinion questions?"

Jawon grunted without looking at her.

"I take that grunt to mean, 'oh god, why doesn't this old bag just leave me alone with her silly questions. I'll answer one or two, but she better make it quick.'"

Jawon was slightly taken aback by her boldness. He turned to get a second look at this woman. Lucinda leaned back slightly, crossed her legs, and did not bother to tug down her worsted wool dress. Noticing her broad, soft-calf leather black belt with the bold gold buckle, Jawon assessed she was probably some kind of leather freak who liked to tie down men or spank them with a black riding crop. *Nah, it's not worth it* was his final appraisal.

"If our ages were reversed," Lucinda leaned forward again, bracing her flawlessly made-up face with the back of her exquisitely manicured hand, "if you were a mature man and I were a young attractive woman, would you be offended if I brushed you off without so much as a civil hello?" Sporting a self-assured smile, Lucinda looked directly at Jawon, awaiting his answer.

Acid cruelly dripped from Jawon's thickly mustached lips, "I think you ought to be at home baby—sitting with your grandchildren instead of out here trying to rob the cradle."

"Ah ha. Well, Jawon, ten years from now, I hope you're not sitting on the other end of this question, and if you are, I hope the lady whose attention you're trying to attract is just a bit more understanding than you are now. That's all. You may go now."

Jawon backed off the stool and walked away, leaving a dollar tip on the bar while offering no further acknowledgment of Lucinda.

Lucinda turned to face the mirror behind the bar and in its reflection caught sight of Roderick, the genial bartender, standing discreetly to the side, dressed in black slacks, a crisply starched white shirt topped with a hand-tied black bow tie, and a black and white checkered vest highlighted by a metal name tag which mirrored the bar's multicolored neon-and-florescent-lit interior. There was neither smile nor smirk on Roderick's placid face, nor did his eyes give any indication that he had watched the drama unfold. Without bothering to look directly at him, Lucinda sat her drink on the dark wood of the bar and familiarly addressed Roderick. "Well, Rodney, don't just stand there. Freshen my drink, please."

As Roderick moved toward her, Lucinda glanced at her watch. It was almost midnight in Portland. Lucinda mischievously decided to call Billy Jo and disturb whatever little excitement in which he might be engaged. Before Roderick could pour the freshener, Lucinda waved him off. "Rodney, I've decided to go home instead of sitting here and getting my feelings hurt. Be the gentleman that you are and call a cab for me please."

Lucinda never, never ever drove her white Lexus when she went alone to paint the town. A solitary woman cruising down the avenues late at night was like flashing a baked ham in front of hungry bulldogs. Any man that she might meet would pay more attention to her car than to her, and assume that where there was a Lexus there was a big bank account that he might access. Besides, it was safer this way. Not that she had ever done much more than flirt, just to see if she still had what it took to attract a man ten years younger than she. Most of the time . . . oh, why think about it.

Pulling two crisp, new twenties from her purse, Lucinda waved them at Roderick, "I assume this will cover my tab for three doubles and also adequately provide for your well-being."

Roderick nodded affirmatively as he received the bills with a smile. His clean-shaven head was oiled to a soft, attractive sheen, and were it not for the gaucherie of two gold-capped teeth, Lucinda might have found him attractive as well as personable.

"Will there be anything else I can do for you?" he asked Lucinda in a charming tone that implied he was both a trustworthy listener and a resourceful procurer.

Lucinda's liquor got the better of her normal disinterest in what other people did or didn't do. "Does diabetes run in your family, Rodney?"

"Not that I know of. No, I don't believe so. A little arthritis is all I've ever heard about, but then my folks are from the country, out Vacherie way. Don't a day go by they don't walk at least a mile and all their food is fresh, home cooked."

"You're fortunate, Rodney. Did you know the treatment for diabetes is deleterious to the libido?"

"So I've heard."

"Watch your diet, young man. We wouldn't want your libido going south before you're sixty-five."

"Ah, no, ma'am. We certainly wouldn't want that to happen." Roderick had been idly wondering if she were single or out for a fling, or both. Without her having to say any more, he knew that she was grieving for a husband or lover who was no longer sexually active. Someone called to him from the other end of the near empty bar. Roderick waved an acknowledgment to the customer while he was wrapping up with Lucinda. "Is there a particular company you prefer?"

"Company?"

"Cab company."

"No. How would I know? I don't usually take cabs."

"OK. I'll be right back." Roderick walked briskly down to the waiting customer, served him, reached under the register, pulled out the bar's phone, and rotely punched in the White Fleet number as he walked back to where the matronly woman sat.

"A cab is on the way. The dispatcher will ring me when they're outside."

"Such an efficient young man you are."

"Thank you," said Roderick with a graceful bow of his bald head.

"Rodney, one more thing."

"Yes. At your service."

"Might I use your phone to make a quick long distance call?" requested Lucinda while removing another crisp twenty from her purse, along with the note page on which Billy Jo had written his hotel telephone number. "My husband would just love to hear from me at this particular moment." Roderick took the twenty with his right hand and handed the phone to her with his left.

"Take your time," Roderick said over his shoulder as he moved to the far end of the bar.

"Mr. William James Brown, please. He's a guest." Lucinda smirked at the thought of calling Billy Jo from a bar.

Although she felt her mood turning foul, when Lucinda heard Billy Jo answer the phone, she brightened her voice. "Hello, my lover. Wherever you are."

"You know where I am. I gave you the number and you called it."

"I miss you."

"I miss you too, honey."

Then there was an awkward hush as Lucinda waited for Billy Jo to indicate interest in her. And waited. And waited.

"Other than missing you, I'm doing all right, thank you." Lucinda finally broke the stalemate, not bothering to mask her sarcasm.

More silence.

"I'll be home late Sunday night."

"Should I wait up?"

"You don't have to."

"Billy Jo, why do you . . ." Her words trailed off into a strained silence. Something was in her eye. She paused to dab the edges of her left eye with the heel of her hand. "You know where I am now?"

"No, I don't, Lucinda. Where are you?"

"I'm sitting in a bar, but I would rather be somewhere with you."

Again, silence.

Something else was in her eye now. "Billy, I just want to make you happy. Be good to you. Make it all good to you . . ." Lucinda abruptly stopped babbling. "You see you've got me babbling. Would it excite you if I told you I wanted you so much that we could have phone sex right now. And . . ." Lucinda paused. "I started to say something really naughty but this is a mobile phone and anyone could be listening."

Silence.

The liquor kept her talking long after she normally would have stopped. "I'll be forty-nine next week, and in another four months or so, you'll be forty-six, and that's not so old. I was thinking maybe some other medication might help you, I mean, maybe, make you feel less, or, I mean, feel better, or . . ." His tight-lipped silence was not making it easy. "Are you sorry that I couldn't have children?" As Lucinda questioned Billy, she instantly regretted saying anything and wished that he would say something. Anything. "Billy, are you there?"

"Yes, I'm here."

"And I'm not."

"Lucinda, I think you've had too much to drink."

She had not realized she was slightly slurring her words.

"It's all right. I'm catching a cab home."

"See you Sunday night, honey."

Lucinda held the phone to her ear long, long after the dial tone sounded following Billy Jo hanging up. As Lucinda lowered the phone from her ear, Roderick moved toward her. Before she could hand the phone back to him, it rang and startled her. She almost dropped it. Roderick grabbed it, also catching hold of her hand in the process of securing the phone.

"It's OK, I've got it." She left her hand nestled in Roderick's as he used his free hand to expertly hit the talk button, shift the phone to his ear, and answer, "Hello." While he listened to whoever was talking, Lucinda tightened her fingers on Roderick's hand. "Thanks. She will be right out."

Roderick hit the talk-off button and leaned on the bar without trying to pull his hand away. "Your cab is outside."

"Is it?"

"Yes, it is."

"Rodney, you wouldn't be interested . . . ?"

"I don't get off until four and I've already promised . . ."

"Just kidding," said Lucinda unconvincingly as she reluctantly released his hand. "Have a good night."

Lucinda slowly descended from the stool, studiously attempting to maintain her balance and walk as straight as she could. Roderick shook his head. She didn't have a ring on her finger and she was calling her husband from a bar at almost two in the morning; Roderick had seen so many like her. *The world is full of lonely people.*

At the door Lucinda paused before heading out into the chilly dark. Who was she fooling, she had never cheated on Billy Jo. And never would; even if she did like to sometimes pretend she would enjoy being promiscuous. No, what Lucinda really enjoyed was being desired. Desired like Billy Jo used to do before his illness flared and . . . Lucinda didn't want to think about it.

So why did she keep thinking about how unfair it was that she had been a virgin when she first married, stayed married for five miserable years, spent seven wasted years so-called "dating" until she found Billy Jo floundering in a marriage that was all but legally over; so terribly unfair that now that she had found the man she wanted, he didn't . . .

Lucinda had salvaged Billy Jo from Betty's neglect. That woman was so . . . beneath Billy Jo, so incapable of helping him achieve the finer things in life. Unfortunately for Billy and Betty's children, all three of them looked like their mother and, worse, acted like their mother. They were all parasites; they just wanted what little money Billy Jo had saved, which wasn't much. What was a measly $78,000 anyway? It's amazing what one can think of when opening a door.

Betty didn't understand Billy Jo, what he wanted in life, what a legal career could mean. She was uneducated and Billy Jo deserved more. Betty undoubtedly didn't know how to do all it took to keep a man— Lucinda used to say to "keep a man happy." These days she cynically just placed the period after man. Later for this happiness crap.

But wasn't she entitled to happiness? People admired her—she came from a good family, was well educated, took care of herself. That thing with her uterus didn't stop her from being a woman. And my, my, my, wasn't she some kind of woman? Exactly the woman Billy Jo needed as a helpmate to eventually become a judge.

Lucinda loved Billy Jo. He would be a public success, and God knows he was privately terrific. Lucinda loved the way Billy Jo made love to her, even though she knew he was not as interested in loving her as she was in being loved by him . . . Oh, this was all too . . . Lucinda pushed against the burnished brass plate etched with the club name, Black Diamond.

As the door swung open, an early morning gust sent a shiver through Lucinda and she suddenly remembered asking Billy Jo to turn around. "I want to suck too," she had said while he had been patiently slurping her wetness with an almost disinterested expertness.

In her dating career, which seemed like another lifetime ago, she had had the opportunity to sexually examine maybe twelve dicks. Ah, the variety of the male sex organ, the little differences, particularly when aroused. She liked the feel of some, especially the way they throbbed when she squeezed or how they jumped as she teased the scrotum with her fingernails; for a couple of others it was how they looked, the veins pulsing on . . . what was his name, yes, Andre, light-skinned Andre, with the thick veins crisscrossing the surface of his thing, or the hooded darkness of Jerome's uncircumcised penis; and then there had been the size of Harold's tool. A basketball player's big dick, but he hadn't known what to do with it, or without it, for that matter.

Lovemaking with Billy Jo had been the biggest turn on, surprisingly so—oh, you could never tell just by how a man looked, or even how he danced; you could never tell if he knew how to make love without using his dick. Billy Jo knew. And Lucinda really, really liked that.

Moreover, Billy Jo wasn't squeamish about her freaking him. He hardly moved the first time she inserted a forefinger in his rectum, while she was sucking him and he was busy down there giving her head. Why was she like that? What did it look like? She supine, he on top of her, his head bobbing between her quivering thighs, his knees astride her head, his member in her mouth, her nose just beneath his taut testicles—Lucinda really liked that he was clean so the smell was never suffocating—and her hand spread across his bottom, one long finger deep inside him. What would a photograph of that look like?

He never questioned her, or made her feel embarrassed or feel anything but happy to have her way with him—not even the time she reminded him to shower and have a bowel movement before they jumped to it when they had been out on that wonderful weekend at the spa in Nevada, and had had a big lunch, and a scrumptious dinner, and had been out all day and dancing half the night, and . . . her finger was all the way in him, plunging at him, and the more deliberately she pushed, the more he nibbled at her clitoris, and she sucked him so hard she was afraid she was going to hurt him, but it felt so good. Why? Why all of that? Why did it take all of that?

At the curb, the cabdriver held open the back door of his maroon Toyota Camry. Lucinda slid in, thanking the driver by flashing a wide smile and making no attempt to hide her thighs as, one by one, she slowly swung her legs into the sedan. She would have really given him a good peek but he was studiously not looking, and Lucinda was not sure whether he was just being a gentleman or if, for some unfathomable reason, he really didn't want to catch sight of what lay between her legs.

Lucinda slid all the way over to the driver's side of the backseat so that she was directly behind him when he got in. After she gave him the address, Lucinda folded her arms, briefly; she made sure the door was locked and then pushed her body deeply into the corner of the backseat.

Lucinda knew what she was going to do. Lucinda knew what she shouldn't do.

She scooted down, lay her head on the fabric of the backseat and pretended to sleep.

Her hand crept under her dress. She had not worn panties.

"Any particular way you want to go?"

"Oh, whatever. I'm sure you know how to do your job. Take whatever route. This time of the morning, what difference does it make? Are you . . . ?" Lucinda stopped herself. She didn't want to make small talk. She wasn't even mildly interested in this young foreigner. She certainly didn't want to know what country he was from with his African accent. What did that matter?

Yes. Her left hand was there.

"Ma'am?"

"Don't mind me. I babble sometimes after a drink or two. I'm not used to drinking."

Good, he was taking the expressway. No lights. No stops.

If he turned around and saw her—*God, I would be so embarrassed*, Lucinda lied to herself, halfway hoping he would look at her, would . . . "Oh." She scooted down further and gapped her legs wider. Forefinger in the hole, thumb on the button.

She was beginning to breathe heavily—is that why he turned the radio on? "Is OK I play radio?"

"Yes. Of course." Their eyes met briefly in the rearview mirror. Could he imagine how smooth her thighs were? The treadmill and the exercise ball were really an effective way to keep her legs toned. What would he think if he turned and saw her, saw down there. The way she kept her private hair close cropped. How the dark of her looked in the shadows, the deep chestnut of her bulging labia major set off by the cream of her dress bunched up almost to her hips. Would he pull over and try . . . even on the expressway? What would he do if he could see the glistening sheen of the beginnings of a mildly musky flow dripping down there?

Lucinda smiled wanly. The guy looked away and pretended to be just driving a woman home. But Lucinda knew. Maybe he could smell her arousal. "Billy." Barely audible, her utterance was more a release than a sounding. Lucinda wanted to touch her nipples, to rub them between her thumb and the side of her pointing finger. She could smell the driver; he reeked of Old Spice or was it one of those obscenely colored (whoever heard of quality perfumes in those garish shades), one of those obnoxious body oils those unkempt street merchants hawked? Lucinda closed her eyes.

Lucinda imagined Billy Jo's lips sucking her breasts. Could you call this sex? A short tremor shot through her. Lucinda's legs jerked and she bumped against the back of the driver's seat. She knew she should stop. Billy. Just thinking about him.

She turned slightly sideways, as though she was going to curl up on the seat or like she was trying to get comfortable, or look out the window. Or anything but . . . "Oh." Why was she doing this to herself? She never usually made sounds during sex with Billy Jo because she usually had him in her mouth when she came. Lucinda wanted to stop, wanted to move her hand. But. *"Oh!"*

"You OK, lady?"

"I'm OK." Lucinda caught her breath and held the air inside her chest, tensing to enjoy the sweetness of the release that was just about to happen.

Lucinda paused, turned, and looked up at the rearview mirror; she was certain the man was leering at her. But he wasn't. At least he was pretending he wasn't. Lucinda was sure he was waiting for her to close her eyes and then he would stare. *"Oh."* A sudden contraction caused her to jerk. Her free hand flew to her mouth. She bit her fist.

Lucinda knew that men got off on watching women please themselves; however, she no longer cared whether he was furtively observing her. Lucinda squirmed as she continued and her thumb press hit just the right rhythm. "Oh-Ohhh." She turned her head just as the driver adjusted his rearview mirror.

Patrick Orobio saw the woman fling her head back and open her mouth, like she was, well, like she was . . . No, she couldn't be. These crazy American women. He didn't like that they were so out of control.

Meanwhile, in Portland, Billy Jo lay on his side in the dark, Sandra firmly massaging his back.

"That was Lucinda."

"What did she want?"

"Nothing. She was drunk."

# Vodka and Viagra

(From the novel-in-progress
*A Piece of Cake*)

## Al Young

"Just half a Viagra, Sidney," KoReena whispered, and then said it again with a squeal. "One half'll do it. That's enough. You don't have to be no Bob Dole."

Now, you know how funny it can get when people start talking and carrying on while they having sex. Remember back when the politicians were out to impeach Mr. Bill Clinton, when they were shining the spotlight on him and Miz Monica? You'd had to been either Stevie Wonder or Ray Charles not to see what was going down. Me, I was looking at how Larry Flynt was dropping a cool million on every woman that wanted to step forth and snatch the covers off some hypocrite congressman or senator. Come to find out, the rascals that was out to destroy Bill Clinton were hypocrites and liars their ownself.

I bring up all this just to say: Not only do people lie *about* sex, they lie *while* they actually be having sex.

"Aw, baby," I said, "can't nobody else but you do what you do like you do it."

To KoReena's credit, she didn't say anything. She just ooo'd and ahhh'd and wrapped her thighs around me so hard I knew I'd be feeling the effects of our workout for days. You know that old riff of Macbeth's: Tomorrow and tomorrow and tomorrow. For me doing the thing's the best exercise there is. It'll beat doing crunches anyway. For a sucker that's been around since World War Two, I ain't doing half bad. I'm still a pretty good stick man—with a little help, you understand. See, you get to your seventies, you can still get it up. Sure I can get it up—or, to be truthful, feel it get itself up. That's not the problem. The problem is how long can you keep it up? And that's where these pharmaceutical tools come in. Every time I go in to get a read-just, I thank the doctor, my chiropractor, who writes me out prescrip-tions. All this prostate trouble a lotta men my age be dealing with, KoReena made me read this article in a woman's health magazine, for crying out loud, that was about how semen if you don't discharge it will just go to laying up in your prostate gland until it go bad. You got to keep moving it outta your testicles. So I consider myself lucky to still have somebody around me that still likes to make love as much as I do. KoReena, mind you, she fifteen years younger than me, but, from what buddies tell me, it's a whole lotta women her age that's plain out-and-out given up having sex—not with hardlegs, not with men anyway.

Just the hot dampness of KoReena's breath in my ear, the dab and stab of her tongue, was enough to light me up inside like a laser. I felt ready to shine and cut thru all them carefully delivered bits and bytes of hers, and play her whole sweaty CD all the way thru, all over again. That was the problem that morning: Viagra sometimes get to acting the fool and let you know it ain't got no conscience. What Ko-Reena always served up—to my ears, to my heart, to my johnson, to my crazy way of thinking—was something like music. Name me any-thing that's stronger and stranger than a man and a woman doing ex-actly what a man and a woman can do so beautifully together. And when they been together as long as KoReena and me, what more can I say? Did I say strange?

All of a sudden—clean through all the thundering and lightning that was rumbling and flashing from the rainstorm outside—I heard KoReena cry out: "Good old heterosexual love!" That's exactly what my woman said, half grunting, half shouting, half whispering it to the room. Never mind that all this was taking place in good old San Francisco, where it's got to be more gay men and women per city block than in the whole of ancient Greece. Even I, a rusty senior that's seen just about everything life can throw at you, even I thought it was funny when KoReena groaned this.

Heterosexual love? Sound like a song Marvin Gaye, if he'd lived, might've gotten around to writing. Where did that come from? In the twelve years we'd been married and, like they say, *practicing* sex, Ko-Reena'd never hollered out anything like that. Where was it coming from? When you making love, tho, it's hard to ask questions. But for some reason, I spoke up anyway.

"What's that you say, baby?"

"Huh?"

"What'd you just now say?"

"Did I say something?" she asked. From the way she let her eyes ease open so they could make contact with mine, I got it that she hadn't heard herself talking.

"You might've been just thinking out loud," I told her. "But I thought I heard you say something about 'Good old heterosexual love.'"

KoReena laughed. "Come to think of it, now I do remember saying something like that."

"And what did you mean by that?"

Now KoReena opened her big brown eyes all the way. That little round, fleshy neck of hers, where it pooches out just under her chin—which I always tease her she got from her Mexican grand-daddy—it went to quivering. To me that was sexy, like when she got around some of her folks and she went back to talking in Spanish.

"Sidney," she said, "are you thinking maybe I've been keeping something from you?"

"No," I lied. "It just sounded peculiar to me that you would blurt that out."

"And what's so peculiar about it?"

"Well, hell . . . Yes, this is heterosexual love we're dealing up in here. That's all we ever dealt. I don't have anything personal against homo-eroticism, but—"

"Now that we're rich, I'm going to have to stop you from taking all those community college courses."

"Look, Koko, I knew that word before I ever stepped onto a campus. It's not a day go by in the Bay Area you don't hear or read that word."

KoReena, who is nothing if she's not smooth, she just looked at me and smiled. Then she pulled my face down to hers so she could kiss me all sloppy and for real on the mouth. When her hand slid down under the sheets and Mister Johnson felt her cool fingers wrap around him, it made me a little mad that I wasn't really in control of any of this. I felt like arguing. Back with my first wife, Squirrel, when we would get to arguing, that turned me on and her, too. I would get as hard as she got wet. And with my bourgie artist girlfriend JoJo, who died about a year before I met KoReena at the blues festival, it was the opposite. You get JoJo pissed off, you ain't gon get no what's-name. KoReen, she was slick. It was some kinda way she kept parts of herself curtained off in mystery, you know.

"KoReena," I said, "I know you done laid up here and got your-self a nut offa me. But I don't believe Mister Johnson is ready to call it a night."

"A night, my foot," my baby said, laughing. "It's already nine o'clock in the morning, and if we don't get up from here, get cleaned up and go to that investment seminar at the Holiday Inn, then you talk about missing the boat."

"Baby, just because that man's slick infomercial charmed you so don't mean he knows any more about investing than me or Willie G."

"I liked his presentation. It was far more intelligent than the ones where they trot out those borderline people talking about how they bought them a house—two houses, three, four, five houses—with no money down, then rented them out or sold them for a fortune."

"Baby, can we get back to the subject at hand?"

KoReena rolled her eyes and said, "You mean, back to the subject I just happen to have my hand around right now."

"OK," I said. "All right then, you wanna be like that."

All my woman did was shake her head and slither down under the sheets, making good and sure her titties jiggled against me all the way down.

I know when to stop fighting and switch. Soon it was gonna be my turn to cry something crazy.

I knew when to kick back and zone out, too, and just let lying dogs sleep. Dozing off, I wondered again if we deserved to be as rich as we became after me and Willie G. wiped out the Lotto, I mean, *slaughtered* it? I spent too much time turning that one over in my mind and talking with my baby about it. KoReena's family—since on her mother's side they came here from Mexico—they strived and tried to make something outta themselves, so she was brought up, you know, kind of on the outer edges of the middle class. They had that house down in Milpitas. They'd let it get rundown, but it was

still theirs. They owned it. Me, my children and grandchildren pros-
pered. Don't ask why, but I never did want much of anything except
to be healthy, peaceful and be able to do anything I wanted to whenever I felt like doing it.

You ever thought about the power that someone that's dressed
has got over somebody who isn't? As my grandkids say, it's awesome,
and then some. KoReena was good at making that kinda power-move
on me. I mean, she could *play* it!

I didn't realize how deep into sleep I'd slipped until I felt her
bending over me, saying, "It's all right, sugar. You can stay here and
sleep. It's pretty nasty out there, and I've been worried about how
you let your immune system get run down on that plane back from
France."

Sniffing hard, I drew in a heady hit off my wife's expensive perfume, snorted it all the way up inside my brain on the sly the way
JoJo used to snort that profane cocaine in her very last days on earth.
Willie G. always talking about how he thought somebody'd put some
kinda whammy on JoJo since she spent so much money on psychics.
Willie figured somebody must've slipped her some goofer dust or
something. She did leave here pretty quick. And just when her draw-
ings and paintings were starting to sell, and she was getting famous
all up and down the state. But I always will believe it was that happy
dust that stopped Jo cold in her tracks, killed her dead. Laying out
$400 a bottle for KoReena's scent at the Duty Free Shop, Orly Air-
port, Paris, didn't distance me one inch from how good it made her
smell. Like something good to eat.

"You smell like dessert," I said.

"I know," she said, "like those Rice Krispies squares we used to
cook up with marshmallow. You gonna roll your tired, gray boodie
outta bed and go hear this talk, or what?"

"You still got that little digital recorder you ordered off Home
Shopping Network last week?"

KoReena fished the thing out of her purse and waved it at me.

"Then," I said, "why don't you make a recording of everything the
man say. I can play it back and maybe learn something about high finance."

"Maybe that is the thing to do," said KoReena. "Better that than you falling asleep in the middle of the man's presentation and start snoring and stuff."

I sat up and hoisted one leg out from under the comforter. "Look, baby," I began, and I meant every word I was about to say. "Sometimes I get tired of this rich-wealthy-affluent bullshit. James Brown was right. Money don't change you, but time will move you on."

"Wrong," snapped KoReena.

"You calling me wrong, or you calling James Brown wrong?"

"The words go: 'Money *won't* change you, but time . . . will *take* you on.' There's as much difference, a big difference, between *don't* and *won't* as there is between *move you on* and *take you on*. You messing with my song, Sidney! My moms used to play that record and dance us to death."

"Hold on," I said. "I'm making a point."

"Which is . . . ?"

"The best investment I see happening these days is to take all your money out of the stock market and the money market and anywhere else where it's trading going on."

"And do what with it?"

"I don't know," I said. "Maybe just let it sit up in a CD or a savings account and draw whatever little interest it can. Better than losing it, like that two hundred thousand we lost last year, fooling around with MCI and Gateway."

At this, KoReena yelled, "Whoa! So that's where I left them!" Hustling into the bedroom bathroom, she snatched up her key ring and jangled that at me, too.

"I'm sorry, honey, but I gotta go."

"All right," I said, "but you better take the big umbrella, the golfing umbrella I bought you at Nordstrom's."

"To satisfy you, I'll take it. Women aren't as crazy about those big-ass umbrellas as you men are. I was out on Montgomery Street the other day when it was raining, and there were so many yuppies with their golf umbrellas opened out that we couldn't hardly get past one another on the sidewalk."

"Are we talking about the Holiday Inn in Civic Center or the one by the Embarcadero?"

"How come all of a sudden you have to get specific details?"

"Because I might just surprise you, get myself together, and get over there late and meet up with you."

"No, darling, no favors, please. Just stay here, take yourself a long hot shower or a bath, fix yourself some breakfast, and be here safe and sound when I get back. I know you're worn out."

"Worn out? I just needed me a catnap, that's all."

On her way out, KoReena looked back and said, "It's a good thing we got us a little money. Otherwise, we might be living in one of those mobile home estates, trying to get by on social security, with you spending every spare nickel you can get on vodka and Viagra."

"What a perfectly evil thing to say. What's the matter with you this morning, baby?"

"Just feeling my oats, I guess. The moon might be in Jupiter."

All the way out the bed at last, I said, "You never know. The moon might just be in Milpitas."

# The Statue of Liberty

(From the short fiction collection *Fever*)

## John Edgar Wideman

One of the pleasures of jogging in the country is seeing those houses your route takes you past each day and wondering who lives in them. Some sit a good distance from the road, small, secluded by trees, tucked in a fold of land where they've been sheltered thousands of years from the worst things that happen to people. A little old couple lives in this kind. They've raised many children and lost some to the city but the family name's on mailboxes scattered up and down the road, kids and grandkids in houses like their folks', farmers like them, like more generations than you'd care to count back to England and cottages that probably resemble these, Capes, with roofs pulled down almost to the ground the way the old man stuffs on a wool cap bitter February days to haul in firewood from the shed. There are majestic hilltop-sitters with immaculate outbuildings and leaded glass and fine combed lawns sloping in every direction, landmarks you can measure your progress by as you reel in the countryside step by step jogging. I like best those ramshackle outfits—you can tell it's an old farm two young people from the city have taken over with their city dreams and city habits because it's not a real farm anymore, more somebody's idea of what living in the country should be at this day and time. A patched-together look, a corniness and coziness like pictures in a child's book, these city people have a little bit of everything growing on their few acres, and they keep goats, chickens, turkeys, ducks, geese, one cow—a pet zoo, really, and a German shepherd on a chain outside the trailer they've converted to a permanent dwelling. You know they smoke dope and let their kids run around naked as the livestock. They still blast loud city music on a stereo too big for the trailer and watch the stars through a kind of skylight contraption rigged in the tin roof and you envy them the time they first came out from the city, all those stars and nobody around but the two of them, starting out fresh in a different place and nothing better to do than moon up at the night sky and listen to the crickets and make each other feel nice in bed. Those kinds of houses must have been on your jogging route once. You look for them now beneath overloaded clotheslines, beyond rusted-out car stumps, in junk and mess and weeds, you can't tell what all's accumulated in the front yard from where you pass on the road.

A few houses close to the road. Fresh paint and shutters and shrubs, a clean-cut appearance and you think of suburbs, of neat house after house exactly alike, exactly like this one sitting solitary where it doesn't fit into the countryside. Retired people. Two frail old maids on canvas folding chairs in the attached garage with its wizard door rolled up and a puffy, ginger-colored cat crossing from one lady's stockinged feet to the other lady's stockinged feet like a conversation you can't hear from the road. Taking the air in their gazebo is what they're thinking in that suburban garage with its wide door open.

In the window of another one only a few yards from the road you can't tell if there's a person in the dark looking out because the panes haven't been washed in years. A house wearing sunglasses. You have a feeling someone very very old is still alive inside watching you, watching everything that passes, a face planted there in the dark so long, so patient and silent it scares you for no good reason. A gray, sprawled sooty clapboard swaybacked place a good wind could knock over but that wind hasn't blown through yet, not in all the time it's taken the man and woman who live here to shrivel up and crack and curl like the shingles on their steep roof that looks like a bad job of trying to paint a picture of the ocean, brushstrokes that don't become stormy ocean waves but stay brushstrokes, separate, unconnected, slapped on one after another in a hurry-up, hopeless manner that doesn't fool anyone.

A dim-shouldered, stout woman in a blue housedress with a lacy dirty white collar is who I imagine staring at me when I clomp-clomp-clomp by, straining on the slight grade that carries me beyond this house and barn people stopped painting fifty years ago, where people stopped living at least that long ago but they're too old now to die.

Once I thought of an eye large enough to fill the space inside those weather-beaten walls, under that slapdash roof. Just an eye. Self-sufficient. Enormous. White and veiny. Hidden in there with nothing else to do but watch.

Another way jogging pleasures me is how it lets me turn myself into another person in another place. The city, for instance. I'm small and pale running at night in a section of town I've been warned never to enter alone even in daylight. I run burning with the secret of who I am, what I'm carrying, what I can do, secrets no one would guess just watching me jog past, a smallish, solitary white woman nearly naked on dangerous streets where she has no business being. She's crazy, they think. Or asking for it. But no one knows I can kill instantly, efficiently, with my fingers, toes and teeth. No one can see the tiny deadly weapons I've concealed on my person. In a wristband pouch. Under a Velcro flap in my running shorts. Nor would anyone believe the speed in my legs. No one can catch me unless I want to be caught.

When the huge black man springs from the shadows I let him grapple me to the ground. I tame him with my eyes. Instantly he understands. Nothing he could steal from me, throwing me down on the hard cement, hurting me, stripping me, mounting me with threats and his sweaty hand in my mouth so I won't scream, none of his violence, his rage, his hurry to split me and pound himself into me would bring the pleasure I'm ready to give of my own free will. I tell him with my eyes that I've been running to meet him. I jog along his dangerous streets because I've prepared for him. He lets me undress him. I'm afraid for a moment his skin will be too black and I'll lose him in this dark alley. But my hands swim in the warmth of him. His smell, the damp sheen tells me he's been jogging too. It's peaceful where we are. We understand each other perfectly. Understand how we've been mistaken about each other for longer than we care to admit. Instead of destroying you, I whisper to him, I choose to win you with the gentleness in my eyes. Convert you. Release you. Then we can invent each other this quiet way, breath by breath, limb by limb, as if we have all the time in the world and our bodies are a route we learn jogging leisurely till the route's inside us, imagining us, our bodies carried along by it effortlessly. We stand and trot off shoulder to shoulder. He has Doberman legs. They twirl as if on a spit.

For weeks now they've been going by each morning. Crooker hears them first. Yapping and thrashing, running the length of her chain till it yanks her back to reality. A loud, stupid dog. I think she believes she's going to escape each time she takes a dash at her chain. She barks and snarls at them and I'd like to rubber-band her big mouth shut.

Quiet, Crooker. Hush.

Leave her be, Orland grumps to me. Barking's her job. She gets fed to bark.

We both know Crooker's useless as a watchdog. She growls at her reflection in the French doors. She howls at birds a mile away. A bug can start her yelping. Now she's carrying on as if the Beast from Babylon's slouching down the road to eat us all for breakfast and it's nobody but the joggers she's seen just like I've seen them every morning for a week. Passing by, shading to the outer edge of the road because they don't want to aggravate a strange, large country dog into getting so frantic it just might snap its chain.

Nothing but those joggers she's barking at. Shut up, Crooker.

How do you know those people ain't the kind to come back snooping around here at night? Pacify the dog and them or others like them be right up on top of us before we know it.

Orland, please. What in the world are you grumbling about? You're as bad as she is.

I pay her to bark. Let her bark.

She's Crooker because at birth her tail didn't come out right. An accident in the womb. Her tail snagged on something and it's been crook-ended since. Poor creature couldn't even walk through the door of life right. But she was lucky too. Molly must have been spooked by the queerness of that tail. Must have been the humped tail because Molly ate every other pup in that litter. Ate them before we caught on and rescued this crook-tailed one.

When they pass the window Orland doesn't even glance up. He doesn't know what he's missing. Usually he's gone long before they jog past. I forget what kept him late in the morning I'm recalling. It's not that he's a hard worker or busy or conscientious. For years now the point's been to rise early and be gone. Gone the important part. Once he's gone he can figure out some excuse for going, some excuse to keep himself away. I think he may have another place where he sleeps. Tucks himself in again after he leaves my bed and dreams half the day away like a baby. Orland misses them. Might as well be a squirrel or moth riling Crooker. If he knew the woman looked as good as she does in her silky running shorts, he'd sure pay attention. If he knew the man was a big black man his stare would follow mine out the window and pay even more attention.

They seem to be about my age more or less. Woman rather short but firm and strong with tight tanned legs from jogging. She packs a bit more weight in the thighs than I do, but I haven't gained an inch anywhere nor a pound since I was a teenager. My face betrays me, but I was blessed with a trim, athletic high school beauty queen's figure. Even after the first two children Orland swore at me once when he pulled my nightie, Damned Jailbait.

The man's legs from ankle to the fist of muscle before the knee are straight and hard as pipes, bony as dog's legs then flare into wedges of black thighs, round black man's butt. First morning I was with the kids in the front yard he waved. A big hello-how-are-you smiling-celebrity wave the way black men make you think they're movie stars or professional athletes with a big, wide wave, like you should know them if you don't and that momentary toothy spotlight they cast on you is something special from that big world where they're famous. He's waved every morning since. When I've let him see me. I know he looks for me. I wasn't wearing much more than the kids when he saw me in the yard. I know he wonders if I stroll around the house naked or sunbathe in the nude on a recliner behind the house in the fenced yard you can't see from the road. I've waited with my back close enough to the bedroom window so he'd see me if he was trying, a bare white back he could spot even though it's hard to see inside this gloomy house that hour in the morning. A little reward, if he's alert. I shushed Crooker and smiled back at him, up at him the first time, kneeling beside Billy, tying my Billyboy's shoe. We're complete smiling buddies now and the woman greets me too.

No doubt about it he liked what he saw. Three weeks now and they'd missed only two Sundays and an odd Thursday. Three times it had rained. I didn't count those days. Never do. Cooped up in the house with four children under nine you wouldn't waste your time or energy either, counting rainy, locked-in days like that because you need every ounce of patience, every speck of will, just to last to bed-time. Theirs. Which on rainy cooped-up days is followed immediately by yours because you're whipped, fatigued, bone and brain tired living in a child's world of days with no middle, end or beginning, just time like Silly Putty you're stuck in the belly of. You can't shape it; it shapes you, but the shape is no real shape at all, it's the formlessness of no memory, no sleep that won't let you get a handle on anything, let you be anything but whatever it is twisted, pulled, worried. Three weeks minus three minus days that never count anyway minus one Thursday minus twice they perhaps went to church and that equals what? Equals the days required for us to become acquainted. To get past curiosity into *Hi there.* To follow up his presidential candidate's grin and high-five salute with my cheeriness, my punch-clock punctuality, springing tick-tock from my gingerbread house so I'm in sight, available, when they jog by. Most of the time, apparently. Always, if he takes the trouble to seek me out. As if the two of them, the tall black man and his shortish, tanned white lady companion, were yoked together, pulling the sun around the world and the two of them had been circling the globe forever, in step, in time with each other, round and round like the tiger soup in a Little Black Sambo book I read to my children, achieving a rhythm, a high-stepping pace unbroken and sufficient unto itself but I managed to blend in, to jog beside them invisible till I learned their pace and rhythm, flowing, unobtrusive, even when they both discovered me there, braced with them, running with them, undeniably part of whatever they think they are doing every morning when they pass my house and wave.

He liked what he saw because when they finally did stop and come in for the cool drinks I'd proposed first as a kind of joke, then a standing offer, seriously, no trouble, whenever, if ever, they choose to stop, then on a tray, two actual frosty tumblers of ice water they couldn't refuse without hurting my feelings, he took his and brushed my fingertips in a gesture that wasn't accidental, he wasn't a clumsy man, he took a glass and half my finger with it because he'd truly liked what he saw and admired it more close up.

Sweat sheen gleamed on him like a fresh coat of paint. He was pungent as tar. I could smell her mixed in with him. They'd made love before they jogged. Hadn't bothered to bathe before starting off on their route. She didn't see me remove my halter. He did. I sat him where he'd have to force himself to look away in order not to see me slip the halter over my head. I couldn't help standing, my arms raised like a prisoner of war, letting him take his own good time observing the plump breasts that are the only part of my anatomy below my neck not belonging to a fourteen-year-old girl. She did not see what I'd done till I turned the corner, but she seemed not to notice or not to care. I didn't need to use the line I'd rehearsed in front of the mirror, the line that went with my stripper's curtsy, with my arm stretched like Miss Liberty over my head and my waist daintily cocked, dangling in my fingers the wisp of halter: We're very casual around here.

Instead, as we sit sipping our ice waters I laugh and say, This weather's too hot for clothes. I tease my lips with the tip of my tongue. I roll the frosted glass on my breasts. This feels so nice. Let me do you. I push up her tank top. Roll the glass on her flat stomach.

You're both so wet. Why don't you get off those damp things and sit back? Cool off awhile. It's perfectly private.

I'll fetch us more drinks. Not too early for something stronger than water, is it?

They exchange easily deciphered looks. For my benefit, speaking to me as much as to each other. Who is this woman? What the hell have we gotten ourselves into?

I guide her up from the rattan chair. It's printed ruts across the backs of her thighs. My fingers are on her elbow. I slide open the screen door and we step onto the unfinished mess of flagstone, mismatched tile and brick Orland calls a patio. The man lags behind us. He'll see me from the rear as I balance on one leg then the other, stepping out of my shorts.

I point her to one of the lawn chairs.

Make yourself comfortable. Orland and the kids are gone for the day. Just the three of us. No one else for miles. It's glorious. Pull off your clothes, stretch out and relax.

I turn quickly and catch him liking what he sees, all of me naked, but he's wary. A little shocked. All of this too good to be true. I don't allow him time to think overly long about it.

You're joining us, aren't you? No clothes allowed.

After I plop down I watch out of the corner of my eye how she

wiggles and kicks out of her shorts, her bikini underwear. Her elasti-
cized top comes off over her head. Arms raised in that gesture of
surrender every woman performs shrugging off what's been hiding
her body. She's my sister then. I remember myself in the mirror of
her. Undressing just a few minutes before, submitting, taking charge.

Crooker howls from the pen where I've stuffed her every morning since the first week. She'd been quiet till his long foot in his fancy
striped running shoe touched down on the patio. Her challenge
scares him. He freezes, framed a moment in the French doors.

It's OK. She's locked in her pen. All she'd do if she were here is
try to lick you to death. C'mon out.

I smile over at the woman. Aren't men silly most of the time?
Under that silence, those hard stares, that playacting that's supposed
to be a personality, aren't they just chicken-hearted little boys most
of the time? She knows exactly what I'm thinking without me saying
a word. Men. Her black man no different from the rest.

He slams the screen door three times before it catches in the
glides that haven't been right since Orland set them. The man can't
wait to see the two of us, sisters again because I've assumed the same
stiff posture in my lawn chair as she has in hers, back upright, legs
extended straight ahead, ankles crossed. We are as demure as two
white ladies in broad daylight displayed naked for the eyes of a black
man. Her breasts are girlish, thumb nippled. Her bush a fuzzy creature in her lap. I'm as I promised. He'll like what he'll see, can't wait
to see, but he's pretending to be in no hurry, undoing his bulky shoes
lace by lace instead of kicking them off his long feet. The three
chairs are arranged in a Y, foot ends converging. I steered her where
I wanted her and took my seat so he'll be in the middle, facing us
both, her bare flesh and mine everywhere he turns. With all his
heart, every hidden fiber he wants to occupy the spot I've allotted for
him, but he believes if he seems in too much of a rush, shows undue
haste, he'll embarrass himself, reveal himself for what he is, what he
was when Crooker's bark stopped him short.

He manages a gangly nonchalance, settling down, shooting out
his legs so the soles of three pairs of feet would kiss if we inched just
a wee bit closer to the bull's-eye. His shins gleam like black marble.
When he's jogging he flows. Up close I'm aware of the joints, angles,
hinges, the struts and wires of sinew assembling him, the patchwork

of his dark skin, many colors, like hers, like mine, instead of the tar-baby sleekness that trots past my window. His palms, the pale under-pads of his feet have no business being the blank, clownish color they are. She could wear that color on her hands and feet and he could wear hers and the switch would barely be noticeable.

We're in the place now and she closes her eyes, leans back her head and sighs. It is quiet and nice here. So peaceful, she says. This is a wonderful idea, she says, and teaches herself how to recline, levers into prone position and lays back so we're no longer three wooden Indians.

My adjustment is more subtle. I drop one foot on either side of my chair so I'm straddling it, then scoot the chair with me on it a few inches to change the angle the sun strikes my face. An awkward way to move, a lazy, stuttering adjustment useful only because it saves me standing up. And it's less than modest. My knees are spread the width of the lawn chair as I ride it to a new position. If the man has liked what he's seen so far, and I know he has, every morsel, every crumb, then he must certainly be pleased by this view. I let him sink deeper. Raise my feet back to the vinyl strips of the leg rest, but keep my knees open, yawning, draw them toward my chest, hug them, snuggle them. Her tan is browner than mine. Caramel then cream where a bikini shape is saved on the skin. I show him the bottom of me is paler, but not too much paler than my thighs, my knees I peer over, knees like two big scoops of coffee ice cream I taste with the tip of my tongue.

I'm daydreaming some of the things I'll let them do to me. Tie my limbs to the bed's four corners. Kneel me, spread the cheeks of my ass. I'll suck him while her fingers ply me. When it's the black man's turn to be bondaged and he's trussed up too tight to grin, Or-land bursts the bedroom door, chain saw cradled across his chest. No reason not to let everything happen. They are clean. In good health. My body's still limber and light as a girl's. They like what they see. She's pretending to nap but I know she can sense his eyes shining, the veins thickening in his rubbery penis as it stirs and arches be-tween his thighs he presses together so it doesn't rear up and stab at me, single me out impolitely when there are two of us, two women he must take his time with and please. We play our exchange of smiles, him on the road, me with Billy and Sarah and Carl and Augie at the edge of our corn patch. I snare his eyes, lead them down slowly to my pearly bottom, observe myself there, finger myself, study what I'm showing him so when I raise my eyes and bring his up with me again, we'll both know beyond a doubt what I've been telling him every morning when he passes is true.

No secrets now. What do you see, you black bastard? My pubic hair is always cropped close and neat, a perfect triangle decorates the fork of the Y, a Y like the one I formed with our lawn chairs. I unclasp my knees, let them droop languorously apart, curl my toes on the tubing that frames my chair. She may be watching too. But it's now or never. We must move past certain kinds of resistance, habits that are nothing more than habits. Get past or be locked like stupid baying animals in a closet forever. My eyes challenge his. Yes those are the leaves of my vagina opening. Different colors inside than outside. Part of what's inside me unfolding, exposed, like the lips of your pouty mouth.

The petals of my vagina are two knuckles spreading of a fist stuck in your face. They are the texture of the softest things you've ever touched. Softer. Better. Fleece bedding them turns them subtly damp. A musk rises, gently, magically, like the mist off the oval pond that must be included in your route if you jog very far beyond my window. But you may arrive too late or too early to have noticed. About a half mile from here the road climbs as steeply as it does in this rolling countryside. Ruins of a stone wall, an open field on the right, a ragged screen of pine trees borders the other side and if you peer through them, green of meadow is broken just at the foot of a hill by a black shape difficult to distinguish from dark tree trunks and their shadows, but search hard, it rests like a mirror into which a universe has collapsed. At dawn, at dusk the pond breathes. You can see when the light and air are right, something rare squeezed up from the earth's center, hanging over this pond. I believe a ghost with long, trailing hair is marooned there and if I ever get my courage up, I've promised myself I'll go jogging past at night and listen to her sing.

# The Boxer and the Lotus

**Christopher Chambers**

Another succulent memory oozed into Derek Stone's brain before he stepped into the ring. Of course, his arena wasn't a roped canvas square. It was his reserved booth in the dim bosom of a cigar-and-martini bar called The Havana Club. The clink of glasses and slow syncopation of Latin jazz melted together; faces blurred. He dropped his fists, and let his past swallow him whole.

*Lilac. Bergamot. Jasmine. Sweet, pungent, sultry. She swirls the oils together in her palms, smooths it into her skin. Copper-colored skin. Or burnished brass? No—those are loud metals in which my baby sheathed herself during the day. Her tone is muted, warm. Sculpted, kneaded by her fingers that soon beckon me. In reply, my cock parts the folds of my robe. And now my own fingers play the blended oils onto her skin. Sliding along the curve of her back, testing the thickness of her thighs, weighing the fullness of her breasts, coaxing the nubby attentiveness of her violet nipples. I glide from the nape of her neck to her toes. And stop. Lick those toes. Retreat. There, to the timbre of musk and sweat. Black lambswool, pink flesh. My tongue feathers her clit. Then I suck it. I cradle that heart-shaped ass in my palms. Legs shoot askew and painted toes point like a ballerina's. A cry, shrill. Then, guttural. Candle-light glints off her wedding band . . .*

Derek composed himself as the cold seeped back into his soul. Time went toe-to-toe with memory! Tonight, the main event, fifteen rounds, was black women's mindless cupidity. Fists clenched. Pugilist's pose attained. Highball of Glenfiddich strategically placed for refreshment between rounds. Ring the bell!

"You sisters need to jettison the bullshit you're spoon-fed in *Essence*!"

Kwame Brooks, sandwiched between two pairs of women at the table, entreated him, "Don't bite the hand that feeds you. *Essence* had you on their bestseller list for nine weeks."

"Man shut th'fuck up! See, ladies, love is booby-trapped because the male is hardwired to coddle and cuddle only so long as it takes to nut, then he books. Might take him twenty minutes, or twenty years. It will happen. And predictably, the female demonizes him—because she needs him, like Heaven needs Hell. You idolize the idyllic. Such is the duality of women. Such is the *duplicity* . . . of women."

Bell rung. Round over. He drained his highball. Bell rung, round started. He snarled on—the soliloquy sounding less like human words and more like the age-addled bark of a senile German shepherd. Mean. Weary. Haunted.

The women glowered and nudged each other. They were all in the typical professional sister's winter uniform: tight Banana Republic mock turtlenecks, hip-clinging gabardine skirts, spike-heeled Joan and David boots, bangles jangling on their wrists.

One named Amahri hissed, "My sister and my secretary read your novels. I was going to buy your latest. Thanks for dissuading me." She slid away with a second woman in tow, sashaying to the bar, slinging their Kate Spade purses.

"Later," Derek huffed. Then he shouted for the waitress, "Shirleeey. 'Nother round for the faithful! Single malt for *moi*, Cyrano . . . Don Quixote. Hennessey for my Sancho Panza here. A Cosmo and a Cuban *mojito* for Dulcinea and Roxanne."

Kwame cheesed, "Uh, ladies, did y'all catch Derek on Charlie Rose on PBS? 'CBS Sunday Morning' last week? 'BET Tonight with Ed Gordon'? *Honey* magazine named him one of the ten sexiest brothers in America!"

"Kwam," Derek croaked, "you're the fruit of the William Morris Agency's affirmative action program: white literary agency . . . and dumb-ass Knee-go sycophant."

A woman named Tracy slurped down her cosmopolitan and said, "Ya know, Amahri and Lisa are, um . . . at the buffet, and—"

"Oh, they can wait," her companion interrupted. She spoke in a voice quavering from lilting tones, like a flute, to sharp tonics, like a trumpet. "I'm Hope Chen-Lee—the one who recognized you. I teach third grade over at Sojourner Truth. I'm a substitute."

"Starved for grown folks' company?"

She smiled graciously. "Moved here two months ago. Tracy and I are sorors."

"Two months, huh? You coincide with my bad Karma."

Hope parried that riposte, again with a smile. An inexplicable smile. She had huge oval eyes. A round face. Broad brown cheeks, short-coiffed, bone-straight black hair. She spoke with full, cherry lips as she studied Derek's sallow face. "No such thing as bad Karma, according to *The Dao of the Lotus*."

Tracy groaned, "Aw, Hope . . . not tonight with that New Age mess, *please*?"

Hope said, "Any brother who'd refer to us as 'Dulcinea' and 'Roxanne' knows his classics, and *The Dao of the Lotus* is—"

Derek cut her off. "Is *bullshit*." He lolled his head like an effete academic. "Written in 650 A.D. during the Manchu Invasions. About loss, rebirth. Howya like me now?"

"It's more about the continuity of the spirit." Hope smiled, wryly. "And *boning*."

"Hey I *like* this girl, Kwam," Derek chortled. "Even a Daoist would say I got *boned*—five book rejections in two months, the latest from my own editor." The waitress brought the drinks, then circumcised a Monte Cristo for Derek. He mouthed the snipped cigar. "I'm not writing who's-fuckin'-who's-baby's-mama soap opera shit anymore. I don't care if it's all niggahs wanna read, and all white people wanna publish. *Yeah, I said it!* I can say what I want in here, 'cause this is *my* house. My Sloppy Joe's, and I am Ernie Hemingway in here."

Hope leaned in very close, ensnaring Derek with the scent of ginger and vanilla. "Hemingway didn't write *Thinkin' Wid tha Small Head,* or *Tube Steak Boogie*," she crooned, grinning. Then the grin hardened. "Mr. Stone, a brother as deep as you were . . . you *are* . . .

can contribute more. Hemingway, Zora Neale Hurston, Fitzgerald—they didn't give up, give in."

Derek answered in a whispery voice. "Hemingway ate his twelve-gauge. Zora and F. Scott died broke, insane. Me? Amex rolls like I'm Bin Laden; the IRS has a hit man after me. Had y'all known that, would you've scooted over here, all starry-eyed and impressed?" He crushed the unlit $8 cigar into the ashtray.

"He's tripping," Tracy mused aloud.

Derek stood, swaying. "Haven't scared you off yet, Ms. Chen-Lee?" He sauntered to the men's room. Familiar scene. There is nothing more pathetic than weeping into a urinal cake. Praying for grace. Starved for hope.

He returned to the booth to see Tracy hastily scribbling her cell number on the back of her business card and handing it to Kwame. "Your boy needs therapy."

"Nah, an exorcist," Kwame quipped before noticing Derek's presence.

Sliding into his seat, Derek growled, "Tell 'em about the book."

Kwame swallowed hard. "Dee . . . c'mon. Lemme take you home, bruh."

Derek ignored him. "An historical novel about the Boxer Rebellion in China, 1900. That might be over most folks' heads."

Kwame jumped in. "Uh . . . yeah, 'Buffalo Soldiers' from the Twenty-fourth Infantry fought in the American contingent at Peking, with the Europeans, Russians, Japanese. Carving up China. A tough-ass sergeant—the regiment's boxing champion—falls in love with a mixed race Chinese girl. An outcast, servant to prostitutes. Her father was the African houseboy to a white merchant." Hope raised a slender eyebrow as Kwame continued. "War, imperialism, racism, love, murder, redemption. In another universe, it'd win m'dawg a Pulitzer." Kwame sighed. "Got so desperate, I tried to pitch it as *The Last Emperor* and *The Joy Luck Club* meets *Training Day* and *Waiting to Exhale*."

As Kwame spoke, Derek closed his eyes and wished away everyone in the bar. Except Hope. Yet he said nothing to her. Hope seemed to take the cue. She gathered her coat, but lingered when it looked like Derek had passed out.

"Mr. Brooks, where will Mr. Stone be tomorrow?"

"Day-um . . . if he's sober, in Limbo. I mean . . . Manny Limbo's Gym, off Market Square, near Chinatown. Old school, sweaty-stinky place like in *Rocky*."

"Yeah. I don't live too far from there. Thanks. Ya ready, Trace?"

Kwame called to Hope as she and Tracy moved away. "Sister, my advice: stick to your pee-wees at Sojourner. Derek's given up hope."

Derek circled his hulking sparring partner like a wolf loping around a wounded bear. Time to finish him. Jab, jab, cross. Feint. Jab. *Pop!* A right hook crashed into the bear's chin, staggering him. Manny Limbo didn't jump between Derek and his prey fast enough. Another hook, and the big man fell like a cut pine.

Manny cried, "Stone, jou mudda-fockeeng *vato loco!*"

Derek spit out his mouth guard and crawled through the ropes. But as he yanked off his padded head gear, he heard a softer voice.

"*Xhiang Xhi.*" Hope Chen-Lee stood before him, hands thrust in the pockets of her billowy trenchcoat. She smiled. He didn't. "Xhiang Xhi means 'mud girl' in Manchu, Mr. Stone. That should be the name of your female lead character."

"Pass me that towel." When she obliged, he snickered, "Ah, we were feelin' each other at Havana, then? Shoulda ended up in my bed last night."

Hope chuckled. "If I were in your bed last night, judging from your condition, all I'd have been doing was holding a plastic bucket under your mouth."

"What do you want?" he barked. "Besides offering unwanted literary advice?"

"Hot tea on a cold day, Mr. Stone."

Derek masked his soul's approval with a stern grunt. "Wait till I shower."

She did, and she led him the few blocks to Chinatown, under a milky gray sky, wet with snow flurries. Hope halted before a Chinese butcher shop, headless ducks hanging in the window.

"Got a loft upstairs," she explained as she unlocked a red door. "And don't worry—you won't smell a thing from this shop!"

Derek rolled his tongue against his cheek. *Yeah, right—tea's up in her crib, not in a Chinese tea shop or Starbucks! She's no different than the rest of these needy tricks. She's just bringing a new game I haven't seen yet.*

Hope's slender finger stroked the walnut banister as she and Derek ascended the stairs to the loft's door. "My parents are from Trinidad, via Toronto. You know, 'Coolies' or 'Chinie Royal' as the Jamaicans call them. Mixed black and Chinese." They reached the landing; Hope spun around. "Why boxing? No lies today."

"I beg your pardon?"

She opened the door; the scent of mint, citrus wafted out. "No truth, no entry."

The oval eyes washed over him, rinsing away the meanness that compelled him to label her a "needy trick." Oh yes, he wanted to go inside. Badly. He shrugged and shared, "Cool. I was ten years old, coming out of the library with *Treasure Island* and *The Last of the Mohicans* under one arm, poetry by Hughes, Bontemps under the other. Not good in my neighborhood. Got the books, then my ass, knocked to the ground. I resolved that somebody else's ass would fall next time."

Hope smiled and beckoned him in. She peeled off his leather jacket as he recounted: "Got a scholarship to Indiana. Then it became the white frat boys and townie rednecks knocking my books to the ground. It stopped when I became intramural middleweight champion. Do it now to keep in shape. Clear my mind."

"Not very effective at the latter, now, is it?"

Derek finally got his bearings: an eclectic mélange, like its occupant. Exposed brick walls, hung at intervals with West African weaves and masks. Chinese silks and porcelains adorning finely carved West Indian mahogany end tables. In the air: citrus, mint, and the vanilla and ginger of her perfume. Four plush chairs and a futon were arranged in a circle. A stand of live bamboo and flowers behind one, African ceramics and polished stones behind another, a steel lamp next to another chair, a smoldering oil lamp beside the fourth chair, and, over the futon, a huge yet delicate balsa-and-tissue mobile—a Chinese carp.

"*Feng shui?* It figures."

Hope brushed past him with a wicker tray holding two empty teacups. "Five elements, five corners. Water. Fire. Metal. Earth.

Wood. Focuses the *chi*. The spirit. Intensifies touch, breath, heat, smell . . ."

Derek sat on the futon, soft with a white goose-down comforter. Straining his neck, he watched Hope move to the stove. She lit the burner, measured out purplish tea leaves. Mundane motions, but every bit as worthy of study as . . . *yes* . . . the bounce and fall of her breasts under her sweater . . . sculpted thighs and a round ass manifested through tight knit Capri leggings.

With another match, Hope lit candles to fight off the afternoon pall; snow was falling heavier outside. The pot whistled. Hope returned with it and poured. The brew's scent was strange.

"Hold up . . . this *isn't* tea," he said with a grimace.

"Lotus tea," she murmured as she gently steeped the mesh ball. She was bending over, almost grazing his cheek. Derek labored to refuse a peek down that sweater. He gave up. Underneath the sweater, a T-shirt. Underneath the T-shirt, no bra. Just plump breasts hanging like a tree groaning with ripe fruit. A flash of plum-colored areoli.

She knew exactly what he was doing. She rose very slowly. "The lotus is an allegory for life. Use it in your novel. It grows from the muck, the slime, into a magical flower. Heals. Restores the *chi*. The mud flower, for the mud girl, Xhiang Xhi. You'll get your Pulitzer." She moved to the CD console, popped in a disk. The music was oriental. *Lilting*, as when Hope first spoke. "This is a *pipa*—the Chinese lute."

Hope fell back onto the futon, kicked off her clogs and stretched her toes, painted glossy apple-red. Derek drew a heavy breath. Toes were like candy. But he'd yanked out his sweet tooth long ago.

"Why am I here, Ms. Chen-Lee? No bullshit."

She moved closer, licking her full lips. The smell of ginger and vanilla embraced Derek. He awaited the rush to his lips. Instead, he heard a sigh. "Do you answer that, or do I?" Hope asked. "You're here because you're either curious or horny, right? I want you here for neither reason. I want you here, in my bed, to give you what you've lost." When Derek scowled and slid away from her, she pressed, "Yes, you're better than what you've become. Too many women have tried to scour off that patina of yours. No, all you need is a gentle wash."

"Now you're talking crazy! And who the hell are you to say what I need? You been stalking me? Wanna tell your girls how you sucked a celebrity's dick . . . notch on the MAC lipstick case? Or is this some twisted head game!" He shot up. "You gonna help me, huh? I'm out!" The boxer, the mean old German shepherd, had returned.

Hope didn't move while he flailed around for his jacket. "Anger's punched and bitten your heart too long. I know what hopelessness can do."

Derek whipped around. *Punched, bitten*? It was as if she could decipher his pain. "And . . . and now I'm supposed to be *Hope*-full?"

"All I want you to do is drink. It's not poisoned and I'm no sick female with an agenda. Then leave and go on you bitter goddamn way. But not until you *drink*."

Derek's breaths slowed. He walked to the futon, lifted a cup off the tray and sipped the brew. It tasted like stewed grass mixed with honey, but Derek drained the cup. And instantly, he felt the warmth, the succulence, ooze through his body just as in his *memories*. His knees buckled as if he were jabbed in the ring, in Limbo. But he was here, with Hope. And he sat, slowly, on the futon.

Hope said, "The lotus came to China from East Africa, along the first silk and spice roads, three thousand years ago, when white folks were still painting themselves blue and worshipping peat bogs."

Her voice and the *pipa*'s melody swam in Derek's head as he took another sip, this time from Hope's proffered cup. This time, no stewed grass. It was sweet, pungent, sultry. Familiar. Hope draped her arms onto his square shoulders. "Rest," she murmured. She moved the futon slats and lowered the redwood frame flat, then pushed Derek back. She curled up next to the now prone boxer.

Derek said, playfully, "All of my relationships end when I wake up the next morning, so you've been warned, Ms. Chen-Lee."

"*Shush*." Hope giggled. Both smiles evaporated when she added, "Not all of your relationships ended that way. I did my homework on you. Tell me about the one that didn't. Tell about losing . . . Grace."

The boxer and the old dog punched and bit their way back into Derek's soul. The lotus battled them back, and Derek spoke in a slow, pained cadence: "Met Grace Johnson fifteen years ago, at one of her law school parties in Chicago . . . I went back east with her, to Philly, where she's from. Perfect, because I'd gotten into Wharton. Got my MBA. Got married in City Hall, in a thunderstorm, and laughed how that statue of William Penn looked like it was peeing on us. Little did we know . . ."

Hope rose and pulled off Derek's socks, tugged off his turtleneck. He offered no resistance. Her warm palms massaged his biceps, his sore lats; he turned over on his back, and she lightly passed over erect nipples and downy chest hair to soothe his pecs. "Let it out. You're the storyteller."

"Maybe three months after the honeymoon . . . she was fatigued, run down. She'd had some rashes even when we were in Antigua. These . . . splotches . . . had come out in the sun. Told her to go to the doctor. Lord that girl's shit was always together, but when it came to her health . . . *nah* . . . procrastinating. More splotches, weight loss, joint pain."

By candlelight, Derek watched Hope tug off her sweater, then her T-shirt. She knelt beside him; lowered her mouth to his. He swelled under the crotch of his khakis, until she drew away and said, "You thought it was HIV."

The words snapped him to his senses. "*No!* I-I mean . . . she'd told me about these . . . boyfriends . . . roughnecks she'd dated in school, but . . . "

Hope stroked his forehead. "But you made stupid comments, and you thought she never forgave you for it. You were wrong. She did."

"No . . . no . . . no . . . " His voice trailed off. "Blood work came back. It was . . . Hodgkin's lymphoma. Aggressive . . . " He was fighting back tears now. Hope had already unlatched his web belt buckle. "Six months . . . six fucking months, and she was stage four. And I couldn't do a thing."

"I know, baby . . . Let it out."

"If I could have changed places with Grace . . . I would have."

Hope shed her leggings and thong; she laid them next to his clothes on the parquet floor. She straddled him, though his penis had gone limp from his torment.

"She was scared . . . She needed me and then . . . God . . . I'd leave and box in the gym for hours . . . till I was bloody, couldn't move. And I fucked around. Her old roommate. Guess that's how we dealt with grief. The only thing we had power over. Oh, her roommate busted me, all right." He grinned, pained. "Penance, I guess. Grace told me to stay away from the hospital, or later, from her parents' house. Got a certified letter from a lawyer. Separation agreement; medical power of attorney went to her father, not me. I started my new love affair with single malts, pills, weed . . . got fired from my job. Her parents slapped a restraining order on me." Tears flooded his eyes. Hope lowered her head to his chest. "I-I couldn't . . . couldn't even come to my own wife's funeral. And I didn't deserve to!"

"The Dao says, the body's just a rice husk that the wind blows away when we die." She was listening to his beating heart. "But dying angry, or living cruelly—traps our seed in that husk. The cure is to moisten the seed once more." She cooed, "Moistening . . . to quell the anger. Yours. *Hers*. So that something will grow from the muck. The lotus."

Hope swung her body around. That round ass was now in his face; a musky, wet cleft of flesh enveloped his nose. He raised his head to taste her, while his penis grew in her slender fingers. Fully engorged, she devoured it, with relish. Two husks, moistened.

They writhed as they feasted, but it was Hope who stopped first. Her back and ass still toward him, she edged down to his groin. All Derek saw was the curve of her hips as she lowered herself onto him. Her toes touched his armpits; she grasped his ankles.

"W-Wait," he gasped. "We don't have any protection . . . Lemme get some—"

"Protection from what?" she said, looking over her shoulder, voice in a bedroom rasp. "From me? Trust me, Derek. Trust *someone*."

They moved like one sweaty two-headed being. And moans came quicker, though neither could see the other's face. Hope's thighs slid back and forth, consuming him with each forward lunge. Derek met that motion with a circular grind.

Hope cried out. Shrill. Then guttural. He'd heard that before. Long ago.

"*Grace?*" he muttered as her climax peaked, then ebbed. His brain said *stop*. Reconcile the irreconcilable. But his heart refused to do so.

Hope was no longer sliding across his shaft—now she heaved her hips up, thrust them down. Derek grabbed her ass cheeks to double the force. He shuddered; Hope felt the tightness in his scrotum. She lifted herself off his penis as he came, seized it, and adeptly directed the spurts onto her thighs. One great arc painted her left breast.

"There, baby," she trilled. His spasms subsided. And when she turned around, finally, to face him, she saw wide eyes. For Derek Stone expected to see *another* face, beaming at him.

He gulped air. "I'm . . . I'm . . . sorry. I thought—"

"Don't say a word. I'll get a towel. Lie still. Sleep."

"I . . . *Shit* . . . I feel strange. Not sated. More relieved, ya know?"

"I know. More than you could possibly imagine."

The next morning, Derek awoke to find Hope hovering over him. She was wrapped in a plush terry robe; rather than a welcome mug of coffee, she held a small box—embroidered in rainbow-colored silk and cotton—under his nose. "For your trip, to China, to research your book."

He rubbed the sleep out of his eyes and said, "Who said I was going to China?" He took the box.

Hope knelt beside him, stroking his neck. "On your way back, stop at Ft. McClendon, Minnesota, and finish your research on the Twenty-fourth Colored Infantry and the Tenth Cavalry . . . Buffalo Soldiers."

"So maybe, *Xhiang Xhi,* you'll come with me?" When Hope shook her head, Derek shook the box. "What's in here?"

"*Careful!* The water in China's pretty hard, especially in the cities. Rub this oil mixture on your skin. Head to toe . . . pretend it's me doing it."

"Lotus oil?"

"You need to call Kwame Brooks and tell him you're going on a long trip." Hope smiled. "You lost some grace, yes. But you found a little hope, I'd say."

"Will it be here when I get back?"

Derek kept the little box on his lap for most the cab ride home. His mind was awash in sensations, images, music, yet he resisted the temptation to make sense of it. When the cab rounded the corner and stopped at his brownstone, a faint fragrance touched him. He held the box of oil to his nostrils.

Lilac. Bergamot. Jasmine. Two women. One spirit. No more succulent memories, just joyful dreams.

Laughter exploded from deep in Derek's belly. The startled cabbie turned around. Derek composed himself, leaned forward and asked, "Hey, man—know anybody who wants to buy a pair of used boxing gloves?"

# CONTRIBUTORS

(In Order of Appearance)

**Stephen Barnes** is the author of seventeen novels, including the bestselling series written with Larry Niven and his recent books, *Lion's Blood* (2003) and *Zulu Heart* (2003). He has written for the full spectrum of media outlets, including film, television, stage, graphic novels, newspapers, and magazines. His work has been nominated for the Hugo, Cable Ace, and Endeavor awards. He lives in Washington State with his daughter, Lauren, and his wife, novelist and journalist Tananarive Due. Visit his website at www.lifewrite.com.

**Reginald Harris** is the editor of *Kuumba: Poetry Journal for Black People in the Life*. He received an Individual Artist Award in Fiction for 2000 from the Maryland State Arts Council. His work has appeared in several publications, including *African-American Review, High Plains Literary Review, Obsidian II: Men on Men* (Plume, 1998), and *His3* (1999). His work has appeared on the websites of Blacklight Online (blackonline.com), the Black Stripe (blackstripe.com), and Blithe House Quarterly (blithe.com). He lives in Baltimore, Maryland.

**Gary Earl Ross** is an associate professor at the University at Buffalo Educational Opportunity Center. The author of more than 130 stories, articles, and poems, he is a frequent contributor of essays to the *Buffalo News* and WBFO-FM, the University at Buffalo NPR station. He was recently named 2003 Individual Artist of the Year by the Arts Council in Buffalo and Erie County. His other works include *The Wheel of Desire and Other Intimate Hauntings* (2000), *Shimmerville: Tales Macabre and Curious* (2001), and the children's tale, *Dots* (2002). Ross maintains The Writer's Den, a website for writers, at www.angelfire.com/journal/garyearlross. He lives in Buffalo with his wife, performance poet Patrice Ross and the youngest two of his five children.

**E. Ethelbert Miller** has been the director of the African-American Resource Center at Howard University since 1974. He also works as a core faculty member of the Bennington writing seminars at Bennington College in Vermont. Miller is the author of several collections of poetry. His memoir, *Fathering Words: The Making of an African American Writer* was selected by the District of Columbia Public Library for its DC We Read project in 2003. In 2001, he was one of sixty American authors honored by First Lady Laura Bush and the White House at the First National Book Festival.

**Brian Egeston** is a national bestselling author of five novels. He is a commentator for National Public Radio and has been featured in several popular publications. In 2002, his novel, *Granddaddy's Dirt,* was nominated for the Townsend Prize for Fiction and the PEN/Faulkner Award. His most recent work, the novels *Catfish Quesadillas* and *The Big Money Match*, will be released in June 2003. Egeston lives in Stone Mountain, Georgia, with his lovely wife.

**Trey Ellis** has been a professional novelist, screenwriter, and journalist for fifteen years. He has contributed articles to several newspapers and magazines, including *The New York Times, Newsweek, Playboy, The Village Voice, The Los Angeles Times, The Washington Post Book World*, and Salon.com. He has written three well-received novels, including *Platitudes, Home Repairs,* and *Right Here, Right Now,* which won the 1999 American Book Award and was named one of the notable books of the year by *The Washington Post*. His screenplay, *The Inkwell,* was made into a Touchstone film in 1992. Another screenplay, *The Tuskegee Airmen,* resulted in an HBO film starring Lawrence Fishburne and Cuba Gooding Jr. and was nominated for an Emmy for Best Original Screenplay. His screen adaptation of the novel for the film *Good Fences*, featuring Whoopi Goldberg and Danny Glover, premiered at the Sundance Film Festival and recently aired on Showtime. Currently living in Malibu, California, he has traveled extensively through Africa, South and Central America, and has lived in Italy, France, and Japan.

**Phill Duck** grew up in New Jersey, where he currently resides with his wife and daughter. His short stories have appeared in the anthologies *Twilight Moods: African American Erotica* (2002) and *Proverbs for the People* (2003). He is a monthly contributing editor at Suite101.com, an online site for the African-American writing community. Visit him in the cyberworld at www.phillduck.com.

**SekouWrites** is a Brooklyn-based spoken word artist and novelist. He is the creator/editor of the erotic serial novel *When Butterflies Kiss* as well as a performer in the spoken word play *NO good NigG@ BlueZ*. Sekou also produces a monthly seminar, "Black Men on Black Love," which is well attended and has inspired a widespread dialogue on the topic. Learn more about him and his work at www.sekouwrites.com.

**Edwardo Jackson** is a graduate of Morehouse College and has an MBA from the University of Phoenix. The winner of the 1993 NAACP ACTSO Silver Medal in Playwriting, he is an author, screenwriter, and actor, as well as the president of the entertainment promotional company, JAM Entertainment, LLC. His other works include *Ever After* (2001) and *Neva Hafta* (2002), both published by Random House/Villard Books. Forthcoming are the sequel, *I Do?* as well as the story, "And Then She Cried," featured in the anthology, *Proverbs for the People* (2003). Originally from Seattle, Washington, he resides in Los Angeles, California.

**Jemal K. Yarbrough** is a thirty-something attorney in the Los Angeles area, who recently discovered his love of writing. This is his first published work. He is currently working on a collection of short stories, a novel, a screenplay, and a stage play. He is married with three children.

**Michael T. Owens** attended Florida State University, where he obtained a double degree in sociology and communications for business. In 2003, he made his writing debut with *Pick-up Lines,* a novel about a self-proclaimed player's search for his dream girl. He is also the founder of the Scatterbrained Writer's Network, an on-line discussion group for writers of all genres. Currently, he resides in central Florida, where he is busy working on various projects. Visit his website, www.michaelowens.com or e-mail him at www.michaelowens @yahoo.com.

**Mitchell Jackson,** a native of Oregon, lives in New York City. He earned an MA from Portland State University and is completing his MFA in creative writing at New York University. He also teaches in New York University's School of Continuing and Professional Studies. He has published fiction, nonfiction, poetry, and is currently working on a novel, *Luminous Days*.

**David Anthony Durham** earned an MFA from the University of Maryland. His first two novels, *Gabriel's Story* and *Walk Through Darkness*, were both *New York Times* Notable Books. He has won several awards for his work, including the Zora Neale Hurston/ Richard Wright Fiction Award, the First Novel Award from the Black Caucus of the American Library Association, and the 2002 Legacy Award. He lives in rural Scotland with his wife and two children.

**Robert Scott Adams** is a published poet and established jazz critic. A native of Rochester, New York, he attended Morehouse College and has a long career as a radio talk show personality at various stations. His first story, *Where Strangers Meet,* appeared in *After Hours* (2002). He is presently finishing a novel based on the adventures of Miguel and Carlotta. Adams resides in Alexandria, Virginia.

**Cole Riley** gained notoriety as the author of five popular novels, including *Hot Snake Nights, The Devil to Pay,* and *Dark Blood Moon*. Born in the Midwest, he became known as a master of gritty urban noir fiction in the late 1980s with the publication of his novels *Rough Trade* and *The Killing Kind*. His last work, *The Forbidden Art of Desire*, was selected by the Black Expressions book club as a part of the notable *Indigo After Dark* series. He is presently working on a new novel, *Harlem Confidential*.

**C. Kelly Robinson** holds a BBA in finance from Howard University and a master's in business administration from Washington St. Louis. A former corporate financial analyst, he also has experience as a volunteer with Big Brothers Big Sisters, Mentors St. Louis, and Student Venture Ministries. He is the author of two novels, the bestselling *No More Mr. Nice Guy* and the critically acclaimed *Between Brothers*, both published by Random House/Villard. He lives outside Dayton, Ohio, where he is working on a new novel, *The Perfect Blend.*

**Cecil Brown** earned a master's degree from the University of Chicago. A native of North Carolina, he has written two acclaimed novels, *The Life and Loves of Mr. Jiveass Nigger* (1969) and *Days Without Weather* (1982), the autobiographical work *Coming Home* (1993), and the recently published critical analysis of a black cultural icon, *Stagolee Shot Billy* (2003). Brown has written a number of screenplays and stage plays, becoming well known for his screen writing for the comic genius Richard Pryor. He lives in southern California.

**Kenji Jasper** is a novelist, screenwriter, and journalist from Washington, D.C. He is a founding member of Black Entertainment Television's teen summit. The author of two novels, *Dark* and *Dakota Grand*, his nonfiction work has appeared in *Essence, Vibe, The Source, XXL,* Africana.com, and many other national publications. He is a regular contributor to National Public Radio. Currently living in Brooklyn, New York, Jasper is now working on his third novel, *Salamanca Mitchell.*

**James Alan McPherson,** a native of Savannah, Georgia, attended Morgan State University, Harvard University, and Iowa University. His work has earned him a Pulitzer Prize, a MacArthur prize, and other awards. He is the author of two collections of stories, *Hue and Cry* (1969) and *Elbow Room* (1977); *Crabcakes* (1998), a memoir; and *A Region Not Home: Reflections from Exile* (2000). He has taught creative writing at the University of California, Santa Cruz; Morgan State University; and the University of Virginia. Currently, he is on the faculty of the University of Iowa Writer's Workshop.

**Kalamu ya Salaam** is a New Orleans editor, writer, filmmaker, and founder of the Neo-Griot Workshop that writes with text (page and Internet), sound (radio and recordings) and light (digital video); cofounder of Runagate Multimedia Publishing Company. He is also leader of WordBand, a poetry performance ensemble and moderator of e-Drum, a listserv for Black writers and diverse supporters of their literature. His latest book is the anthology *360 Degrees: A Revolution of Black Poets* and *The Magic of Juju: A History of the Black Arts Movement* is forthcoming. Salaam's latest spoken word CD is *My Story, My Song*. He can be reached at kalamu@aol.com.

**Al Young,** a native of Ocean Springs, Mississippi, grew up in the South, Detroit, and the San Francisco area. He has written twenty books, including the novels *Who Is Angelina?*, *Sitting Pretty*, and *Seduction by Light*. His other works are: *Heaven: Collected Poems 1956–1990; The Sound of Dreams Remembered: Poems, 1990–2000; Mingus Mingus: Two Memoirs* (with Janet Coleman); *Drowning in the Sea of Love: Musical Memoirs*; and *African-American Literature: A Brief Introduction and Anthology*. He is the recipient of the Guggenheim, Fulbright, and NEA fellowships as well as the American Book Award, the PEN West Award for nonfiction, two Pushcart Prizes, and the PEN/Library of Congress Award for nonfiction. An inveterate traveler, he has taught, lectured, read, and performed his work throughout the United States and the rest of the world. His work has been translated into more than twenty languages, including Italian, French, Japanese, Russian, Swedish, Arabic, and Norwegian.

**John Edgar Wideman,** born in Washington, D.C., was raised in the Homewood section of Pittsburgh, which serves as the locale of much of his fiction. He received degrees from the University of Pennsylvania, and was selected as the second African-American Rhodes scholar to graduate from Oxford University in 1966. Wideman has authored three short story collections and eight novels. His work has earned two PEN/Faulkner Awards, made him a finalist for both the National Book Critics Circle Award and the National Book Award. He was awarded the MacArthur Prize in 1994. Currently, he teaches creative writing at the University of Massachusetts at Amherst.

**Christopher Chambers** is a Washington, D.C., native who served four years as an attorney with the U.S. Department of Justice before turning to literature. His critically acclaimed debut mystery-thriller novel, *Sympathy for the Devil* (2001), was followed by his latest work, *A Prayer for Deliverance* (2003). He has taught as an adjunct professor at Howard University of Law and a lecturer in communications at Queens University. A member of the National Association of Black Journalists and the Mystery Writers of America Guild, he resides in Maryland with his sweetheart, Dianne.

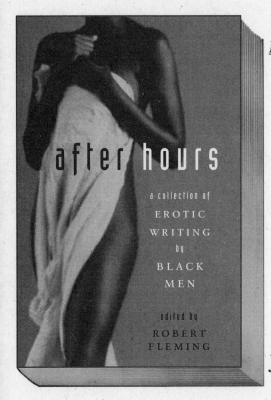